★ ★ ★

DUST ON THE SEA

BOOKS BY

EDWARD L. BEACH

Dust on the Sea

The Wreck of the Memphis

Around the World Submerged

Run Silent, Run Deep

Submarine!

* * *

DUST
ON
THE
SEA

Edward L. Beach

Holt, Rinehart and Winston

New York • *Chicago* • *San Francisco*

Published simultaneously in Canada by Holt, Rinehart and Winston of Canada, Limited.
ISBN: 0-03-076390-8
Library of Congress Catalog Card Number: 79-155503

Published, October, 1972
Fourth Printing, December, 1972
Printed in the United States of America

ACKNOWLEDGMENTS

Steven Kroll—*friend, confidant, editor, and an author himself, who helped form this story.*

Patricia Doolittle—*with astonishing patience she copied all the pages many times over.*

Tia Cronin—*who helped by critically reading and commenting on an early version of this manuscript.*

Edward Beach—*my son, who read and criticized the manuscript and in the process inserted much of his own philosophic, poetic nature.*

Hugh Beach—*my other son, who also carefully went over every word and made many thoughtful comments in the knowledgeable way I have come to value so.*

Ingrid—*my daughter, known as Ping, whose happy spirit and joie de vivre meant so much during the difficult days of composition.*

and

Martin Clancy, Bill Hatch, and Bruce Barr, the three tenders of the boiler room, to whose encouragement, thoughtful suggestions, and tactful criticism I owe such a great deal.

As with *Run Silent, Run Deep*, which it follows, this is entirely a work of fiction. I have striven to portray what submarining was like during the war years, and have held closely to the idea that not only should all the action and motivation be plausible, but also that the reader should receive an accurate description of the instrument in which the work was done: the U.S. submarine. Sometimes I have thought of *Eel* herself as the heroine of this story, but a valid case for this might be hard to make. Nevertheless, the reader will know more about how to operate a submarine of World War II after he finishes this book than he knew before.

None of the events herein described existed anywhere except in the mind of the author. There has been no conscious portrayal of any actual person, nor did a submarine named *Eel* figure in World War II. If some of my old comrades recognize that *Eel* had much in common with *Tirante* and *Piper*, as did *Walrus* with *Trigger*, I can only answer that any author has the prerogative of borrowing from his own experience.

The same holds true for some of the crew of the *Eel*. At one point, as also happened during the preparation of *Run Silent, Run Deep*, I found myself personifying, in her crew, a few of the men with whom I served, and to whom I shall always be indebted. It was not possible, of course, to name them, and in any case there were too many. But I'd like them to know that I thought of them.

Washington, D.C.
May, 1972

Ashes to ashes, dust to dust—so goes the litany as a mortal body is committed to the ground. When a ship dies there is no grave save the devouring sea. However, for a little while there is always a residue—debris, an oil slick, a streak of coal dust, an accumulation of dust and trash floating on a white canopy of air bubbles. This pattern is extensive if she sank suddenly, if catastrophe shattered her compartments, burst her bunkers open, blew her guts out.

Then the white bubbles dissipate, and for a short time longer there is only the streak of dust and a few items of junk to mark the place. Soon that, too, is gone.

The dust on the sea is the grave of a ship. It is only a temporary marker, but it is an indelible one to those who have seen it. And it is forever engraved on the souls of those who have had to be the cause.

★ ★ ★

DUST ON THE SEA

- 1 -

Commander "Rich" Richardson, commanding officer of the United States Ship *Eel*, was luxuriously soaping himself in the cramped officers' shower stall in the after starboard corner of the submarine's forward torpedo room. Two showers of more ample dimensions existed in the crew's washroom, three full compartments aft—about one hundred feet—but these were designated for use by the seventy-two enlisted members of *Eel's* complement. Not only was their use by officers inhibited by location and protocol, but especially today, with the return from *Eel's* first war patrol only hours away, they were doubtless in full use.

The submarine's designers had perhaps felt justified in making the officers' shower smaller than those for the crew, since her eight officers received, even so, far more bathing space per individual; but it might have occurred to them that officers surely must average the same size as their admittedly less privileged crew members. So had Richardson's reflections ranged three times a week during the two months' patrol now ending, as he wet himself down, turned off the water, soaped thoroughly over all his body, and then rinsed—in the water-saving bath routine demanded by the chronically inadequate fresh water evaporators in submarines. Even so, the newer "evaps" were a tremendous improvement over the inefficient travesties of the name which had been installed in Richardson's first submarine, the old *Octopus*. And an objective observer might have pointed out that the skimpiness of the shower clearly had resulted from additional space required in that particular corner of the *Eel* for the larger and more powerful sonar equipment installed in the new submarines. Certainly, the *Walrus*, Richardson's previous command, had had older and less effective sonar, but a bigger shower, than *Eel*.

But logic or objectivity were far from Richardson's mind. The floor of the stall was a marginal twenty-three inches on a side, and apparently the designer had somehow determined that six feet one and a fraction inches was the maximum height that any submarine officer was likely to be. Its top had been capped accordingly, and Richardson had long made a habit of rising on his toes to touch his head against the top plate, as if to measure any possible change in his height. More—al-

1

though this had not been the original designer's fault but instead that of a Pearl Harbor sheet metal butcher—the space above the spray nozzle had been reduced to about half of its original dimensions by a protrusion encasing the heating control panels for the new electric torpedoes which *Eel* had taken on patrol. The man had not even bothered to round the corners or smooth off the beading of his welds. To avoid painful scratches, one's head (granted, of a lesser diameter than the rest of the body) had therefore to be kept carefully cocked toward the torpedo tubes while rotating under the spray.

During the first part of the patrol, Richardson's three baths a week had been his sole recreation while the ship was in enemy waters. The beneficent combination of warm fresh water and his vulnerable nakedness soothed his brain and body. Weeks ago, relaxed after his bath, he would have amused the officers of *Eel*'s wardroom over coffee or a meal with highly ingenious methods of vengeance upon the shower-bath designer, if he could ever be found. During the last three weeks, however, since the destruction of Bungo Pete—Captain Tateo Nakame of the Imperial Japanese Navy—the light-hearted fantasies, which used to come of their own accord, had stopped.

Once, in a transparent attempt to bring him back to his old mood, his executive officer, Keith Leone, had incautiously asked for a description of the latest scheme. The whole wardroom, including Rich, had been embarrassed by the abrupt refusal the query evoked.

Now, however, entrance into Pearl Harbor was only a short time away. Already the submarine was in the Pearl Harbor Defense Zone. *Eel*'s two months of strenuous effort were nearly at an end. Ahead lay two weeks of complete freedom from responsibility, two glorious carefree weeks at the famous Royal Hawaiian Hotel, which, for the war, had been turned into a rest haven for submarine crews between patrols.

Richardson felt almost cheerful as he stood under the slowly dripping shower nozzle, cranium pressed against the overhead as was his custom, neck akimbo, torso contorted to avoid the uncomfortable edge of the boxlike, neck-high intrusion of the control panel, elbows braced against the sides of the stall because of the moderate roll of the ship. The black mood still lay there, not forgotten by the prospect of entering port, but put aside. He felt a touch of gratitude to the hapless shower stall designer, because, for the first time in three weeks, he had just thought of a new and really appropriate torture to inflict upon him.

The man would doubtless be fat, unpleasant-looking, and scared; but mercy would sternly be denied. He would be tied securely with a heaving line and suspended head downward from one of the periscopes.

Then, slowly and remorselessly, the periscope would be lowered into its narrow steel well (it might be better for the designer to be a skinny fellow after all). Rich would stop the periscope before the designer got to the bottom of the well, but he would have a good fright, and it would serve him right. He would also receive an excellent appreciation of the inadequate space in the shower.

Richardson turned on the water for a deep and soothing rinse. There was no need to conserve water this day. The black mood was entirely gone. It was the second such complete relief he had felt, as though a long shut valve in his brain had suddenly opened to flood his being with confidence and euphoria. Two weeks ago it had lifted when *Eel* rescued the three downed aviators in their rubber boat, but this had lasted only a few hours, had slowly seeped away. A week ago it had closed down tight when the enthusiastic but noncommittal message from ComSubPac, welcoming *Eel* back from "an outstanding patrol"—stereotyped phrase!—had arrived.

The idea of the villain being lowered into the periscope well to the fate he so richly deserved brought an unaccustomed grin to Rich's newly shaven, soapy face as, with eyes shut, he plunged it carefully—so as to avoid the metal edge of the boxed-in torpedo control panel—into the gentle spray of warm water. The shower, after all, was not much larger than the periscope well. The sides of the well would be slippery, too, with oil and salt water instead of soap; it was round instead of square; there would be no warm spray of fresh water. . . .

The edge of the control panel protrusion dug into his neck. It was he, Rich, who should be in the periscope well! It was he who should plead for mercy, while Bungo Pete looked on impassively and refused it! He could see Bungo Pete's face. He had looked him squarely in the eyes as he had killed him. Nakame looked exactly like Sammy Sams of the *Walrus'* training days, indistinguishably mingled, also, with old Joe Blunt, his one-time skipper in the old *Octopus*, even with Admiral Small. The ever-changing face never ceased cursing him, beseeching him, condemning him. Everlastingly, it would live in his mind, always changing, taking on the characteristics of others, and yet always remaining the same.

At the base of the well was an inspection plate, and as he came down level with it, it would be removed. Again, the staring eyes of Tateo Nakame would sear into his own, even as they had that day so long ago and every night since. Again, and still, they would pronounce him a pariah among men, fit only for vileness and shame.

In place of the euphoria of a moment ago, black reaction returned. The despairing weight of a situation beyond remedy, for which there could never be a cure, or an expiation, clamped down. There could never have been a way out. He would have had to do it, would always have to do it, exactly as he had done it, given the same set of circumstances. He, the victor in combat, was now forever the victim of the man he had destroyed.

For two weeks Richardson had been unapproachable, virtually a recluse on the bridge, in the wardroom, in his stateroom. His officers—and the crew as well—had ceased to bring little things to his attention as they used to. Now, except for the most formal requirements, they took everything to Keith. This, of course, was probably an excuse to avoid his dour company. Not that he wanted company. Twice he had ordered his meals brought to him on a tray, but both times he had finally yielded to Leone's impassioned protests. But this had not made him any the more approachable, except to Keith, who all along was valiantly trying to pretend that there was nothing wrong.

Nearly three years had passed since that peacetime Sunday when an American battle fleet, beginning its traditional day of worship, was smashed under a surprise attack by Japan's naval air forces. Richardson was then skipper of the *S-16*, an old submarine which he, Jim Bledsoe, and Keith Leone had hauled out of a navy yard back channel in the summer of 1941. Jim, tall and tanned, a natural athlete and a natural submariner as well, was executive officer. Keith, more introspective than Jim and considerably younger, was fresh out of the New London submarine school. Richardson had been in submarines almost since his graduation from the Naval Academy at Annapolis six and a half years earlier. He was thinner, not quite as tall as Jim, about a year older; but his slim body was as fit, without the aura of physical power which Jim exuded. A bony forehead, topped with light brown hair verging on the sandy, surmounted a pair of deep-set eyes. They would have been counted widely spaced, had not the necessary readjustments of *S-16*'s bridge binoculars, which they all used, proved Keith's eyes to be the farthest apart of them all. Beneath Richardson's straight, rather thin nose—marred by a horizontal line above the nostrils giving its tip the spurious appearance of being upturned—there was a set of thin lips defining a wider-than-average mouth, which of late had been compressed into a flat, straight line slashed above the strong chin and prominent jaws.

Keith Leone, executive officer of *Eel*, a veteran of seven patrols in *Walrus*, the first four under Richardson and three more with the redoubtable Jim Bledsoe at the helm, had more war experience than any other person aboard. More, even, than Richardson himself, who had been shunted aside to the hospital with a broken leg, courtesy of a shell from Bungo Pete's destroyer, at the conclusion of *Walrus'* fourth war patrol. Heavier than Richardson, Leone's square-built frame and massive head brought his steady eyes to a level only slightly under Richardson's own. There was an air of competence, of relaxed purposefulness, about everything he did.

The years of war had fired the basic clay of which Bledsoe, Leone, and Richardson were made. Jim was now dead, after a sunburst of glory, lost with all hands on his fourth patrol in command of *Walrus*. During those four patrols he had exploded into prominence as one of the most fiercely combative, supremely successful submarine commanders of all time. Keith, now a lieutenant, was no longer the unseasoned youth of the *S-16* days. His graduation from a midwestern university had been right into the feverish prewar preparation of the summer of 1941, and he had known nothing but submarine warfare ever since. Pressure had formed him quickly, had distilled his youthful verve into mature resourcefulness. Long since, Richardson had recognized that Keith also, like Jim, was a born submariner. He lacked the impetuous violence that had characterized Jim, but in its place he possessed sensitivity, competence, and a cool nerve which bred respect in seniors and juniors alike.

After three years of wartime command, broken by his wound and convalescence, Richardson had, by his own estimation, changed the least of the three. The net effect on himself, the few times he tried to define it, was merely increased self-confidence. Daily inspection in his polished steel shaving mirror prevented him from noting the gradual accumulation of seams around his mouth and in his face, the progressive leanness of his jaw which revealed its musculature, the combination of weather-callus and wind-burn which ended dramatically at the line of his open-necked shirt. The most subtle change of all was not visible: a mellowing of his attitude toward the enemy, even while, simultaneously, his capacity to damage them increased.

Perhaps it could better be described as improved understanding. On the personal level, this was to a large degree because of Nakame; but more important, it was the product of a growing appreciation of the differing national drives which had impelled Japan to initiate the war.

The greatest mistake Japan could have made was the attack on Pearl Harbor: a despicable onslaught while negotiations aimed at resolving the differences between Japan and the United States were at their height. Its sneaky, underhanded execution justified any horror the resulting war might visit upon its perpetrator. It blocked any possible resolution other than calamity to Japan. It eliminated any conceivable terms except unconditional surrender. It would cost Japan her entire way of life before that account was closed.

Yet, in spite of the hatred, Richardson had begun to feel growing compassion for the people of Japan. They were the ones who would have to suffer the sure retribution for what their leaders had unleashed. Which he was helping to bring upon them.

When *Eel* entered the Pearl Harbor entrance channel, her first war patrol at an end, a coxcomb of eight tiny Japanese flags, four of them radially striped naval ensigns, the others the standard meatballs denoting merchant ships, would fly from her radar mast. Richardson had not wanted them, but he had permitted the crew's enthusiasm, as rendered by Keith, to control the decision. The prospect of entering port was, as usual, conjuring up the anticipation of mail, fruit, respectful admiration by the crews of other submarines who were already in port and had already had their moment of attention. Except for Rich. This was part of the bleakness. The patrol had had as its express purpose the destruction of Bungo Pete. He had been extraordinarily successful against U.S. submarines. Early in the war, before anyone had known who he was or what his real name was, Nakame had earned the sobriquet of "Bungo Pete" from those who had experienced his depth charges. He had sunk seven subs off the Bungo Suido, one of the entrances to the Inland Sea of Japan. The last two were the *Nerka*, commanded by Richardson's close friend, Stocker Kane, and the *Walrus*.

It had been a difficult, emotion-wracked voyage. But he would have to relive it yet one additional time for the admiral and his staff, principally his chief of staff, Captain Joe Blunt, and then again, in greater detail, for the debriefing team. It had all been laboriously written into a two-part patrol report—one part labeled "Confidential," the other "Top Secret," but the debriefers would insist on getting it all verbally, too.

From his hospital bed, Rich had used his influence with the chief of staff to give the *Walrus* to her executive officer, Jim Bledsoe. Jim had promptly taken off on three supremely successful patrols to Australia and back. But instead of sending *Walrus* back to the States for a badly needed overhaul upon her return, Blunt had reluctantly ordered Jim to make one last patrol. Admiral Nimitz had directed the Bungo Suido be kept under surveillance. *Walrus* had been the only submarine available.

Nakame had claimed sinking *Walrus* in a Japanese propaganda broadcast on the same day Richardson's new ship, the *Eel*, completed her training prior to departure on patrol. The news came on the heels of the Navy's official announcement that *Nerka* was overdue and presumed lost. Joe Blunt, his first submarine skipper, later his squadron commander in New London, and now chief of staff to the Commander Submarine Force, Pacific Fleet—Vice Admiral Small—had been the emissary of both bits of bad news. The cumulative wound had been deep.

Walrus, Blunt explained, had been reporting weather every three days. Three days previously, Jim had added to the routine report the further information that he had only four torpedoes remaining, all of them aft. The next message, due that morning, had not arrived. Instead, there was a propaganda broadcast detailing the claim that the *USS Walrus* had been sunk by Nakame's forces.

In despair at the news of the loss of his old ship, following so closely on the loss of Stocker Kane in the *Nerka*, Richardson pleaded for assignment to the Bungo Suido. The upshot was that *Eel*'s orders were changed: instead of AREA TWELVE, the East China and Yellow Sea, she was sent to AREA SEVEN, with particular instructions to destroy Tateo Nakame and his Special Antisubmarine Warfare Group.

Richardson soaped himself all over for the second time. Now, *Eel* was returning. He had carried out his mission. Bungo Pete was dead, sliced to bits by *Eel*'s propellers. Sunk, during a storm, were all three ships of Nakame's little squadron: the *Akikaze*-type destroyer, a disguised "Q-ship" (an old freighter with big guns, filled with flotation material), and a submerged submarine behind the pseudo merchantman. *Eel* had expended her last torpedoes on them. Three lifeboats remained, launched, as their destroyer sank, by Nakame and his professional crew.

Of course, the lifeboats. Nakame would weather the storm in them. Less than fifty miles from shore— he'd be back in business in a week: A little boat with oars tossed against the sky. A row of faces staring, suddenly knowing what was to come. Eel's huge bow raised high on a wave, smashing down. Guillotine.

A brief search for the second boat. The bullnose rising, striking it on the way up, smashing it in, rolling it over. Still rising, grinding the bodies and the pieces of kindling down beneath Eel's pitiless keel.

One more lifeboat. Nakame's. Black water driving in solid sheets over Eel's bridge. Somebody in the stern of the boat, heroically fighting back. Rifle bullets striking the armored side of Eel's bridge, shattering the forward Target Bearing Transmitter. Eel's bow alongside, sideswiping, slashing past. Shift the rudder! The boat bumping alongside, dropping on the curve of the ballast tanks, its side bellied in, its ribs crushed. Tateo Nakame: a short fellow with an impassive face; deadpan. A first-class naval officer. A professional. Dedicated. Tough.

Around in a full circle. No avoiding this time. Bungo still fighting back. More rifle shots. The lifeboat in halves. The rifle flying out into the water. Nakame somehow managing to reach Eel's side, get his hands on the slick tank tops—clutching, gripping, clawing to hang

7

on. Grimacing with the effort, and with anguish at finally losing. Washed off by the sea as Eel *hurtled past. Sucked under by the screw current. Doubtless instantly killed by the thrashing, sharp, spinning blades rising under him as* Eel *pitched downward into the hollow of an oncoming sea. . . .*

It was a glorious Hawaiian morning on *Eel*'s bridge as the submarine, coming up from the southwest, rounded Barber's Point and straightened out for the Pearl Harbor channel entrance. The approach from sea was simple; straight in, perpendicular to the shore, past the sea buoy to the two entrance buoys and the black and red channel buoys marking both sides. A straight shot, with only a few easy bends after passing inside the shoreline. Always there was someone patrolling off the entrance, an old destroyer or one of the smaller PC-boats, and Richardson could not recall a day since the start of the war that there had not been aircraft overhead and a minesweeper chugging up and down the channel length.

Today, however, the minesweeper was missing. As *Eel* approached the sea buoy—the farthest marker to seaward—it was noticeable that the heavy swells which the submarine had been feeling since the turn off Barber's Point were considerably intensified near the shore. There was also a perceptible rise in the temperature of the air, a sultry warmth emanating from the shore. Richardson caught Keith's eyes upon him.

"Kona weather," Richardson said. He had once been familiar enough with the moist winds, sweeping from the south, which could pick up the surf and on occasion batter the low-lying parts of the island. Keith had heard of it too, though probably he had never seen a real Kona blow. Keith nodded shortly.

Lieutenant Buckley Williams, wiry and slender, finishing his fourth patrol, was Officer of the Deck and would have the privilege of bringing the travel-stained sub in to her berth. He, Keith, and Richardson stood together at the forepart of the bridge, the two younger officers on either side pressing against the overhang of the windscreen, Richardson in the middle leaning back against the periscope support foundation. Above them, standing on two little platforms built on to the periscope shears, protected from falling by guard rails, four lookouts zealously followed the orders that prohibited them from taking their binoculars down from their eyes. Their postures showed their discomfort as they held the heavy glasses. During the patrol, lookouts had tired rapidly. Perhaps something could be done for them during the refit period. Aft on the bridge deck, on that section still known as the "cigarette deck" from oldtime submarine tradition, when it was the only place where smoking was permitted, Ensign Larry Lasche, finishing his first war patrol, and Quartermaster Jack Oregon, a veteran of *Walrus*, were likewise obeying the ship's standing order which required them, when not otherwise gainfully employed, to maintain a careful, sweeping binocular watch on the sea and the horizon. The order, strictly speaking, said "air" as well, but except for that terrible day when the war began, the air over Hawaii belonged to the United States.

Buck Williams and Keith Leone were also using their binoculars in careful sweeps of the water where an enemy submarine periscope might suddenly and disastrously appear; only Richardson could be considered a passenger, in all the meaning of the word. A feeling of lassitude, of nonparticipation, possessed him. His had been the adamant insistence on the binocular order; now his own pair hung uselessly from their strap around his neck, not once having been used, their focus as yet unchecked from the setting Oregon habitually put on them.

The waterproof bridge speaker, protected under the wind deflector in front of Williams, suddenly blared. "Bridge, this is control. Request permission to open hatches and send line handlers on deck!"

"Permission granted!" bellowed Williams, reaching a thin, muscular arm to the starboard side of the bridge, where the "press-to-talk" button of the bridge speaker was located.

Richardson afterward was never able to explain what it was that pierced through to his consciousness at this precise moment. Perhaps it was some long-submerged recollection of his training under Joe Blunt in the *Octopus*, his first submarine, now, like *Walrus*, a casualty of the war. Perhaps it was just that things simply did not seem right, that some sixth sense was in rebellion. He jerked upright from his indolent pose of a moment ago. "Belay that!" he shouted.

Buck Williams' reaction was characteristically quick. "As you were! Belay my last! Do *not* open hatches!" he shouted into the speaker. Then he straightened up, looked at Richardson. "Sorry, Captain," he said. "What's the matter?"

Keith was also looking at him inquiringly, the widespread gray eyes in his sensitive face—no longer boyish after eight war patrols—showing startled surprise.

All Richardson's senses were suddenly alert. Something was dreadfully wrong. The empty channel must somehow be involved, but his rational senses gave no clue to what it was. "Make sure that all hatches stay shut!" he said. Then he raised his binoculars and for the first time swept deliberately around the area. *Eel* was passing the sea buoy, had passed it. Less than a mile ahead, the red and black entrance buoys beckoned. Deliberately, as though in the grip of some greater comprehension than his own, he stepped to the side of the bridge and peered astern.

Lasche and Oregon were also staring uneasily astern. No one could have said what it was that was bothering him—and then, suddenly, clearly, there it was! He swung around.

"Buck!" he said savagely, "Get everybody off the bridge! Put Oregon in the hatch, ready to shut it on order!" Keith waited to hear no more, dived wordlessly below to his station in the conning tower.

"Clear the bridge!" bellowed Williams, the timbre of his voice showing his wonder. "Oregon!"—as the quartermaster raced past him—"You wait till last, then stand on the ladder and be ready to shut the hatch on orders!" Wide-eyed, Oregon stepped aside, let the lookouts precede him, looked questioningly at Williams and his skipper.

"I'm staying up here, Oregon," said Richardson. "I just want you to be ready to shut the hatch if necessary!" The quartermaster scuttled down the ladder.

"In the space of twelve seconds the bridge had been abandoned, except for the Officer of the Deck and skipper. "What is it, Captain?" said Williams.

"Take a good look aft, Buck," said Richardson, putting his own binoculars back to his eyes.

"I don't see anything, Captain—nothing, really—the horizon does look a bit strange out there, though. . . ."

"That's not the horizon, Buck. It's a lot closer than that!"

"But it is too the horizon! There's nothing beyond it!"

"No, Buck. It's the top of a big wave. It'll be breaking here in a couple of minutes!" Richardson's voice held a calmness that surprised even himself.

Williams stared at him. "I don't get it, sir," he said.

"Once in a while this happens in what they call Kona weather, Buck. A big wave sweeps in from the sea, and unless you're ready for it, it can do a lot of damage. There must have been a couple already today. That's why there was no minesweeper in the channel. We're going to be pooped in a minute. Better be ready to hang on. . . ."

"Should we send for a line to lash us to the bridge?"

"That would have been a good idea if Pearl had thought to warn us about this, but I don't think we'll have that much time now. Matter of fact, here it comes!" Mesmerized, the two officers stared aft.

Suddenly Richardson reached behind Williams, pressed the bridge speaker button. "Conning tower! Keith! You have the conn! Keep us on course through the periscope!"

"Conn, aye aye!" said the speaker in Keith Leone's unmistakable voice. "The 'scope is up! What's going on?"

"Kona wave about to poop us, Keith. We may not be much good up here. You've got to keep us in the channel!"

"I will keep us in the channel. I have the conn! Should we shut the main induction, Bridge?"

The question was an eminently logical one. Judging from the sudden precautions taken on the bridge, it was evident that massive flooding was expected from the pooping wave. While the main induction valve, thirty-six inches in diameter, and its associated piping were as well protected from the sea as could be arranged, the four big ten-cylinder diesel engines running in *Eel's* two enginerooms sucked an enormous quantity of air into the ship. Were the induction valve to be submerged, water instead of air would be sucked in and flood the engineering spaces. Prolonged flooding—for several seconds—might even endanger the ship, not to mention much delicate electrical machinery. By shutting the induction valve, Keith also inferred the obvious shift to battery propulsion, which, of course, required no air.

"Affirmative, Keith!" Richardson responded. "Here comes the wave!"

In the space of less than a minute since Richardson had triggered the first alarm, *Eel* had traveled approximately one-quarter of the distance between the sea buoy and the main channel entrance buoys. Now it looked as though she were crossing a narrow, shallow valley of water. Ahead, on the far edge of the trough, watched the Pearl Harbor channel entrance buoys. It was mandatory to pass between them, for they lay on either side of the dredged and blasted passage into the harbor. Astern, what Buck Williams had thought was the horizon was now clearly the crest of a large wave, racing toward land. Already it was drawing water from the area ahead of it, creating a depression in the water level through which the submarine was passing, and adding to its own crest at the same time.

"Rich!" called Williams. "It was nice knowing you!" The comment was made in a jocular tone, but it was the first time Richardson had ever heard one of his juniors use his nickname. Buck Williams would be a damned good submarine skipper someday, if somebody didn't cashier him first for irreverence in the face of danger.

The two men braced themselves in opposite corners of the bridge. Astern, the wave had crested, foaming at the top, formed into the shape of a huge breaker. Moving shoreward at a speed far greater than that of the submarine, it began to lift her. *Eel's* stern rose. Her bow depressed, until water was within a foot or two of flowing over her slatted main deck forward. But the wave rose much too rapidly for *Eel*'s stern to follow, and the huge breaker began to submerge the submarine's after parts. Still it came on, curling higher, standing on the main deck nearly as high as the tops of the periscope supports.

Richardson had heard no orders given to shut the induction, but the thump of the valve beneath the bridge deck, as the hydraulic mechanism closed it, could be mistaken for nothing else. Keith had shifted to the battery. Except for the hatch on the bridge, the submarine was as tight as she could be.

"Buck! Get below!"

"I'm staying with you!" shouted Williams. To confirm his determination he leaned under the bridge overhang, shouted to Oregon, whose worried face could be seen framed in the bridge hatch. "Shut the hatch!"

The bridge hatch slammed shut. The wheel on its top twirled to the shut position as Oregon spun it from underneath. Williams and Richardson were now isolated on the submarine's bridge. The breaking sea, curling in mighty splendor, stood on the *Eel*'s main deck. The wave's forward progress slowed as it gathered strength from the shallow water it had scooped up into its corporeal self. Its forward face became steeper—"A wonderful surfboard comber if one dared to ride it!" thought Richardson. The wave touched the after end of the cigarette deck, bellied up from beneath, leaned forward even more. It foamed at the top, became suddenly concave, with a million lines of curved vertical ribbing, and broke.

"Hang on!" shouted Richardson, and as he did so he heard Williams shout the identical words to him. Both men gripped the bridge railing and took a deep breath.

Afterward, Richardson would recall an impression that, though there was no noticeable temperature to the sea, he suddenly found himself standing in water to his waist and for a second looked straight up inside the hollow of the breaker. He saw its crest strike the top of the periscope shears, adding yet more spray to its descending, broken, frontal edge. Then he was engulfed in roaring water. There was a sensation of color, of white mixed with streaked lightning, and of pressure. His feet were no longer securely on the deck. He was weightless, buffeted. His hands strained to hold the rails, were swept free. Something hit him on the back of his head; whether he blacked out for a moment he never knew, but his next recollection was a sudden awareness of the solid structure of the bulletproof front plating of the bridge pressing against his back, the slatted wooden deck driving upward against his thigh and buttocks.

12

Water, draining freely between the slats, held him immovably in place. He could see its shiny surface above him, exactly as it looked so often through the periscope when a sea rolled over its eyepiece—except that this time it was tilted at a crazy angle. Then his head broke through, and in a moment he could move and pull himself upright. Surprisingly, he had felt no need for air. Perhaps there had not been enough time.

A wet, disheveled Buck Williams was still gripping the bridge rail where he had been before the wave struck. The ship was heeled far over to port; Richardson, on the port side, had gone farther under than Williams. The bridge speaker was blaring something. It sounded choked and garbled, because water was still draining from its perforated bottom, but it was unmistakably Keith's voice.

"Bridge! We're way off course! Are you all right?" With the ship already knocked off her ordered heading, if anyone had been swept overboard the thing to do was to continue the unexpected turn and go after him directly. Doubtless Keith would have someone on the other periscope helping him look for people in the water—yes, both 'scopes were up, describing great arcs across the cloudy sky as *Eel* rolled in the aftermath of the huge sea—but of course it was not possible to depress the periscope optics sufficiently to see what had happened on the bridge directly beneath them.

Richardson made as if to reach for the speaker button. The quick-thinking Williams, nearer to it, pressed it for him. "Keith! This is Rich!"—unconsciously he also used his nickname—"We're both okay up here. Carry on!"

"Conn, aye! That comber rolled us over thirty degrees and took us forty-five degrees off course! We're coming back to channel heading now!" Keith sounded relieved, despite the distortions of the speaker.

Several hundred yards ahead, broad on the port bow, the entrance buoys danced as the breaker hit them. Strangely, they seemed no closer than they had been before the pooping sea, though they had then been dead ahead, with the submarine making quite respectable speed. As Rich watched, the two buoys steadily swam to the right, settled down a few degrees on the starboard bow. Keith was compensating for the distance *Eel* had been pushed off track, obviously planning to get the ship centered in the channel and on the right course before passing between the buoys.

"That looks like the only wave, Skipper!" said Williams. "I sure wouldn't have believed it if I hadn't seen it!"

"Me, too, Buck. That was the biggest comber I've ever seen, or heard about, either!" Richardson paused. "After we get secured let's

13

look up this Kona business. I've seen it before. But never this rough!"

Both officers had been shaking their binoculars dry, now put them to their eyes and began looking steadily aft. "Well," said Richardson, "that was it, I guess. Only one wave, but that one nearly creamed us."

"Open the hatch, Captain?"

"Negative, not for a couple minutes."

"Aye aye, sir." The conversation, clipped and monosyllabic, carried out with binoculars against their eyes, had shifted to officialese. A full thirty seconds of silence ensued, each man absorbed in his own search of the water and horizon astern.

"Bridge! . . . Conn! We're steady on base course, about to pass the entrance buoys!"

Buck glanced at his skipper, caught his imperceptible nod, pressed the bridge speaker button. By mutual understanding of the watch officers, merely pressing the button—which allowed a certain amount of feedback to enter the ship's speaker system for a moment—had become accepted for a routine acknowledgment, making unnecessary the additional distraction of words. In a silence that was almost eerie, for *Eel* was still on battery power and the customary mutter of the diesel engine exhausts was absent, the sub moved ahead. The two buoys, the red conical one to starboard and the black can-shaped one to port, swam alongside. Only a moment ago they had seemed quite close together, thought Richardson, and now they seemed far apart. He was totally oblivious to the fact that he had made this identical observation at least a dozen times before.

"Skipper . . ." Buck again, in a conversational tone. "Why didn't you clear the bridge entirely when we saw the wave coming? There was time for both of us to get below, I'm sure." He still held the binoculars to his eyes while talking.

Richardson put his own glasses down, let them hang on their strap around his neck. "There probably was enough time, Buck," he said, "but of course I didn't have any idea how big that wave would be. We were in a narrow channel. Entering port, the skipper is supposed to stay on the bridge. But why didn't you obey me when I told you to go?" He was not being entirely frank; he'd been thinking that perhaps the wave had been meant for him, that it might bring peace for all time.

And then he wished he had not asked his own question of Williams, for there was a hint of hesitation as that normally self-possessed young man answered, too smoothly, "I just figured that since I had the deck, I'd better stay up too." Williams' binoculars remained against his eyes as he spoke, and he was inspecting the shore to starboard.

14

"Bridge! . . . Conn! Permission to open the main induction and answer bells on the engines!"

Richardson was grateful for the distraction from a conversation which had taken an uncomfortable turn. "Conn! . . . Bridge!" He held down the speaker button, bellowed into it, supporting himself with the ruined Target Bearing Transmitter. "Open the induction! Answer bells on three engines! Open the bridge hatch! Lookouts to the bridge!"

The clank of the induction valve, immediately below the after part of the bridge deck, was his answer, even before Keith made the customary acknowledgment. Then came the familiar clatter of the engines rolling on air, and the hearty power roar, accompanied by sprays of water from the mufflers, when the diesel fuel was cut in. The handwheel in the center of the hatch spun; it banged open: crash of heavy steel against lighter steel. Four lookouts, followed by Lasche and Oregon, dashed by him and to their stations. Last up was Keith.

"I still have the conn, Captain," he said. "Request permission to turn over to the regular OOD"—with a glance at the drenched suit of what had only a few minutes earlier been inspection khakis—"if he's ready."

"It's up to Buck," began Richardson, but Williams beat him to it, spoke at the same instant. "I'm ready to relieve you," he said to Keith.

As the traditional ritual of turning over the duties of Officer of the Deck took place—truncated in this instance because of the short time Keith had held the conn—Richardson raised his binoculars and surveyed the channel. So far as he could see, *Eel* was the only ship in it. The entrance buoys were now astern. Ahead two more red and black buoys were in sight, similar to but smaller than the first pair. The visibility held a hint of haze, and he could barely make out the third pair. *Eel* was still proceeding through open water, but ahead the shoreline closed in except for a patch of water in the middle toward which she was steering. Unseen in the distance and the haze, the otherwise straight channel made a couple of small bends between banks of hibiscus-laden shore, and to starboard around one of them would be Hospital Point, with usually some convalescing patients and a few nurses watching the ships pass in and out. No doubt there would be a crowd of people today, curious to see what the Kona weather might do to the outlying reaches of the channel and to any ships caught in it. They would have noticed the absence of the usual sweepers and patrol craft, the lack of other ships going in or out (Keith had commented on this after things had returned to normal). From her appearance they would know *Eel* was returning from patrol, and they would guess the significance of the display of Japanese flags flying from the radar mast. They would probably wave a greeting as the ship rounded the

15

point. Perhaps, with their own injuries, with *Arizona*'s flag still raised every morning over the 1100 men still aboard the silent, shattered hulk, they would be pleased if they could know that this particular submarine had deliberately run down three lifeboats filled with enemy sailors.

Almost, for a blessed instant, there had again been a feeling of peace and normality, an ordinary gladness at the return from patrol at once safe and successful, relief from the latest emergency passed, anticipation of the good times in store for the next two weeks or so until the demands of getting ready for another patrol would take up all their time and energy. But, as usual, the mood could not last. Richardson would not go to the Royal Hawaiian Hotel. He could not join his officers and crew there. He would remain aboard during the refit, perhaps ask for a room in the submarine base BOQ if things became too impossible on board. His lips unconsciously compressed into the hard line which had recently become so often his expression. He released the binoculars, allowing them to drop with unaccustomed disdain on their leather thong and strike his chest. Keith was beside him.

"I've been relieved of the conn, sir. Buck has it again." Then, in a less officious tone, looking squarely at him, Keith added "We hope you'll be able to join us at the Royal tonight, Skipper. ComSubPac and Captain Blunt will probably want you for dinner, but will you promise to come on out after?"

Instead of the petulant negative he intended to utter, Richardson found himself answering, "Well, there'll be a lot to do here, but maybe . . ."

Keith didn't let him finish, maintained a note of heartiness which instantly betrayed itself as a substitute for anxiety. "Come on, Boss, you can't let us down. Al Dugan and Buck and I have planned a big party to celebrate the boat's first run. If you expect me to let anyone put any paperwork in front of you today, you're crazy!"

Probably the party had been less than a minute in the planning stage. It was even possible that Keith and some of the others had set up some sort of cabal to keep him from brooding over the lifeboats, to see to it that there was always one of them with him. Perhaps that was why Buck had refused to go below. Clever of them! Well, he would not be taken in.

"You know I'll probably not be able to make it, Keith—It's almost routine for a returning skipper to have to go to dinner at the admiral's house the first night." This was a non sequitur. Keith had already mentioned that probability. But the admiral's dinners rarely lasted late, and in any case the wardroom party would be held in one of the hotel rooms, where Rich too would be assigned.

16

Keith was not giving up. "How about after, then?"

Richardson hardened his voice. "No. It's your party, not mine. I'd be a drag on you fellows. Besides, with the curfew, I'd have to break some of the rules to make it out there after dark. You can all get just as drunk without me, anyway." He gave his voice all the finality he could muster, while pretending to grin.

Keith recognized defeat in the covert contest. "Okay, Skipper. But you won't get away from us tomorrow—by the way, shouldn't we send down for some dry clothes for you and Buck?"

A few minutes later, as *Eel* rounded Hospital Point, there was indeed a larger than usual group watching. Several pairs of binoculars were also in appearance, being handed from one patient to another by solicitous nurses who were not above looking through them themselves as they did so. *Eel* was the only ship they had seen pass their lookout point so far that morning, and they made all the right deductions, save one, having had much experience in the meanings of the signs they could identify. Several among them muttered comments that Kona weather must not be all they had been led to expect: this rust-streaked sub, obviously just back from a very successful war patrol, probably to Empire areas, showed no signs of having been in the least discomfited. The two or three waves they had seen from a distance did not seem big. They were inadequate reason for the lack of other ships in the normally busy channel. Probably the authorities had been overcautious.

But no one was able to give a plausible reason why, as well as could be seen from a distance, there were two naked men among the group on the bridge, toweling themselves and then apparently hastily donning their clothes.

- 2 -

The reception at the dock in the submarine base was exactly as Richardson had imagined it would be, exactly as it had always been for a submarine returning from patrol. The number one docking space in front of the submarine base headquarters had been cleared for *Eel*. A trim and alert crew of enlisted line handlers stood prominently in the foreground, and a ten-piece band played popular music at the head of the pier. A crowd of khaki- and dungaree-clad submariners had gathered around the place where a long bridgelike wooden structure, the Admiral's extra-wide ceremonial gangplank, or brow, its rails wrapped in shellacked white cord, was waiting to be put over to *Eel*'s deck when she came to rest. Conspicuous near the brow, standing in the foreground and a little apart from the others, Rich could see the stocky figures of Admiral Small and his chief of staff, Captain Joe Blunt. Near them a burnished five-gallon milk can stood out among mail sacks, crates of fruit and vegetables, and a large sealed cardboard box which could only contain the traditional ice cream. All these still rested in the small cart that had been wheeled down to the dock, where friendly hands would eagerly pass them across the submarine's rail and onto *Eel*'s deck even while the arriving ceremonies were still in progress.

But all did not seem quite the same as usual. At least, not to Richardson. Greater than ordinary warmth exuded from the crowd even before the docking maneuver had been completed. The smiles of welcome were broad, even broader than usual. Were they lacking a little in spontaneity? The wisecracks exchanged with *Eel*'s crew as her black-and-gray, rust-splotched length slowly eased up alongside the dock into her allotted mooring, on the other hand, seemed less ribald than his memory recalled, somehow more subdued. Everyone present must know how he had destroyed Bungo Pete. His radioed report of the action in which *Eel* had sunk a submarine, a Q-ship, and a destroyer, and then rammed and sank three lifeboats, had been classified Top Secret and was deliberately sparse of details. But the Pearl Harbor grapevine was renowned.

The patrol report, laboriously composed and typed on mimeograph stencil sheets ready for reproduction, lay sealed in Quin's tiny yeo-

18

man's office near the wardroom. Contrary to usual practice, it had been typed in two parts. The second part, labeled "Top Secret Addendum to Report of First War Patrol of USS *Eel*," contained all the details of the fight with Bungo. This, Richardson planned to hand to Admiral Small or Captain Blunt personally.

Williams, as Officer of the Deck, was making the landing. Keith was on the bridge ready to lend a hand. Richardson could not divest himself of responsibility for the safe handling of the *Eel*, but he could clearly demonstrate his confidence in Buck Williams and Keith Leone by ostentatiously paying no attention as they maneuvered the ship alongside the dock.

As *Eel* slowly traversed the last few feet to her appointed mooring space, Richardson quietly left the bridge, climbed down the steel rungs at the break in the cigarette deck rail, and made his way forward to the forecastle.

Instinctively, because he knew exactly what they would be doing and what space they would require, he avoided the practiced maneuvers of the line-handling parties on the submarine deck. As *Eel*'s way gradually petered out through the last few feet of still oily Pearl Harbor water, he found himself exactly opposite the submarine force commander and his chief of staff.

At about the right time—for it would not do to be premature with the ship not yet fully in, nor to be too late, Rich saluted, encompassing both Admiral Small and Blunt with the same salute.

"Good morning, Admiral," he said. "Morning, Commodore."

Neither Small nor Blunt was interested in the traditional formalities. Both returned his salute, Blunt rather condescendingly, Richardson felt. Both called across a welcome.

The admiral's words could not be faulted. "Rich," he said loudly, obviously intending that everyone should hear, "that was a magnificent patrol! I'm delighted you had no trouble this morning coming in. Congratulations on a great run!"

Captain Joe Blunt had been Richardson's greatly admired skipper in *Octopus*, his first submarine, during the years before the war. He was short and spare, though lately the spareness was less evident and his close-cropped salt-and-pepper hair had a lot more "salt" in it. So did the extraordinarily heavy eyebrows. Before the war, sub skippers were older. Blunt must now be in his fifties. His face had always appeared weathered and craggy to Rich, no doubt from the years he had spent on an open submarine bridge. He had been the epitome of the professional submarine officer, considerate and helpful to his sub-

1 9

ordinates, demanding of performance, confident of himself and his ship. He knew more about *Octopus*, and could handle any part of her better, than anyone else aboard. Since the *Octopus* days, he had been squadron commander and training officer at New London for both Richardson's previous commands, the old *S-16* and the new *Walrus*. Now both *Octopus* and *Walrus* were gone, lost somewhere in the Pacific. It was natural that it should be Blunt's greeting which Richardson would afterward recall most clearly. "Welcome back, Rich," he said. "We weren't expecting you until late this afternoon. Didn't you receive our weather warning this morning? We told you to remain outside until this Kona weather passed!"

Four heaving lines flew out to the pier, to be caught in midair by the line-handling parties at whom they were aimed. Swiftly *Eel*'s mooring lines were hauled in, the eye splices on their ends placed over the waiting cleats. The cheerful bustle of warping the submarine in the last few feet until she lay snug against the wooden pilings that formed the edge of the pier prevented further conversation. It was just as well. There could be no answer to Blunt, except the obvious one that a message not received was as if never sent. Somehow Richardson had the idea that Admiral Small had not wanted the matter brought up at all.

In a few moments all was secure, the brow placed aboard, and the crowd of well-wishers, preceded by Small and Blunt, took over *Eel*'s deck.

It was an honor, Richardson realized, for both the submarine force commander and his chief of staff to descend to *Eel*'s tiny wardroom and drink coffee at the table where he and his officers had held so many councils of war. Certainly they wanted to talk about the patrol just completed, but they must have known this could not be. There were too many others milling about during this first hour of return from patrol. There would be time for confidences later. The visit was a ceremony.

In the far corner of the wardroom, ensconced on the settee which sometimes doubled as a bunk for the most junior of all the officers, Keith Leone was already deep in conversation with someone who could only have been the submarine base engineering and repair officer. They started to rise when the admiral and Captain Blunt entered, but there was obviously nowhere for them to go; Small, in a single motion, bade them retain their seats.

Things were no better in Richardson's own stateroom, to which the three adjourned briefly after the coffee ritual. *Eel*'s well-ordered existence had been totally disrupted. There were strangers everywhere bustling up and down the narrow passageway, loud conversation, the general brouhaha of holiday.

"I'm sorry for the confusion, Admiral," said Rich. "It always seems to be this way when you come in from patrol. . . ."

"I know, Rich," interrupted the admiral, "I just wanted to get a feel for how you are after that fantastic patrol of yours, and tell you how proud we are of you. I read all your messages personally, and I want you to know I am in complete accord with everything you did." Small had spent his entire career in submarines, and had many times voiced regret he could not make war patrols himself. He was a short man, though taller than Blunt, and now, in middle age, had begun to verge on stoutness. His face was heavy, elephantine with a prominent hooked nose but his forbidding countenance faded with the genial friendliness he always displayed to his "submarine drivers," as he sometimes referred to them.

"That's right, Rich," said Blunt. "We just want everyone to know we think old Bungo had it coming to him. . . ." Was that a look of disapproval in Small's unexpectedly bleak eyes? Blunt changed the subject. "How about giving me your patrol report just as it is? I take it you've put it on stencils?"

"Yes, sir, Commodore," said Richardson. "Also, we have a special Top Secret addendum, separately submitted."

Admiral Small nodded his eyes shifting back to Richardson. "Good thinking, Rich. We'll take both of them right now." Richardson rose from his seat on his bunk and pressed a button built into the top of his desk. A moment later Quin thrust aside the green baize curtain which had been pulled across the doorway to the stateroom.

"Let me have our two patrol reports. . . ." began Richardson.

"Here, sir. I figured that's what you wanted, Captain," said the yeoman. Quin was always one jump ahead of everybody else, mused Richardson as his guests stood up to leave. In single file, the admiral leading, the three made their way topside.

"Again, Rich, that was a magnificent patrol," said Small, extending his hand. "I won't ask you to lunch. I know you have a lot of things to do. But will you join me for dinner at my quarters tonight? We eat early because of the curfew you know, so come on up about five o'clock for a drink, and we'll see that you get out to the Royal Hawaiian before they chase everybody off the streets at ten."

"I'll be there too, Rich," said Blunt. "The boss has asked a couple of others, too, so you won't have to do all the talking. We'll have read your report by then, and we'll be anxious to hear what went on between the lines."

Richardson forced himself to show pleasure in accepting, saluted four times as the admiral and his chief of staff in turn went through the departure ritual of saluting first him and then the colors. Then they stepped from *Eel*'s slotted deck to the brow and walked swiftly ashore.

Having to go to dinner was an ordeal he had expected. Richardson was grateful to be spared the preliminary of luncheon at the admiral's staff mess, where the current crop of "staffers," most of them either ex-skippers or Johnny-come-latelys awaiting their turn at a fleet submarine command, would have had free access to him. It was thoughtful of Admiral Small to dispense with this portion of the regular routine.

It was just as well, anyway. For one thing, he would have to go through at least the form of turning over to the "relief commanding officer"—the experienced executive officer of another submarine, now waiting his own command, who in the meantime was designated to take over all responsibility for *Eel*. This would permit *Eel*'s own regular crew, except for those to be rotated ashore during the next patrol, to be transported in a body for a two-week vacation at the luxurious Royal Hawaiian Hotel in Honolulu.

Boxes, duffel bags, and a couple of small collapsible suitcases were already appearing on deck, and two large navy buses were parked only a short distance away.

Richardson felt alone, detached from it all. This was not the same as the returns from patrol he had experienced before, the joyous release from pressure and travail. If anything, the pressure seemed greater. He felt indecisive, unable to think or hold an idea. Keith, he noticed, had not asked him for a single instruction. Keith was doing it all. Once he thought he saw Keith cast a worried look, quickly masked, in his direction.

It was impossible to move from the spot where he stood. A group of fellow skippers, nearly a dozen in all, surrounded him. All were eager to ask questions about his battle with Bungo Pete: the sinking of the submarine, the fight with the *Akikaze*-class destroyer, the final destruction of the Q-ship with single shots from stern tubes in a small typhoon.

How had he got *Eel* into position with weather conditions as they were? Why had not the Q-ship or the destroyer been able to hit him with gunfire? How had he known it was Bungo Pete whom he was fighting? What depth had he set on his torpedoes—had he made any adjustment for the heavy seas running? Why had he not shot at the Q-ship first—how had he identified it as a Q-ship and not an ordinary freighter? How in the world had he gotten away with sinking a submerged submarine right out from Bungo Pete's formation without alerting Bungo? What did he consider to be the optimum firing range and depth setting of the electric torpedo? Had Richardson heard of the new periscope radar—a radar made small enough to fit right into a periscope so that a radar range could be obtained submerged, thus facilitating more accurate fire control solutions? Had Richardson heard of the latest fleet submarine design, a bigger, faster boat, with even more torpedoes than the twenty-four which were standard?

The professional conversation, normally of huge interest, had nothing for him. Richardson answered the questions as briefly as he could, only with difficulty remembered the depth settings and firing ranges. He asked no questions in his turn about the radar in the periscope or the new, bigger submarines.

The silent arrival of an ambulance provided an excuse to break it up. The rescued aviators brought back from *Eel's* "lifeguard" stint would have to be tended to. None were ambulatory. All would need stretchers. "Keith," he began—but Keith had also seen the ambulance. Several men were already striding purposefully across the brow toward it. They returned with three metal stretchers with assorted straps for holding the patients in as they were lifted vertically up through one of *Eel's* deck hatches.

Still, the operation needed supervision. Richardson must say good-bye to the Army Air Corps captain and his two men. They would be coming up from the crew's dinette, through the deck hatch just abaft the bridge and conning tower structure, this being the shortest lift. Quickly they appeared. Keith's arrangements had been well made. Richardson shook hands with the lanky pilot, who managed to extend his hand out from under the straps holding him in the basket stretcher. Richardson hoped that the treatment his corpsman had given the westerner's broken leg would prove satisfactory. A little over a year ago his own broken leg—a compound fracture, to be sure—had had to be rebroken and reset after the return to Pearl Harbor. In consequence he had insisted on hours of study of *Eel's* meager medical library by Yancy, the ship's pharmacist's mate, Keith Leone, and himself before the first move was made to set the flier's leg.

He pressed the shoulders of the other two men. More seriously injured, they had been strapped in even tighter. He nodded and smiled at their mumbled gratitude, wished them quick recoveries, and then wandered aft toward the stern, in the vicinity of the motor room, where the skin of *Eel's* ballast tanks began to curve in as the hull narrowed.

It was about here, on the port side, that Captain Tateo Nakame had managed to place his hands on *Eel*'s heaving side, had tried to climb aboard. He would no doubt have continued the unequal fight if he had succeeded in doing so, would have striven somehow to destroy *Eel* and himself with her, had he been able. It was from this spot that he had cast that last look at Rich, the look which expressed all his hatred, his dedication, his desperation at being destroyed after so many successes.

Richardson would never forget the lines on his face, the agony etched there unutterably as he confronted a fate he must have partly expected, which was now arrived. On sudden impulse, Rich remembered, he put down his binoculars, exposed his own face. It was more a symbolic act than a logical one. It was some unconscious memory, some atavistic tribal recollection of ages past, which had impelled him. Respected enemies at their final confrontation, when one was to die, stood face to face.

There was a discoloration on the smooth black ballast tank surface. Some stray streak of harbor oil, splashed up on the way in. The orange and purple hues contrasted with the black skin of *Eel*'s hull, shifted shape as he approached. In the changing colors he could suddenly see the streaked outline of a clutching hand—two hands. Bungo's. It was not possible that the impression of Bungo's hands could have stayed there, persisted, under three weeks of ceaseless washing by the sea as *Eel* voyaged homeward from the coast of Japan! Yet, somehow, the kaleidoscopic image was there, oozing, slipping—the fingernails digging—grasping for purchase. Bungo had made a tremendous effort, a superhuman effort, to climb that impossibly slick curve of steel.

Rich had been the only man to see it, to appreciate it, to gaze heartlessly at him as he died.

This had been the end for Captain Tateo Nakame, of the Imperial Japanese Navy. "A mean old bastard," Blunt had called him. He might well have been all of that; he was also a dedicated officer of the old school who had given his all for his country. At some other time, in some other context, he might have been a friend, a man to admire. He had his counterpart many times over in the U.S. Navy.

"Captain?" he did not recognize the voice. The handprints were dissolving, drifting, were no longer recognizable. "Captain?" Through the fog, it was Keith. "Captain, we've got everything set to disembark the crew and shift them over to the Royal Hawaiian. Will you be coming over with us?"

"No, Keith, I've got a few things yet to do. . . ."

"Matter of fact, I do too, sir. They've secured the galley, but I had them lay on some sandwiches and there's some coffee left, so we can have a fair lunch. Aren't you going up to the admiral's mess?" Whatever Keith's intention, he had broken the spell. Maybe this was what he had meant to do all along. "There's only a few of us left aboard, Captain; everybody else is in the bus. Okay if I shove them off? Then I'll join you down in the wardroom."

"Okay, Keith." Now that he had been reminded of it, he *was* hungry. Breakfast had been early that morning. The crowd on deck had pretty well dissipated. *Eel* was now just another submarine among the many tied up at the docks in various stages of refit. Soon she would be moved over to a routine berth, to free the space in front of the ComSubPac headquarters for another submarine due to return from patrol. But this would not be his responsibility, nor Keith's. Someone else would do it—the "refit commanding officer" (who was he, anyway? He should know; the man must have been in that crowd he had tried to talk to on the forecastle, must have introduced himself). Richardson climbed down the ladder into the crew's dinette. At sea it had always been filled with an active throng of men, either reading, seeing a movie, playing some game, or eating. Now it was deserted, vacant, like the whole submarine. Already silent, devoid of life. Stagnant, the way life usually became. And smelling a little stagnant, too.

He moved forward into the wardroom. There was a pile of official mail, some newspapers, a sheaf of patrol reports of other submarines. By custom, all of it—even the official letters—would be looked at during the next patrol. Things demanding answers immediately would be brought to him by the refit skipper. No point in worrying about it now. No point in thinking about any of it. Keith would be waiting and was probably hungry.

Submarine skippers returning from war patrol generally got the use of an automobile from the ComSubPac motor pool during their stay in port. Favorite skippers always got the best cars, but of course they had to drive them themselves. None so far as he knew, Richardson reflected as he arrived in front of the admiral's house on Makalapa Hill, had ever been given the admiral's own car and driver.

"What are your instructions, driver?" he said as he stepped out of the car.

"Deliver you, sir, and return when you or the admiral send for me," replied the sailor. He was dressed in immaculate whites. His sleeves bore several hashmarks denoting successive enlistments. He wore a silver submarine insignia.

Struck by sudden curiosity, Richardson bluntly asked the obvious question. "How is it that an experienced submariner like you is pushing this sedan around Pearl Harbor?"

"I was on the *Nerka*, Commander," said the man, suddenly sober. "They took me off just before Captain Kane took her out on her last run. This is my relief crew assignment, and I guess I was just lucky. In a couple of weeks I'll be getting my orders back to a new sub in the States."

"Thanks, sailor," said Richardson, solemn in his turn. "I'm sorry. Captain Kane was a damn good friend of mine."

"I know it, sir." The driver seemed to have difficulty in speaking. "Thank you for what you did for him and my buddies."

The man wanted to say something more. There was a hint of embarrassment in his eyes, as if ashamed to be caught in a sentimentality. He avoided those of his passenger, stared through the windshield as he began to speak, then wrenched himself around to face Richardson. "We know what you done out there, sir," he said, "and why you done it. I was with Captain Kane on the *R-12* before, and I put in to go with him on the *Nerka*. He was a great skipper. Everybody on that boat loved him. Now I'm supposed to go back to Mare Island for a new sub, but I was just wondering—my buddies are all out there with him. It's almost like I jumped ship on them. I should go out one more time, before I go back, because of that. So—I was wondering—do you have room for a spare auxiliaryman on the *Eel*?"

Richardson made note of the man's name, service number, and organization in the thin notebook he habitually carried. He had walked nearly the entire distance to Admiral Small's front door before the despairing realization struck him. "We all know what you did," the man had said. Richardson should have expected this. Of course everyone knew. Certainly the *Nerka*'s auxiliaryman did not condemn him, would even support him because of his own feeling of loss. But he knew him for what he was: the man who had killed Bungo Pete by running down the lifeboats of a torpedoed ship.

The admiral's door swung open before he reached it. A white-jacketed Filipino steward held out his hand for Richardson's cap. Was there something behind his smile? A smirk? But there was no time to think about it. The party was already going on. Admiral Small had evidently arranged for the other guests to be there before Richardson's arrival.

Among them, to his astonishment, were three women.

"Rich, you're the lion of the evening," said Admiral Small, taking him by the arm. "Let me introduce the others—ladies first; we have to remember our manners. This is Mrs. Elliott, Lieutenant Wood, Miss Lastrada—oh, you already know each other?"

The last time Richardson had seen Joan Lastrada she had been Jim Bledsoe's date at a hectic between-patrols party just before *Walrus* had departed on her last voyage. Richardson had felt it before, but even so, when their hands met at the formal introduction, he was unprepared for the sexuality which she was able, wittingly or not, to put into a simple handshake.

Mrs. Elliott, it turned out, had a home in Honolulu, and had somehow avoided being evacuated to the States at the beginning of the war. She was a navy wife, obviously a socially prominent person, and her husband was apparently an old friend of the admiral's.

Miss Wood, or Lieutenant Wood, to give her correct army title, was a WAC officer, perhaps in her early thirties, stationed at Fort Shafter. Blond and attractive, a little large of feature and a little heavily made up, she was no match for Joan Lastrada, whose slender waist, gently out-thrust bust, and softly rounded hips complemented a finely structured face. Joan still had the overwhelming femininity which Richardson had first noticed, which since the beginning of the world has made men forget the face and figure and follow blindly after that subtle essence.

In addition to Captain Blunt, Admiral Small had also invited two other captains from his staff. And it was immediately clear that Rich was the only operating submariner present. The same white-jacketed steward who had opened the door was now attentive with a tray of drinks. Succulent little canapés were passed around. Richardson found himself telling freely how he had enticed Bungo Pete out to search for him, how he had almost blundered into his own trap, but, by good fortune, had identified the Japanese submarine before it dived, and sank it with a single torpedo fired on sonar information alone.

Perhaps it was the drinks. With the eager attention being paid to him, he found himself very quickly with his second amber-colored drink in his hand. The Jap submarine had dived just outside the entrance to the Bungo Suido. He had seen her dive, and Stafford had picked her up immediately on sonar. Once she had gained a submerged trim, she would be at periscope depth, ready to attack any American sub making a surface attack on the nearly unsinkable Q-ship. She would be on steady course, not zigzagging. There had been no reason to silence her machinery: the submarine she expected to attack would be on the surface. *Eel*, entirely shut down for silent running, found it absolutely simple to maneuver into perfect firing position. He had not dared to use his active sonar to obtain a "ping" range, had estimated the range, instead, by the ancient triangulation method. But he had compensated for this by firing on a ninety track angle—his torpedo aimed to hit at exactly ninety degrees to the target's course. In such a case, range drops out of the calculation. No matter what the range, any properly aimed torpedo will hit, if it runs long enough, for the angular geometry of the firing triangle remains identical regardless of its size.

Suddenly aware he was the only one speaking, that he was being loquacious, he stopped, momentarily embarrassed. There was a ring of attentive, eager faces around him. He had set down his drink, was illustrating the maneuvers with his hands. Even the steward, a blue embroidered submarine insignia conspicuous on his starched white jacket and three blue hashmarks on his sleeve, lingered unobtrusively within earshot. Admiral Small, his eyes alight with interest, forced him to continue.

Stafford had switched the sonar from earphones to loudspeaker. Everyone in the conning tower had heard the torpedo running, had heard it merging with the enemy sub's propeller beats and machinery noise, had unconsciously held his breath waiting for the explosion. It came with startling loudness, eight seconds after the computed running time of the torpedo. Everyone heard the grim results: the water hammer within the doomed hull, the frenzied speeding up of the motors, the blowing of tanks, the bubbling escape of the precious air. All heard the sudden cessation of the propellers, thought they heard but more likely imagined the violent arcs of electricity as sea water shorted out the motors or their controls. The last clearly identifiable sound was the crunch as the now overweighted hull crashed into the bottom. There was no hope for any of the Japanese submariners; the depth of water was too great for escape even if they had escape gear. Admiral Small shook his head solemnly; they had no such equipment, according to the best intelligence reports.

Richardson's description was followed by a rush of questions. What depth had he set on the torpedo, and how had he made the determination? The submarine had seemed to be about the same size as the *Eel* herself, and he had simply set the torpedo for what he thought would be the best setting had *Eel* been the target. Did he know the Japanese submarine periscopes were slightly shorter than those of United States submarines, and that he should have set the torpedo a little more shallow? No, he had not. The few feet involved would have made no difference anyway, provided the torpedo ran at the intended depth which now they all uniformly did.

Why had he not fired a spread of three torpedoes at the submerged submarine instead of only one? Because three torpedoes would be three times as noisy as one. They might have alerted the submarine, given it time to maneuver. Three explosions would undoubtedly have alerted Bungo if all three had hit, or if those which missed had exploded when they reached the end of their runs, as they still so frequently did.

There was no talk about the lifeboats at first, and Richardson had already finished his second drink, or perhaps it was his third, when suddenly the subject was raised. The drinks had been very strong. Already he was feeling their effect, knew he would feel it more. He glanced uneasily at the women.

"It's all right, Rich," said the admiral. "Everybody in this room has read your dispatches and your patrol report. The three girls here have a higher clearance than you do." Mrs. Elliott looked startled. Rich was sure that he caught a sharp glance from her directed at Admiral Small.

The dinner was delicious, the wine warming. Richardson realized that he had been garrulous, had fully described his decision to ram and sink the lifeboats. He had not intended to describe this part of the fight. Suddenly there was release in speaking of it, justifying what he had done. The battle had taken place only a few miles from the coast of Japan. If Nakame had been allowed to return to port, with his primary personnel and their precious expertise, he would have been back in action almost immediately. Measured against the value of Bungo's services, even with the growing shortage of ships because of the war losses, replacement vessels would not have been a large problem. Merely sinking the *Akikaze* and the other two ships he was employing that day could have practically no effect on his long-range campaign against U.S. submarines. It would have been a minor setback, nothing more, and he would have come back more dangerous than ever.

Why had Richardson not captured them, taken them on board the *Eel*? Not possible. The sea was too heavy. It would have been impossible even with maximum cooperation from the Japanese—not to be expected under the circumstances. Nakame still had his rifle, and he had not given up. The Japanese were superior in numbers. They were so close to shore. Picking them up would have exposed *Eel*'s crew to unacceptable hazard, even assuming, in the storm then raging, they could have been gotten aboard.

The others were nodding agreement. Rich found his highball glass refilled yet another time. It was after dinner. "Time for the movie," said the admiral. The same steward who had opened the door, served the drinks, and then put on the dinner, now busied himself with rigging a movie theater in the living room of the house. At least, it had been a living room, but it was apparent that Admiral Small had been using it for an office. The room had no rug, but there were a couch and sufficient comfortable chairs. A screen was set up in the entrance hallway, and a small projector was mounted on the top of the admiral's desk. And now the steward showed himself to be a movie operator in addition to his other talents.

Four people had to sit on the couch intended for three, shoved in front of the desk. Automatically, Richardson was sitting beside Joan. The euphoria induced by drink and the obvious importance which everyone attached to his words throughout the evening had had their effect. The crowding was not uncomfortable.

The movie was a silly story with all the love-conflict clichés. It had no relation to anything that anyone present in that room had been doing for the past several years, received all the more attention because of it, and gradually Rich became more and more conscious of Joan's thigh pressed close against his as they watched the convoluted situation unfold to its predictable conclusion.

His palms were sweating. Nervously he wiped them dry along the crease of his trousers, felt the backs of his fingers traveling along the smooth softness of Joan's leg under her light skirt. She was not offended. His hand groped for hers. She returned the tentative pressure of his fingers.

The movie ended. The normally efficient steward seemed to have trouble finding the light switch. During the delay there was a slight bustle from the other two people who had shared the couch, Captain Joe Blunt and First Lieutenant Cordelia Wood.

Admiral Small was looking at his watch, suggested another drink. Mrs. Elliott and the two staff officers refused politely, swiftly bade their adieus, and were gone. The efficient steward appeared again at Richardson's elbow with yet another very dark highball. But this time, knowing that he had already drunk far too much, and that very possibly it had been the admiral's and Captain Blunt's deliberate intention to get him tipsy, he took perverse pleasure in refusing it. Probably the plot had been kindly intended. He was, after all, the submarine skipper home from the wars. In addition, his host might just possibly have divined some of the inner tensions which still possessed him. Joan was standing very close to him, had been since the movie.

"Maybe we had better call it an evening too, Admiral," Blunt said. "No need to call your driver. Rich and I will take the girls home in my jeep."

"Okay, Joe," said Small. "But remember, you're not so much younger than I am!" The admiral's smile was genial, but Richardson suddenly sensed something else in it, some reserve. There was an unspoken warning in it, a measure of disapproval. But it was not directed at him. Blunt's quick, eager grin in response seemed a little strange, out of

30

place. Richardson's intuitions were not working. The expression on Blunt's face was not quite the right one. Something lay just beneath the surface, out of reach, some tension of which he was unaware.

There was some difficulty in opening the door. The light-lock, a jerry-built structure of boards and heavy painted canvas, intended to prevent light from showing outside when the door was open, would permit only two to pass through at one time. To facilitate getting through, Joan took Richardson's arm as a matter of natural course. She did not release it as they passed into the dark outside, instead hugged it to her a little tighter and strode out with him. He could feel her hip against his thigh as they walked toward the street.

The back seat of a wartime jeep will hold two people if they sit very close together. It is high and hard, with only a padded board for a backrest. It is a lot more comfortable if one puts his arm around the girl. Joan curled against his shoulder.

Blunt started the motor. "My quarters are right on the way," he said. "Why don't we stop there for that nightcap?" Nobody said anything.

There was a sentry box at the foot of the hill. The curfew sentry was already there. Perhaps it was later than Richardson had realized.

Driving slowly with lights out—in fact, there were no headlights at all on the jeep—Blunt braked to a near-stop. A grin, with a clear trace of envy, showed on the sentry's face as he saluted and waved them on.

Captain Blunt's house, like all the others in the general housing area, had been built before the war as quarters for married personnel. The largest houses were on Makalapa Hill, and they ranged on down to near barrackslike triplexes and quadruplexes, ranked row upon row, in the enlisted men's area on the flat some distance away. Blunt's house was smaller than Admiral Small's and there was no steward in evidence. It was even more sparsely furnished.

In conformity with the blackout regulations, there was a light-lock arrangement at the entryway to permit passage without showing light outside the house. Inside, as in the admiral's house, all the windows had been covered with heavy black paper.

"Rich, you and Joan make yourselves comfortable while Cordy helps me in the kitchen." Instantly Joan was in his arms.

The man standing inside Richardson's body who had always been the dispassionate and detached observer, was unaccountably missing. All Richardson's senses were concentrated on feeling the hard outline of Joan's hips, the soft tips of her breasts against his chest. One of her hands caressed his ear. Her mouth was partly open, soft, inviting.

This would not do. The others were only in the next room. They would be coming back in a moment. Joan seemed to anticipate his mood. Her tongue flicked the edges of his lips as she swung away.

There had been no sound from the kitchen. "Yoo-hoo," called Joan.

This brought results. Noise of sudden movement. Ice clattered into glasses. Liquid poured.

The living room contained a slip-covered day bed made up as a sofa with pillows along the wall, and a single overstuffed armchair. Blunt and Cordelia Wood arranged themselves side by side on the day bed, backs to the wall.

Rich found himself seated in the overstuffed chair, with Joan perched on its broad arm. A single dim light burned in a corner. All four were quiet. The other couple was out of Rich's view, off to the right beyond Joan, whose thigh stretched tight the fabric of her skirt, and whose bronzed legs, unfettered by stockings, dangled and occasionally touched his own.

"Rich," said Joan softly, "you know I knew Jim?"

"Yes."

"And that I know how terrible you feel about those lifeboats?"

This he could not answer. He had tried to be matter-of-fact, to avoid being defensive, as he described the action. Obviously he had not fooled Joan.

"You had to do it, Rich. There was no other way."

Curiously, Richardson felt no objection to Joan's probing. She held her drink in her right hand. Her left arm rested on the back of the chair, and now he could feel the tips of her fingers gently touching the back of his neck, gently rubbing behind and below the ear, softly stroking. "Jim used to talk about you some, you know, and little by little I came to know how much he admired you. The last time I saw him, he said you were his best friend." Rich said nothing.

The tapering fingers on his neck stopped, then resumed their gentle stroking. "You haven't asked me about my job, and please don't, but what the admiral said is true. I knew about Captain Nakame and how much it meant to you to get even for what he did to the *Walrus* and the *Nerka*, and all the others."

"It wasn't just to get even . . . ." Rich began.

Imperceptibly, the stroking fingers pressed a little harder. "Hush up, Rich, of course not. It was for Pearl Harbor, and the war, and the *Octopus*, too. But some of it was for the *Walrus* and for Jim, and for your old crew. You know that."

The fingers were doing their work. He felt an ease he had not known for weeks, since that fatal battle with Bungo Pete.

"You're probably thinking about that German submarine in the Indian Ocean that machine-gunned survivors a couple of years ago.

32

They were merchant seamen, noncombatants. The German skipper did it out of just plain fear for his own skin if they got back to port with the news that a submarine was in that area. Maybe there was some sadism in him, too. With you it was different. The men you ran down were all navy men, combatants, specialists in fighting submarines. You were fighting them, not just their ships. They had not stopped fighting you."

"Yes," said Richardson.

His sensuous reaction to Joan's near presence was as great as ever, but a feeling of relaxation was spreading over his body. The tightness in his mind was subsiding.

"Probably I shouldn't tell you this, but we know all about what happened to the *Walrus*. Nakame was riding the submarine that day. His other two ships stayed in port for some reason, so he sent out an old tub of a freighter for bait. It was night, and after Jim sank it, he hove to among the survivors to pick them up. There were only six men on the whole ship, and he had their life raft alongside when the torpedo hit. Everybody on it was killed, too."

Again the faintly increased pressure of the fingertips, the message of surcease.

Joan said no more, allowed her fingers to speak for her. So this had been Jim's undoing! An errand of mercy, perhaps an expiation of that time so long ago when the blood lust was on him, and Richardson wrestled his gun away!

There had been no quarter at Pearl Harbor. No quarter for the *Yorktown* at Midway. No quarter in two wars for submarines of either side. Nakame had even sacrificed his own men.

The fingers continued their restorative work. He did not need the drink, had not touched it. There was no indignation, no despair, no further sorrow. The silence continued: easy, comfortable, warm, intimate. Blunt's voice broke it. "My God, it's already past curfew!"

Richardson had forgotten about the curfew, but no one seemed much upset. He had heard that in one form or another this situation happened not infrequently. The rule forbade traveling after 10 P.M. If you were not home by curfew, you simply spent the night where you were.

"I've got a spare bedroom upstairs with two bunks in it for you girls. Rich, you can sleep on the couch down here in the living room. We'll have to make an early reveille, though, and start for Shafter right after daybreak."

Rich was surprised—perhaps he should not have been—to see that Cordelia had twisted around so that she lay almost in Captain Blunt's lap. Her arm was around his waist, her skirt hiked up carelessly above her knees, her face flushed. Blunt's mouth and cheek seemed fuller and redder than usual. There had been no attempt to shift back to a more conventional pose. Neither Blunt nor the girl appeared at all disturbed over missing curfew, and suddenly Rich realized that this was not new to them. Indeed, the whole situation might well have been premeditated. Joan appeared not the least disconcerted. Her fingers had not interrupted their soothing massage.

Stripped to his undershorts, Richardson lay under only a sheet. With lights out he had dared to open a window at the foot of the day bed, but this did little good in the sultry subtropical climate. His body tingled where Joan had last touched him. He knew what must happen, what was going to happen. There was no hurry. He could hardly wait, and yet he could wait. It was her move. There had been no words exchanged, but she would come. He would not rush her. Time did not matter. He could wait for her. She would come when she was ready.

Less than twenty-four hours ago, he had also lain sleepless, in the narrow bunk of his stateroom in the *Eel*, reliving the battle with the lifeboats. A combination Bungo Pete and Sammy Sams, cursing, had fired a machine gun at him. Tonight Bungo Pete was gone. Again he was sleepless and uneasy, tingling, acutely conscious of his hands and his feet, and the tiny nipples of his chest where the sheet touched them.

But his uneasiness was for an entirely different reason. He could remember solitude, camping in the mountains. Youthful plans formed by a dominant father, suddenly diverted into a new and more exciting world, still disciplined, but beset with bigger priorities. Until Laura, girls were not a serious thing. But Laura was forever unattainable. . . .

It was a warm night. No breeze, but perfumed. The distant murmur of never-ceasing industry, barely miles away, presided over by the Pearl Harbor odor: crude fuel oil mixed with water and earth. Flowers outside the window vainly sending their fragile aroma into an unheeding world. Ozone from the ever-flashing electric arcs. Hard flux burning, flowing off the welding rods, carbonizing, melting steel plates, joining them, urgently forming them into new and unexpected shapes. Tortured machines, dismantled, revitalized, restored for future torture. Joan's lingering, subtle fragrance. The gentle pressure of her fingers, that spoke so many words.

The crew of the *Eel*. The workers in the Navy Yard and Submarine Base shops. The driven—and the common drive that drove them. Reek of old sweat burned into uniforms and work clothes. . . .

The only life he had known. Ultimately, he would follow Jim,

Stocker, even Tateo Nakame. This was what everything had aimed him for. He had expected to lose himself in the intense concentration of it all. The huge machine covered half the earth. It had not been made for the parts to have anything for themselves. That was not what it was for. The parts were intended only for the whole machine to work better. . . .

Soft footsteps on the floor above. Sound of a door opening, then shutting. Sound of another door softly clicking shut.

He waited. The door again. Soft footsteps on the stairs. Slow, a little hesitant. "Shy" was a better word, for they did not hesitate.

She came down the steps barefooted, on tiptoe, heels high above the floor. Her luxuriant black hair hung down on the left side of her face. She wore a light cotton bathrobe several sizes too large for her.

He was trembling, holding himself quiet under the sheet. Easy, said the inner voice. Take it easy. She is doing something she has to do. Don't rush her.

He closed his arms about her. Her lips parted softly when his touched them. Her quivering mouth was a refuge. He felt himself disappearing into it. All other motion in the world stopped. Beneath the cotton robe was only Joan.

- 3 -

The ride from Fort Shafter to the submarine base after leaving off Joan and Cordy would have been pleasant, Richardson decided, if only old Blunt had not been so talkative.

The first phase of the morning's excursion, in the early light—the hour after sunrise was always the loveliest—had been quiet, but it, too, in its own way, had been unusual, vaguely uncomfortable. Richardson's pulse was no longer leaping. Everything was matter-of-fact. From the look on Joan's face one would have thought nothing had happened. Perhaps nothing had.

He was unable to guess what was going on in her mind. Had she any conception of the turmoil, the emotional crisis in his which she had helped assuage? His extra self, that part of his brain which seemed to function of its own, more objectively, more cool than he was himself, was telling him that everyone, Admiral Small and Captain Blunt included, had been conspiring to help. Keith and Buck and Al Dugan—all the crew of the *Eel*, in fact—had done so too. Each in his own way, as it came to each to understand. Even the admiral's driver had tried—how did he know? Was the story of the lifeboats all over the base?

Last night Joan had seemed intuitively to understand more than anyone. She had been wanton, had deliberately given herself. It had been a deeply generous, totally personal effort to lift him from the purgatory into which he was drifting. And yet—of this he was sure—there had been something driving her, too. But could the explosion of feeling with which he had responded be called a cure? Or was it merely a compound of too much to drink—that, too, kindly intended by his friends—and the natural reaction of the sailor, just ashore?

The warm sensuousness of night was gone. During day, one retreated into convention, into formality. Maybe this was the barrier. Last night he thought he knew her. Today he was not so sure.

The *Eel*—complicated, intense, an example of man's genius, pound for pound the most complex instrument modern technocracy and cleverness could devise—was simple by comparison. With the *Eel* he felt safe. Once you had mastered her, learned her needs and capabilities, *Eel* was always predictable. You could use her, play upon her, exploit her strengths and protect her from the consequences of her weaknesses. She was a comfort, because she was always the same. But why had sailors, from time immemorial, always personified their ships as female?

Ships were not enigmas. Women by contrast were. He had no idea what Joan was thinking, or even if she was thinking at all, behind the restraint imposed by the morning.

They kept conversation alive because it was what you did. It meant nothing, had no sequence. Whatever the sentry at the entrance to the Shafter compound may have thought, his expression betrayed nothing. Richardson climbed into the front seat of the jeep beside Blunt. They set out for Pearl Harbor, driving a little faster than before.

Blunt's mood had changed, or it might only have been suppressed earlier. He was ebullient, talkative, almost effervescent. Mired in his own thoughts, Richardson at first paid only enough attention to respond when response was necessary. He wished Blunt would stop, or at least shift to professional matters.

"You sure are a lucky man, Rich," Blunt was saying, slapping the steering wheel of the jeep for jovial emphasis. "Half the guys I know would have given a year's ration of tax-free booze to be in your shoes last night!"

Startled, Richardson could think of no answer appropriate to the remark. Something unknown, unexpected, had grated across his consciousness. This was, at the very least, out of character for the Captain Blunt he had known! Uncertainly, he gave him a searching look, did not reply.

Blunt took no notice. "She's supposed to be the best piece on the island, but nobody knows who's getting any of it. They say there's some airdale in Lahaina—and then you come along, and your first night ashore . . ."

Maybe if he pretended not to hear what Blunt was saying he would get off this kick. A deep uneasiness clutching at him, Richardson managed to find something of interest in a rocky field off to the right. There was something strange, a different quality, almost a babbling note, to the incisive familiar tones. It was the last thing he would ever have expected to hear in that voice!

"When this story gets out, Rich, you'll be more famous around here than if you sank two Bungo Petes!"

This could not be allowed! A burst of rage flooded to Richardson's brain. In growing unease at the trend of Blunt's conversation, he had been about to make another spare, noncommittal comment. A depth of anger which startled even himself boiled to the surface instead. "Commodore, if I hear one word about last night from anybody, I will punch you in the nose! Publicly!"

Blunt, about to say something more, stopped, took a long look at Richardson. The fury in his junior's eyes was all too evident. He surrendered.

"Oh, hell, Rich, you didn't think I'd go around telling about this little soiree we just had, do you? After all, I was in on it too, remember. That Cordy Wood, now, she's really something. You know she's a damn good wrestler. Slippery as an eel, and quick as greased lightning . . ."

But Richardson had found something else of interest in the area of sand and scrub bushes the jeep was now passing. His disquietude was complete. Surely Blunt had not intended to imply that he might boast about the previous evening! Yet he had done exactly that. And the balance of his remarks had been equally uncalled for. This was a side of his character which Richardson had never seen and could not, even having seen and heard, bring himself to believe was a part of the man he had so admired for so many years.

The old Joe Blunt was deeply sensitive, deeply understanding of his men and junior officers—and of their wives or girls as well. Richardson would never forget Sam Fister, his immediate superior in the *Octopus*, and what Blunt had done for him. When Sam's girl wrote frantically that she was in trouble as a result of the submarine's unscheduled stop in San Francisco, Sam had had the good sense to go right to his skipper. The letter was received in Cavite weeks after it had been mailed, as *Octopus* moored following a month-long simulated war patrol. No matter that Sam's supervision was needed for the upkeep to be performed at Cavite, or that nearly six months remained before the prewar navy regulations allowed him to marry. Joe knew his way around, and he called in a good many of his I.O.U.'s that night. Next day, Sam was designated courier to Washington, and boarded the Pan-American Clipper with priority two orders. In three weeks he was back, a married man and ready to give his soul for Joe Blunt.

Later, purely by accident, Rich was present when Admiral Hart, Commander of the U.S. Asiatic Fleet, told Blunt that someone's wife had written her suspicions to someone else's wife. Hart was justly feared as one of the toughest officers the navy had ever produced. Richardson, completely forgotten by his two superiors, stood marveling as Blunt laid his own career on the line to block investigation of Sam's putative violation of regulations. He marveled even more when Admiral Hart agreed, somewhat unwillingly, but agreed nevertheless, that until he received official notice—as he would if Sam claimed quarters allowance for his bride—he had no obligation, at this time of increasing tension, to inquire into officious rumors that concerned neither the battle readiness of the Asiatic Fleet nor the safety of the United States.

Blunt, a model of rectitude himself, had always been tolerant of people and their problems with one single exception: when they hurt his ship or the navy. Although, through their men, women sometimes interfered with the smooth operation of *Octopus*, Richardson had never heard him speak of a woman in other than chivalrous terms. Yet this morning he had been callous, even degrading, in his comments about the two girls with whom they had just spent the night, and for no reason.

No doubt, in the course of her time at Pearl, Joan had given herself to more than one man. Certainly, she must have to Jim. It was probably true that there were many, for there could not be a man who, meeting her, did not want to possess her. Emotions and pressures of war affected both the male and the female, and considering the differences in their wartime roles, it probably affected them about equally. Joan, far more than most women, was actually participating in the war, and her outlook, correspondingly, might well be more like a man's. Her job, obviously, had something to do with breaking down enemy coded messages—though this was his own intuitive deduction and could not be discussed. Doubtless, such employment must have its pressures.

Yet, how could you figure out a girl like Joan? Their lovemaking had been swift, fierce, and unrestrained, each seeking something for himself, or herself, at the same time as each gave to the other with the most unselfish and vulnerable completeness. Once, when both were for the moment sated, she murmured that she had planned how they would finish the evening from the instant she had seen him. He was different from the others, she said (astounding how frank she was!), for while they also had the drive of the war and of the risks and the fighting, none had so clearly, so plainly, needed that little thing she could do for them. Rich had never thought of a girl in quite this way. Joan was totally feminine, totally desirable. A very private person, yet completely honest about herself. In her own very womanly way, she was as aggressive as any man, but unfeminine she clearly was not; completely the opposite. Promiscuous, his instincts flatly denied. Free, most certainly; but his every apperception told him the freedom was hers, not that of others. Many men would campaign for her and fail—and some would salve their egos by groundless leers and innuendos.

A woman like Joan, despite her natural privacy, would generate gossip from disappointed men and jealous women alike. But to know Joan was to realize that those who had been allowed to feel the real abandon of which she was capable would not be the kind who would lend themselves to gossip. While Jim was drunk, Rich remembered, he had once—and that was the only time—nearly alluded to his relationship with her. But the inferences had all been Richardson's. Jim had actually said nothing, had never actually mentioned her, had only scourged himself for some unstated failure regarding Laura.

Rich had a warm feeling at the thought that at first sight Joan had trusted him. Blunt's extraordinarily crude comment, when he expressed surprise at Rich's "success" his first night ashore, had been far more right than he would ever appreciate. Then Rich remembered that Jim had (her own words) spoken highly of him.

Oddly, the inner glow remained. Perhaps both he and Joan were brutalized by the war. He had killed Nakame in defiance of the still honored code of the sea, which prescribed forbearance for men in lifeboats. He had also violated the code which his father, the preacher, had so thoroughly inculcated. It should be degrading to think of himself as only one among many in Joan's life, but in a seldom visited corner of his soul he felt cleansed of something. Somehow, the thought that Joan was not and perhaps never could be for him alone made no difference. It made no difference at all.

He would have to be grateful for her favor, to be one of those she admitted to her private inner circle. He could not hope to be the only man to be with her. Certainly, she would not sit alone while *Eel* was at sea! But she had done a lot for him, could do a lot more. After last night, he had hopes that he might also be able to do a little for her.

The rest of the trip was in silence, for which Rich was at first grateful and, gradually, a little concerned. Perhaps Blunt had been hurt, perhaps angered. Perhaps it had all been a game. It would not be the first time Blunt had acted a part to get someone's goat. That must, on second thought, be the explanation! Almost, Richardson convinced himself; but in the back of his mind there lingered something unsatisfied, something unexplained. Probably it would eventually go away. The strain of the just-finished patrol must have made him overquick to react.

The realities of the night before receded more and more as the gate to the navy compound at Pearl Harbor approached. In their place, the harder realities to be faced during the day—the war and the submarines—once again reasserted their predominance over Richardson's thoughts.

The chief of staff, no doubt, had a desk covered with papers and messages accumulated during the night watch.

For his own part, Richardson wanted to read the daily file of dispatches from submarines on patrol which was maintained in a room off the Operations Office. He needed to see *Eel*'s refit started; and he wanted to investigate any new devices or technical improvements which might be applied during the two-week repair period. Particularly, he resolved, he must look into that new radar periscope.

By the time Blunt stopped the jeep at the head of the pier where *Eel* now lay—she had been moved late the previous afternoon—the old relationship seemed almost restored. "Rich," said Blunt as they shook hands, "will you come to my office about 10 o'clock? There's some things we should talk over." With relief Rich promised, saluted, walked down the pier and across the narrow working gangplank to his ship.

Already, much work was going forward. The shattered Target Bearing Transmitter on the bridge, he noted, had been removed during the night. This was a vitally important instrument. Consisting of a specially waterproofed (and pressure-proofed) pair of binoculars, mounted permanently in what amounted to a set of gimbals so that they could be trained on any bearing, it very accurately sent this information to a set of dials near the Torpedo Data Computer in the conning tower. Thus the "TBT" permitted torpedoes to be aimed from the bridge as accurately as the periscope could aim them when the submarine was submerged.

Walrus had a much smaller and less accurate TBT in which the OOD's own binoculars had to be fitted into a bracket to send the bearings to the conning tower. The new design, bulkier but much more precise, also had the convenience of a built-in buzzer—to give the "mark"—in one handle. Being solidly attached to the ship's structure, it additionally gave physical support to the man using it in bad weather—a matter for which Rich had been most grateful a few weeks ago. Tateo Nakame had destroyed *Eel*'s forward TBT (there was one forward and one aft, necessitated by the periscope supports which obscured all-around view). It was good to see that its replacement had high priority.

Among the items Richardson had requested in his refit book, submitted on arrival, was installation of an additional five-inch gun on the main deck forward to match the one *Eel* already had aft. To go with it, Buck Williams had suggested a rudimentary fire control system, making it possible to use the TDC for coordinated control of both guns from the bridge during gun action. An aiming system could easily be devised if the submarine base could be persuaded to mount the two TBTs side by side, port and starboard, instead of fore and aft.

But moving the TBTs would be quite a job, involving moving electrical connections and making structural changes to the heavy steel plating of the bridge bulwarks. Rich could show the desirability of the new system, but strong arguments would be needed to get the submarine base to alter the standard arrangement. It would require his personal and primary attention.

There would be a conference later on today, at which Keith and the other officers would all be present, to review and plan the refit work. Most critical of the repairs was the matter of the ship's hydrau-

41

lic system. During the latter stages of the previous patrol the frequency of its recharging cycle had nearly doubled. This presaged trouble; a thorough overhaul was mandatory. *Eel* had many more hydraulic devices than the old *Walrus*. Her torpedo tube doors were hydraulically operated, for example, and her periscope hoist mechanisms had long, thin hydraulic hoist rods in place of *Walrus'* electric motors and wire hoist cables.

In response to the increased demand for hydraulic power, the hydraulic plant in the newer subs had been redesigned and enlarged. But the load was twice as great. Maybe the plant still wasn't big enough. . . .

Eel was a refuge, his home, his occupation. All he had in life, really. But she also carried memory, especially of the past three weeks. Fortunately there were many new faces in the relief crew performing various tasks about the ship. That made a difference. The boat herself also indefinably felt different alongside the dock instead of at sea. His own stateroom, untouched by any of the work going on, and yet so constricted, so crammed with memories of tormented hours, and so alien with the ship in port, was where it was worst.

He could feel the brownout closing back down upon him. Joan Lastrada's ministrations the night before had been extraordinarily successful, but no woman, hours in the past, could compete with the here and now of the tiny metal-walled chamber in which he had for so many days sat in front of his desk or lain brooding in his bunk. Nor could any woman compete with the great steel hulk of congested machinery which he had used to smash the lifeboats.

Half an hour after he stepped aboard, he was ashore again, reading the message files.

At ten he was in Blunt's office, a sparsely furnished, white-walled room in the bomb-proof building constructed for the ComSubPac headquarters. It was exactly as he remembered it, except for the addition of a large bookcase with glass doors. On its shelves, instead of books, was an assemblage of mementos, some of which Richardson recognized as dating from *Octopus* days. The majority, however, were new, evidently recent acquisitions. The single large window, deep set in heavy concrete walls, looked out toward the Pearl Harbor Navy Yard. Immediately below it, Pier One, now empty, was ready for the next submarine to come in from patrol. Blunt's desk was in front of the window, the back of his chair exactly in front of the glass.

The chief of staff was standing, gazing out the window, his hands massaging themselves behind his back. Characteristic gesture. Suddenly it was reminiscent of that night, two months ago, when, standing in the same pose, Blunt had told Rich of the loss of his old boat. Different in only one thing: night instead of mid-morning. Then the lights of the navy yard had been strong spots of brilliance in the distance, beneath them the black waters of the harbor. Now the bright sun of a late fall morning streamed through the window, tingeing the waters beside the pier an unaccustomed powdery green.

Blunt turned as Richardson announced himself. The pipe in his mouth was freshly lighted, drawing well. He held it between clenched teeth, spoke by moving his lips, articulated behind artificially rigid jaws. "Rich," he said, "that was a tremendous patrol you turned in. You have no idea of the effect here when your message came in about Bungo Pete, and then the later one when you rescued the aviators. Admiral Small made a special report to Washington about it. I want you to know that."

He could have used some of this knowledge a week ago. But this was not why the chief of staff had asked Richardson for a conference. He waited.

"How are you feeling, Rich?"

Why should Blunt ask this question at this time? "Fine, sir. I've never felt better. . . ."

"No, I don't mean that, Rich. I'm thinking about your state of mind. This patrol took a lot out of you I know—now wait . . ." as Richardson began to protest. "Any war patrol takes a lot out of the skipper. Most of them don't realize how much they've had to drive themselves, but you really had a particularly tough deal."

Maybe old Joe Blunt had read a lot more between the lines than Richardson had meant to put there in the patrol report. Or maybe, under the influence of the admiral's whiskey, he had revealed himself far more than he had intended. Joan, he knew, had guessed. And no doubt Keith understood. Perhaps Blunt still possessed that sensitivity of understanding which had made him so beloved of his junior officers in the *Octopus*.

"We were wondering whether the fight with Nakame had really gotten to you. You should have sent someone else to unlash the rubber boats when that Jap patrol plane came over. Doing it yourself doesn't seem the smartest move. You left Leone in charge of *Eel* under enemy attack. There was a damned good possibility that you might be killed, along with the aviators you were trying to rescue."

"Commodore, there wasn't time! The boat was diving! Keith was already below. The patrol plane was practically on us. . . ."

"Plane! Plane!" The foghorn blast. Men dashing to the bridge, tumbling below. Eel's vents open, air whistling out of them. Con-

43

*sternation: the heaving line fast to one of the bow cleats, the other
end still attached to the rubber boats.* As Eel *submerged, the line
would drag the boats under, dump the injured fliers in the water.
Richardson the last man on the bridge, seconds left in which to get
below before* Eel *went under. "Shut the hatch, Keith! Take charge!"
Jumping down on deck, running forward to free the line, Blunt's old
aphorism reverberating through his mind as the diving submarine
took him under with her:* "Take it easy, take your time, do it right;
take it easy, do it right!" *Many feet under, water pressure on his
back from* Eel's *forward motion bending him over the cleat, he at
last managed to get his fingers under the rapidly tightening heaving
line, pull it free. It was murder pushing himself clear of the huge
cleat digging into his abdomen.*

*Reliving it, Richardson could remember the pain all over again.
For a few minutes he thought the heavy rounded cleat had emascu-
lated him. He passed out, must have bobbed to the surface practically
under the rubber boats. The flier caught his arm, undoubtedly saved
his life.*

*The Japanese aviators were playing the cat-and-mouse game, hop-
ing to entice Keith to surface. When their plane came close, he would
dunk the 'scope and not raise it again until they were back on their
way to the horizon. Richardson timed the plane's movements, motioned Keith to bring* Eel *as close as he could, snagged the periscope
as it went by, signaled for* Eel *to surface as soon as the plane went
out of sight. Keith neatly brought the boat up directly beneath the
two rubber boats, landed the three wounded fliers and the painfully
bruised Richardson on deck. The bang of the hatch opening, men
racing down on deck, recklessly gathering up the four temporary
castaways, pitching them down the open hatch, slamming the lid,
opening the vents, getting her back under. Haste. Haste. The plane
coming back.* Take her down! *Take her deep fast! Lean into those
diving control wheels! All ahead emergency!* For God's sake, get
some down angle on her!

Blunt was still talking. The tone of his voice was the one he used
when he was displeased. "Why didn't you radio the task force to
provide air cover? You should not have made Leone surface your boat
right under that Jap Betty to pick you up!"

The direct accusation caught Richardson unprepared. This, of all
matters, he had not thought would be brought under unfriendly scru-
tiny.

"But I was in the rubber boat, Commodore! There was no way I
could tell Keith to send a message! He couldn't have sent one submerged anyway. Maybe we should have sent one before, but we were
occupied with getting those men aboard. There just wasn't time to set

up and send a message!" Lamely, Rich added the word "sir" to the sentence.

"Well, maybe not," said Blunt. "But you should have had a message ready beforehand. That's the way it's got to be in submarines, Rich. You've got to think of everything, all the time. Trouble with you young skippers is that you don't look ahead. You could have lost your boat, or been lost yourself, along with the three fliers you were trying to help!"

Years ago, Blunt had used that same tone of voice to upbraid Rich for a poorly executed dive in the *Octopus*. Afterward he had praised him for quickly diagnosing and remedying the trouble, improper compensation of the after trim tank. Richardson felt the sudden return to the attitudes of eight years ago, when he had been the inexperienced new arrival to Blunt's brand-new submarine. He sat uncomfortably in his chair. Blunt was being a little hard. It was almost contrary to tradition to rake a newly returned skipper, especially on the day following return from a successful patrol.

Apparently Blunt had come to the end of his chastisement. "Anyway, it came out all right," he said. "You were lucky and got away with it. So let's forget about it."

But Rich could not forget about it. There was something behind Blunt's words. Was there a hint of vindictiveness in his manner? Could he have been reasserting himself, his superiority, after the night in his quarters and the conversation in the jeep? And what about Blunt's reaction to his personal risk in casting loose the rubber boats—that, at least, had brought him the most peace and contentment of the entire patrol. So far as leaving Keith in command for a time, that had been an incident of combat. Keith had long since qualified for command; else he could not have been exec. Richardson would have trusted him anywhere. Was there, in truth, a real reason behind Blunt's probing? Richardson himself had secretly wondered whether there had been a subconscious wish to risk death underlying his action. Had Blunt sensed this? Even yesterday, when Rich could have gone below, he had remained on the bridge when the Kona wave had pooped the boat. He might well have been washed overboard. Was that part of the same underlying wish?

Some of his thoughts must have shown on his face. Blunt continued in a kinder tone. "Nearly all our skippers are young, like you, Rich," he said. "You're not the only one with a few problems and frustrations. Here in Pearl some of us at least get a chance to relieve some of them. Maybe you need a little more of that stuff you got last night."

"Goddammit, Captain!" burst out Richardson, half rising in his chair.

"Oh for Christ's sake, take it easy, Rich. This is a world war we're in. Everybody's in it, the men and the women too. And don't forget the women are giving it all they've got, just like you are. Just who do you think those girls were, anyway?"

"You're not trying to tell me . . . ." Richardson stopped. Was this a hint at the puzzle about Joan's work at Fort Shafter?

"They just happen to know more about what's going on in Japan than either of us ever will, unless we take over the admiral's job, but I'm not going to say anything more, so forget what I said." He had long since removed the pipe from his mouth. It had gone out, unnoticed, on his desk. Now he palmed it, tamped down the contents of the bowl, gently shook out the loose ashes, relighted it.

A deep, satisfied puff. A curl of smoke gently rising toward the ceiling. "Anyway, that isn't what I wanted to talk to you about. Have you heard about the wolfpacks we've been organizing?"

"Yes, sure," said Richardson, relieved that Blunt had shifted the conversation away from the events of the previous night.

"Mason's Marauders turned in a pretty good combined patrol, and so did Tremaine's Tigers, but others haven't been so lucky recently. It all depends on the area they get, and how well they've been trained beforehand, naturally. Also on how much dope they get in the area, and how aggressive the boats are themselves."

Rich nodded.

"Anyway, what I'm telling you is that the admiral is giving me the next wolfpack, and I was wondering whether you would like to be in it."

"Us? The *Eel?* We won't be through our refit and training for three more weeks!" Suddenly Richardson realized he did not want to be in a wolfpack under his old skipper. A day ago he might have welcomed the idea.

"Timing is no problem. We've already picked the other two boats: *Chicolar* and *Whitefish*. The *Chicolar* is a brand-new sub, due to arrive from Mare Island in a couple of days. She has an experienced skipper, though, so she'll need only routine refresher training. She'll be okay. The *Whitefish* is an older boat and her skipper is due for rotation this time in. They're already here, got in a couple of days before you did, so the timing is really pretty good. We'll need the three weeks to plan our coordinated tactics."

There had been hesitation, less than enthusiastic acceptance, in Richardson's manner. Had Blunt noticed? Had he expected a greater expression of pleasure at the prospect of being shipmates again? But even if so, this could not explain Blunt's negative attitude toward the rescue of the aviators, for the wolfpack, at that point, had not yet been mentioned.

Blunt was still talking. "Most of you young skippers say Jap convoys are too small for wolfpacks. Since the poor results from the last couple we sent out, the Old Man hasn't been too willing, either. But last week he had a conference with Nimitz, and since then we've been putting this one together."

In Richardson's opinion, the damage done by a single three-submarine wolfpack generally was not equal to what could be accomplished by three aggressive boats operating over a wider area independently. Furthermore, higher risk of detection and counterattack resulted from the wolfpack's need for radio communications between its members.

The disquiet, allayed a moment ago, was back. Blunt, who had taken the bewildered ensign on board the *Octopus* and made a submariner out of him, who had publicly qualified him with his own dolphin insignia in front of the entire crew, had always been a source of admiration and strength. This had been no less true later, at New London, and until very recently, at Pearl. But there was a subtle difference between the Blunt of today and the Blunt of even two months ago, when Richardson had last seen him. The voice, the mannerisms, the countenance, were exactly the same; yet, there was a new slackness about his jaws and a never before noticed unreality to his conversation.

Only someone who had served under Blunt, who had experienced his vitality as a superior, would be able to see the difference. Admiral Small, obviously, had seen nothing untoward, for he would not otherwise have designated him as the commander of a wolfpack, in charge of three submarines on war patrol.

Suddenly speculation took off on another tangent, and simultaneously it became certainty. Wolfpack commanders were commonly drawn from among underemployed squadron commanders, of whom there were a number in Pearl. Submarining was a young man's game. The navy—the war—was passing the older men by. They were in the middle; they had had their boats before the war, and there could be but one force commander. The Germans controlled their wolfpacks entirely from shore. It was an American idea to put a wolfpack commander aboard one of the subs. The opportunity was much sought after. There were too many claimants. No one got more than one crack at it. No doubt Blunt had also been restive, perhaps even a little envious, like some of the others. But the chief of staff, of all the officers in Pearl, could not complain about being unemployed. There had to be a substantial reason for ComSubPac to deprive himself of his right-hand man. Something really important must be intended for this wolfpack. That conference between the two old submarine colleagues, Small and Nimitz, had done it!

Then the inner voice of logic began to speak. Richardson should realize that his own perceptions were overdrawn, too finely sharpened by the pressures of the patrol just completed. Admiral Small had had far more opportunity to observe Blunt than Richardson. His view must be the correct one. If anything, he would be aware that Blunt was wearying under his heavy desk duties. The chief of staff's job was essentially one of paperwork, a despised chore for a man of action, especially for a man of the sea. An assignment carrying with it unusual responsibilities of a completely different nature, at sea on submarine war patrol, doing what his entire career had been preparing him for, would appeal to the admiral as exactly the sort of change his valued assistant needed. This would clear the cobwebs from Blunt's mind. And it would give him a taste of the action for which the admiral had many times expressed his envy. Joe Blunt might well have felt the same, might have asked for the assignment.

Only one more question to ask, for which Rich already knew the answer. "Have you decided which boat you'll be riding, Commodore?"

"I figured you'd ask that. The admiral and I think I should be on the most experienced boat, with the most experienced skipper. This adds up to yours."

Perhaps, in the process of doing something really big, something of real significance in the war effort, the old Blunt would reassert himself. Once away from Pearl Harbor and its invidious subtleties, the old relationship Richardson had so valued could be revived.

He could feel himself pulled in two directions at the same time, but all the decisions had already been made. Admiral Small of course knew that Blunt had once been skipper of the *Octopus*, and that Richardson had served three years under him there, as well as an additional time in New London. Obviously, it was Small who had decided that Blunt would ride the *Eel*.

"Great," said Rich, this being the only reply he could think of. "What do we have to do for training? And when can we start?"

"There'll be a little more work in it for you and some of your officers, of course, and you won't have as much free time in the Royal Hawaiian Hotel as maybe you'd hoped. I want all of you to study all the reports of all the previous wolfpacks. And I want you three skippers to get to know each other pretty well, too. Then we'll set up a training period to work out our tactics."

"Is our area picked already?" Rich asked.

"AREA TWELVE, the Yellow Sea and East China Sea. That was where we were going to send you, remember, when we diverted you to the Bungo Suido last time. Matter of fact, we've not had a submarine in there since, and by now the Japs must be running a lot of traffic through there. There should be plenty of targets, at least in the beginning. As soon as we hit them, of course, they'll close off again. So I want to go in and hit them real hard right away. Good thing they won't have old Bungo to shift over there."

"Fine," said Rich. "It sounds like a lot of fun." "Fun" was the wrong word, but Blunt did not seem to notice. If Richardson's latest evaluation was on target, there would be a lot more than "fun" involved. He hoped he had sounded convincing. "When do we start getting ready?"

"Right after the *Chicolar* gets in, day after tomorrow. I'll call all three of you skippers together, along with your execs. It won't be too tough a schedule. You'll have plenty of time off. There'll be plenty of time to see the Lastrada dame, if she has any free time. After sixty days at sea you must really have had lead in your pencil last night. . . ."

Somehow, Richardson managed to make a quiet retreat. There was something wrong, all right.

To Richardson's surprise, at the afternoon-long refit conference there was no resistance at all to his proposal to move the two Target Bearing Transmitters into little bulges built into the sides of *Eel*'s bridge. He had prepared himself with diagrams showing the increased arc which could be covered by either TBT in the event of failure of the other, and he was psychologically ready to discuss the loss of aiming capability from the forward TBT after Nakame's rifle had smashed it.

In this instance, *Eel* had no torpedoes remaining forward—or aft either, for that matter—but the principle was valid. Rich would use this argument last, had begun to describe his intended use of the side-mounted bearing transmitters for director control of the two five-inch guns, when he realized here was no opposition to his proposal. So far as the refit people were concerned, it was only the question of the physical capability to do the job.

The reaction to his other primary request, that extra skids be provided for stowage of ten torpedoes in the after torpedo room, instead of the standard eight, was the same. He had been prepared for opposition, for no submarine had yet taken twenty-six torpedoes on patrol.

Sufficient space existed, but the designed load was only twenty-four fish. Should *Eel* be unlucky enough to have a "dry run," be forced to bring her full load of torpedoes back to her base, expenditure of fuel—lighter than the water replacing it—would cause her to be so heavy that submerged trim would not be possible without using Safety tank as a part of the trimming system. The extra gun forward compounded the problem. Well, Safety had been designed with a view to this potential necessity. It was already piped and valved into the trim system. If necessary, he would use it.

Keith put it into words. "Skipper," he said, "they'd give you ten TBTs on the bridge if you wanted them, or fifty torpedoes. If you asked them, I think these guys would jack up the periscope and build a new submarine underneath it for you!"

It was true, and the amount of work agreed to be accomplished upon *Eel* in the period of two weeks was nothing less than prodigious. The clue—it was more than a clue, it was a plain statement—came as the conference was ending, as the base repair officer shook hands with Rich. "All of us lost some friends in AREA SEVEN," was what he said—and then his face showed dismay as he realized that somehow he had said the wrong thing.

The biggest problem concerned the hydraulic plant and what to do about it. *Eel* was a new submarine. The patrol just finished had been her first. She was also, however, one of the first to have the new enlarged hydraulic system. There had been no previous experience with this particular design. Much was known about the older hydraulic plants, which involved a smaller hydraulic accumulator and an entirely different hydraulic pump, but *Eel* presented completely new problems.

Al Dugan had carefully maintained the operational history of the plant, especially after difficulties had begun to appear. It was apparent that there was gradually worsening leakage of some kind taking place, perhaps in the accumulator itself, very likely elsewhere too. The expenditure of replacement hydraulic fluid had increased alarmingly in the last few days of the patrol, and the time between recharging cycles of the accumulator had reduced correspondingly.

It was agreed that the hydraulic plant would be completely disassembled and carefully tested. This was to be the principal job of the refit.

Richardson also found, to his surprise, that apparently as an afterthought Keith had requested a survey of the officers' shower with view to restoring the head room. If the heating control panels for the electric torpedoes could be relocated anywhere else in the compartment, Keith pointed out dryly, it might be possible to do away with the commanding officer's discomfort while bathing. Richardson had not spoken of the shower design, or joked about revenge upon the designer, for weeks. Changing the heating panels would be a large job for a marginal result. Keith must have done some negotiating with the base repair shop. Clearly, he expected the base to agree to do the work. He must have considered the job important.

Another conference was scheduled for the following morning, at which only Keith, as the ship's personnel officer, need be present. This was to review the rotation of crew members. Even though *Eel* had finished only one patrol, in order for the crew rotation policy to work it was necessary to replace some 20 percent of *Eel*'s complement by new people.

Richardson remembered his conversation of the previous evening with Admiral Small's driver, He fumbled for the page in his notebook where he had written his name. Lichtmann. "It's as good as done, Skipper," said Keith. "I told you they'll do anything they can for us around here. If we wanted Captain Blunt himself to go out with us next time, I bet he'd come."

"He is coming!"

"What?"

"We're going to the Yellow Sea on a three-boat wolfpack, with Blunt as wolfpack commander. This is all confidential, for now, so don't repeat it around where you can be overheard. We'll be flagship, so he'll be riding with us. You and I are going to be his right and left hand, I suspect, to help put this thing together."

"Oh, hell, Skipper, I was hoping to have another chance to go off by ourselves."

"Me too, Keith, but that's the way the ball bounced this time. Anyway, you know Blunt's an old friend and ex-skipper of mine. It will be great having him along with us."

The look on Keith's face showed his doubt. Clearly, Keith shared his skipper's silent reservations.

The chief problem of coordination between submarines, as all parties to the wolfpack well knew, was that of communication, Submarines patrolling close to an enemy shore spent their days submerged, surfacing to recharge their batteries under cover of darkness. When well away from land they might extend their daylight patrol radius by remaining on the surface, but they had to be ready to dive instantly if in danger of detection.

Once a radio circuit was established between surface ships, transmission and receipt of messages could be virtually assured. Because one never knew when a submarine might be submerged, however, such certainty could never exist between the members of a wolfpack. Very long wave signals from a powerful nearby shore station could be received to a shallow depth with a specially insulated antenna, but the high frequency radio signal of even a nearby submarine could not be heard beneath the surface; nor could a boat transmit while submerged. Furthermore, a receipting system was mandatory, for otherwise there would be no assurance that a particular message of extreme importance had been received by one's wolfpack mates. A submarine required to make an important transmission, for example an enemy contact report, very likely might have only seconds available before combat or initimate danger. But she could never be sure the message had been received until at least one other boat transmitted a radio receipt signal. She would have to wait, possibly repeat the message, and thus further compromise herself.

The longer the radio message, the greater the chance of its interception by an alert enemy. This could lead to location of the transmitting submarine by a direction-finding station, even to breaking down the code of the message. The result would be a paucity of enemy traffic through the suspect area and a greater likelihood of anti-sub sweeps. Some wolfpacks had developed special codes to reduce the lengths of their radio transmissions. Keith had been an interested follower of the systems devised, and several times he had stated they did not go far enough. Communications between its members, he said, was the crucial weakness of all wolfpacks. It had been left almost entirely to the communications officers and senior radiomen, whereas clearly it should receive the personal attention of the wolfpack commanders and skippers. Keith's impassioned presentation easily convinced Richardson, who had long harbored the same thoughts himself. The interview with Blunt ended as Keith and Rich had hoped, with Blunt's approval of Keith's ideas. But, beyond giving support to the project in general terms, the prospective wolfpack commander had displayed surprising passivity, almost disinterest.

"You'd think he thinks it's easy!" burst out Keith, once safely out of earshot.

"He's just depending on us, especially you, since it's your idea. He's paying you a compliment."

"I don't read him that way at all. He just doesn't realize how tough it is to talk to another boat out in the area!"

"Come on, Keith. Neither have we experienced the problem so far. He knows what he's doing. Anyway, we've got his backing. Isn't that what you wanted?" Richardson's words were mild enough, but there was a snap of finality to them. His protective instinct regarding Blunt had overreached; he had overdone it. Keith had felt the slight degree of asperity and was giving him a troubled look.

Two days after the new *Chicolar* had been welcomed from Mare Island, the three skippers and their wolfpack commander met for their first formal conference. Blunt had decided, he said, that the first submarine to detect a convoy would not attack. It would instead trail the enemy and send position reports to help the other two boats to make contact also. The second submarine to make contact would be the first to attack. Then it would fall astern to perform the trailing duties. Not until at least one other sub had attacked and had fallen behind, out of the immediate vicinity of the convoy, was the original "trailer" released to make an attack of her own.

Attacks were to be made on the surface at night as a matter of preference, with due regard for the location of the trailer, who would presumably be keeping station from a sufficiently great distance that no one could mistake her on the radar for a patrolling enemy escort. In addition, narrow sectors directly ahead and directly astern of the convoy center were designated as safe sectors. No submarine could attack another ship in such a sector without positive visual identification. Other larger sectors were designated as unlimited attack zones, where attack on any target was permitted no matter how it might have been detected.

Whenever possible, day or night, Blunt stressed, all submarines should stay on the surface in order to facilitate both communication and positioning for attack.

Richardson found that the ideas of the other two skippers as to how to carry out night attacks in the surfaced condition were quite at variance with his own. Les Hartly of the *Chicolar*, a rotund and very intense officer, the senior of the three submarine captains, had only one method, to which he held strongly. At the beginning of the war he had commanded an S-boat in the Asiatic Fleet, undeniably an experience to confirm anyone's latent qualities of self-sufficiency. Lack of a TDC in the S-boats had led to development of more rudimentary approach techniques, based mostly on time-honored concepts of the "seaman's eye." Even though Les had later commanded the more modern *Porpoise* for several patrols, the presence of an early TDC in her control room had not caused him to modify his notions. After three runs in the *Porpoise* he had been granted leave, to which all Asiatic submariners were clearly entitled, and had then been sent to Mare Island to commission and bring out the new *Chicolar*.

Hartly by consequence had been more than a year away from the war; but his ideas were nonetheless positive. He spent far more time expounding on their advantages than in listening to those of others. Blunt was the only one who might have commanded his attention, but even the wolfpack commander, with no war patrols to his credit, was at a disadvantage. Only Keith, with eight, topped Hartly's record of seven war patrols, and Hartly quickly disposed of all suggestions differing from the conclusions he had already fixed on.

The way to handle a convoy, he said many times, was to attack instantly, if possible as soon as contact was made. In this way the risk of counter-measures would be least. He thought of *Chicolar* as a huge torpedo running on the surface which he would steer at high speed directly for the enemy, continually altering course to keep bows on to the ship he had selected for primary target. Hartly's attack course was thus always a long sweeping curve. At the last minute he would shoot his torpedoes and then put the rudder over hard in whatever direction looked best.

Since Hartly wasted no time in preliminaries, other than seeking a feasible attack position, his method had the undeniable advantage of being finished very quickly. Another strong point was that *Chicolar* never exposed more than a bows-on silhouette to her intended victims.

Vainly, Richardson stated the counter arguments. The curved attack course deprived Hartly's plotting parties of a reasonable opportunity to determine the enemy course, speed, and zigzag plan. The emphasis on immediate attack compounded the plotters' difficulties. Lack of previous study of the enemy's movements would prevent them from detecting an unexpected zig until some time afterward, if at all. A large zig away would put the submarine far astern, with a long chase or loss of the opportunity inevitable. A zig toward might put the submarine suddenly dead ahead of the enemy—which usually had one escort out in front—in a bow-to-bow situation with a closing rate equal to the sum of the speeds. This was the most serious of all the contingencies. A surface attack was no longer possible; discovery and counterattack were virtually certain.

It was a matter of individual submarine tactics, professional expertise. Because of the large divergence in views the subject was tacitly avoided in Blunt's presence, but several times, until it became an incipient cause of acrimony, Rich brought a more general discussion between the three skippers around to this topic. In desperation, and against his better judgment, he finally began to extole his own procedures, which were to track at about seven miles' distance, and a little ahead of the beam, until all the variables had been as well determined as could be. Then, immediately after the convoy had settled upon a favorable zig course, so that there would be several minutes before the next zig, he would turn in for a deliberate, calculated attack. An inestimable benefit Rich saw in his method was that anything out of the ordinary on the part of the target would instantly be detected by plot, for by this time the plotters would have nothing else to worry about.

But there was no convincing Les Hartly. And he roundly condemned *Eel*'s extra torpedoes and the second five-inch gun.

Whitey Everett, the new skipper of *Whitefish*, must have been assigned that particular submarine by someone with a sense of humor. The nickname had been bestowed years ago for his extraordinarily blond hair, now shading into premature gray. The *Whitefish* was a relatively old submarine, having been completed at the Electric Boat Company yards in Groton, Connecticut, only a couple of months after the *Walrus*. Rich and Keith had watched her launched and had known many of her original crew.

She was essentially a carbon copy of *Walrus*, with slightly greater austerity in her interior appointments because, unlike the *Walrus*, her construction had been ordered after the war began. Everett, a year senior to Richardson, was in fact her third skipper. This was to be his first command patrol. Slow-moving, taciturn, he had early developed a reputation for wisdom. He had been executive officer of a fleet submarine at the beginning of the war, but had then spent some time in New London as skipper of one of the training boats. Subsequently he had returned to the Pacific for a "make-ye-learn" cruise as a prospective commanding officer—a "PCO"—and now, somewhat to his chagrin, had drawn the *Whitefish* instead of one of the newer, heavier-built submarines like *Eel* or *Chicolar*.

Whitey had never participated in a night attack on the surface, Rich quickly realized. Perhaps the aura of deliberateness which he had so long cultivated actually masked inner insecurity. Despite all the theory he had been subjected to and all the discussions he had engaged in, he really had no confidence in his ability to engage in a high speed night action. Patently, he felt most comfortable submerged. On the game floor, whenever the choice was left to him, he elected to attack submerged at daybreak, having used up the whole night waiting for this single opportunity.

The gaming sessions were made as realistic as possible. Each of the three subs was given its own headquarters, with charts, navigation tools, and encoding equipment, and was permitted to communicate with the other submarines only by simulated radio messages. All messages were required to be in the special submarine attack code which Rich and Keith had devised, and no submarine could send or receive messages while it was "submerged." Players were permitted to view the game floor only when, according to the tactical situation, they were actually in a position to do so. Even then, they could see only that portion of the game floor which, supposedly, would have been in sight through the periscope, or on their radar, under the conditions of the moment.

By the time the long game days wore to an end, Richardson felt mentally exhausted. It was not so much that he was physically tired. Keith rightly put it to boredom. "Dammit, Captain, this is just a communication drill. All we're doing is writing messages on pieces of paper. It's almost a waste of time!"

"Not quite true, Keith," said Richardson, again alertly ready to defend Blunt. "We're getting to know how the other fellows think and work. We've noticed quite a difference between Les Hartly and Whitey Everett. Another thing it's doing is to give all of us a workout in your new code."

Again there was the slightly abashed look on Keith's face. Twice, within a very few days, he had thought he understood what was running through his skipper's mind only to find that, somehow, he had missed a signal, had gotten unaccountably off the track. "Well, I guess that's right," he said uncomfortably. "But you've got to admit this is sure tiresome. I suppose it will be a lot different when we try it aboard ship at sea."

"It's pretty tiresome, all right. But it will be better when we take on that convoy from San Francisco." Richardson was feeling twinges of conscience for not having let his most loyal supporter know more of what had been troubling him, but of this he could not speak. He would, however, have continued with a few more encouraging words had not the approach of the unwitting cause of the misunderstanding, Captain Blunt, cut short the conversation.

In addition to the preparations for wolfpack operations, a great deal was going on exclusively concerned with the *Eel* herself. The relaxation and ease of the Royal Hawaiian Hotel could not compare with the supreme interest in seeing that she was properly gotten ready for the forthcoming patrol. Most of her officers, particularly as the two weeks off the ship drew to a close, found more and more reason to spend long hours on board. Al Dugan, heavyset, phlegmatic, methodical, a submarine engineer to his fingertips, nearly matched Richardson's own devotion to *Eel*'s reconditioning. The most important thing he had going, he several times told his wardroom mates, was the hydraulic plant. There was no question in his mind that the problem would be discovered and solved, but as the days wore on and the week of refamiliarization training approached, he gradually began to devote most of his time to watching the work and participating in it. His responses to Richardson's questions on the subject, while still full of confidence, betrayed his concern. To assist Al in his other responsibilities, he was given full use of the new officer just assigned, Ensign Johnny Cargill. In size, shape, and temperament a younger Dugan, Cargill had graduated from the submarine school at New London only weeks before. His orders to *Eel* in his hand, he had been an unnoticed member of the group which met the submarine upon her arrival in Pearl Harbor and had automatically landed in her refit crew. He was eagerly trying to be useful and, according to the engineer, despite his youth and complete lack of experience was proving to be of real help. It became accepted that he would be assigned under Al as assistant engineer.

Richardson himself took on the problem of relocating the two Target Bearing Transmitters—one of them new—on either side of *Eel's* bridge cockpit. A segment of the bulletproof side plating had been cut out of each side, and new bulged pieces to accomodate the instruments inserted. To get it done right, Richardson went over to the Pearl Harbor Navy Yard with the sections of heavy steel plate which had to be bent into a particular shape to fit his drawings. When the TBTs were mounted he personally supervised their location, height and precise alignment. Finally, with Buck Williams and Keith Leone assisting him, he spent hours carefully "bore-sighting" the transmitters, so that they accurately transmitted the angles of aim to the repeater dials in the conning tower.

The two-week refit at Pearl Harbor, supposed to be rest and relaxation for submarine crews between patrols, had been something less than restful for him, *Eel's* skipper realized, when he and his crew rendezvoused back aboard their submarine. First, of course, there had been the coordinated tactics training, the "convoy college." Then there were the demands of the refit itself, theoretically carried out in entirety under the supervision of the relief commanding officer. Obviously, however, the real commanding officer of any particular submarine could never be unconcerned about the work in progress.

And finally, of course, there was the time spent with Joan. Blunt had been right in one thing. She was indeed sought after. She must have especially made herself available for him—otherwise he'd have had no time with her at all. He found it difficult to analyze his feeling for her. The tensions of war and his own psychic needs were a part of it. So was her tremendous physical attraction. But this last was not special for him alone. Many had felt it. Jim Bledsoe, for one.

Deliberately, he had made his second evening with Joan as different from the first one—only the day previous—as he could. There was a nightclub in Honolulu which catered to the young-officer set, with a maximum of privacy and a dance band. Ostentatiously, it was placarded to the effect that it would close its doors half an hour before the curfew, to make sure that everyone had plenty of time to get home. For most of its habitués, Richardson found, this only adjourned the evening somewhere else. Hesitantly, he confessed that his ingenuity had not extended that far, and that he had not wanted to be with Captain Blunt a second night. Joan dimpled, and made it come right. Her room in Fort Shafter was only a convenience, a place to sleep should she have to remain late on some special project. She had a private apartment in the Moana Valley, with a private entrance.

The apartment was tiny, secluded, tastefully decorated, austere rather than luxurious. All Joan's possessions, she told him, had been lost when she had had to leave Japan on the eve of war. Her father was in the diplomatic service, but she did not know where he was and thought he might be dead. (Richardson felt this was not strictly true.) Her mother had died some years ago. (This must be true.) It was not until several days later that Richardson realized this was the extent of the information he was likely to learn about her. She was adroit at making him talk about himself, his time at Annapolis, his first duty after graduation, his boyhood in California, his father's zealous career as a Presbyterian minister, the often expressed ambition for Rich to follow in his footsteps. The bad times of 1930 had wrecked the traveling preacher's hopes of sending his son to divinity school, and he had died within the year. The appointment to Annapolis had come as a chance for an education which the new widow would have been unable to provide from her meager estate. It also answered a deep personal dilemma. Rich, even as a boy, had sensed that he lacked his father's dedication to the ministry. His mind ran to mechanical things. He loved machinery. The complex machinery of a submarine was a constant source of delight, and operating it, or watching someone else operate it—if he did it well—was sensuous pleasure.

It was peaceful listening to Joan's records and talking quietly about the years before the war, when things (from the present view, at least) were much less complicated. He even told her one day about his girl while at the Naval Academy, his "OAO" (the initials were for "One And Only" in the schoolboy lexicon). Sally and he had had fun together. Undoubtedly, she had made someone a fine wife. His classmate Stocker Kane had married immediately after the expiration of the two-year rule, two years to the day after they had graduated. At one point Sally and he had planned the same; but as the two years stretched out ahead, and the demands of a navy life occupied all his interest, he had realized that his own confidence had not matched Sally's.

"It was just that you didn't really love her, Rich," said Joan. "It was too soon for you." He had to admit to himself that this was true.

Inevitably, even during their closest moments, when the war seemed so distant and Joan's nearness so fulfilling, that cursed second self of his, which had forced the break with Sally, which sometimes took possession of him or, most often, merely stood there, watching, would evoke the thought of Laura.

Laura. Jim Bledsoe's widow. Richardson could clearly remember the moment when he first met her. A near disaster during training operations. A trip to the bar at the New London Submarine Base Officer's Club afterward. Jim bringing forward a smiling girl in a green dress. "This is Laura." Gray-green eyes. Tall. Slender. Cool hand in his. Blond hair—natural. Rich's nerves still jumping from the near-collision during a practice approach that afternoon, had responded magically to her presence. She was the first girl, in fact the only girl, who had ever affected him to such a degree. Had she not been Jim's, had Jim not been his exec in the *S-16*—if there had only been more time—he might have dared to pursue the strong emotion Laura had so suddenly awakened in him.

The coming of war, a few weeks later, had telescoped everything. A cold, rainy Sunday at the club at New London. A chance encounter with Laura and Jim. The voice on the radio in the next room, sounding somehow different from the regular announcer, letting it be known, even though his words could not be distinguished, that something was radically wrong. Laura, sent back to New Haven. *S-16*, bravely, uselessly, girding for a possible sneak attack in the Thames River. A short time later, still in December, the terribly bad moment over Jim's qualification for command of submarines. Laura, once warm and friendly, now cold. Still perfect, but even the coolness was perfection. Then it became apparent that she and Jim still hoped to snatch out of the jaws of war at least a few normal, or near-normal, months together. Before the *Walrus* was ready to go to sea, Jim had come in with a request for transfer to a New London–based submarine. It had been totally unexpected. Jim was petulant, antagonistic. In a release of long-suppressed emotion he had cursed the *Walrus*, Richardson, the whole naval establishment.

Perhaps Richardson should have approved the request and sent it forward. The official response would have been automatic; it would have been approved. But Jim's position would have been understood as unwillingness, or fear, to enter the active war. His career in submarines

5 9

would have been finished. He would have carried the black mark with him forever. Richardson already bore some of the responsibility for the unfortunate qualification fiasco. He could not do more to Jim than he had done already, however inadvertently.

He had made his voice cold, devoid of emotion. Standing at his desk, he tore up Jim's paper, threw it aside.

The effect on Laura was something Rich knew he would have to endure in silence. Whatever she knew or surmised about the workings of the navy, she must certainly have been bitter at the hand the navy had dealt her. She must have stated it to Jim. It just wasn't fair. Jim should have been allowed to stay in New London a while longer. Someone else, despite the black mark of his earlier failure, surely would have given him a second chance to qualify for command. Both of them must have known it was Richardson who had blocked that road.

And then there had been the emotion-charged day of leaving New London for the war zone. Memorial Day, 1942. Laura had been a guest for lunch in *Walrus'* tiny wardroom. She and Jim had been married for only five days. It was the last time they were to see each other. Here, with *Walrus* on the point of departure—forever, as it had turned out—Richardson received a flash of pure personal insight. It was an affecting moment for all hands, with most of the crew saying longing and fearful farewells to their loved ones. He, on the other hand, the captain of the sub, had no one to bid him good-bye except the admiral at the submarine base, who routinely did this for all departing boats; Captain Blunt, his squadron commander; and a few other skippers.

It was at that instant, for the first time, that he was able to identify the strange feeling he had for Laura. She was Jim's. They had pledged themselves to each other. Richardson had grown to love her, and that was the beginning and the end of that, too.

Through it all, something of which he could never speak, Laura had come to personify the girl he would one day want to marry. Gradually he had come to know it, to accept it. But why had he opposed Jim's request for transfer? Why had he insisted on taking a disgruntled, potentially disloyal, second-in-command to sea with him? Was it only, as he tried to make himself believe, and as Jim had apparently at last been convinced, that he felt a responsibility to protect Jim from the full consequences of his ineptitude? Was this the only reason, or was there something underlying it, something deeper, more basic? Could he have wanted to separate Jim from Laura?

Buried within every soul lies a capacity for evil. Could that have been his real, his (even to himself) unadmitted motive? It was the first time he had followed this train of thought. It scared him. It was monstrous, diabolical. He, Edward Richardson—"Rich" to Jim and Laura—was not capable of such an act, much less the thought of it. Yet now he had thought of it. The question was whether he had also thought of it, somehow, subtly, unconsciously, before the *Walrus* got underway from New London.

Joan had sensed something. She was withdrawing from him, growing indefinably more distant. There was something cold inside him. The second self was telling him to stop this morbid thinking. He had acted honestly, without conscious thought of self, or Laura. He had salvaged Jim's submarine career. It was because of him that Jim had had the chance to find himself. He could hold himself to no responsibility for Jim's death. Good men had died in the war. Jim had simply been one of them. So had Tateo Nakame.

Joan accepted his mute apology. No word had been spoken. He wondered whether she had guessed he was thinking about another girl.

The in-port routine between patrols always involved, at its end, a third week of exercises at sea. With three submarines designated to travel out to the same exercise area and there operate as a coordinated team, the at-sea period became a strenuous rehearsal for the tactics they had practiced on the game floor. A supply convoy was due in Pearl Harbor from San Francisco. The three boats spent the entire week lying in wait for it, planning its interception, trailing it. For two days and two nights, simulated attacks were carried out. At the end of the time, when the ships arrived at their destination, the eight-ship convoy had twice been theoretically wiped out. Richardson and Leone, who found themselves almost without supervision laying out the problem and the tactics for all three submarines, were so short on sleep as to be virtually wiped out themselves. Blunt, on the other hand, having delegated both minor and major decisions to his two subordinates, made up for long nights of pursuit and attack by equally long naps during the days. At the conclusion of the training he felt better rested, he said, than he had for years. Being at sea again, he repeated several times, was a tremendous tonic.

It was already dark when *Eel* slid alongside her berth at the submarine base. The training period had been pronounced a complete success. A staff car was waiting for the freshly shaven and showered wolfpack commander, who promptly disappeared. Keith gave Richardson a long, silent look as the two wearily dropped on their bunks.

ComSubPac was holding a conference. The reason was clear when the only attendees turned out to be a Captain Caldwell, the operations officer now temporarily also filling in as chief of staff, Blunt as wolf-

61

pack commander, and the skippers of the three submarines assigned to him. "This is top secret," Admiral Small cautioned them. "You may not speak of it outside this room, not even to your execs. After you get to sea and are beyond Midway, you are authorized to let them know, but not until then, and no one else under any circumstances."

The three skippers nodded their understanding. Rich shot a glance at Blunt and Caldwell. They were looking steadily at the admiral. From their expressions, they already knew what was to come. This interview, then, was for the benefit of Les Hartly, Whitey Everett, and himself. It would prove the rightness or wrongness of his deductions regarding the importance of the mission they were to be sent on.

Even as the thought raced through his head, Admiral Small confirmed it. "The purpose of this meeting is to inform you three commanding officers of your special mission. You will commit it to memory. You may make no notes of any kind. It will not be mentioned in your operation orders. While I'm speaking, go ahead and ask questions on any points you wish. This is the only notification you'll receive."

Small motioned to Caldwell, who rose to draw back the curtain covering the wall chart. It was a different chart from the one Richardson had seen only a few months ago. Larger, more detailed as to land topography. Evidently a metal backing had been installed when the chart was changed, for Caldwell next selected several items from a box and placed them, with a noticeable metallic click, upon its vertical surface. Even Blunt leaned forward attentively.

A red ring had been placed around a tiny island almost at the southern tip of the Nampo Shoto chain—the Bonins—and, almost due west, a large red arrow pointed to a much bigger island at the southern extremity of the Nansei Shoto, the Ryukyu group. Below the arrow, hand-lettered on a piece of cardboard mounted on a large magnet, were the words, "OPERATION ICEBERG."

The red ring covered the name of the small island, but Rich had plotted his way through the Nampo Shoto too many times to fail to recognize it instantly. Iwo Jima.

The other island, almost directly west of Iwo Jima, was equally familiar: Okinawa.

The admiral was talking. "Gentlemen, Operation ICEBERG is scheduled to begin in January. It is only the first move, and perhaps the most important, in the campaign which will end in Tokyo, we hope, in the fall. First, we are going to take Iwo Jima by assault. Its garrison is already isolated. There will be a heavy bombardment by naval ships and the army air corps, and then our Marines will move in. The Japanese general there is a dedicated soldier and will fight to the last, but we expect to take it fairly quickly after his troops are softened up. Immediately afterward, before the Japs have time to catch their breath, we will move on Okinawa. That's our real objective. It will be the staging area for the attack on the home islands." He paused. His listeners were staring at the wall chart. His voice, measured, flat, emotionless, each sentence carrying the impact of an explosive charge, continued.

"We believe the enemy is unaware of our specific intentions, but by now he must have a pretty good idea of our Pacific strategy. The commander on Iwo has been told he can expect no reinforcements, that if attacked he must defend the island with what he's got. Once we take Iwo, however, Okinawa will clearly be one of our most likely objectives. Undoubtedly Japan will do her utmost to bolster its defenses. But she'll not expect a one-two punch, and that's why we plan to move so fast." He paused again. Richardson could hear Everett breathing beside him. No one spoke. The wall map held death for thousands of men, Japanese and Americans. Admiral Small was pronouncing their death sentences, though of course he had little to do with it. The decision must have been made in Washington, perhaps by the President himself, certainly upon recommendation by the Combined Chiefs of Staff: that extraordinary combination of the military leaders of all the allied nations in the war. Most of the men who would die would not know even that much. *Eel*, *Chicolar*, and *Whitefish* had a part to play. Other submarines, doubtless, had their parts too.

Perhaps the admiral had expected questions. There were none. He went on. "Our mission is to prevent reinforcements to either of these islands." Now he was coming to cases. "Special submarine patrol areas are about to be established around both Iwo and Okinawa. They will be kept occupied until each campaign is over, or, in the case of Iwo Jima, until it is clear the enemy is not going to send any more troops or supplies. Most of the Japanese forces are already pretty well tied down where they are anyway, with a single exception, the Kwantung Army. That's the one that has us worried, and that's where your three boats come in." Again Admiral Small paused. He looked steadily at the four sitting before him.

Rich nodded shortly, not bothering to note whether the others did also. The Kwantung Army was in Manchuria. Originally formed to safeguard territory seized from Russia, it had been the basis of Japan's political power in China's northern province. This was the army which had attacked China in the early thirties, and until Pearl Harbor the Kwantung Army had done nearly all of Japan's fighting. It was here that most of her top soldiers had received their early combat training.

Since 1941, however, the Kwantung Army had been employed only to hold the ground against the possibility of combat against either China or Russia. It had seen little if any action. Yet Japan kept huge forces there, forces she badly needed elsewhere. If the admiral was hinting that a combat role for the Kwantung Army was in the offing, was expected, there must be important business for any submarines in the Yellow Sea. Small was speaking again.

"Shipping in either direction between the home islands and Manchuria is critically important to Japan. Most significant, and of most importance to our forces, is any movement of troops out of Manchuria. We have received indications that the enemy may be contemplating shifting several complete divisions, but as yet we have no idea where to. As soon as they begin to suspect our plans for Okinawa, that's where they'll go for sure. They might even ship some of them to Iwo Jima. No matter where they go, they will be bad news for our men. They're well trained and well equipped. Their officers are fanatically eager to get into the war. It's up to us—to you fellows and your boats—to stop them from getting there.

"We'll keep you advised as well as we can, of course, via 'Ultra' messages. As you know, we're able to get certain extremely valuable information from a special group at Fort Shafter"—Small's eyes for a second flicked directly at Richardson—"and anything pertaining to the Kwantung Army or Manchuria in general will be sent to you immediately. Washington has directed that a coordinated submarine group be kept in the Yellow Sea. You are to try to cut off any traffic between Manchuria and the home islands of Japan. Generally speaking, there's quite a lot. We suspect most of it is moving close inshore. You can hurt them severely by sinking the ships carrying supplies and replacement cadres to or from Japan. Most important of all, however, are the organized divisions of that army in Manchuria. If we get wind of any movement involving them, you'll be expected to make a maximum effort to stop it. Carry out normal area coverage until you hear from us. But be ready to take decisive action if and when you do."

The large eyes in Admiral Small's heavy face fastened on each of his listeners in turn. His voice took on an even more somber tone. "Until and unless you hear from me differently, you will carry out a regular patrol. From that moment, however, this wolfpack becomes a special mission force. I do not have to tell you how important it is that these reinforcements, if the Japs attempt to send them, do not arrive. We don't yet know when they'll be sent, or if they will be, but to stop them, gentlemen, will immediately become the primary mission of this wolfpack. If they go, they must go by sea. They will hurt us badly if they reach Iwo Jima or Okinawa. It is up to you to see that they do not."

ComSubPac had finished his speech. "There are a couple of more items," said Caldwell. "First, we have been expecting to see more air activity in the Yellow Sea than has been the case. Perhaps the Japs are running low on aircraft, or perhaps they are conserving them for some other purpose. The low level of air activity may continue for you, or it may increase dramatically. In any case, be prepared for anything.

"Second point, watch the sampans. Some of them are not fishing boats at all, but specially built, big new patrol boats. They have sonar gear aboard, and they carry depth charges. Their main purpose is to detect and report submarines to the main ASW forces. They're built of wood and look like fishermen, but they're a lot bigger. So don't let that fool you. They have a pretty good size gun, about thirty-seven millimeter, and it's as good as our forties. Your operation order says to grab any good opportunity to knock them out with your guns. But be sure you catch them by surprise, because they can hurt you pretty badly with that gun. Their radio will alert the whole area that you're around, too, unless you're lucky enough to knock it out right at the beginning. So don't take one on until the area is already pretty well aware of your presence.

"Third thing, they don't have anybody as good as old Bungo in the Yellow Sea" (the bald mention of the name startled Richardson; he hoped his face did not betray him), "but they've got a pretty efficient antisub outfit. Several of our boats have had a bad time from them. They very nearly got the *Seahorse*, you know. That was after Cutter was detached. She was so badly damaged we've had to take her off the firing line, probably permanently. We think the wooden patrol boats and ASW tincans are all part of the same organization. The tincans are fairly small, about a thousand tons, but they're good sea boats with good sonar sets, plenty of depth charges and well trained crews. They're diesel powered, so they have good cruising range. They usually operate in groups of three; so if you run into one of them there's likely two more around somewhere, and they're not good news at all. Some time ago the Jap Navy began building a new and better antisub destroyer, or frigate as they call it. The first one was named the *Mikura*, and we think these boats in the Yellow Sea are probably *Mikura*-class tincans. They have a four-inch gun. Watch yourselves if you tangle with one."

There was not much more to the briefing. A few questions, a final exhortation by Admiral Small. When it was over, Richardson felt Whitey Everett's eyes upon him. Everett's face was unnaturally set, even for him. His cultivated austere appearance of competence was belied by the worried manner in which he shifted his eyes from one participant in the briefing to another. To Rich, the unexpected reference to Bungo Pete had been sudden and unsettling. He wanted only to go away, began to excuse himself, and then realized he could not. This would be Whitey's first patrol in command. He wanted reassurance about the *Mikuras*, wanted to suggest means of mutual support against them.

It was the last night in port. Preparations for going to sea were complete. Nothing more needed to be done, except see Joan one last time. He could still make some time for Whitey. He would be late, but Joan would understand.

- 4 -

It was with a sense of calm, even peace, that Richardson gave the orders for getting *Eel* underway the next afternoon. Actually he had little to do with it. Keith had already handled all the arrangements. Al Dugan, the engineer, would have the honor of being Officer of the Deck and giving the commands which would take *Eel* to sea once more.

By custom, submarines departing on patrol got underway in the midafternoon. If more than one left the same day, the most senior departed last. This, of course, was *Eel*. *Whitefish* and *Chicolar*, at adjacent piers, had backed clear a few minutes before, and *Whitefish* had already rounded Ten-Ten Dock on her way out the Pearl Harbor entrance channel. *Eel* was the third of the three submarines to get underway, befitting her status as flagship for Blunt's Bruisers, the wolf-pack code name.

Admiral Small was the last to say good-bye. He shook hands with Richardson, then Blunt. "Good luck and good hunting," he said. A warm smile for Rich, a meaningful one for Blunt. He stepped quickly ashore.

From the bridge, Al Dugan: "Take in the brow!"

Four sailors, who had stepped into position alongside of it—again the ceremonial brow was in use—seized its rails in unison. In one co-ordinated movement they yanked it clear of *Eel*'s forecastle.

The mooring lines had already been singled up, reduced to a single strand from each of the four cleats on *Eel*'s deck to corresponding cleats on the pier. "Take in all lines!" said Al. "Rudder amidships! All back one-third!"

Eel's engines, idling quietly with a small spatter of water from their mufflers, took on a slightly deeper note when her controllermen in the maneuvering room put the motors in reverse and began to draw power from her generators. Slowly she moved backward. When clear of the pier, Dugan ordered the rudder full right. *Eel*'s stern began to curve to starboard as she entered the harbor waters.

Richardson stood alongside Blunt on the cigarette deck. At just the right moment Dugan shifted the starboard propeller from "back one-third" to "ahead two-thirds," and a moment later the rudder from "right full" to "left full." Now well in the channel, *Eel* began to twist on her heel, continuing to cast to port. Her backward motion slowly ceased. She began to gain headway.

The crowd on the dock had not yet begun to dissipate. The band was playing "Sink 'Em All." How many times had he heard it? Originally it had been "Bless 'Em All." Some submariner had written new words for it.

Under Buck Williams' rapid direction, order was appearing on deck. All topside gear not necessary to the patrol had already been removed, and now the remainder was swiftly stowed. As *Eel* rounded Hospital Point in her turn, and caught sight once again of *Whitefish* and *Chicolar* in column ahead, the last man went down below and the last hatch on deck was dogged shut.

Williams appeared on the bridge. "Main deck secured, anchor secured for sea, sir," he said to Dugan, with a nod to Keith. He stepped a few feet aft. "Main deck secured, topside secured, Captain," he said to Rich. He gave an unnecessary salute, probably for Blunt's benefit.

Gravely, Rich returned the salute. "Very well," he said.

Williams returned to the fore part of the bridge to where Al Dugan had assumed his watch station behind the windscreen. "There are no unauthorized personnel topside, Al. The captain, wolfpack commander, and executive officer are on the bridge. . . ."

"I know about the bridge, Buck," said Dugan in a tone of friendly sarcasm. "But thanks anyway."

"Oh, go to hell, Al." Williams grinned. "Permission to go below, sir."

Dugan grunted assent and Buck disappeared down the hatch into the conning tower. This hatch, the main induction, and the engine exhaust valves were now the only openings not tightly closed.

In a few minutes Rich would hear from below decks, "Ship is rigged for dive!" From that moment he, or any Officer of the Deck, had but to give the order to submerge to have it happen. All main vents would instantly spring open; the main engines would shut down; the main induction and engine exhaust valves would be closed; the motors, which had been getting their power from the generators on the ends of the diesel engines, would begin drawing current from the battery. Bow planes would rig out, and the ship would plunge precipitantly beneath the surface of the sea.

Richardson's feeling of well-being persisted as *Eel* passed the channel entrance buoys. It was here the Kona wave had nearly swamped the ship. Here was where he might have been swept overboard. He might have been able to swim to shore, or he might have drowned. It would have been a test. He might even have welcomed it at the time. . . .

Eel felt taut beneath him. Clean. Fresh-smelling. She had been re-painted. The two TBTs in their new locations on either side of the bridge had proved their increased convenience during the week-long exercises just completed. In place of the after TBT there was now located a twin twenty-millimeter machine gun mount. The guns them-selves, not sufficiently corrosion-resistant to stand submergence, were stowed in cylindrical tanks installed vertically under the bridge deck. They could be brought up and made ready in less than a minute.

On either end of the bridge was a forty-millimeter automatic gun. These were too heavy to manhandle for stowage and hence had been permanently mounted. Cadmium plating protected their unpainted sur-faces. Ranged about them were various strategically located racks to hold extra ammunition.

On the main deck there were now two stubby, five-inch guns, one forward and one aft of the bridge. Near them, built into each end of *Eel*'s bridge structure, were two large cylindrical tanks with hatchlike closures. Each held twelve shots of ready five-inch ammunition, and a rough bore-sight tool of Buck Williams' invention. Submergence or depth charging might ruin the delicate alignment of the pointer and trainer telescopes, Buck had warned. This could easily be checked by fitting his new tool, which contained a small telescope with cross-hairs, into the open breech, then check-sighting the guns on designated marks on deck forward and aft.

On the forecastle, also at Williams' suggestion, the forward torpedo room hatch now carried emplacements welded on either side to accom-modate a fifty-caliber machine gun. The gun would be served by two men standing on a plank placed across rungs inside the opened hatch. The forward hatch trunk was ideal for this "foxhole" function, as Buck had enthusiastically explained, because it was fitted with a lower hatch which could be shut to preserve watertight integrity while the gun was engaged. If the ship were forced to submerge suddenly, its crew had only to shut the upper hatch to be safe inside. And if they couldn't make it, the lower hatch would at least protect the rest of the ship from flooding.

Six fifty-caliber mounts had been installed on the bridge also, three on each side, with stowages for the three demountable guns arranged nearby. From the center area of the bridge, protected by its armored siding, a very respectable fusillade could be maintained in case of necessity. Repeated drills had been held for all guns. All-in all, *Eel* could fire a great arsenal of weapons if it came to surface gun action.

Under Keith's supervision, the bridge lookout platforms now had an upturned edging, or rim, that the men could feel with their toes. This would give them a feeling of security when the ship began rolling in a seaway, and in consequence they would keep a more effective watch. To facilitate quick descent from the lookout stations, sections of pipe had been installed in the manner of firemen's poles. The guard rails within which they stood had been made smaller and raised several inches so that they could also function as arm rests while binoculars were held at eye level. Reduction of arm fatigue and of concern for holding on as the ship rolled, Keith had argued, was the answer to the lookout weariness which had worried them.

Below decks little visible change had been accomplished, except that the top of the shower in the forward torpedo room had been restored to its proper dimensions. Richardson had thought of offering his own stateroom to Captain Blunt in deference to his rank, but after discussion with Keith had not done so. "You're still captain of this ship," Keith had said. "You'll need all those dials, call buttons and squawk boxes, and he won't. When the OOD needs you, he'll need you very much, and we've got to have you right at the other end!" It was this last argument that convinced him.

The matter had never been discussed with the wolfpack commander. Perhaps it should have been, thought Richardson uneasily, when, to everyone's surprise, Blunt insisted on taking the least desirable bunk, that on the wardroom transom, even though there was a spare bunk in one of the staterooms. It was not until determined protest had been made, pointing out that this would greatly reduce the usefulness of the wardroom for early breakfasts and late coffee, as well as its myriad other functions, that he permitted himself to be assigned one of the three bunks in Keith's room, across the passageway from Rich.

During the refit the biggest job, involving the most anxiety, had been the overhaul of the hydraulic system. It had been taken apart completely and thoroughly inspected. Nothing specific had been found wrong except slight scoring on the inner walls of the accumulator. When put back together, the entire system had been pronounced perfect. All during the training period it had functioned as predicted, its cycling time restored to the original specifications. It would cause no further trouble, the relief crew skipper had said. Al Dugan, when asked privately, expressed the same opinion, but Richardson, looking back later on their brief conversation, could recall a fleeting impression that Dugan had less than full confidence in his own words.

The other major improvement was the installation of one of the new radar periscopes. Unfortunately, its top was considerably larger than that of the original night periscope which it replaced; inclusion of radar had necessitated a four-foot reduction in effective length, and removal of the optical range-finder. To obtain a radar range, which was the only kind it could get, the now club-headed instrument had to be raised several feet higher out of water than had been necessary with the old optical periscopes.

But the radar periscope did give very precise ranges, and Richardson had practiced assiduously with it, along with Rogers, the teen-aged operator who came aboard with it from the Fleet Radar School. Fortunately, the attack periscope was still the old type with a very thin, tapered head, almost invisible if adroitly used. For the latter stages of a submerged attack, Richardson had resolved, he would revert to the optical system to gain the advantages of deeper submergence and a less visible periscope.

In sum, a truly extraordinary amount of work had been done on *Eel* during the refit period. Her new paint job topside and all her new equipment had virtually made her a new submarine. Satisfaction filled her skipper, tempered by the realization that with Blunt aboard he would not be entirely her master. Something else was nagging the back of his mind also, something unstated, unarticulated. The controversy over Blunt's bunk had been a minor thing. But was it indicative of something, a state of mind maybe? Surely it was not worthy of further thought. Blunt probably had not intended to appear disappointed. Probably Richardson had misread him. Best put all this behind, lay it to the pressures and problems of Pearl Harbor.

He would concentrate on the thought that a certain degree of relaxation would be his during the patrol to come, for the big decisions to attack or not to attack, to risk his life and that of his crew, or not to do so, would be made by someone else. And as his own responsibility decreased, his freedom of mind to think through the dilemmas of the past two months would be correspondingly greater. He should be able to follow Blunt's lead implicitly, as he had before in the *Octopus*. Once Blunt had shaken off the miasma of Pearl Harbor, he would be his old self again. The weight of Richardson's responsibility would be confined only to the efficient operation of the *Eel* as a submarine.

Even as he rehearsed the thought, however, it occurred to him that on the other hand perhaps the worst thing would be to have nothing to occupy his mind as he lay sleepless in his bunk, studying the shadowed metal walls surrounding him. This had been his trouble on the way back from the last patrol. It had become progressively worse the farther *Eel* voyaged from the battle zone.

As night came on, he almost dreaded the prospect of once again lying there sleepless, the memory of Pearl Harbor's activity—and Joan —fading, while all the familiar objects and sounds associated with that difficult trip home were free to reassert their depressing dominance.

7 1

The three submarines, proceeding on parallel but well separated tracks, did not sight each other until they rendezvoused for refueling at Midway Island.

Next morning they set forth again, running separately and in radio silence. Blunt had decided there had been adequate exercise in convoy techniques and there need be no drills en route to the patrol area. All submarines were to run as fast as they could consistent with safety and conservation of fuel, remaining on the surface at all times except for morning dives to get a trim or—after entry into enemy waters—when submerging to avoid detection.

The days passed with monotony as the three submarines approached the far western Pacific. With increasing urgency Richardson began to make the point that some coordinated drills were essential to maintain the unity of the newly created wolfpack. There need be little loss of time, virtually no additional expenditure of fuel. The three members of Blunt's Bruisers had had no joint operating experience except for the short time together at Pearl. To his surprise, his arguments had no noticeable effect. Blunt listened, but with scant attention, saying only that rest was necessary for everyone before entering enemy controlled waters. Then everything would fall into place.

The second cup of coffee after dinner in *Eel*'s tiny wardroom became the occasion for a daily discussion. Near-pleading by Richardson, stubborn refusal by his superior. Twice Richardson privately cautioned Leone not to try to help. Emotion was creeping into the disputation; it would be the wrong thing to do.

With the first landfall on Japanese-held islands due in four days, Richardson changed debate tactics, concentrated on the needs of *Eel* herself. Every skipper had the right and duty to satisfy himself as to the state of training of his crew. This was his responsibility, not that of the wolfpack commander. The skippers of *Chicolar* and *Whitefish*, traveling out of sight, were making such decisions for themselves. *Eel*'s crew must not be allowed to go stale. It was purely a matter for each individual ship. He would carry out a full day's drill, lasting from before dawn until long after sunset. Convoy exercises were not involved. Blunt need pay no attention, could remain in the wardroom.

It was obligatory, however, to inform Blunt that he had determined to devote a day to drilling *Eel*'s crew. Acquiescence was surprisingly reluctant, even for this unassailable position.

It had never been a part of his old skipper's previous character to oppose training or drills of any kind. Quite the reverse. There was something under cover, some syndrome of fatigue in him, which Richardson must think about and try to alleviate. The voyage across the Pacific had been more of a strain than Richardson remembered from previous patrols, but as the day's work began, with Buck Williams on the TDC, Keith Leone as assistant approach officer, Stafford on the sonar, and Quin, the yeoman, wearing the battle telephone headset, he began to renew the confidence he had felt the last days in Pearl. Larry Lasche was assigned to the automatic plotting table in the after part of the conning tower, opposite the TDC—unfortunately with his back to Buck, with whom he was to coordinate, but this could not be helped. Young Rogers, fresh out of high school and an electronic hobbyist since childhood, was on the radar console. In the forward end of the conning tower, Scott was on the helm as before, with Oregon, senior quartermaster, on one side keeping the log, and Quin on the other.

Immediately beneath the hatch leading to the control room, on the port side of the control room, was the ship's diving station, where at battle stations Al Dugan held sway, assisted by Chief Starberg at the hydraulic manifold a few feet to his right. Sargent, number two in the auxiliary gang under Starberg, operated the air manifold across the compartment, on the starboard side of the control room. Communication with Dugan was through the open hatch or by telephone—or by the ship's general announcing system.

As the day's drills progressed, Richardson could feel the sinews of control tighten, their cohesiveness renew itself. The sharp edge of readiness, so painstakingly instilled, had been whetted.

During night surface approaches, the fundamental difference in stations was that Dugan and Richardson, along with a specially selected set of lookouts, moved to the bridge. Should it be necessary to dive, Richardson would drop into the conning tower, while Al Dugan and the lookouts, descending an additional level, would simply shift to the submerged condition at the diving station.

For surface gun action, day or night, however, the procedure was very different. Certain deck hatches would have to be open. A large number of men would be on deck to serve the two five-inch guns, plus extra men on the bridge for the automatic weapons. Immediate diving would not be possible. In an emergency it would be necessary to sacrifice guns and ammunition left topside. Exercising the guns with *Eel* already near to possible enemy air patrols would be unnecessarily hazardous. Richardson decided against it. The guns, so seldom used anyway, would have to go with whatever residual readiness remained from the training already received.

Deep in Richardson's mind, underlying the strenuous activities of the day, were Admiral Small's words about the impending operation against Iwo Jima and Okinawa. It was of maximum importance to the U.S.

cause to prevent any possible Kwantung Army reinforcement of the troops already in these two islands. The day's workout was just what *Eel's* crew needed to get them fully geared up for what might lie ahead.

Two weeks after leaving Pearl Harbor, having transited at night through the Nampo Shoto south of Iwo Jima, the three submarines separately passed north of Okinawa, timing their transit of the Ryukyu chain again for the dark hours. After a short detour to avoid a reputed mine field, they headed up on a northwesterly course into the operating area. During the entire voyage, neither ship nor plane had been seen.

That night, after the debris of the evening meal had been cleared away, Richardson deliberately brought the conversation around to the business at hand.

"Commodore," he said, "Keith and I have been studying our area and reading up on the dope ComSubPac put in the operation order." Keith produced a rolled up chart which he spread out on the table. "The two main Japanese focal points for shipping to and from China are Shanghai and Tsingtao. There is a little traffic, too, out of Tientsin, up here in the Gulf of Pohai. These three ports are pretty far apart."

"Yes, I know," said Blunt, stuffing tobacco from a pouch into his pipe.

"So it looks to us that the smart thing for the Japanese to do, considering the submarine danger, is to stay as close inshore as possible. These island chains shown here along the coast of Korea, west side and south side, practically provide an inland passage for them. There's a beautiful one here on the west coast, the Maikotsu Suido. The track charts of subs previously in the Yellow Sea show that our boats have seldom gone after them there.

"Any ships departing Tsingtao for Japan will most likely hug the coast of the Shantung Peninsula on a northeasterly course until they get to the narrowest part of the Yellow Sea. They'll run across at full speed, up here near the tip of the peninsula, and then head south along the Korean coast and through the Maikotsu Suido. The shortest route is of course straight across to the southwest tip of Korea and then into the Shimonoseki Strait and the Inland Sea, but from their point of view it's also the most foolish. The smart thing for all ships, including those from Shanghai, is to run up the coast of China and cross at the narrowest possible place. Once they know we're in the area, they might run even farther north, into the Gulf of Pohai."

Keith nodded his agreement.

Richardson dropped his voice. "Almost surely, Tsingtao will be the departure point for Kwantung Army divisions deploying to the war zone. That's the place we should watch most closely. But we don't want to be too obviously blockading it, because that would alert the enemy and increase the escort forces they'll provide."

Blunt, using his thumb to pack the tobacco into his pipe, said nothing. After a moment's pause, Rich continued.

"So, what we should do is blockade Tsingtao from a distance. We should send one boat into the Maikotsu Suido right away. It will be the ideal place to start. The other two, patrolling outside to the north and south, will be in position to take care of any ships diverting outside. If we hear anything from ComSubPac, all of us will be able to reach Tsingtao very——"

"Maybe so," interrupted Blunt, lighting his pipe and puffing. "But we haven't had any submarines in the Yellow Sea at all for a while. I think the Japs are probably running straight across, where there'll be more sea room. Anyway, that's where I want to start, where we can surface patrol for maximum coverage. Set up the regular patrol line, oriented north and south. We should be in position by morning. Something will turn up in a couple of days."

Abruptly he heaved himself up from the settee, drained his coffee cup, and walked out of the wardroom.

Richardson found Keith looking at him with a puzzled expression. "What was that about?" he said. "He didn't even listen. What's this business about sea room? Is he ticked off about something?"

Richardson shook his head. "Not that I know of," he said. "Probably he knows a lot about what they're doing that we don't." But the uneasy feeling had begun to grow again.

Shortly before dawn next morning, Richardson climbed up on the bridge. Keith was there with Oregon, still shooting his morning stars for a careful fix of position.

"Ready for our morning dive for trim, Keith?"

"Nearly, sir. One more star."

Swiftly Leone inverted his sextant, sighted on one of the pinpoints still showing through the rapidly graying atmosphere, with his left hand made a quick rough adjustment on the inverted sextant arc. Then, reversing the sextant to its correct position, he squinted at the star, gently rocked the sextant from side to side, carefully twirled the vernier scale knob with the thumb and forefinger of his right hand. "Stand by," he said. "Stand by—mark! Did you get it, Oregon?"

"Got it," said the quartermaster. Oregon held a notebook and a large pocket-watch in his left hand, was writing in the book with a pencil with his other hand. "Watch time was six thirty-seven and twenty-one seconds."

"Sixty-one degrees, fourteen minutes, and three-tenths," read Keith from his sextant scale. "That's it, Skipper. I'll figure it up right away. We're not far off our dead reckoning position, though. Should be right at our patrol spot."

Then to Buck Williams, who was Officer of the Deck, "Navigator and quartermaster going below, Buck." Keith and Oregon swung down the hatch.

Dawn was breaking rapidly. It was becoming perceptibly lighter. There was a muggy haze to the atmosphere, grayness creeping into the sky. The stars were already too dim to be viewed. The horizon was becoming more visible, though its outline was still far from clean. Keith must have had considerable difficulty in getting a sharp enough horizon for his sights. *Eel* lazed gently ahead, a single exhaust pipe aft burbling.

Rich put down the binoculars through which he had been surveying the sky and the sea, looked at Williams.

"We're ready to dive, Captain," reported the OOD. "We have two hundred fifty feet of water under the keel, going ahead one-third on one main engine. Battery charge is completed. So far as I know, we are on station."

"Very well, Buck," said Richardson. "Take her down."

"Clear the bridge!" yelled Buck. At the same time, he reached forward to a switchbox placed on the center of the bridge overhang just behind the windscreen, placed his entire mittened hand upon it, pressed distinctly two times. Simultaneously he shouted "Dive! Dive!" down the open hatch. The sound of the diving alarm reverberated loudly twice on the ship's general announcing system. At the order "Clear the bridge," the four lookouts posted on the periscope shears behind Williams hastily tucked their binoculars into their windbreakers, stooped through their lookout guard rails, grasped the fireman's poles, and slid swiftly down the intervening eight feet to the bridge deck. They landed with a thump. Half doubled over, protecting their binoculars with their left arms, they dashed forward to scramble one after the other down the hatch.

Quartermaster Scott and Larry Lasche, now a lieutenant (junior grade), who had been standing their watch on the after part of the bridge, walked forward more deliberately, waited until the four lookouts were below, and then themselves disappeared. Scott would wait in the conning tower alongside the bridge hatch to assist in closing it when the last man came down.

At the instant the diving alarm had sounded, a series of small geysers —mainly air, but with a little water mixed in—appeared in quick succession on either side of the main deck from forward to aft: the main vents, jerked open by hydraulic power from the control room.

7 6

Simultaneously, the exhaust noise from aft ceased. There was a clank as the main induction valve, the air intake both for the engines and for ventilation, seated itself under the forty-millimeter gun in the center of the cigarette deck. There was increased turbulence of water astern. In accordance with standard diving procedure, the electrician mates in the motor room had put both motors on "ahead full." Up forward, the bow planes were beginning to rig out and take a bite into the water.

Eel's bow began to slide down toward the water's surface. The sea burst through the large bullnose casting on her bow.

Richardson grinned at Williams. Seeing the bullnose go under had always given him a small thrill of pleasure. It provided a means, also, for testing or hazing his officers. Calmly, Williams put his binoculars to his eyes, made a pretense of taking another look around the horizon.

"Okay, Buck, I'll go below," said Rich, knowing that he had lost this little game of chicken. It was, after all, the Officer of the Deck's duty, as well as his prerogative, to be the last man off the bridge. Rich gripped the hatch hand rails, dropped lightly down the ladder into the conning tower. Williams, a couple of seconds behind, swung down on the wire lanyard attached to the hatch, bringing it down with his weight. The hatch latched shut. Scott swiftly remounted the ladder, reached up, and twirled the handwheel on the underside of the hatch, extending the dogs and locking it securely shut.

"Hatch secured!" called Scott. Instantly there was a loud noise of air blowing from the control room below. A rapid increase in air pressure was noticeable in the ears.

Williams released the lanyard, stepped swiftly to the control room hatch, and a moment later was at the diving station where the lookouts had preceded him. The first two had their hands on the large chromium bow plane and stern plane wheels. The submarine had already taken a five-degree bow down attitude. Williams held up his right hand, palm and fingers open in the habitual signal, scrutinized an aneroid barometer on the diving instrument panel.

"Secure the air!" bellowed Williams above the noise, clenching his fist and shaking it for emphasis. The roar of air blowing from an open pipe stopped. Air pressure stopped rising. Ears adjusted. There was a pause as Williams carefully watched the barometer. "Pressure in the boat is two-tenths, Captain. Holding steady," he announced up the hatch. Then, raising his voice, he called over his shoulder, "Blow negative to the mark!"

Lichtmann, standing watch on the air manifold on the starboard side of the control room, was expecting the order, promptly twisted the blow valve open. The roar of high-pressure air, slightly more muted

7 7

because it was blowing into a tank under the pressure hull instead of freely into the control room, again filled the compartment. The chief petty officer to Williams' right, facing the main hydraulic control manifold with its triple row of handles, stood up to inspect a gauge on the panel above them. He traced the needle with his finger as it slowly moved counterclockwise, suddenly held up his clenched fist. The blowing stopped.

"Negative blown to the mark, sir." Klench, the chief, sat down on his padded tool bench, his hand on one of the shiny levers before him.

"Shut negative flood valve!" said Williams.

Klench pulled the lever toward him. There was a faintly perceptible thump somewhere below. "Negative flood valve is shut," he said.

"Vent negative!" Klench leaned forward, pulled another handle. There was the low-pitched whoosh of a large volume of air issuing from a big opening. Air pressure in the control room again perceptibly increased. When the blowing noise stopped, Klench pushed back the lever he had been holding open. "Negative tank vented, sir. Vent shut," he reported.

"Negative tank is blown and secured, Conn. Passing sixty feet. Trim looks good." Williams tilted his head back, projected his voice through the open hatch so that Richardson in the conning tower could hear him. Negative tank, always kept full of water when the submarine was surfaced, gave her negative buoyancy when the ballast tanks were flooded on diving. Thus it increased the speed of submergence, after which, to achieve the desired state of neutral buoyancy, the tank had to be emptied again. This would be done after *Eel* had broken clear of the surface and was adequately tilted down by the bow, but it was important also that the tank not be blown at too deep a depth, for to do so would cause a tremendous volume of air, at a relatively high pressure, to be vented back into the submarine.

Williams tilted his head back again, snapped an order up the hatch. "All ahead two-thirds!"

"All ahead two-thirds answered, sir." The helmsman, Cornelli, was a new quartermaster just taken aboard from the relief crews. He was inexperienced, but he had worked out well in the training period before departure. Richardson noticed, however, that Scott, the quartermaster in charge of the watch, was standing by him at his post in the forward end of the conning tower. He appeared to be totally engrossed in writing something in the quartermaster's notebook, but his eyes had flickered more than once in the direction of the new helmsman. It was a good thing to see.

Approximately a minute had passed since the dive had been initiated. *Eel*'s decks still held a steady five degree down angle, as measured by the curved bubble inclinometers on the diving stand and in the conning tower.

"Passing one hundred feet, Conn," said Williams. "Trim still looks good, sir."

It was unnecessary, but Richardson felt impelled to say something in reply. He leaned over the open hatch so that he could see the top of Williams' head. Buck was supporting himself on the ladder with one foot on the lowest rung, intently watching the action of bow and stern planes, depth gauges, inclinometer bubble, the diving crew about him and the auxiliaryman behind him. "Level off at one-five-oh feet, control. Let me know when you have a one-third speed trim."

"One-five-oh feet. One-third trim, aye aye," responded Williams, as though he did not already know that this was exactly what he was expected to do. "Passing one-two-five feet, Conn."

Richardson also had a depth gauge in the conning tower, did not need this piece of information, but he seized the opportunity to note that his own depth gauge registered the same amount as that which Williams had just announced to him.

"Ease your bubble," Buck said suddenly to the stern planesman. "Watch it! Don't overshoot!"

Leaning back and raising his voice, he called up the hatch, "All ahead one-third!"

"All ahead one-third answered," came the reply from Cornelli, a split second after the annunciator clink.

To the bow planesman Williams said, "Ease your bow planes. Try to hit one-five-oh feet with a zero bubble and hold it."

"One-five-oh feet, sir, zero bubble," responded the man operating the right of the two large shiny wheels in front of Williams. He had been progressively lightening himself, removing his binoculars, divesting himself of foul-weather bridge jacket and at the same time holding the bow planes on full dive with a free hand or occasionally a knee. Now he took the bow plane wheel, leaned into it counterclockwise. The bow plane indicator rose toward the zero position.

A moment later, Williams swung to his left, spoke to the man on the trim manifold, pointing to him for emphasis. It was the first order he had given him. "Flood forward trim from sea, one thousand pounds."

"Flood forward trim from sea, one thousand pounds," echoed the man, fitting his wrench to the manifold and turning it. Watching one of the gauges above it, in a moment he reported completion of the operation.

Buck Williams continued to concentrate on the diving panel. "Stern planes on zero," he ordered.

The stern planesman put his planes exactly on zero, held them there.

Attentively, Williams watched the gauges. His concentration increased.

"Pump from forward trim to after trim, five hundred pounds," he ordered. This maneuver completed to his satisfaction, he continued watching the instruments, his posture gradually relaxing.

"Pump from auxiliary tanks to sea five hundred pounds," he ordered. This done, "Bow planes on zero."

The ship's speed, as indicated on a dial on his diving panel, had dropped below four knots. Keel depth was a fraction less than one hundred and fifty feet. For a long minute Williams watched his dials, said nothing. Then, leaning back again, he called up the hatch to the conning tower. "Final trim, sir. One-five-zero feet, one-third speed."

To Klench he said, "Damn good compensation, Chief. You were right on, fore and aft. I figure she was only five hundred pounds light overall, maybe less, once she starts soaking up a bit."

"Thanks, sir," said Klench, obviously pleased. "I did figure she'll soak up about five hundred pounds when she gets settled down."

"Control," called Rich from the conning tower. "I have the conn. Make your depth six-five feet. Bring her up easy." To the sonarman in the conning tower he said, "Search all around. Let me know when you have completed your search."

With planes on full rise, her propellers turning over at minimum speed, *Eel* slowly swam toward the ordered depth. It took several minutes to get there because of the slow speed, and the further fact that on the way up Rich ordered ten degrees right rudder in order to permit the sonar to listen on the bearing which had been blocked by *Eel*'s screws. Satisfied, he allowed Williams to bring her all the way up without interference, raising the tall attack periscope as the ship passed seventy-five feet in order to take a quick look as soon as its tip broached the surface. He was rewarded by the sight of the underside of the water, now under full sunlight, looking exactly the same as it would from above the surface. The Yellow Sea obviously deserved its name. The water was not yellow, but the color of light brown mud.

The periscope broke the surface, surged upward. With his right elbow crooked around one handle, holding it to his chest, his left hand pushing on the other, he quickly walked it around, inspecting first the horizon, then the air. Nothing in sight.

He walked around a third time with the periscope elevated at maximum elevation. Nothing.

Back to the horizon for a more leisurely search. Still nothing. He lowered the periscope.

"Control," he ordered. "Five-eight feet. Prepare to surface."

The radar periscope had better optics than the attack periscope because of the larger diameter and greater simplicity of its lens system. His next search would be through it.

"Five-eight feet, aye aye. Prepare to surface, aye aye."

Buck Williams had come one more step up the ladder from the control room. "Captain, how soon do you figure to surface?"

Williams, who had been up since 3:30 that morning, was really asking whether he would have to bundle up again and go back on the bridge, or whether he could turn that chore over to Al Dugan. Al, no doubt, had already been called and was probably having breakfast at that very moment.

"Sorry, Buck," said Richardson. "You'll have to take her up yourself. The visibility is excellent. We can triple our area coverage on the surface, and I want to get back up there."

"Aye aye, sir," said Buck.

Suddenly Williams stepped off the ladder to make room for someone to come up to the conning tower. Blunt. "Rich," he said. "Why are you surfacing?"

"Your orders, Commodore. We're just finishing our trim dive. We're on station in the middle of the area, with no land nearer than a hundred fifty miles. Visibility is excellent, so we'll have no trouble seeing enemy aircraft before they see us."

"I gave no such order, Rich. I said you should use your best judgment about running on the surface in the area. I also said I don't want to be detected."

Rich was uneasily conscious that Scott and Cornelli, the other two persons in the conning tower, had expressions of irresolute surprise on their faces. "Let me show you on the chart, Commodore," he said. Perhaps if he could get Blunt into a low-voiced conference in the back of the conning tower it would be possible to straighten things out with no further damage to morale.

A large-scale area chart was already laid out on the plotting table. "Your written orders say remain on the surface whenever possible, and last night you sent the wolfpack a message to conduct surface patrol on a north-south line," said Rich. He indicated a lightly penciled dot with a small circle around it. "Here's our morning dead reckoning position. Saisho To, here, or Quelpart Island, is the nearest land. There are no airfields indicated, although I suppose there could be some. Here are the other two boats—*Whitefish* is twenty miles to the north of us and *Chicolar* is twenty miles to the south. We are in the middle of the area, right on the line between Shanghai and Sasebo. If anybody comes through here, one of the three of us should see him and be able to vector at least one other boat into position for a submerged attack."

"I know," growled Blunt, testily sucking his pipe. "But they don't know we are in the area yet. That's why we have to stay submerged. I don't want to be detected or have our presence known until we get our first big convoy."

Richardson stared at him. Blunt's cheeks were sagging, his eyes streaked with tiny red veins. This was exactly the opposite of what he had said the previous night. "But Commodore," Richardson protested, "we sent the 'surface patrol procedure' signal to the other boats last night, along with the coordinates of the patrol line!"

"Well, countermand it, then. I want to patrol submerged! I can't stay up all night and all day, too!" Blunt turned away from the chart, stuffed his pipe in his mouth, and went below.

Dilemma: to send a message, *Eel* would have to surface; but if Rich was any judge of Blunt's state of mind, it would be necessary to gain his specific approval to surface even for a short time.

In the meantime *Whitefish* and *Chicolar* would be surfacing after their own trim dives. At this very moment, in obedience to orders, they would be setting a daylight surface patrol routine. Squatting on his heels to talk through the control room hatch to Williams, who, once the wolfpack commander had passed, again had partly mounted the ladder, Richardson explained that surfacing would be delayed slightly. Then he sent for Keith.

"Keith, how's your fix coming? Can you take over the conning tower for a while?"

"Sure. The computation is finished. Oregon can plot it. We can't be more than a mile off our dead-reckoning position anyway. What's up?"

"Fine. Make routine periscope observations and put this message in our wolfpack code while I go talk to the commodore." He handed Keith a piece of paper.

"Captain Blunt won't let us surface?" guessed Keith.

"That's right. He's changed his mind from last night."

"You know, Skipper," said Keith as Richardson stepped on the ladder rungs preparatory to descending into the control room, "he must have been up all night. The chiefs say he just wandered back and forth, and sat up in the wardroom drinking coffee. He never even lay down. Maybe he's not feeling well."

"Maybe so," said Richardson as he ducked down the ladder. He had the feeling that Keith had not said all he might have liked to say, that his eyes were trying to convey something to him.

Ten minues later, when he returned to the conning tower, Keith handed him the completed message. "How are we going to get it out?" Keith asked.

"I'll take over again, Keith. The commodore has okayed our broaching long enough to get the message off. You take the message to the radio room, and as soon as your antennas will load up, send it out. Let me know on the bridge speaker when you get a receipt."

"Will do," said Keith.

Richardson crossed to the control room hatch, squatted on his heels again. "Buck," he said, "are you ready to surface?"

"Yes, sir."

"All right. We're not going to surface all the way; I just want to broach on high pressure air. We'll not cut in the main engines, but flood negative tank in case we have to make a quick dive."

"Got it," said Buck. "Do you want lookouts?"

"Yes, we'll need the lookouts, but nobody else. Send them up to the conning tower now. We'll shut the control room hatch before we come up, just in case she ducks under again."

Rising to his feet, Richardson said to his exec, "Better get below, Keith. . . . Another thing . . ." as Keith stood poised in the control room hatch opening, "in case we have to dive suddenly, she might go down pretty fast, so you might find yourself in charge for a while. Don't worry about us up here. We'll get in the conning tower somehow."

In a few moments the four lookouts, in full foul-weather gear with binoculars slung around their necks and inflatable belts around their waists, were in the conning tower. A jacket and belt had been handed up to Richardson also. "Scott," said the skipper, "I want you to remain in the conning tower and stand by the bridge hatch. Shut it if water comes in. You got that?"

"Yes, sir."

"Shut the lower hatch!" Williams pulled the control room hatch lanyard from below. It slammed down. Scott stepped on it, held it down with his weight on one foot as he kicked its two dogs home with the other.

Richardson made a final sweep with the periscope, pressed the toggle on the intercom. 'Control, this is conn. When ready, broach the ship."

The whistle of high pressure air. A springlike lifting effect. The depth gauge needle began to revolve counterclockwise. Richardson swung the periscope around rapidly several times, stopped momentarily, looking dead ahead. "Bow's out," he said. He swung aft. "Stern's coming up."

Williams had already stopped blowing. Now came the noise of negative tank taking on the water which, when ballast tanks were again flooded, would give *Eel* thirteen tons negative buoyancy.

"Stern's up," said Rich, still looking aft the periscope. He swung it around forward. "Bow's going under . . . good!" The noise of high pressure air again could be heard from the control room. Watching his depth gauges and bubble inclinometers, Buck was giving another shot of air to the forward ballast tanks to compensate for the water taken into negative tank.

Rich snapped up the handles on the periscope. "Down periscope," he said. One of the lookouts pushed the hydraulic control lever. "Crack the hatch!" Scott, already standing on the rungs of the ladder, quickly spun the handle. There was a slight hiss of escaping air as the small volume of air in the conning tower quickly equalized to the atmosphere. "Open the hatch," ordered Rich. Scott released the latch, shoved the hatch upward, stepped back. In three quick leaps up the ladder rungs, Richardson was on the bridge.

A swift look around with his binoculars: all clear. "Lookouts!" The four men clambered up the ladder, climbed to their places. One of them ran to the after part of the periscope shears, tugged briefly on the rope knotted there, released the whip antenna. A spring swung it upward into a vertical position.

The skipper and lookouts surveyed the horizon and the air. There was nothing in sight. *Eel* rode easily on a quiescent mud-brown sea, her main deck at the water's edge, her main structure, except for bridge and periscope shears and the two five-inch guns, visible only from directly overhead.

From the bridge one could see tiny little rivulets of water sloshing among the slats of her wooden deck, or swirling alongside as the submarine moved sluggishly ahead under the leisurely thrust of her motors.

The bow planes were still rigged out. They would be kept on rise for their planing effect. The sky was gray, not overcast. Simply gray and dank. There was a musty odor to the atmosphere. The sun could not be seen, but visibility, Richardson judged, was at least fifteen miles, maybe more.

Water still dripped from the bridge structure as a multitude of tiny pockets slowly drained away. With unaccustomed clarity of sound, because there was no engine murmur from aft to preempt the ears, the water streams could be heard dropping directly on the sea which half-covered the conning tower beneath Richardson's feet.

The Yellow Sea is far from the coldest body of water in the world, but Richardson was beginning to feel the December chill. He hunched his shoulders inside his jacket, put on the mittens which he customarily kept ready in its pockets, checked his rubber lifebelt for the carbon dioxide cartridges which should be there to inflate it on need. What could be holding up the message, he wondered.

"Bridge!" Keith's voice. "*Chicolar* has the message. We can't raise *Whitefish*."

He might have guessed. Whitey Everett was taking his own time about surfacing. No doubt he would greet the instruction to patrol submerged with pleasure, maybe relief, but in the meantime his being submerged and out of communication was keeping *Eel* on the surface and in a very uncomfortable cruising situation.

Rich had argued strenuously with the wolfpack commander for a normal surfacing operation, pointing out that the ship was customarily able to dive to periscope depth in about forty-five seconds, even with a start at slow speed. But Blunt, already climbing into his bunk, had refused to permit it, had finally agreed to broaching as the only compromise he would accept. Well, he, as well as the rest of them, would simply have to wait.

There was one thing which had not been discussed, however, and it could therefore be accomplished without disobeying any order. Rich pressed the bridge speaker button. "Control, this is bridge. Equalize pressure through the main induction."

"Control aye aye," from Buck Williams.

The quiet on the bridge was eerie. Richardson could clearly hear the remote operating gear engage the inboard induction flapper in the forward engineroom. Then came a whoosh of air under the cigarette deck, in the midst of which, barely distinguishable, was the clank of the thirty-six-inch-diameter main induction valve. There had been a lot of air inside the submarine, what with negative tank twice having been vented into the hull. The noise lasted about three seconds, was followed by the clank of the main induction shutting and the further noise when the engineroom flapper snapped shut on its spring.

After half an hour Richardson, inadequately prepared for cold weather with only his jacket, guessed that Whitey Everett must be having breakfast submerged. Nearly an hour after *Eel* broached, by which time he had decided Whitey had added a nap to his breakfast schedule, the welcome news came from Keith in the radio room that *Whitefish* had received the message.

"Clear the bridge," he said. The lookouts went below. He took a last look around with the binoculars. This would be a good drill, he thought. "Take her down!" he shouted, a spurious alarm in his voice. He hit the diving alarm twice, jumped for the hatch. Scott slammed it shut behind him, dogged it. He could feel the bow planes reversed to full dive, digging in, the increased drive of the propellers as the motors suddenly went to full speed. The main vents were open, but there was understandably little noise of air vented and water entering, since the ballast tanks had been only partly emptied.

"Did you start a watch?" he asked Scott. Without replying, the quartermaster held out his left hand. In it, suspended from a piece of cord which he had looped around his thumb, lay a stopwatch. The hand was passing fifteen seconds. At that moment the sea, which could be heard gurgling around the outside of the conning tower, closed over it. Several more seconds passed. "Forty-seven feet," said Rich, who had crossed to where he could watch the depth gauge.

Scott stopped the watch. "Twenty-four seconds flat, Captain," he said, holding it out for him to see. "Not bad, sir."

Rich nodded, pleased. He would say something congratulatory to Buck Williams also.

A quiet discussion with Keith confirmed what he had suspected. "I know darned well he was submerged," said Keith. "Either that or his radio had broken down. When we finally heard him, he came in loud and clear."

Nelson, the chief radioman, shook his head. "He wasn't broken down, sir," he said. "I could hear him loading down his wet antennas when he answered us. He had just surfaced."

For a short time Rich worried about what he should report to Blunt when the latter asked him the reason for his long delay on the surface, until it came to him that the wolfpack commander must have slept through it all.

At the end of four days Richardson realized that he had become distinctly restive. So had Keith, and so, he could see, had Buck Williams and a number of the other members of the crew. They would quickly go stale, lose their fine edge of alertness and training, if some change in the deadly routine could not be made. Every night for four days, with the area chart spread out on the wardroom table, he had gone over the same arguments with Blunt.

"They have to come through here," Blunt would say, banging his pipe on the chart in the approximate center of the area, scattering ashes and sometimes small glowing tobacco embers on it. Richardson would argue the Japanese had long ago learned that the shortest distance between two points at sea was not necessarily the straight line which crossed the center of a submarine patrol area.

"Look," he would say, "the only things we've seen since we've been here are wooden sampans. Maybe some of them are on antisub patrol, as they told us about at the briefing. The big cargo ships must be going up and down the coast of China close inshore. We've not seen any out here. They probably enter harbor at night, anchor in the mud flats off the Chinese coast, or travel inshore of some of these small islands. The chain of islands off Korea forms almost a protective barrier against submarines."

For four nights in a row Keith and Richardson had pored over the combined contact and patrol track chart which someone in ComSub-Pac headquarters had compiled from all submarine patrol reports for the area. The chart clearly showed that of all the submarines which had been assigned AREA TWELVE since the beginning of the war, most had patrolled in the center of the area. By far the majority of contacts, however, had been made on the periphery. The submarine which had turned in the best patrol to date had never been in the center of the Yellow Sea except to cross it en route from one side to the other.

The arguments had no effect on Blunt. The wolfpack commander would not permit them to patrol surfaced during daylight, nor to shift their patrol areas closer inshore. Several times he pointed out that a submarine built for a test depth of four hundred feet, like *Eel*, was not able to realize her entire potential in the shallow water of the Yellow Sea. Even in the deepest part of the area it was impossible to achieve maximum submergence. Richardson decided not to bring up the fact that this was known before the Yellow Sea had been selected for their combined patrol area, and that unless ComSubPac was to abandon AREA TWELVE altogether, some submarine would have to patrol it.

The fifth night, however, brought a change. Ensign Johnny Cargill had the coding watch. "It's one for us," he said simply, handing a decoded message to his superiors.

The message said: SPECIAL TO BLUNT'S BRUISERS 151800z x SIX SHIPS 34 DEGREES 10.1 MINUTES NORTH 127 DEGREES 30 MINUTES EAST x COURSE WEST x SPEED TEN 151016z x

"That's three o'clock tomorrow morning our time," said Leone.

"How long will it take to get there?" demanded Richardson.

Using a pair of dividers Keith picked off the distances. "One hundred twenty miles for us," he announced. "About one hundred three miles for the *Whitefish* and one hundred forty or so for the *Chicolar*."

"It's nearly twenty hundred now. We have seven hours. Barely time," calculated Richardson. He seized a piece of paper and Keith's thin wolfpack code book.

"*Chicolar* and *Whitefish* will have got the message too, don't you think?" said Keith.

"They're supposed to. . . . Johnny, tell the officer of the deck to shift the battery charge to one main engine and the auxiliary diesel, and go to full power on the other three engines on course zero-two-five. Tell him we'll adjust the course later. Tell him also as soon as we can put that fourth main on propulsion, I want him to do it." As he spoke, Richardson was busying himself with the code book, in a moment handed two separate pieces of paper, one in plain language, the other coded, to the wolfpack commander.

Through the entire rapid exchange, he suddenly realized, Blunt had said not one word. Carefully Blunt read, perhaps for the third or fourth time, the message Rich had drafted: REFERENCE COMSUBPAC 151016Z X PURSUE AT MAXIMUM SPEED X JOE This was what they had trained for in Pearl Harbor. Exactly this situation had been foreseen, this message sent in drill. Time after time, under various different contingencies, they had rehearsed how they would respond to exactly the contingency now before them.

As Blunt held the two papers in his hands, Rich could hear the air discharge signaling the starting of two more main engines. The gyro-compass repeater in the overhead of the wardroom began to spin. He could feel the different motion as *Eel* changed course and began to pick up speed. There had been two main engines on battery charge, with just a trickle of electricity going to the motors. The time fully to recharge the battery would unavoidably be longer when one of the charging mains was replaced by the auxiliary, but three main engines wide open on propulsion would drive *Eel* at nearly seventeen knots. Already he began to feel the drumming of the water along *Eel*'s sides. There was a low shriek of blowers from the control room area. The OOD had ordered the low pressure blowers put on to expel the remaining water in the ballast tanks. In anticipation of another night of slow cruising on station, they had not been entirely emptied.

"We should send the message as soon as we can, Commodore," said Rich urgently. "The other boats will be expecting orders."

Still Blunt said nothing. His face looked strained, the jowls on either side of his chin more prominent. Intuitive understanding struck Richardson. Despite all his years in submarines, Blunt had never been at sea in the war zone before. This was his first experience! He held authority, but he had never been tried. How many other wolfpacks must also have had this specific problem! Strange that no one had mentioned it. . . . Obviously, the flagship skipper must carry the load for his neophyte superior—this must be why Admiral Small had insisted *Eel* be Blunt's flagship! But it was an intolerable burden; it was not fair. . . .

Rich hesitated, his brow furrowed. He tore a third sheet off the pad, copied the encoded message on it. "I'll be right back, Commodore," he said, stepping swiftly out of the wardroom and walking aft.

In a moment he was at the radio room, a small compartment just off the passageway in the after portion of the control room, "Here, Nelson," he said, handing the message to the chief radioman, "get this out right away to the other boats. Commodore's orders."

Back in the wardroom he picked up the dividers, a pencil, and a plotting protractor. "Here's our position, sir," he said. "And here's this convoy. It's just south of the island chain on the south coast of Korea. My guess is they're going to round the southwestern tip of Korea and head north. Anyway, where they are right now—or will be at three this morning if this dope is correct—they can't head north yet, and it would make no sense to go south. So I figure if we head for this spot, right here, we'll be in good shape to pick them off. At their speed of ten knots we ought to be able to overtake them pretty easily even if they do pass through there a little ahead of us; and if we get there quickly enough, we'll intercept them before they get to the point on the tail of Korea where they'll probably change course and head up through the Maikotsu Suido. That's why we have to go to full speed, sir."

For the first time Blunt spoke. "I can't risk my submarines in the shallow water around those islands," he said.

"You won't have to, Commodore. Look." Rich pointed with the closed dividers. "These islands aren't all that close together. The water around the outlying ones is as deep as it is anywhere in the Yellow Sea. If these ships are closer inshore than the message says, we can trail them from seaward until we find a spot where there's enough room to attack."

Blunt stared at the chart, still said nothing. Richardson wondered how he could state the clincher argument without being too obvious. "Maybe they won't be there at all," he finally said, "and we'll have to send a message to ComSubPac that his dope was no good."

Just possibly, Rich later concluded, Blunt realized he was really telling him their explanations of failure would also have to carry proof of adequate effort. He well remembered the sarcasm with which Blunt himself had in the past occasionally referred to certain submarines which, for one reason or another, seemed to have so much difficulty finding the enemy.

The race for position ran on through the night and into the morning. Around midnight, the rate at which *Eel*'s two main storage batteries could continue to accept a charge had diminished to such a degree that the charging rate could be carried on the auxiliary engine alone.

Thenceforth, on four big ten-cylinder diesels, trailing four exhaust plumes behind her, she raced at full top speed for the designated spot on the chart.

Everyone not on watch or actively engaged had been directed to try to get some sleep. Richardson lay down at about 11 o'clock and actually dozed off, to awaken, momentarily confused, a couple of hours later. Keith, he noted, turned in the moment he knew his skipper was on his feet. Blunt remained virtually in the same place he had been, drinking cup after cup of coffee and incessantly smoking his pipe in the wardroom.

At about two in the morning, first carefully adjusting his red goggles to protect his night vision from the white lights, Richardson took one last tour through the ship. As he had expected, nearly everyone was already in the vicinity of his battle station, some dozing quietly, others intensely alert.

Immediately abaft the control room, on the after side of the dividing watertight bulkhead, was the ship's galley, with the operating mechanism for the main induction valve directly above the stove. Here he found the entire complement of ship's cooks manufacturing a mountainous pile of sandwiches. "Just figured we might be needing 'em, Skipper," said one.

In the crew's dining space adjoining the galley were the gun crews of both five-inch guns and the ammunition resupply team. Some of them, he saw, were already wearing red goggles. There was no one in the sleeping space abaft the dinette, but in the next compartment aft, the forward engineroom, there was a double watch of engineers, most of them standing around idly. Here and there a toolbox had been opened, its contents laid out for easy access.

The after engineroom was the same. Both enginerooms were thundering with the full power of twenty huge diesel cylinders and twice that number of pistons in each. The compartments were also frigidly cold—windswept—as the frosty atmosphere of the Yellow Sea whistled in through the main induction outlet in the overhead of each, was sucked into the voracious engines, and spewed overboard through their exhausts. Beyond, in the electrical maneuvering room, steaming hot from the loaded electric motors and control systems, again there was a double complement of engineering personnel, in this case, electrician's mates. And down below, through the open hatch leading into the cramped motor room, he could see two men watching the temperature gauges.

The last compartment aft was the after torpedo room, with its four large bronze torpedo tube doors matching the six in the forward torpedo room. Counting the four torpedoes in the tubes and the six reloads —two more than the designed load—the after torpedo room had ten torpedoes compared to the forward torpedo room's sixteen.

With approval the skipper saw, already laid out as in the forward torpedo room, the special equipment which Keith and Buck had designed to make possible a torpedo reload even with the ship pitching and rolling on the surface.

Still wearing the red goggles, Rich returned to the control room, passing forward through the broiling hot maneuvering room with its two huge motors beneath the deck, and the contrastingly cold engine rooms with their roaring diesel monsters and whirling electric generators on either side.

In the crew's dinette, one of the mess tables now held a large oval tray with a mound of sandwiches covered with a dampened cloth. Several were already being eaten, Rich noticed, and he filched one from under the cloth as he went by. In the galley two more loaded trays had been put aside for use later. They would be needed.

The watertight door to the control room was closed to protect its darkened condition. Rich lifted the latch, stepped over the coaming, relatched it. Through the goggles he was instantly aware of the red lights glowing about, but at first could see very little else. In a moment, however, thanks to the protection given by his goggles, he was able to distinguish the familiar objects.

Since the ship was on the surface, the diving station was secured. The bow planes were rigged in, the stern planes locked on zero. Al Dugan was loitering about on the diving station in desultory conversation with the battle stations bow and stern planesmen, who were sitting on the toolboxes which doubled as seats when they were operating the planes. Al gave a thumbs-up signal as Rich started up the ladder into the conning tower.

It too was dimly lighted, had been "rigged for red" since surfacing. The roar of the engines came more clearly here through the open hatch in its forward starboard corner. Also could be heard the rush of the sea through which Eel was cleaving, the muttered monosyllabic words of the watch on the bridge deck above, the occasional response from the helmsmen or the quartermaster in the forward part of the conning tower.

The speed indicator, mounted on the forward bulkhead just above the helmsmen's head, stood at just a shade below twenty knots. Its needle indicator, in reflective paint, stood out sharply in the soft glow of the instrument lighting.

Eel pitched softly, rolled gently, but there was a purposefulness to her motion. The very steel fabric of the submarine exuded a determination to go about her deadly business.

In the after port corner of the conning tower, the Torpedo Data Computer—the TDC—purred softly, its instrument panel lights glowing. It had been turned on for hours, and the automatic inputs from ship's own course and speed had been checked and rechecked. Buck Williams had long ago reported the TDC in readiness to receive the observed inputs of target course and range, plus the all-important item of exact target bearing from radar, sonar, the TBTs on the bridge, or the periscope. With this information it could help determine target speed and automatically make the necessary computations to set the correct gyro angles on the torpedoes. Then, when the firing key was pressed, the selected torpedoes would be sent on their deadly mission aimed with the most accurate information the human mind and the mechanical computer together could devise.

On the starboard side of the conning tower, opposite the TDC and a little forward of it, was the radar control console, glowing with suppressed green, orange and red lights. Faint flashes shone through crevices in the light shrouding covering it. A figure stood bent over the console, his face pressed into a conical rubber hood shaped to fit a man's forehead and the bridge of his nose. The man, his two hands on the face of the instrument, fingering its dials, was relaxed but simultaneously all attention. In the darkness above the bridge, at the top of the periscope shears, the rotating electronic antenna was searching the area, probing the night, bringing in the information down to this vitally important instrument.

Rich recognized the slight figure peering into the radar receiver as he stood beside him. "Quin," he said, putting his hand on the yeoman's shoulder, "how is the watch going? See anything yet?"

"No, sir," said Quin, keeping his face against the hood. "I've been up here since midnight, and all I've got is Quelpart Island, off on our starboard beam about forty miles away. Also, there's radar sweeps coming in on our starboard and port quarter."

"Our friends, right?" said Rich.

"Yessir. They've got rotating radars just like ours, and they're on the same frequency. I can see them sweep across, so I figure it must be them."

"Let me see, Quin."

Quin stood up, stretched gratefully. Rich pulled the red goggles from his eyes, let them hang on their elastic thong around his neck, leaned into the hood. He was looking at a large circular dial, perhaps twelve inches in diameter, from the center of which a white shaft of light the thickness of a pencil line rotated ceaselessly in a clockwise direction. Faint concentric circles—the range markers—were visible as the moving pencil line illuminated them in passing.

At the 2 o'clock position, out near the periphery of the dial, the jagged outline of land appeared clearly every time the rotating wand passed it, slowly faded as the wand continued around the circle, was regenerated when it passed over it again. Rich watched as the radiant wand made several passes, noticed when from slightly below the 5 o'clock position there appeared the faint evidence of another wand, also sweeping. When it intersected *Eel*'s wand, a series of dashes was produced. The 8 o'clock position had a similar, fainter wand rotating from it which could occasionally be seen.

"That's *Chicolar* over on our starboard quarter and *Whitefish* on our port quarter, Quin," said Rich. "That's where they should be. It looks as though we're out ahead of both of them."

"The one to port seems to be dropping behind," volunteered Quin. "But the one to starboard—it's been there all the time I've been up here."

Theoretically, *Whitefish* should be a shade faster than either *Eel* or *Chicolar*, or so Whitey Everett had argued. Perhaps her battery had been more depleted and he had not yet been able to put all four main engines on propulsion.

Richardson mentally projected himself out into the space covered by his moving radar beam. To starboard, silent and massive, the bulk of Quelpart Island, a mountain rising out of the water, divided the Yellow Sea into two parts. The ships he sought were coming toward him north of the island. Ahead, not yet near enough to be picked up on the radar, the rocky coast of Korea formed a corner projecting into the sea, its long side extending nearly due north, the short side stretching eastward to create a funnel through which the convoy passing to the north of Quelpart must come. Strewn about the Korean coast, extending northward and eastward, many small islands, rocky and inhospitable, stood like protective sentinels guarding the mainland. Soon one or more of them would become a jagged blob on the radar. *Eel*, scenting game, was racing toward them. In a little while a group of tiny symmetrical pips would appear among the jagged blobs. They would be arranged in some man-designed, coherent way, and they would move, whereas the islets would only grow nearer. Then would the prey be flushed, and the wolf of the sea gather her pack together. They had already been called to follow. They would pursue it, fall upon it like the ravening wolves they were, rend it to pieces. Man would eat man. It was as though Richardson stood omnipotent in the heavens, searching the sea below and seeing both the past and the future.

The same scene was being duplicated in the conning towers of *Chicolar* and *Whitefish*. Perhaps both skippers were standing in their conning towers, their stations for most of the battle to come, also peering at their radar scopes, also waiting, possibly also seeing in their own allegorical conception what it was they were about to do. The call of the wild wolf had been heard. The pack was gathering.

Richardson straightened up, indicated to Quin that he should take over the radar again, replaced his goggles. He stood silently as his eyes once again began their acclimation to the dark. Momentarily he had been blinded by the considerably brighter lights of the radarscope, his mind distracted by contemplation of the hell he was about to unleash.

The PPI 'scope, as the dial he had been watching was called, had been designed with a view to use at night. Its predominant color was red. Beside it was another hooded dial, the A 'scope, which gave precise ranges but had a profusion of green lighting guaranteed to produce instant night blindness lasting many minutes. Richardson had avoided looking at the A 'scope, but even so it would be some minutes before his night vision was fully restored. He readjusted the red goggles more comfortably, returned to the forward part of the conning tower, stopped with one foot on the ladder leading upward. "Scott," he said to the quartermaster, "I'm going up on the bridge. We'll be getting some kind of a radar contact before long. We'll be picking up some islands up ahead, too, but I'm expecting ships. We might be shooting torpedoes before daybreak."

The radar operators had all been thoroughly briefed as to the prospect of getting a return on land or small islands which would resemble ships. The whole submarine was already keyed up. His prediction about imminent combat, confirming the knowledgeable guesses already rife, would be known throughout the ship within seconds. Tension would increase, but so would alertness and readiness.

Eel's speed might even increase a fraction of a knot as the electricians once more sought carefully to balance the loads on her four generators and, if possible, slightly increase the output of the four big diesels.

Already he could see better. One last look around the conning tower. It was businesslike, calm, efficient. This was the way a submarine should be. He climbed the few steps to the bridge, ducked under the overhang. "Permission to come on the bridge," he called.

"Permission granted, Skipper." Buck Williams, Officer of the Deck, had his elbows on the overhang, binoculars to his eyes, peering over the front of the metal windscreen. Richardson stood beside him, the goggles dangling again around his neck, binoculars also to his eyes.

"We should get contact pretty soon, Buck," he said, sweeping the murk with his glasses. "We've got Quelpart on the radar. I guess you know that. And there's a flock of little islands that will show up dead ahead pretty soon now. What we're watching for is a formation of ships moving between the land formations."

"How long before we're in radar range of the first island?" asked Williams.

"Not sure. Maybe half an hour. Time to get my night vision settled down, I hope."

Eel's bow, lowered nearer to the water's edge by the powerful thrust of her propellers, steadily, almost hypnotically, drove apart the quiet sea. Two white streamers of roiled water, several feet abaft the bullnose and on either side, formed an inverted V. In the center of the V, her bow forming its point, lay the submarine. Little else could be seen of the sea. The hollow of the bow wave formed just forward of *Eel's* bridge. Aft, the returning bulge of seawater tended to sweep up the submarine's rounded sides and occasionally lap into the base of her free-flooding superstructure. Farther aft yet, four exhaust pipes, two on each side, spewed forth a thunder of spray and steam. Occasionally a wave gurgled toward one of the yawning openings of the pipes, to be hurled backward in white confusion under the force of the exhaust gases. All the way aft, abaft the stern mooring line chock, there was a white ribbed disturbance in the sea, a burbling from below. Immediately beyond, coming in from the sides, the dark waters hurled themselves into the cleavage behind the submarine. The only note of her passage was the straight white wake stretching out astern, growing less in the distance as quiet returned to the Yellow Sea.

The air as usual was dank, still, and cold. Richardson's night vision was returning, but he still found it difficult to distinguish the horizon, where the sky and the water met. All was the same dark grayness. Overhead, no stars to be seen. As before, he had the impression that visibility was not unduly restricted, but that somehow there was a salt content to the air, a thin concentration which gradually brought haze of sky and haze of sea together in a unity that defied piercing.

He had no feeling at all. It was as though he were watching from somewhere else. His second self, the buried one of which he was so keenly aware, was about to take charge. This was his profession, his metier. This was what he was a master at: the relentless power of *Eel's* four big diesel engines, her spinning propellers, the unimaginable potential for destruction in the ten torpedo tubes she was about to use;

himself, the controller of it all—the controller, and yet as much as any one of them, controlled.

From whence had come the intelligence sending *Eel* on this deadly errand? Admiral Small, of course, but where did he get it? The admiral had mentioned Fort Shafter as being a special source of information. This must be what he was referring to. This must be why Mrs. Elliott, Cordy Wood, and Joan had such high security clearances. They all worked there. One of the peculiar things about Joan's job was the strange hours. Frequently she would spend several days in a row inside the Shafter compound, never leaving, sleeping at odd times in the room assigned to her. Then she would be off for several days. Joan had once lived in Japan, and she could both read and speak Japanese. Her father had been in the diplomatic service. She said she thought he was dead, but she never talked about him. There was more to his story. Could he have been in intelligence? Could he still be? Could that be the reason for Joan's reticence? Was she, also, in intelligence work?

It must be so. She had known about the lifeboats even before Rich had told about them. She had known about the *Walrus*, and what had happened to her. Submarines had been benefitting from special information about convoy movements since nearly the beginning of the war. Joan's knowledge of Japanese would be needed to translate the messages into English. There must be a large group involved with just this part of the work, and it would be very highly classified. No wonder Joan had been so reluctant to talk about herself!

Little bits of information began to piece themselves together. Joan's seeming familiarity with the names of the submarine skippers, for one thing. She knew who was on patrol, and who had just returned. And she knew how well they'd done and what their problems had been, almost as though she, as well as Rich, had been reading the daily dispatches. Several times he had had the feeling that she was pretending ignorance simply in order not to appear too well informed. The last night before sailing, he was suddenly struck by the notion that she knew of Operation ICEBERG. It was intuition, nothing more, and he had been trying to think of a way to find out without violating the secrecy imposed by Admiral Small, when she interrupted him in the way she knew so well, which always led to other things far removed from submarines and the war.

Obviously, if these deductions were correct, Joan must know what submarines were assigned to the various patrol areas. Although this sort of information was considered top secret by the submarine force, she would know that at this very moment *Eel* was patrolling the East China and Yellow seas, along with the *Whitefish* and *Chicolar*. She would know of the message about the convoy. It might even be she who had decoded it, or translated it. And she would be aware that it was sending *Eel* into combat and mortal danger. Now that they had been so close, that she knew Richardson so well, what would she think, or feel, about the risks she was subjecting him to? Would she worry about his safety? Or was it all part of the job? What about Jim Bledsoe and the *Walrus*? Through some tacit understanding, some regard for her privacy—and Jim's, though he was dead—he had refrained from bringing Jim up. She had told him what she felt she ought, and he had resolved to be satisfied with that.

Now it occurred to him to wonder whether Jim's last, fatal attack on Bungo Pete's decoy freighter could have resulted from a similar message. If so, it meant that it had been planted, and therefore that the enemy had finally realized their convoy routing code had been broken. If so, this convoy *Eel* was now pursuing might also be a decoy. If so, he and the other boats might be steering at full power into a gigantic trap!

But his mind refused to follow the train of thought. It could not be true. It was too far-fetched an idea. Admiral Small and the Fort Shafter people would have to be trusted not to be taken in. Anyway, it made no difference. No matter what his imagination concocted, *Eel* and the other two submarines had received an order for battle. They had been pointed toward the enemy, and they had been unleashed. From here on, ComSubPac did not exist. Joan did not exist. Nothing existed but the sea, and *Eel*'s slender prow cutting it into halves as she sped through it. Only he existed, at the center of the universe, and even he did not exist. There was not even such a thing as the will to do what he was in the process of doing, what he had been trained for so many years to do. There was only the fact of doing it.

Time had been, years ago, when he worried whether he would be able to fire torpedoes set to kill; whether he would be able to nerve himself to see the effects; whether he could hold himself together, still function, disdain the terror of the inevitable counterblow. Before the war a perfect torpedo shot was a professional triumph. It had required meticulous preparation of equipment—the angle solvers, the tubes, the ancillary parts of the submarine which brought them to the firing point, the torpedoes themselves—and lengthy, boring, often lonely practice. Success was achieved when the target signaled the torpedoes had passed beneath her keel. A bull's-eye: accolades for all, qualifications, promotions, favorable comments in fitness reports, a conspicuous white E on the conning tower. What happened when the bull's-eye produced instead a catastrophic explosion, a column of white water mixed with death and debris, a shattered hulk which a moment ago had been a fine ship—that was something he had thought of as happening in another world. It was imaginary, not real. It was not part of the prewar drill. He had, of course, known that ships would sink. But, before the war, he had never been able to visualize what it must actually be like.

Now he had seen it. Being the cause of it was easy, for in the process something had happened to him, too. He was split into two people, both of whom were present at the same time inside him, both able to react. But the two, the automaton and the spectator, were entirely different from each other. The automaton had been trained to be a nerveless perfectionist. The devastating result of the automaton's perfectionism was a clinical certainty it accepted with detachment. The automaton always shouldered the spectator aside, took over the periscope or the bridge TBTs at the start of any action. Beside it, inside it, stood the spectator, observing, marveling, saddened at the destruction and the loss of life. Once in action, the automaton could not be stopped, except by the interposition of some external superior force, and if the opportunity arose, it would inevitably respond with some deadly riposte of its own. It could coldly aim a torpedo that would rip the vitals out of a ship and send it reeling to the bottom of the sea. It would watch the carnage with cool concentration, ready to wrest instant advantage from whatever developments there were.

The spectator, seeing through the same eyes, would always see the dust left floating at the spot where a ship had sunk, would mourn the doomed round black spots—the heads of men—clustering around floating wreckage. The spectator could feel compassion, imagine himself among them, wish they had not, by appearing before his sights, wrought their own destruction. Yet the spectator also had his hardness. These were the enemy. They sought his death. Though the targets of the moment were merchant ships, they were part of the enemy's total war effort. They would not hesitate to try to bring about his own destruction with depth charges, bombs, any weapons they might happen to possess. They were not above breaking the rules of war. There had not even been a war with the United States on December 7, 1941.

They had killed Stocker Kane in the *Nerka*, and Jim Bledsoe in the *Walrus* at a moment of mercy while they were rescuing the crew of an old freighter. Its crew, part of Nakame's outfit, had desperately signaled for rescue. The torpedo from Nakame's carefully positioned sub struck just as Jim was bringing the life raft alongside.

What rules could there be in total war, if Stan Davenport and his men had to die in *Oklahoma*'s enginerooms even before that war existed? Stan's body was found at his station near the port throttle when the big old battlewagon finally was rolled upright. Japan had initiated the war by an unparalleled act of international treachery. She had thrown away the rule book. Surprise, shock, irresistible power: these were the only currency left between Japan and the United States. The reckoning for that brutally cynical act would be cut from similar cloth. No negotiations could stop it, for whom did Japan have who could be trusted as a negotiator? After Pearl Harbor, who in America would be willing to take a similar risk again?

The spectator could even talk with the automaton, but the conversations were always one-sided, always subject to the superior demands of combat. The night was clear and beautiful, the spectator might say. The sea air was clean; the salt dust blowing was refreshing. The Japanese were admirable seamen. They built fine ships, and they knew how to operate them. He could not say they were a fine, honorable people: not after what had happened at Pearl Harbor, and then later at Bataan and Corregidor; but they were industrious and hardworking. The automaton would grimace frigidly through the TBT or the periscope, call out the crucially important observations, maneuver the critical weapon, the *Eel*. It never answered the spectator's observations. It acted, with finality. Its actions were the only answers it ever gave.

Long ago, Richardson had learned that he was as much an instrument of his submarine and its torpedoes as they were of him. There was no room for emotion, no room for thinking. Yet he did think, and observe, in a strange, set-aside corner of his mind. During combat, there was only room for the trained reaction to do what had to be done quickly, effectively, and with precision. After it was over there would be again, as there had always been, a coalescence of personality. The spectator and the automaton would merge into one, and the stern compulsion would disappear. Afterward there might be a reaction to what he had seen and done. But only afterward.

A moderate breeze came over the top of the bridge windscreen, doubtless entirely the product of *Eel*'s speed, for the air was as still as the sea. This time he had properly prepared himself for the cold, with boots and heavy trousers in addition to his heavy jacket. The air had a bite to its chill. He spread his mittened hands to cover as much of his face as he could, held the binoculars to his eyes, elbows resting on the little dashboard behind the windscreen, scanned the nothingness ahead. Beside him, Williams silently did the same.

Above the still figures on the bridge towered the two metal cones

9 9

which were the periscope supports. During daylight the four lookouts stood on little platforms high on the side of each cone. Now, swathed in foul-weather gear, they stood at the bridge level, protected by the bulwarks, binoculars still sweeping steadily.

Above them all, impervious to fog, darkness, or weather, the best lookout of all ceaselessly rotated, sending its invisible radar beams out over hundreds of square miles of ocean surface, to show by a pip on a dial in the conning tower any unusual phenomenon on the surface of the sea.

Rich had been on the bridge approximately half an hour when, from the slight bustle going on beneath the conning tower hatch, he knew that some sort of word was coming.

"Radar contact, Bridge!" Scott, relaying the word, no doubt from Quin. "Looks like land! Port and starboard. Twenty-five miles."

"Bridge, aye aye," from Williams. "Those are the islands we're expecting. Keep the information coming, but look carefully between them. We're looking for ships, Conn."

"Conn, aye aye," responded Scott. "Radar has the word."

It was perhaps another ten minutes before anything new showed on radar.

"Radar contact!" Quin's voice, bellowing from his position at the console.

Instantly Buck pushed the bridge speaker button. "Where away, Radar? Range and bearing!"

"Zero-four-zero, Bridge. Fifteen miles! Looks like six ships, sir!"

Williams looked at his skipper. Richardson nodded. "Station the radar tracking party," the OOD briskly called into the bridge speaker.

More bustle below decks. It could not have been more than twenty seconds before the bridge speaker blared once again.

"Radar tracking party manned and ready, Bridge."

"Track target bearing zero-four-zero," ordered Buck on the loud-speaking system. Then, pitching his voice to reach the helmsman down the hatch, "Steer zero-four-zero, helm. All ahead two-thirds!"

The roar of the engines eased. *Eel*'s bow swung slightly to the right, steadied. Richardson nodded with approval.

Putting *Eel*'s nose directly on the target would accentuate any discernible relative motion, enable the plotting party more quickly to determine in which direction the target was moving. Slowing down was routine—to avoid blundering prematurely into close range. Later, depending on which way the targets seemed to be moving, it might be necessary to turn around to put *Eel*'s stern toward them.

The TDC in the conning tower was, of course, the heart of the plotting effort. Normally Buck Williams would be operating it, but since for the time being he was occupied as Officer of the Deck, Keith would be running it for him.

Rich picked up the bridge hand-microphone which had been sent up when the radar tracking party was set. Rigged with a short extension cord, it permitted him to speak to the conning tower, control room, and maneuvering room without the necessity of fumbling for a button and leaning over to speak into the bridge speaker. Responses, of course, came as previously on the announcing system. He spoke into the mike: "Conn, this is bridge. I don't want to get closer than fifteen thousand yards."

"Recommend you slow down even more, Bridge," said Keith on the bridge speaker. "The range is closing rapidly."

Williams had heard too. With a quick look at Richardson he gave the order. "All ahead one-third!"

Several minutes passed. The bridge speaker blared again. "Bridge, conn." Keith's voice again, "We have six ships. Looks like three big ones and three little ones. The three big ones are in a column, and there's a little one ahead and on each flank. Estimated speed ten knots. Estimated course two-seven-oh. The range is now twenty thousand. The way we have them set up, they'll pass about ten thousand yards away at the closest point of approach."

Blunt was on the bridge. Rich was conscious of his presence even though he had not voiced the customary request to come up.

"Buck," said the skipper, "they're going to pass us too close aboard. Reverse course and put our stern on them." Speaking into the microphone he continued, "Conn, this is the bridge. We're reversing course to put our stern to the target."

"Conn, aye aye," from Keith.

Buck, as was his right as OOD, gave the orders. Slowly *Eel* swung to the right, her port side diesels muttering a little louder than before in response to the small speed increase he had directed.

"When you get around, Buck, go to all stop. We're at a good range now. Then go ahead just enough to keep the range at fifteen thousand."

All this had been rehearsed before. Should the range begin to decrease radically, indicating a zig toward, it would be easy to increase speed and pull off the track. Should plot indicate a zig away, now that a firm radar contact had been obtained it would be a simple matter to reverse course once more and maintain the desired distance.

"Commodore," said Richardson, "it looks like we're the trailer."

Blunt seemed not to have heard. Rich waited a moment, then spoke into the bridge microphone, "As soon as we're around and steadied on the new course, Conn, give me another reading on enemy course and speed. I want to send a message to the other boats as soon as possible."

In a few moments Keith reported that enemy course appeared to be 260, speed ten. "Range is now seventeen thousand. Closest point of approach about thirteen thousand."

"Better kick her ahead a little, Buck," said Richardson.

Then to the mike, "Keith, do you have tactical communications with the other boats?"

"Yes, sir. All set."

"Make up the contact report."

Keith clicked the bridge speaker switch twice. In a few minutes he read the message aloud: TALLYHO X THREE AND THREE X COURSE TWO-SIX-OH X SPEED TEN X POSITION QUEEN FOURTEEN X RICH ONE X

"Let her go, Keith," called Richardson through his microphone.

He could visualize Leone speaking into the radio microphone which had been installed in the conning tower. It must have been less than a minute before he announced, "Roger from Les, Bridge. Roger from Whitey."

Minutes passed. Keith again, "Bridge, Conn, zig to the convoy's right. It looks like they're going to pass north of the closest island. New course three-zero-zero. We're getting speed eleven now. I've made up another message to send to the other boats."

"All right, Keith, go ahead and send it. What course do you recommend to maintain contact?"

"With the island shielding them, we should come in closer, Captain. Recommend we close at full speed to get around to the other side and pick them up as they come in the clear again."

"Right," said Richardson. He motioned to Buck. With the latter's order, the main engines once again lifted their wild monotone. The propellers began their thrashing. *Eel* swung around again to the right, steadied on a course a little west of north.

During all of this Blunt had been a quiet but interested observer. Now he spoke. "Rich, why did you turn tail to the enemy when you first contacted him?"

Richardson was surprised at the question. "That was agreed procedure, sir," he said. "We made first contact, so we have to trail and avoid getting too close ourselves."

"It looked as if you were avoiding combat. But now you're closing in again, and you're getting in among the islands, too. I don't like it, Rich, it's too shallow. Our charts aren't that good."

He spoke rapidly. His voice had a nervous quality.

Richardson stared his amazement. It wouldn't do to let Buck Williams or the lookouts hear this exchange. He crowded over toward Blunt, dropped his voice, "Commodore, this is actually the deepest place in this whole section of the Yellow Sea! Take a look at the chart. These islands are narrow pinnacles coming up out of the bottom. It's over fifty fathoms where we are right this minute! Besides, there's plenty of sea room around and between these islands. We can see them on radar, and we can see them with the naked eye. This is our chance, sir. Your chance to start this patrol off with a real bang!"

"We're on the surface too close to land, Rich," muttered Blunt. "What if a plane takes off from one of these islands to provide air cover?"

"They'll never see us at night, Commodore. We'll soon merge in with the land return of these islands so their radar won't work, either!" Richardson terminated the exchange by putting his binoculars to his eyes. Fighting the ship was his responsibility, not the wolfpack commander's. Later there might be more to discuss, even recriminations, but this was out of place now. The sweep of events was beginning to move too rapidly.

Eel was again at full speed, throwing spray from both bows. Holding the now clearly outlined bulk of a relatively steep, slab-sided land mass on her starboard bow, she raced to regain contact on the other side. In the meantime Keith was sending another message to the other two submarines. When contact was regained, the message explained, *Eel* would slow down again, remain close inshore, wait until the convoy had passed on ahead, and then follow from astern at a greater distance.

In between observations of the convoy the radar kept swinging about, searching in all directions. It was during one of these searches that Rich saw the wolfpack training bearing fruit.

"Radar contact!" Rogers' boyish voice. He had relieved Quin when the tracking party was called. Rich could hear him clearly, without benefit of speaker.

"Radar contact, bearing two-zero-zero! He's got a radar too. I think it's the *Chicolar*!"

"I'll check it, sir." Keith. In a moment the exec reported, "It is the *Chicolar*, Captain. He acknowledges with his radar."

During convoy college a means had been devised for handling the radar of two submarines for precisely this eventuality. "Now that we have him on the radar, Captain, I'll give him a vector to the target."

In a few moments Keith's voice again on the bridge speaker, "Bridge, conn, tallyho from *Chicolar*. He's going in on our vector, figuring to pick them up on his own radar on the way."

This was, of course, just like Les Hartly. Richardson would never have attacked with so little information on the target. He was surprised to hear Blunt mutter approvingly.

Once out from behind the island, and again with a good radar contact on the enemy convoy, *Eel* slowed down, closed the island shoreline. Her diesels growling softly, she lay to in the quiet water, her stern again toward the enemy. Her radar still ceaselessly patrolled the night, and short contact reports still went out to *Whitefish*.

Chicolar, now in contact on her own, needed no further information except possibly early notification of any change in enemy course and speed. In any case, she would be monitoring the transmissions to *Whitefish*.

"Captain"—Keith's voice on the speaker—"We've got the whole picture on the PPI 'scope. *Chicolar* is going in on their port bow, and she's about ten thousand yards from firing position right now."

"Commodore," said Richardson, "why don't you go down and watch it? I can't because it would hurt my night vision. We'll go to battle stations as soon as *Chicolar* finishes. . . ."

Blunt dropped down the hatch. Several more minutes passed.

"Bridge, conn! Target has zigged to his left!" This was bad. If it zigged far enough, this could put *Chicolar* dead ahead, and the leading escort would be upon her in a matter of minutes.

"Bridge, conn. Target course checks at two-four-five! *Chicolar* is now sharp on their port bow!"

Richardson had to fight the impulse to run down below to see for himself. He could visualize the situation well enough. The enemy bearing, which had steadily been drawing left for *Chicolar*, had suddenly stopped drawing to the left and was now steady. Because of Les Hartly's approach technique, they were almost dead ahead of him. The target was coming directly for *Chicolar*, making eleven knots, and *Chicolar* was heading for the target at twenty knots.

He grabbed the bridge microphone, "Commodore!" he yelled. "Recommend an emergency message to *Chicolar*! Target is heading right for him!" *Chicolar* had held radar contact on the enemy such a short time that his plotting party could not yet have fully assessed the enemy's zigzag plan. He very likely would not discover the sudden deterioration of the situation until long after *Eel*'s tracking party had seen it in their plot.

No answer from the conning tower. The commodore must be there. Keith, alone, would have answered immediately. If necessary he would have sent the message in name of the wolfpack commander. There was no time to lose, not even time to encode a message in their simple wolfpack code.

"Keith!" bellowed Richardson. "Emergency message to *Chicolar*!"

No answer. Cursing, Rich shouted to Williams, "Take the conn, Buck! I'm going below!" He dashed down the ladder, rushed to the after part of the conning tower.

The commodore's squat bulk blocked the radar. He had pushed both Rogers and Keith aside, was staring at the PPI 'scope. Its hood had been removed. In his right hand he held the radio transmitter microphone. Keith, his eyes much bigger than usual, looked at him helplessly.

"Commodore! We've got to warn Les!"

Blunt did not move. Peering over his shoulder at the unhooded 'scope, Richardson could take in the entire panorama of disaster at a glance: the single gleaming pip with swirling, spiral-dotted radar indications emanating from it; and only a little distance beyond, three or four miles on the radar 'scope, six pips arranged like the head of an arrow— three large pips in a column, three small ones in a triangle formation around the leading pip—headed directly for the pip that was *Chicolar*.

"What did Blunt say?" he hissed to Keith.

"Nothing," whispered Keith. "He hasn't said anything. He just grabbed the radio mike and won't let it go."

Richardson turned to Blunt, "Commodore, there's barely time—he can still dive. . . ." He reached for the microphone, grabbed it. Blunt's fingers were clenched. No time to wrestle for it. Rich fumbled for the button, leaned over, shouted into the microphone, "Les, this is Joe. Emergency! Zero angle on the bow! Get out of there! Les, this is Joe. Emergency! Zero angle on the bow!" He repeated the message twice. Still no sign from Blunt. He could feel Keith crowded against his right shoulder. Rogers, too, on the other side. The range could now be no more than three miles.

Some division was occurring in the enemy convoy. The three smaller pips continued as before, but the three larger ones, still in column, were drifting to the right. In a minute the shaft of the arrow had broken away from its head, had headed up more to the north. The three little ones, however, were converging directly upon the little pip from which the dotted sweeping wand of radar emanated.

"Captain!" Buck Williams' voice on the bridge microphone. "Gun fire to the north!"

"All ahead flank! Right full rudder!" shouted Richardson. He broke away from the group in the conning tower, dashed to the bridge. "Buck," he said, "I'll take back the conn. Sound battle stations, and take your post on the TDC. Get your gun crews ready also. They're shelling the *Chicolar*. We'll have to go and help."

"Roger, Captain. We're lying with our head one-seven-oh, all stop, except for your last order."

"Right, Buck. I have the conn. . . . Keep your rudder right full!"

"Can you see all right, sir? Maybe I'd better stay up with you a few minutes."

"Okay, Buck, do that. Go ahead and sound battle stations anyway, right away."

The pealing notes of the general alarm rang through *Eel*. Within seconds the report came up. "Battle stations manned and ready!"

"Conn!" Richardson shouted into his bridge microphone. "Range and bearing of *Chicolar*!"

There was some delay. Finally Keith replied, "Range to *Chicolar*, eleven thousand yards!"

"Buck!" said Richardson savagely, "I can see well enough up here! Get down there and get Blunt away from the radar!"

Williams dashed below.

"Helm!" Richardson called down the hatch to the helmsman, "make your new course three-five-zero!"

"Three-five-zero, aye." Scott. The helm was his battle station. Richardson did not know the exact bearing of *Chicolar*, but 350 would do for a start. He picked up the microphone, "Conn, bridge; bearing and range to *Chicolar*!"

"Three-four-five, Bridge. Range eleven thousand two hundred."

"Steady on three-four-five, helm!" ordered Richardson.

Under the thrust of four suddenly aroused diesels, *Eel* was picking up speed swiftly, curving to the right, straightening out on the ordered course. Up ahead Richardson could see flashes on the horizon.

Damn Les Hartly and his all out bows-on approach! This was exactly the situation which had been predicted, and now he was caught! Maybe *Eel* could get there in time to create a diversion, but *Chicolar* needed only one shell through her pressure hull to end her career. He leaned over, pressed the bridge speaker button. "All hands hear this," he said. "*Chicolar* has been caught on the surface by enemy tincans. They are shelling her now. We're going over to try to help. Gun crews stand by in the control room and crew's mess!"

Rich was conscious that the battle lookouts, men specially designated to take lookout stations during surface action and who were also trained to operate the two bridge forty-millimeter guns and the twenty-millimeter pair, were coming up one after the other and taking their stations.

Al Dugan would be coming shortly, was there. "I'll keep the deck, Al," he said. "You run the routine. If we can get close enough to open fire with all weapons, maybe we can take the heat off *Chicolar* and they can dive."

"What are you going to do about the convoy, Rich? Are you going to let them get away?" Blunt's voice. He had again come on the bridge without anyone being aware of it. "Rich," he went on, "I have a report to make about your executive officer. I want you to relieve him of duty and confine him to his room. He was insolent to me just now, pushed me, even."

Rich could feel his eyes narrowing. He answered rapidly, "Can we talk about that later, sir? We've got to see what we can do to help *Chicolar*!"

"That's what I mean," said Blunt, shifting back to the first subject as though he had never mentioned the second. "We've got three ships now that are about to get away. They're unescorted, too. Those are our targets. That's what we came out here for. Leave the *Chicolar*. Go after them. That's an order, Richardson!"

"Commodore, the *Chicolar* is worth a dozen of those old ships! She's in trouble!"

"You heard me, Richardson! The *Chicolar* can take care of herself. You go after those three ships. Do I make myself clear?"

"Bridge"—this was Keith on the speaker—"*Chicolar* has dived."

"Keith, what's the range and bearing of the convoy?"

"Convoy has reversed course, Bridge. They bear zero-zero-zero, thirteen thousand yards, course zero-nine-zero, speed twelve." In one way Blunt was correct. Unescorted, the three freighters, or whatever they were, would be easy meat.

No doubt the three escort ships would depth charge the area where *Chicolar* had dived. They would be out of action for some time. Whatever *Eel* did had to be done immediately.

Raising his voice, Rich shouted into the bridge hatch, "Come right to zero-three-zero. . . . Keith," he said into the hand mike, "give me a course to intercept the convoy."

"Zero-three-zero looks good, Bridge!"

In the distance, far on the port beam, the flashes of gunfire had ceased. Richardson could hear the detonations of explosions. No doubt they were depth charges. Keith confirmed it. "We can hear distant depth charges below," he reported.

Richardson's night vision was returning rapidly. At ten thousand yards he could see the dark blobs of three ships on his port bow. With her superior speed *Eel* drew abreast of them, maintaining her distance.

"Conn, bridge. Target course?"

"Steady on zero-nine-zero, Bridge," Keith responded. "Convoy is not zigzagging. Three ships in column. Speed twelve."

Obviously they were trying to make as much distance away from the scene of action as they could. Anticipating only a single submarine in the area, they had ceased to zigzag, had probably gone to emergency speed. Rapidly *Eel* opened out on the convoy's starboard bow.

"We'll fire two fish at each ship," Rich said to Keith. "Give me a course for a ninety track on the middle ship. We'll shoot all fish to hit, and take them in order from forward aft."

"Aye aye, Captain. Looks pretty good right now, sir; come on around anytime. Recommend course north."

All this time *Eel* had been plying along at nearly twenty knots through a calm, motionless, almost oily sea. Richardson felt again the curious sense of detachment he always felt at just this moment. "Stand by," he ordered. "Left full rudder. Helm, make your new course zero-zero-zero! . . . All right, Keith," he called into the bridge microphone, "we're making our approach now. Call out the ranges as we come in!"

The range closed swiftly. At seven thousand yards Rich ordered two-thirds speed ahead. He could see the large bulks of the three ships looming clearly, shadowy shapes in his staring binoculars. Swiftly he swept from one to the other. They were running in very close formation, hardly three ship-lengths apart. Two were relatively new ships, not large, perhaps three thousand tons each. Engines aft—probably the products of a war construction program. The third ship was a trifle larger and looked older, an old-type freighter with a tall stack and a small deck house amidships. Possibly four-thousand-ton size.

Eel was now as committed as *Chicolar* had been, with three basic differences: she knew a lot more about the enemy, having tracked them for a considerably longer time, she was coming in for attack on their beam, and there were no escorts.

"Range four thousand yards"—from Keith on the bridge speaker. *Eel*'s speed had been reduced to about ten knots. At three thousand yards range, with the leading ship just on her port bow, Richardson ordered the outer doors to the forward torpedo tubes opened. He could almost hear the six consecutive thumps as the hydraulic mechanism banged them open.

"All ahead one-third! Stand by forward!" he ordered.

"Range twenty-five hundred yards!"

"Why don't you go ahead and shoot, Rich?" Blunt. He had not spoken for more than a quarter of an hour. Richardson had completely forgotten his presence on the bridge.

From the high plane of the objective professionalism which somehow possessed him, Richardson heard himself say, "I seem to remember an old skipper of mine saying once you get in there to take your time and do it right. They can't see us."

"Range to leading ship sixteen hundred. Gyros six right. Torpedo run one-six-zero-zero!"

"Conn, bridge, we'll shoot with the port TBT," continued Richardson into the bridge mike, setting his left shoulder into the bulge built in the port side of the bridge. "Bearing, mark!"

"Port TBT, aye aye. Range sixteen hundred. Torpedo run one-five-two-five. Gyros ten right. Ready number one!"

"Stand by, forward," said Rich once more. He looked through the TBT binoculars, thumbed the button buzzer with his right thumb. "Shoot!" he said into the microphone hanging on its wire looped over the top of the pressure-proof binoculars.

"One's away"—Keith from the conning tower. He could hear someone counting seconds. "Two's away."

"Shift targets," said Rich. He swung the TBT to the second target. "Bearing, mark!" He pushed the button.

Keith answered as before, "Ready with number three!"

"Shoot!" he said again.

"Three's away! Four's away!"

"Shift targets! Bearing, mark!" He thumbed the button a third time.

"Ready number five!"

"Shoot!" said Richardson for the third time.

"Five's away! Six away! All torpedoes fired forward!"

Richardson had felt the mild lurch as each torpedo was ejected. *Eel* was firing electric torpedoes and therefore there was no wake, no sign that anything had happened in the water, but he knew that six times three thousand pounds of highly complicated mechanism, carrying a total of twenty-four hundred pounds of TNT, was running in the dark water.

"Aren't you going to maneuver, Rich?" asked Blunt.

"No, sir," said Richardson. He felt perverse detachment. Standard tactics called for maneuvering to avoid, but he would not do it. He had dealt death again, and now he must watch it happen. "These ships have had it," he growled in justification. "Besides, they're unescorted. There's nobody there who can hurt us."

There was a flash of light at the water line of the first freighter. The ocean was riven as a huge plume of water and air suddenly obscured the doomed ship's midsection. Seconds later another similar plume covered the after portion. Then the noise of explosions came in—three times; three loud booms.

"What happened, Rich? I distinctly saw you fire only two torpedoes at the first ship."

"We heard them through air and water both, Commodore," rapidly responded Rich. "The middle two probably overlapped each other and reached us around the same time." He shifted his attention to the second ship just in time to catch the two explosions enveloping her.

109

He shifted the TBT to the third ship. Nothing. The torpedoes could not have missed!

Then, as he watched it, the ship seemed to divide into two parts. Her midship section disappeared. Bow and stern rose toward the sky, closed together, swiftly shrank. Both sections were already half under water when the thunderous explosion of the torpedoes beating in the old freighter's ancient bottom reached them.

"Six hits for six torpedoes! Bully good shooting, Rich!" shouted Blunt ecstatically, slapping him across the shoulders and slamming his eyes unexpectedly into the rigid rubber-protected eyepieces of the heavy TBT binoculars. "Great work!" Blunt was almost babbling with excitement and pleasure. Curiously, Richardson felt totally let down. This had been ridiculously easy. The ships had had no defense whatever. *Chicolar* had taken the escorts out. His attack had been made without warning, and he had had all the advantage of modern technological science. It had been nothing but murder.

"All ahead, flank! Left full rudder!" he ordered.

"Where are you going now, Rich?" said Blunt.

"Back to the *Chicolar*. Maybe we can help her a little." He spoke into his command microphone. "Conn, bridge, what have you got on the *Whitefish*? And where are the three tincans working over *Chicolar*?"

"Nothing on the *Whitefish*, Captain. We've not seen her radar for quite a while. Maybe she's dived. Morning twilight will be in half an hour. The three tincans are where they were before, still in a group fifteen miles bearing two-six-five true."

"Make your course two-six-five, helm," said Rich.

"Rich, they're fifteen miles away. Day will be breaking before we get there."

"Then we'll dive and make a submerged approach. They won't be expecting a second submarine."

"After what you did to that convoy? By the time we get there they'll know what happened to it, and that another submarine was responsible!" Blunt seemed totally oblivious to the fact that four lookouts, a quartermaster and Al Dugan were all crowded together on *Eel's* tiny chariot bridge and could not avoid hearing every word that was said.

"Commodore," muttered Rich, trying to give his voice an urgent piercing quality while at the same time lowering his tone so that only Blunt could hear, "Commodore, they won't have any idea what has happened to their convoy! Besides, the *Chicolar* is in trouble! She may have been hit before she dived! We're still recording sporadic depth charging over there, and the radar shows the three Jap escorts still clustered around the same spot. We'll be able to dive outside visual range and make a dawn attack. . . ."

"Absolutely not, Rich, I forbid it! That's an order!" Blunt spoke as loudly as before. "Our mission here is to sink Japanese ships, not to go off shooting at windmills on some wild goose chase! *Chicolar* can take care of herself. Les Hartly is an experienced skipper. I want this ship to remain undetected. *Whitefish* is already submerged, and you are to do the same. I want you to head southwest and return to your patrol position. This was a good night's work. I won't let you spoil it now!"

Night was beginning to give way to the gray haze of the approaching dawn. Blunt's face was seamed, its once craggy lines now only sagging gray flesh. His eyes had a strange intensity, a hint of fervid determination. Rich had never seen him this way before. Abruptly Blunt turned. He stooped for the grab rail above the hatch to the conning tower, swung himself below.

After the commodore disappeared there was silence on the bridge. Dugan, not a loquacious individual anyway, wisely was using his binoculars and paying no apparent attention to the exchange between his skipper and the wolfpack commander. Obviously the strain of the war patrol, Blunt's self-isolation on board the submarine, and his background in prewar submarine tactics might contribute to a sort of bewilderment which could be responsible for his present attitude. It was also possible, Richardson had honestly to admit to himself, that he had deeper information, better knowledge, than possessed by the submarine skippers. One thing sure, he was the senior officer present. The three submarines in effect were his fleet. His orders must be obeyed.

"All ahead two-thirds. Come left to course two-two-five," Rich ordered down the hatch. In the stillness on the bridge, the clink of the annunciators answered him before the acknowledging call came from the helmsman. "Al," he said to Dugan, "take over the deck. Check with the forward torpedo room to be sure that no torpedoes are loose in the room. When you're satisfied that everything is secure, go ahead and dive. Take a quick sounding first. We should have at least forty fathoms under our keel."

Richardson fought down a feeling of bitterness as he descended the ladder into the conning tower. He waited there, withdrawn and uncommunicative, as Dugan gave the necessary orders, received the correct responses, and supervised the operation of submerging. Instead of the wild exultation of successful combat, the satisfaction over destruction of three enemy cargo ships without having received a shot or a depth charge in return, gloom enveloped him. The three ships sunk had been far less offensive than Bungo Pete. They had not shot at him, had not even known he was there. Their only offense was that they happened to be on the other side of a war.

They had had nothing to do with starting the war, nor, for that matter, had he, nor had Bungo Pete. Perhaps, as Blunt had once suggested, he spent too much of his time thinking about the lifeboats. Was that why he had wished to rush to the aid of Les Hartly and the *Chicolar*? Was he still impelled to rush headlong into danger in order to satisfy his unconscious craving for absolution? If so, perhaps Blunt was right. He had no right to risk his men or his ship to fulfill some inner psychological compulsion of his own.

He waited in the conning tower until the dive was complete, and *Eel* was cruising quietly at periscope depth. Suddenly he felt tired. Keith had been standing silently in the after part of the conning tower alongside Buck Williams, facing the now quiet TDC. Neither had said a word to him. Perhaps they had some inkling of the inner turmoil which possessed him.

"Keith," he said in a low voice, "secure from battle stations. Set the regular submerged watch. I'm going below."

He swung himself onto the ladder leading to the control room, went down with his back to the ladder, his heels on the rungs, supporting himself from falling by hands on the opposite side of the hatch coaming.

In the control room, Al Dugan obviously wanted to say something. He beat him to it. "Al," he said, "Keith has the conn in the conning tower. We'll be securing from battle stations in a minute. He'll turn over to you."

"Aye aye, sir," said Al. "Can I talk to you for a minute, Captain?"

"What is it?"

"We have a problem coming back, Captain; it's the hydraulic system. I didn't want to bother you about it before with all that was going on, but she's recycling fast again. If we're going to have a few hours, I'd like to turn to on it with a couple of men. We'll have to put the planes in hand power, and secure the plant. You won't be able to use the periscopes for several hours." Dugan's normally stolid face was clearly worried.

- 5 -

Al Dugan's plan of attack on the hydraulic system was to isolate all of its parts and methodically inspect each one. "We're lucky to have that fellow Lichtmann aboard, Captain," he said. "Our boat was built in Portsmouth, and *Nerka* at Mare Island. She was an earlier boat than this one, but Mare Island builds to Portsmouth designs, and it turns out he was *Nerka*'s hydraulic plant expert. Starberg and Sargent are pretty good at it too; so we've got our three best men on it, and we'll go at it systematically. There must be something basic wrong with it."

"How long will it take you to put the plant back in commission if we need it? If we can't use the periscopes, we'll be in trouble if something turns up."

"Depending upon which part we take down, we should be able to get the vital parts of the system working again in an hour. To find the problem, though, may take several days. I'd like to begin with the periscope hoists, and that's why I thought maybe we could go deep for a while. I'll let you know if we strike any trouble. We'll have it ready for surfacing by sunset for sure."

"Okay, Al. Let me know if there's anything at all anybody else can do to help." He felt a deep yawn arising from the depths of his being. Going deep for a few hours would give the whole crew a rest. He wanted nothing so much as to surrender to the demands of sleep.

Blunt, as usual, was sitting in the wardroom, unlighted pipe in his mouth.

"Commodore, we're going to have to stay below periscope depth for a while. I'm turning in. You should do the same," said Rich.

"I'm not sleepy," said Blunt. "You go ahead. I'll call you if anything turns up."

So far as anything turning up in any way connected with *Eel*, Rich thought, he had better be informed of it before Blunt, who was, after all, sort of an official passenger, not involved with the operations of the ship. But it was a small matter, not worth worrying about. He removed his outer clothing, climbed in his bunk, and was instantly asleep.

Al Dugan awakened him several hours later. "We think we may have

113

found at least some of the trouble in the system," said the engineer. "The accumulator ram may be scored again—she's not holding pressure like she ought—but the main trouble seems to be in the overload bypass system. This new design has a complicated valving setup. I think some of the valves are sticking. We don't know which ones, though."

The clock on Rich's stateroom bulkhead was indicating nearly noon. "I must have been asleep quite a while, Al. What shape do you have the plant in now?"

"Well, we're still checking some of the parts, but unless we find anything more, we'll have to go with what we've got. We'll have it ready to surface by sunset," Al promised.

It was with gratitude for a long comfortable rest that Richardson brought *Eel* to periscope depth several hours later, and, just at sunset, took a careful look around through the periscope. Nothing was in sight. The sea was flat, calm as before. The murky gray atmosphere was unchanged.

The worrying in his mind had been growing stronger as the uneventful day wore to its close. The overcast sky reflected his mood. "Keith," he said, "be sure Rogers has the radar all peaked up before we surface. I want to see if we can pick up the *Whitefish* and *Chicolar* radars on ours. No telling where they'll be. Both ought to be north of us, I think."

As it grew dark, the familiar surfacing routine took place and Richardson was on the dripping bridge. "There are no stars, Keith," he called down the hatch. "You'll have to work on dead reckoning." This had been anticipated. No stars had been seen through the periscope either. Keith clicked the bridge speaker button from the conning tower twice.

The deep rumble of two main engines recharging the battery and providing steerageway was always comforting to hear. *Eel* settled into her surface cruising routine. Another night of tense watchfulness in enemy waters lay ahead. It felt almost better this way than to be submerged deep below periscope depth, with 'scopes inoperative because of lack of hydraulic pressure. Rich looked up at the shears. On their after side, just above the topmost periscope support bearing, the slotted oval dish which was the radar antenna rotated ceaselessly. Evidently it was seeing nothing, not even the radar of another submarine, for otherwise it would have been searching right and left of the suspect bearings, looking for confirmation in short, jerky sweeps.

"Permission to come on the bridge and dump trash and garbage!" a shout from the conning tower. Part of the surfacing routine. Since the

114

captain was on the bridge, permission for such matters had to be sought from him—an authoritarian obligation he would abdicate the moment he passed below. Buck Williams cast a quick look at his skipper, received a nod in return.

"Permission granted to dump trash and garbage," Buck called down the hatch. In a moment two men dragging filled gunny sacks behind them appeared on the bridge. The OOD and skipper moved out of their way to permit them clear passage to the cigarette deck, where the two men in a practiced maneuver flung each sack in turn clear of the side and into the water. "One more coming up, Bridge. A juicy one." There was someone in the conning tower boosting the sacks up to the bridge. A little more gingerly, the third sack was carried aft, thrown overboard also. Wiping their hands on their shirts, the two men stood for a minute, sucking in deep lungfuls of the salt-laden air, then in turn went below.

Richardson waited a few more minutes. Still no sign from the radar. It was now completely dark. The visibility was less than the previous night, perhaps five miles. Surely by now *Whitefish* and *Chicolar* would be surfacing.

"Going below, Buck," he said abruptly. He reached for the rail above the hatch to the conning tower, with distaste found it covered with a slimy, sticky substance. "Buck," he said sharply, "get this rail wiped off, and have some words with the cook. One of the garbage detail always ought to have a rag with him and wipe the rails down when they're finished. Otherwise somebody is sure to slip and hurt himself sometime. Especially if we make a sudden dive." He realized there had been a slight irritation in his voice, more than he wanted to show.

Rogers looked up as Richardson approached the radar console. "No contact," he said. "Nothing at all. No pips. No sweeping radars. Just lots of grass, and land to the northeast."

"We're too far away to pick up any of those tincans who were depth-charging *Chicolar* last night," Keith said, "unless they've decided to head down this way. But if conditions are right, we should be able to see one of the other boats' radars as far as fifty miles, maybe more."

"I know," Rogers said. "Except you can't figure out these atmospheric conditions. Just now we got contact on land over sixty miles away which Mr. Leone says must be Quelpart. I've never seen this kind of range on this radar. It's got to be atmospherics!"

Suddenly he looked closer at the radar, crowding alongside Keith, also bent over the unhooded dial. "Mark!" he said. "Look at that!"

Richardson moved in. The sweeping wand rotated slowly clockwise, passed the 6 o'clock position, the 9 o'clock position, and then, nearly at 12 o'clock, it was broken into a series of short dashes. "There it is," all three men said almost simultaneously.

"Steady on it, Rogers," said Keith. "Give us a bearing!"

In obedience to Rogers' manipulation of the control handle, the moving wand steadied, swept back and forth over the area it had been crossing, was broken again into dots as the unseen outline of another sweeping wand far off the scope to the north intersected it.

"Who is it?" asked Rich.

"Don't know, sir," said the radarman. "If he steadies on us maybe we can exchange calls."

The alien wand continued its periodic sweeps for several minutes, then at last hesitated uncertainly, swept jerkily back and forth, finally beamed directly at the wand emanating from *Eel*.

"There he is, sir. He's on us now," said Rogers. "Shall I give him the recognition signal?"

"Yes, go ahead."

The code name for each submarine was her skipper's nickname, and its initial letter had been settled on for radar recognition purposes. A standard radio-telegraph key, shorting out the transmitter, made it possible to key the radar pulses. Deliberately Rogers pushed the key three times, holding it down for approximately one second the first time, five seconds the second, and one second the third.

On the 'scope *Eel*'s wand suddenly vanished, came back on, was interrupted for a longer period, came back on, vanished for a third time, and then returned to its normal intensity: a dot, a dash, a dot; the letter R in Morse code.

They waited a full minute. "Send it again, Rogers," said Rich. Once again the radarman tapped the radio gate key. Again they watched. At last there was an answering interruption from the alien radar—a dot and two dashes.

"That's a W for 'Whitey,' " said Keith. "I'll bet *Whitefish* has just surfaced."

The feeling of disquiet in Rich's mind was stronger. "Resume your normal radar search, Rogers," he said. "See if you can pick up *Chicolar*. He should be to the right of *Whitefish*." For several minutes the trio stood in front of the radar, inspecting it carefully whenever it swept over the northern arc, but nothing was seen.

Dinner in the wardroom was a gloomy affair. At the conclusion of the meal Keith excused himself from the wardroom, returned a moment later. He shook his head slightly as he looked, gravely and unblinkingly, at his skipper.

116

"Commodore," said Rich slowly, "I'm worried about the *Chicolar*. We've been unable to raise her. We have the *Whitefish* okay—she's up somewhere to the north of us—and I figure that *Chicolar* ought to be up there too, but she hasn't come in yet."

"There are lots of reasons why Les Hartly may not have been able to check in with us yet, Rich," said Blunt. "There's no cause to worry, at least not yet."

"He may be in trouble, Commodore," said Richardson.

Blunt said nothing, puffed his pipe impassively. He was sitting exactly where he had been all day, exactly where he had placed himself after the convoy action of the night before. For all Richardson knew, he might have sat in the same place all day long.

"Commodore," he said, "anything could have happened. They were caught on the surface, remember. They might even be on the bottom and unable to surface."

Blunt palmed the pipe bowl. "What do you want to do, Rich?" he said. His gravelly voice was smooth, too smooth.

"I still think we should have tried to do something this morning," said Rich quietly.

"So? Well, why didn't you?" Blunt squeezed the pipe bowl. His hand was trembling slightly. "Do you mean to say that you would have been willing to take this crippled submarine, with a bad hydraulic system, up against three alerted enemy antisubmarine ships?"

There was an unreal undercurrent in the conversation. "But Commodore, the hydraulic system trouble wasn't reported until after. . . . Besides, we didn't have to tear it down right then. It could have lasted——"

"But you had trouble all the same, didn't you? Somebody has got to have some common sense around this submarine! I absolutely forbid your taking her into action against enemy combatant ships in the shape she's in!" Again there was that look of strained intensity. "The subject is closed," Blunt said. "*Chicolar* will probably show up in due course, and we'll all wonder why we made such a fuss about it."

Looking back on them later, the next several days were for Richardson probably the most uncomfortable he had ever spent. The vision of Tateo Nakame with both hands planted on the skin of *Eel*'s ballast tanks on the port side near the stern returned in full force. Combined with it, however, was an even more vivid vision, that of *Chicolar*, damaged, leaking, wracked by depth charges, her pressure hull—probably the conning tower—ruptured by shell fire. A bad leak or other damage would have driven her to the bottom. There, once her location

117

was precisely determined, it would be marked with a buoy. The Japanese escorts would slowly and deliberately cruise back and forth across the spot, sowing depth charges with the depth setting devastatingly determined for certain.

Every night, during the ritual planning and strategy council in the wardroom, the discussion would begin on the subject of *Eel*'s hydraulic system. Al Dugan reported that at least two bypass valves in different return lines seemed to be sticking occasionally and might be responsible for the continual bleeding down of the accumulator. This was apparently the cause of the rapid cycling and might have led to the scoring and other troubles. If nothing of greater seriousness developed, he thought, the system could be kept under careful surveillance and give satisfactory service for the remainder of the patrol.

As to where enemy ships were going, the arguments were no different from before. Everything had been said several times. Adamantly Captain Blunt held to his mid-area patrol thesis, insisting that sooner or later ships must cross the Yellow Sea. In the meantime, it became distressingly evident that something serious had happened to *Chicolar*. At the very least, her radar and radios must be out of action, a theory hopefully advanced by Larry Lasche and seized upon by Blunt. But after the first day, no one made further mention of this possibility.

After the second night without news, Richardson hesitantly brought up the need to reorganize the combined operations of the two remaining members of the wolfpack. Blunt became agitated at the suggestion, peremptorily ordered it dropped. Only when it became *Eel*'s turn to send the routine weather report for the Yellow Sea area did he permit a single terse sentence concerning lack of word from *Chicolar* to be included at the end of the message.

Rich could sense the dropping of morale throughout the ship. Years ago he had learned that no secrets could be kept from the crew of a submarine. This was axiomatic. *Chicolar* and her crew had gone to join *Nerka*, *Walrus*, and the other submarine casualties of the war. The fact cast gloom upon all of them, particularly *Eel*'s skipper, since he could not rid himself of the thought that just possibly, if he had persisted a little more strongly in his initial impulse to go to her assistance immediately, he might have won the argument with Blunt. Clearly, he should have insisted on returning to the spot after sinking the three freighters. A submerged approach at dawn might have been successful in picking off one of the destroyers, or even two, had he been lucky, but, most important, a sudden salvo of torpedoes would have distracted them from the wounded *Chicolar*, even perhaps convinced them she had got away. Then, if she were indeed disabled on the bottom, it might

118

have been possible later to communicate on sonar and render some help. At a minimum he could have stood by to rescue those of her crew able to escape via the rescue breathing apparatus.

Over and over in his mind Richardson revolved the alternatives that might have been. Every time he did so, his thoughts went back to the same point: he was the captain of the *Eel*, and he held the responsibility for what she did, or didn't do, to help her consort. Was this not, indeed, what Blunt had almost said? But it was all too late now.

After the fourth fruitless day of patrolling with nothing but fishing boats of various sizes sighted, and no messages from ComSubPac, he tried a new approach.

"Commodore," he said, once again pointing out the various salient features of the shore topography around Korea and the coast of China, "we've been in the area eleven days. We have only nineteen days more before we have to pull out. So far, *Whitefish* hasn't made a single contact. He's got a full load of twenty-four torpedoes, and we need to figure out some way to give him a chance to shoot some of them."

"What do you suggest?" asked Blunt.

"Well," Rich said slowly, trying to speak matter-of-factly, "this is Whitey's first patrol as skipper. He's never made any night surface attacks, but he always was good with a periscope. So maybe if we could find a deep spot close in to shore somewhere, where ships might be pretty sure to pass, we could send him in there. He'd still be in radio contact at night, so we could coordinate our operations if a big convoy came by."

Richardson was startled at the alacrity with which the wolfpack commander seized upon his suggestion. Within an hour *Whitefish* receipted for a message directing her to proceed close into the coast of China south of Tsingtao, where, the chart showed, relatively deep water extended fairly close to the shoreline.

Again there was the waiting, the deadly boredom of readiness with nothing happening. Two nights later a message arrived from *Whitefish*: SANK FIVE THOUSAND TON FREIGHTER X DEPTH CHARGED X PROCEEDING TO CENTER OF AREA TO REPAIR DAMAGES X FOUR TORPEDOES EXPENDED

"Good for Whitey Everett," said Blunt when the decoded message was placed in front of him.

Rich tried to press his advantage. "Commodore," he said, "this at least proves that there are ships moving. The total bag for the patrol so far is four, but they're all relatively small coastal freighters. Maybe that's all the Japanese have left. Anyway, now that *Whitefish* is back in the center of the area, it's our turn to go close into shore, and I was thinking that this spot off the west coast of Korea . . ."

"With your hydraulic system in the shape it's in?" said Blunt. "Not on your life! I forbid it!"

"Commodore," Rich spoke sharply, "this submarine is not a cripple. We're perfectly able to carry out our functions. If not, there's a submarine tender at Guam, and we should go back there for repairs. We've been two weeks in the center of the area now, sir, and we haven't seen a thing come through here. The four ships our wolfpack has sunk were all picked off close to shore." There was a bite to Richardson's voice, a compound of annoyance and of frustration.

"No!" said Blunt, slamming his fist on the table. "I'm running this wolfpack, and as long as I'm in charge you will operate in accordance with my instructions!"

This time it was Richardson who, in scarcely concealed anger, abruptly rose and left the wardroom.

He climbed to the bridge, seething. There was no question that something was wrong with Blunt. He had been a highly competent peacetime skipper of the *Octopus* eight years earlier, and he had been a source of strength and support with the old *S-16* and the *Walrus*. Beginning with the recent period at Pearl, however, Blunt seemed to have changed, and he had not bounced back upon going to sea. The stimulus of a patrol had not had the hoped-for effect. His thought processes were not as incisive as they once were. He looked older, acted older, spoke in unaccustomed clichés. Rich also was convinced he was getting far from enough sleep. His eyes always looked blurry and tired, and he spent hours in the wardroom drinking innumerable cups of coffee, morosely speaking to no one. No doubt Admiral Small had thought getting him to sea, away from the routine of his desk and the distractions of Pearl Harbor, possibly also away from Cordy Wood, would restore him. But the problem obviously was deeper. Something else was wrong.

Perhaps the loss of *Chicolar* had begun to prey upon his mind, but Richardson had truthfully to admit to himself that he, at least, had begun to notice disturbing signs before the patrol began.

"Permission to come on the bridge?" Keith's voice. Evidently he had followed him, having waited a decent interval first. Rich welcomed the opportunity, walked quietly to the after part of the cigarette deck, leaned against the rail, waited for him.

"Skipper," said Keith in a low voice, "I have to talk to you about the commodore. He's got me worried, sir."

"How, Keith?" said Richardson wearily.

Keith was his confidant and best friend on board, but years of navy training and of ingrained respect for his former skipper were behind the deep reticence Rich now felt.

"He's not the same as he was back in New London, sir. He was different this time in Pearl, too. Ever since we left Pearl Harbor he has been acting more and more strange. He hardly ever sleeps, and he hardly ever talked to you, or anybody, until lately. But now he's beginning not to make sense."

Richardson could think of nothing to say. The idea would have been startling a few days ago. Not so now.

"He's your old skipper and all that, and I worried a lot about whether I should tell you this. He's driving us all batty."

"Oh, come on, Keith," said Richardson uncomfortably. "He's got a lot more on his mind than you know."

"No, that's not it." Suddenly Keith spoke with a tone of passionate vehemence. "He doesn't usually talk much, as I said, but for the last two days, when you're not in the wardroom, he's been talking a lot. All he talks about is maybe somebody is sabotaging our hydraulic plant!"

"Now, wait a minute, Keith. You don't expect me to believe that a member of our crew is deliberately trying to wreck the hydraulic system!"

"Nobody's trying to sabotage anything! That's only the commodore's idea. We're all trying to help Al figure out what's wrong. The best man we've got on the hydraulic plant is Lichtmann, but lately the commodore has decided Lichtmann must be the saboteur. Don't ask me how he came up with this one, but it's all he's talked about for a day, now, and it's giving us a fit!"

On the forward part of the bridge, the quartermaster and Officer of the Deck maintained their vigil, while behind them the four lookouts stood motionlessly, elbows on the bridge bulwarks, binoculars steadily sweeping the murky horizon, which could hardly be seen. One part of Richardson wanted badly to continue the conversation, but he could not, would not. "Keith," he said, "I don't want this subject to be talked about. Not anywhere, and especially not in the wardroom. It's up to you to keep the rest of the wardroom in line when I'm not there. Blunt may be passing through a tough time—but he does have a lot on his mind, remember that. Anyway, I don't want you or any of the others worrying about him. He's my problem. I'll handle him. He's an old friend, and I'll take care of him."

Having made a decision, Richardson was surprised at the ease with which he was able to placate Keith. Perhaps Keith also felt he had said enough. Rich searched his mind for a new topic of conversation, found it. "Keith," he said, "have you thought much about what types of ships those three escorts were that got the *Chicolar*?"

"Only what I've already told you. Nobody saw them. They must have been pretty small, because on the radar scope they were only half as big as the freighters. The three pips all looked exactly the same, so all three escorts could be the same type of ship. They increased speed from ten to eighteen knots, by our plot, when they closed in on *Chicolar*. They weren't just patrol craft, that's one thing sure. We counted over ninety depth charges, so that means each one carries at least thirty and probably a lot more. Anybody carrying that many depth charges——"

"Must have been designed for ASW work," broke in Richardson. "It's a good thing for us, sitting here charging batteries in the middle of the Yellow Sea, that they aren't out patrolling, instead of sticking to convoy escort duty."

"One of those new *Mikura* class escorts, if that's what they were, might waste a lot of time just patrolling an area," said Keith. "We could avoid him pretty easily. He'll give us a big enough silhouette at night that we should see him before he sees us, and anyway, we should have him on radar long before he's onto us."

"Right, Keith, but the Jap Navy won't pass up the duty to patrol. Remember the fishing boats. They're made of wood, and wood doesn't give as good a radar return as steel. I daresay the three escorts who got *Chicolar* were *Mikuras*, all right, but I'm beginning to wonder whether we might be seeing one of those big sampans they warned us about just before we left Pearl. Twice we've seen a pretty big one. Sea-going junks, I'd call both of them. Or maybe we saw the same one twice. It could easily be a patrol boat."

"Our operation order says the big ones are. They're on patrol to spot submarines. Their hulls are low to the water, and our radar doesn't see them very soon, either, that's for damn sure."

"They aren't worth a torpedo, but ComSubPac is worried about them. That's one reason for the extra five-inch gun they gave us."

Keith thoughtfully nodded his head. The musty atmosphere of the Yellow Sea, muggy, laden with salt, crowded around them, isolated them where they stood. They had moved close together, draped their arms over the forty-millimeter gun barrel. There was a hint of fog in the air, but then, there was almost always a hint of fog in the Yellow Sea at night. Richardson and Leone, standing with their heads inches apart, could see each other clearly enough in the faint illumination from occasional greenish-white phosphorescence in the water, or the gray reflection from some part of the ship's structure. They spoke in low voices, barely loudly enough to hear each other above the muffled diesels spewing their exhaust into the sea astern.

Eel rode easily on the placid sea. Weather in the Yellow Sea apparently was rarely stormy, although, like any body of water, it must have its bad moments.

"You know, Skipper," Keith was saying, "this darkness is deceptive. You can't see the horizon. Taking my sights in the morning and evening I've almost always had to guess at it, and right now, in the middle of the night, you can't tell sky from water. If the Japs were smart, they'd get those two-man submarines out looking for us at night. They know darned well where our patrol areas are. The way we patrol right off their main harbors, their crews could sleep all day in a barracks on shore and come out at night just looking for us. We'd look like an ocean liner to them. One torpedo from a Jap two-man submarine would finish us."

"Maybe that's one reason why the commodore won't let us go in closer. I imagine the two-man subs would have trouble patrolling this far away from harbor."

"Guess so, but now that the Japs know there's submarines back in the Yellow Sea, it would seem to me they would want to send someone out looking for us. They could use the two-man subs close in to shore, and have patrol boats disguised as fishing sampans farther out."

"Could be, Keith. How'd you expect to handle a sampan?"

"Well, he'd probably have a gun, so maybe doing a battle surface exercise alongside him during daylight might not be a good idea. Even a small gun could do a lot of damage if he got it going in time. At night, though, we ought to be able to take him by surprise and pretty well knock him out with our guns before he's able to do us any damage in return—that is, provided the commodore will let us."

"Most sampans I've seen are dark in color, and so low in the water that our gun crews are liable to shoot right over them. Besides, how do you tell a fishing boat from a patrol boat? Maybe we could get them to cooperate by painting 'His Imperial Japanese Majesty's Ship' somewhere on their side. I don't suppose they would be that helpful, though!" Richardson smiled wryly.

Keith gave an amused chuckle. The two remained on the bridge a few minutes longer, but for the time being all had been said that could or needed to be said.

It was the very next night that disaster struck. Surfacing had proceeded without incident. As was his custom, Richardson was the first one on the bridge, followed by Oregon, the quartermaster of the watch. Al Dugan, who would be Officer of the Deck, had not yet finished the routine in the control room and would be up directly. It was a dark night, even darker than the night before, overcast, hazy, neither stars nor moon to be seen. Because of the low visibility and the clear impossibility of taking star sights, surfacing had been delayed until virtually the end of the twilight period. Richardson was attentively surveying the horizon through his binoculars, as was Oregon, standing alongside of him. The view through binoculars would undoubtedly be superior to that which the periscope had just provided, and since the radar would take a few seconds to dry off and produce peak performance, it was important to assure with maximum certainty that there were no small ships lying close aboard that, in the gathering darkness, had not been noticed through the periscope.

Neither Richardson nor Oregon was paying any attention to the submarine wallowing beneath them. The accustomed routine had become so much a part of Richardson's senses that he could register it by hearing and by feeling. Because of the concentration of his binocular search, however, as well as the darkness that overshadowed everything, for a moment he failed to notice anything out of the ordinary.

As he thought about it later, the first subconscious awareness that something was not right must have been when the turbo blowers, automatically started from the control room as soon as the hatch was open, seemed to have a somewhat different pitch from the noise to which he had been accustomed.

But this was not specific, not enough really to make an impression upon him. "Open the main induction!" he ordered. Then his senses came alive with a rush, for there was no answering "thunk" under the cigarette deck. About a hundred feet farther aft, the roar of two main engines and a spatter of exhaust came clearly to his ears. Since opening of the main induction was indicated by a light in the enginerooms and was the signal to start engines, obviously the huge air valve must have opened; but it had not made the customary noise. He would wait a moment before ordering the lookouts to the bridge. He lowered his binoculars to his chest, looked about, noticed that the main deck was unusually low to the water. The engine exhaust was splashing more than normally. Its burbling and sputtering was noticeably louder than usual.

He reached across the bridge, past Oregon, who was still using his binoculars, to press the button to speak into the bridge speaker. He was interrupted by a voice from the conning tower. "Lookouts request permission to come on the bridge."

"No!" he snarled. "Permission not granted! Stay below!"

Again he reached for the microphone button, again was interrupted. "Radar contact, Bridge! Radar contact! Close aboard!"

124

His hand on the button, pressed it. "Control, bridge! Blow up with high pressure air!"

The instant he released the button—when energized, on surfacing, the bridge control overrode all other stations—there was a yell from Keith on the speaker. Evidently he was in the control room. "Captain! The hydraulic system is out! The main vents are not shut! Negative is flooded, and we're submerging!"

If the vents were open, the ballast tanks could not hold air. *Eel* had no buoyancy. Worse, flooding negative tank was part of the standard procedure as soon as the submarine reached the surface. There would be thirteen tons of negative buoyance to pull the boat under again!

Oregon had heard too, and instantly understood. Frightened, he dropped his binoculars. At the same moment, Richardson looked up from beneath the bridge overhang where he had stooped to talk into the speaker-mike, saw *Eel*'s bridge alone on a quiet sea. Forward there was no bow, and aft the submarine seemed to end at the cigarette deck. Farther aft, deep white bubbles came up from below to mark where the two exhaust pipes were still faithfully delivering the exhaust from two diesel engines.

"Oregon, get below!" he shouted.

The quartermaster made a leap for the hatch, but at that same instant Richardson felt cold seawater around his ankles and realized he was too late. Water rose relentlessly through the slatted deck of the bridge, poured down into the gaping hole of the open conning tower hatch!

Oregon slipped, stumbled, fell to his hands and knees. Ignoring him, Richardson gripped the hand rails, forced himself over to the hatch. It was already six inches under water. The water was rising rapidly. He took a deep breath. His head bumped the overhang of the bridge. A violent vortex was surging against the open hatch, pouring down the twenty-three-inch-diameter hole! No one could possibly reach the swinging, chattering, hatch lanyard at the far side of the maelstrom! No one could possibly pull it shut against the force of the sixteen-fold fire hydrant holding the hatch wide open! Worse, the cascade of water would strike the lower hatch, the one leading from conning tower to control room, in exactly the same way. This also would be impossible to close. The control room must be flooding too!

Richardson wedged himself directly above the hatch, struggled to get his heels on the rim, pushed mightily. It didn't budge. The latch must still be engaged in the open position! He was now under water. He stopped pushing, reached down. The pressure was rapidly increasing in his ears. Feeling around the top of the hatch, he found the latch with his fingers, pulled it up, felt it come free. Then, with all the strength of his back and legs, he pressed downward with his feet on the hatch rim.

His back was against the overhead. It was the last thing he could ever do for his ship. He concentrated on only one thing: pushing. With one hand he held the latch from re-engaging. The hatch gave, slowly moved down, suddenly slammed home with a rush as water suction took charge.

It would be latched on the underside now. He reached down to the hand wheel on top of the hatch, with a feeling of indescribable joy felt it turning rapidly from beneath. Someone had gotten to the hatch and was desperately dogging it down!

He must be deep under water now. His ears were hurting. There was a roaring sound in his head. He pushed himself clear. His hands struck something, the base of the periscope shears. Above was a small ledge with a row of large bolts, and then a rung upon which the lookouts climbed. He pressed downward on the ledge, reached up for the rung, found it. He gave himself a mighty heave upward.

It was not enough, could not be. He must be too far under. If a normal human body is brought from the surface to a depth of about twenty feet, compression due to sea pressure makes it negatively buoyant. It would be different, of course, had he been breathing air at that pressure—and in such case he would have to be careful to let it out as he came up to avoid bursting his lungs as it expanded. His mind raced wildly, encompassing all the peripheral thoughts, yet a part of it stayed calm, told him what to do. Now that he was clear of the ship's structure, he could safely inflate his belt. He reached for the toggles, squeezed them, felt the grateful pressure around his waist.

It seemed minutes, but it could only have been a few seconds. His head broke the surface of the water. He blew out the deeply held breath which he had taken perhaps half a minute before and replaced it with a satisfying lungful of fresh oxygen. He was alone on the surface of the Yellow Sea. There was no sign of the *Eel* anywhere, nor of Oregon.

From deep inside of him, something like a sob forced its way to the surface. Only about a minute ago everything had been normal! He had been standing on the bridge of his ship, supervising the normal surfacing procedure. Now he knew not what unimaginable disaster could be occurring to *Eel*, submerged beneath him. All depended upon whether or not it had been possible to get the main induction valve shut. This could be done by hand power, but it was a long and tedious procedure during which incalculable amounts of water would be taken into the ship. If Al Dugan had not been swept away from his station in the control room, he would have signaled the engine room to stop the engines. This would have caused the men also to shut the large air flapper valves in each engineroom on the two inboard ends of the huge air-induction line. Possibly, realizing the boat had submerged from the way the engines would be laboring, certainly when solid water came in through the overhead air line, the machinist's mates on watch would secure their compartments of their own accord.

Since the accident to the submarine *Squalus*, some five years earlier, the air-induction lines of all submarines had been redesigned so that their safety valves in the enginerooms snapped shut on a spring when the latching mechanism was triggered, instead of having to be closed by laboriously cranking, as in *Squalus*. In each engineroom, the releasing device for the spring was located some distance away from where the pipe debouched its air—and in case of casualty, water. At the first gout of seawater through the main induction pipe, the engineroom people on their own should yank the quick-release toggles, slam their engine throttles to "stop," and shove the hydraulic control to shut the engine exhaust valves. Simultaneously, they would frantically crank closed the hand-powered exhaust valves which backed up the hydraulic ones.

If they had acted quickly, as they had been trained, there was hope that *Eel* had not been seriously damaged or put out of action. In such case, she might indeed be able to resurface in a short period, and if so would immediately come back to look for him and Oregon.

On the other hand, much more might have gone wrong. *Eel* might at this very moment be lying flooded throughout her length, or, as in *Squalus'* case, half her length, on the bottom of the Yellow Sea. Certainly, her crew would have much to do before they could consider worrying about him, even assuming they were able to resurface at all. All he could do was to try to remain afloat and wait for rescue, if rescue was to come.

Now he blessed the caution which, stemming from his New London days, had made it an inflexible requirement that people going on the bridge during the surfacing procedure, and at any time in enemy waters, should wear the standard rubber inflatable life belts with which all ships were equipped. He felt again for the toggles and squeezed them. Instantly there was additional pressure around his middle. Evidently one of the carbon-dioxide cylinders had previously not been punctured. His body immediately rose nearly chest-high out of the water. The belt pressed around him comfortably. It had slipped upward to just beneath his arms. Keeping afloat, at all events, was not a problem.

The water somehow felt warm. The air was colder. He had not noticed it before, wondered how long he could last in these conditions. He had read that in the North Atlantic in the winter a man could live only minutes in the water before his body temperature became so far reduced that his vital forces simply came to a halt. Here it was not so bad. Maybe he could last until morning, perhaps even longer if he were lucky. Surely the *Eel* would come back soon!

Paddling with his hands, he turned completely about, searched in all directions. His binoculars still hung around his neck. He shook them as dry as he could, tried to use them. They were little help. Although the sea had seemed nearly calm from the deck of the submarine, there was, in fact, a small swell which effectively prevented his seeing more than fifty or a hundred feet in any direction. He debated taking the leather thong from around his neck and allowing the binoculars to sink in the water, decided not to. He might be able to use them after dawn broke. That was, however, nearly twelve hours away.

He thought he heard something, a distant hail, a voice shouting something. Again he turned around, paddling with his hands, tried to determine the direction from which the voice came, listened intently.

"Ahoy!" the voice shouted. He turned toward it.

"Ahoy!" he yelled. He could see nothing. "Ahoy!" he yelled again.

"Here! Over here!" the voice said.

He began torturously to swim, encumbered by his clothes and the life belt around his middle. He had not even removed his shoes, feeling that the maximum protection he could get against the ultimate cold of the seawater would be to his benefit.

He swam several minutes, stopped, and listened. He was making progress. The voice was louder. Soon he was able to recognize it. Oregon, also floating in the sea, also supported by a life belt.

"Jee-sus, Captain! When I saw the ship go under with you perched on top of the hatch under the bridge overhang, I never thought you'd make it out again!"

"What happened, Oregon? What did you see?"

"Nothing, sir. I fell in the water, and when I got up I saw you trying to get the hatch shut, so I started climbing up the periscope shears. She went down like a rock, sir. I could hear water going into the main induction. That must have made her really heavy, and when the periscope shears went under I just floated off the top. After a while I started yelling, figuring if you came up maybe you'd hear me, and anyway, the *Eel* should come back looking for us. They'll be up pretty soon, don't you think, sir?"

"Any minute now, I think," reassured Richardson, but he wondered if he could believe his own words. With the hydraulic system out of commission, whatever the cause, the main vents somehow open—though they could, with difficulty, be closed by hand—and with the main induction system flooded, *Eel* would be having many problems.

But how could the vents have been opened in the first place? Especially without hydraulic power? The explanation, the only possible explanation, was that the last time the vents had been cycled they had not properly closed. Cycling the vents—opening and shutting them— was customary once or twice a watch while submerged, to release any air that might have leaked into the ballast tanks. If they did not close properly, the fact should have been evident on the red-and-green "Christmas Tree" light panel; but it might have escaped attention. When goggles were worn in a redded-out, darkened compartment, green lights could not be seen at all. Without goggles, they were so brilliant as to hurt the eyes, which then, somehow, could not separate the reds. Understandably, the absence of some green lights might not have been noticed!

If so, if this was what had happened, the fault for the casualty could only be one of command. He should have noticed that *Eel* was not floating normally, that her freeboard was decreasing as the air blown into the tanks leaked out through the partly open vent valves. It would have been so easy for Oregon and him to step quietly inside the hatch again! He could blame no one but himself. Dark shadows descended on his mind. His own incompetence, his failure to keep his mind on his job, had brought his ship and his crew to this disaster!

Sensing Richardson's mood, Oregon too was silent. Side by side the two men floated in the Yellow Sea. Several minutes—a quarter of an hour—passed. Rich aroused himself. He still owed a duty to the one member of his crew destined to share with him whatever the uncertain future held. "Oregon," he said, "I shouldn't try to kid you about what shape *Eel* might be in. Even if they do make it back up in a short while, there's no telling if they'll be able to find us with the kind of visibility we've been having around here. Do you have any line on you? We should lash ourselves together. We may be floating here a long time."

"I've been thinking the same, Captain," said Oregon. "You don't lie so good neither, sir. Maybe these lacings from our parkas would do for a light lashing."

Then another thought struck Richardson, dissipated the lethargy that had engulfed him. "Oregon," he said, "there's something else besides *Eel* around here."

"Sir?"

"Remember that radar contact we had just before the boat slipped under? . . . Well, it must have been a ship, probably a small one, because we didn't see it before we surfaced. We didn't have it on the radar right away, either. It could be anything. Even another submarine. But I'm guessing, whatever it is, most likely it's made of wood, and it's got to be Japanese!"

- 6 -

Except for the cold air, his life belt supported him so well that he was not physically uncomfortable at all, thought Richardson. He and Oregon pulled out the strings around the bottoms of their parkas, twisted the cords together into a single strand of double strength, and then lashed themselves together. They left enough slack so that each man could have a modicum of individual motion without discomfort to the other. Perhaps they could last thus several days, but he doubted it. Even though he could feel the cold only slightly, it was already sapping the strength from him. Without food or water, or sleep, the longest he could honestly hope he and the quartermaster could survive was about twenty-four hours. Despite his rather pessimistic second prediction to Oregon, he had in fact privately thought that *Eel* would be back very soon to look for them. Her failure to reappear could mean only one thing: that the situation on board was serious, possibly downright critical. Gradually his secret optimism gave way to a more sober assessment. In twenty-four hours he and Oregon would simply drift off to sleep. They might float for days, dead in their life belts.

Richardson judged it must be about midnight—his watch, advertised "waterproof," had not been proof against depth—when he became aware that he was hearing something. He turned about, trying to orient himself to the slight breeze, equalize the sound in his ears.

There was no doubt about it. He could hear a motor, or an engine, running. The two men strained to hear more clearly: The sound was approaching, grew more defined. Finally both were forced to admit that by no stretch could it be a submarine diesel.

"Maybe it's that contact we had on the radar just before we dipped under," said Oregon.

"That's what I was thinking too," agreed Richardson. He fumbled with his life belt. One of its attachments was a single-cell waterproof flashlight for just such contingencies. He brought it up, held it in his hand, looked at it.

"Going to signal them, Skipper?" asked Oregon.

"I was thinking of it. If we don't, the *Eel* might come back, but then, she might not for a while. How long do you think you can last in this water?"

131

"I don't know, sir," said Oregon. His normally ruddy face showed ghostly white in what light there was. "I'm okay, but I'm starting to feel the cold, I think. Maybe a day, or a couple of days."

"Me too," said Richardson, inspecting the flashlight carefully. Maybe it would be better to let the noise go past and take their chances in the water. At worst they would die a peaceful death as their body machinery slowly ran down. Perhaps this was to be his atonement. Too bad Oregon had to be involved too.

The sound grew louder. The ship, or boat, would pass fairly close aboard. "Well, what do you say, Oregon?" Richardson asked. "If I put on the light, we go to a Jap prison camp, maybe worse. If I don't, we may float around here forever. Maybe the *Eel* will come back in a day or so, maybe not."

The quartermaster did not answer. Richardson hesitated. Oregon's face was working, "I don't know which would be worse," he finally said. "I—I guess you'll have to decide, Captain. It'll be worse for you than for me, I think, anyhow."

"You mean if they find out about the last patrol?"

"No sir, no sir, I wasn't thinking of that—the war can't last much longer, don't you think? We won't be too long in prison camp—it's just that you're the skipper. They always treat the skippers worst, don't they?"

But Richardson was sure that Bungo Pete was exactly what Oregon was thinking about. Japan obviously could not hold on much longer. Soon the island-hopping campaign would bring the U.S. Navy to her front door in force that could be neither denied nor delayed. Imprisonment in a POW camp would be of short duration for the average, run-of-the-mill prisoner. Not so for the man who had killed Bungo Pete. There was little prospect he would live that long.

But that mattered little at the moment, Richardson quickly realized. What mattered, instead, was Oregon's loyal attempt not to permit his own hopes for survival to affect his skipper's thinking.

The noise of the engine—it could now be identified as a lightweight diesel engine, or possibly even a gasoline engine, poorly muffled, besides—approached closer. Richardson waited until he felt it was as near as it was likely to come. Having had no opportunity to test the light, he was surprised it functioned.

Richardson's captor was the biggest and heaviest Japanese he had ever seen, and it was soon clear that the boat he commanded was far more than an ordinary Japanese fishing boat. While superficially similar to a large sea-going sampan, the boat must have been built like an ancient war-junk. She had two masts with the usual mattinglike sails, which were furled on deck, and she was large, half the length of *Eel*, even broader of beam. She was newly built of extremely heavy timbers, with the exception of the masts, which seemed light and spindly for a craft of her size. Between the masts there was a wooden deckhouse with a gently domed roof of long thin reeds. But beneath the reeds there was clearly a strong wooden roof as well. The whole structure of the craft seemed to be much more solid than an ordinary fishing sampan, even a sea-going one, might need to be.

More, Richardson had not been permitted to observe. He now sat uncomfortably on a stool in the deckhouse, arms bound behind his back, facing someone who could be no one else than the Japanese skipper. The man was tremendous in size, and he spoke perfect English.

"So," he said, "will you tell me again, please, how you came to be here?" He carefully pronounced the word "please," but there was otherwise no hint of the traditional Japanese difficulty with the letter L.

"We escaped from that submarine that was depth charged and sunk."

"You're lying!"

"I am telling you the truth. The submarine was disabled. We waited until the depth charging stopped, and then some of us escaped with breathing apparatus."

Without warning the Japanese jumped to his feet, struck Richardson in the face with a clenched hammy fist. He knocked him off the stool, kicked him several times in the stomach. As Rich tried to roll away from him to protect his abdomen, he shouted a stream of orders in Japanese. Two men came in the compartment, picked Richardson up, sat him again on the stool.

"Now," said the moon-faced Japanese captain, "you are going to stop insulting my intelligence!" He held a heavy stick in his hand, waited a moment for Richardson to answer, then struck him across the side of the head with it. Richardson saw the blow coming, ducked his head so that the club struck the upper part of his skull instead of the thin area of his temple. There was not enough room in the tiny compartment for the big Japanese really to swing the timber. It hurt excruciatingly, nevertheless. Tiny amoebalike blobs drifted back and forth in front of his vision. Still he remained silent. He saw the second blow coming, could not dodge it. It struck the side of his face. He could feel the blood in his mouth, the pain along his jawbone and in his head as he lost consciousness.

He came to as he was being carried across the deck. He felt himself being lowered through a companionway, and then apparently a door was opened and he was placed, fairly gently, it seemed to him, inside a small room. His head ached, and there was blood in his mouth, but the surcease from beating felt heavenly. There was not sufficient floor space to lie at full length. He curled up in the position in which he had been placed and, his arms still bound behind him, fell again into a comatose state which gradually transformed itself into sleep.

Morning came a few hours later, and with it Richardson's inquisitor had apparently decided to change his tactics. Richardson was tightly held by the two crewmen who had brought him. He faced him, standing. "Listen carefully," the huge, round-faced Japanese captain said. "Point one, just in case you wondered, I grew up in Berkeley, California, and graduated from Cal before the war. So don't try anything funny with me. Point two, this ship is a patrol unit of the Imperial Japanese Navy. Point three, three of our larger antisubmarine escorts destroyed one of your submarines last week, not far from here. It was damaged and sank to the bottom, where we heard it making desperate efforts to save itself. We located it by dragging with grapnels, and after we hooked it, we blew it apart by sliding depth charges down the grapnel wires. Point four, there were no survivors." He looked Rich in the eye with a malevolent grin.

Richardson still said nothing. He concentrated all his mental forces on resisting the beating which must be coming.

Still grinning, the Japanese produced a pistol, aimed it at Richardson's belly. His grin expanded, and he began to titter. His voice was pitched at least half an octave above his normal speaking voice. "You'll tell me what I want to know if I have to shoot your balls off one at a time!"

The hatred and contempt in Richardson's soul must have revealed themselves in his face, for suddenly the Japanese thrust the pistol forward and fired.

Richardson saw the move coming, nerved himself to take the obscene blow. His every sense jumped to full clarity, and he saw that at the last minute "Moonface" dropped the muzzle of the gun just a fraction. The force of explosion caught him in the groin. He doubled over in pain, but it was only the slap of the powder charge striking his clothing. The bullet had passed between his legs, grazing the right one but otherwise causing no injury.

The pistol slammed against his head. Again the kick in the side, again shouted orders in Japanese. Two crewmen jerked him upright, held him against the weakness in his legs and the pain in his head. "Moonface" (as Richardson had come to think of him) tittered again, struck him across the face with the back of his hand. "Come along," he said, waving his arm in a beckoning gesture. "I'll show you something!"

More orders in Japanese. The two crewmen propelled Richardson out onto the deck, where the first thing that caught his eye was Oregon, who had been trussed up in a standing position against a mast. His hands were pulled hard behind him, evidently tied together behind the vertical spar. His body sagged against the ropes. His chin was down on his chest.

Richardson wanted to shout encouragement to Oregon, but he dared not. There was a stab of ice in his vitals.

Moonface tittered once more. "This is the way your man spent the night," he said. "It is up to you if I treat him more kindly." He raised the pistol, pointed it at Oregon's body, spoke sententiously, spacing the words: "Where did you come from? How did you get here? Are there any more American submarines in these waters?"

"We're survivors from that submarine that was sunk," Richardson said desperately. "We escaped with breathing apparatus. There are no other American subs around here."

Moonface snapped off his mask of mirth. Oregon was looking at them with fearful eyes.

"Is that true?" Moonface hissed to him. Oregon nodded weakly.

Moonface turned to Rich. "This is how we treat liars," he said. He put his pistol against the lower part of Oregon's abdomen, pulled the trigger.

As the shock of the report died away, Oregon began screaming a high-pitched, incoherent cry of torture. Moonface waited two full minutes, fired a second time. Again he waited, fired a third time. Jack Oregon's agony was horrifying to watch. His muscles bulged and writhed within his bonds, tearing the flesh where his arms and hands were pinioned. His shrieks, which had been high and bubbling, diminished in volume, became animal-like. Bloody froth came from his mouth. Richardson, too, was screaming, lunging against the hands that were holding him back, straining at the cords that bound his arms, lunging toward Moonface. The raving torment gave him strength to drag the two men holding him several feet across the littered deck. He had no conscious plan. Had he been able to reach Moonface, he would have attacked him with the only weapon he had, his teeth. He felt another pair of hands join those that held him, and then a fourth pair. He was wrestled to the deck, held immobile.

Great gouts of dark blood were spilling out of Oregon's groin, splattering on the deck. His head had fallen down on his chest once more. His heaving breath was stertorous, his groans nearly inaudible. Perhaps he was unconscious. Richardson hoped so.

"Help him!" shouted Richardson hoarsely. "Get him some help! He'll bleed to death!"

"You're the one who could have helped him, my friend," said Moonface. "However, I shall be merciful." He stepped forward, lifted Oregon's head by the hair, placed the pistol on the bridge of his nose between the eyes and fired one more time. The heavy automatic literally blew off the top of his head. Bits of bloody matter splashed around the mast and some distance beyond it on either side. Some of it fell upon crew members who had gathered in a group of uneasy watchers.

Moonface holstered his gun. "We'll give you a little time to think it over, my friend," he said. "I may not be so merciful to you." He barked a few words in Japanese to the dozen or so gathered crew members, giggled, and grandiloquently stalked away.

Pinioned to the deck, Richardson was vomiting. The four men holding him down picked him up, carried him to the rail, propped him over it until he had finished. Curiously, their hands felt sympathetic, almost apologetic.

Others had cut the ropes binding Oregon's body to the mast, carried it also to the rail. They averted their faces from Richardson. The reckless disregard of consequences still drove him. He stood up, came as near to a posture of attention as his bound arms would permit. "Stop!" he shouted.

Unsure of themselves, they paused. Rich walked over the few feet to Oregon's body, the men detailed to hold him moving uncertainly with him. Not many of the Japanese sailors or fishermen, or whatever they were, would understand English, but they were men of the sea. They would grasp the significance of what he was about to do. Probably the word would get back to Moonface, but he was beyond caring. Rapidly his mind searched over his early memories. Once, before the war, he had been present at a funeral on board ship. He could not remember the words exactly, but that didn't matter.

He stood alongside the ruined body of his friend, raised his face. A furious recklessness drove him. Let them try to stop him in this duty. The unarticulated thought, unformed, only an emotional reaction, defied them, or anyone, to interfere. He almost wished they would try. . . .

The choking words, some of them heard every Sunday at his father's church, then for four years at the Naval Academy and countless times since, came clearly, without conscious effort to remember. There was a stillness in the air, a high gentle note as the inadequate stays allowed the skimpy masts to creak in their steps. A lapping of the water alongside the wooden hull. Twice he faltered, but it was only the inability of his voice to croak out the words.

There was silence on the deck of the little ship as Rich finished. Tears

1 3 6

streamed down his cheeks. He drew himself up, looked around. "Attention on deck!" he snapped. Whether they understood him or not made no difference. A respectful silence had settled upon the dozen Japanese present. He fixed his eyes on the men who still held Oregon's body, with his head motioned toward the sea. They understood, lifted up the body, and dropped it gently over the side.

The men who had charge of him still had their hands through his arms. He turned away from the rail. They led him forward, down through a small hatch into the hold of the ship, and all the way forward to her bows. The overhead was so low that all of them had to stoop, he more than any, and the heavily barred door which they unlocked for him could not have been more than four feet high. He indicated his bound arms. After a moment, one of them untied them. They pushed him in. He could hear a bar placed upon the door, and the click of a heavy padlock.

Moonface had decided to give Rich plenty of time to think things over, he decided. Perhaps he intended to add hunger to his efforts at persuasion. Clearly he suspected Rich and Oregon must have come from a second submarine, possibly hoped confirmation would redound to his favor. Richardson cursed himself for not having had the wit to remove his parka before he was picked up. It was marked "CAPT," while Oregon's parka had been correspondingly marked "QM." Assuming Moonface had realized he must be the captain of a submarine, the only logical purpose behind his insistent questions must be to establish the existence of a second sub in the area. Perhaps he hoped to gain personal credit for the discovery. This must be only the beginning of the interrogation Richardson could look forward to.

After what he had seen in the twelve hours or so he had spent aboard the little wooden craft, there could be no illusions as to the sadistic lengths to which Moonface might go, unless the rewards for bringing home an American submarine captain alive and reasonably well appeared more substantial than any information he could wring out of him by torture. Even here, there was something irrational. What could Moonface do with any such information that could not be better done by Japanese naval authorities at headquarters? The patrol boat could reach the naval base at Sasebo, for example, in two or three days, or rendezvous even more quickly with one of the faster destroyer types with which she must be associated. But the motion of the patrol boat gave no indication of any purposeful movement. Her tiny engine still maintained the same cadence which Rich and Oregon had noticed the night before in the water, and twice already he had felt her reverse course. During daylight, if fishing was the patrol boat's cover, she would of course have lines out. She might in fact actually do some fishing, although Richardson had seen no evidence of fishing gear during his few fleeting glimpses about the decks.

His arms were numb. The bruises on his face and head, and in the abdominal area, ached with a dull monotony. The inside of his right leg smarted in the path of the bullet which had grazed it. Squatting on the floor of the tiny compartment, for he could not stand upright, he rubbed the injured places. Sufficient light came through the clouded glass of a tiny porthole, about six inches in diameter, to reassure him that the bullet wound was superficial. He was not bleeding. The skin had barely been scraped by the flaming powder grains.

The compartment, if it could be called one—it was no more than five feet in any dimension—was some kind of a storeroom. It was roughly triangular in shape, larger at the top than at the floor level. Two sides, one of which contained the door, were vertical and met at right angles. The third side was in effect the hypotenuse of the triangle, had a slight curve, and was itself almost triangular, being much longer at the top than at the bottom.

This was the port bow of the boat. Its side flared outward, and there was a small porthole. He could hear the gentle lapping of the sea on the other side of the planking. Shelves had been built along the unpierced straight wall. The other one consisted primarily of the heavy door through which he had entered. He pushed on it. It was solidly secured. He inspected the porthole, a very simple contraption which was easily opened. Gray light streamed through the hole. The smell of sea air came with it, refreshed him. Quietly he swung it shut again, latched it.

On the shelves stood an array of nondescript items. A few cans of paint tightly sealed, some boxes that looked as if they might contain scouring powder. A sack of rags, open and half empty, lay beneath the shelves. There was nothing that could serve as a weapon. With a weapon, a paint scraper perhaps, he could attack Moonface, and in the ensuing fatal struggle bring final retribution to both of them for everything that had gone before: the war, the killing, Nakame, and now Oregon. What a mistake to have used the flashlight! Far better for both of them to have quietly died in their life belts in the middle of the Yellow Sea! He wished Moonface would send for him again, get it over with.

He should try to sleep, if he could. He jackknifed himself on the floor, drawing his knees almost up to his chest, pillowing his head on the sack of rags. Some of them smelled faintly of paint, and more strongly of turpentine. He could not sleep. His pulse, pounding with what he had seen and the hatred he felt, would not quiet. Resolutely he closed his eyes, but through his brain danced fleeting images of *Eel*, half-flooded with water, lying in the mud on the bottom of the Yellow Sea, her crew—those who had survived—led by Keith (Blunt would be no help), trying to repair damages, pump out the water, bring the crippled sub to the surface. If they had been able to get the air inlet shut in the enginerooms, the engine exhausts closed, she might not be too badly injured. If water could be kept out of at least one of the battery compartments to give power, the drain pump could be run. Partly flooded compartments could be pumped dry, provided only that someone was able to enter and dive into their bilges to open the drain valves. But if the motor room were even partly flooded, it would be impossible to put the sea-soaked main motors back into commission. *Eel*'s propellers, in this case, would never turn again.

He must have dozed after all. Someone was fumbling with the door to his prison. He scrambled to his knees. The door opened: Moonface, grinning. "Are you ready to tell me what I want to know?"

Richardson remained silent. His loathing for the contemptible animal confronting him made him tremble. It would be a relief to attack him with his bare hands. But not yet. Not until there was a chance of hurting him.

Behind Moonface was one of his crewmen with a wooden bowl in his hands. Richardson wondered if he detected a hint of compassion around the eyes set in the sailor's otherwise impassive face. Moonface took the bowl, held it toward him. It was food, soup of some kind. The aroma filled the little cell. Moonface's grin was more evil than ever. "Japanese Navy regulations say I must feed you. Would you like this?"

It must have been twenty-four hours since Richardson had eaten. He reached for the bowl. Moonface jerked it back, laughing his high-pitched laugh, flung its contents in his face. A spoon fell clattering to the floor. The door closed, was bolted. Something heavy, a cross bar, was set in place. The click of the padlock. He could hear Moonface still tittering loudly as he walked aft.

Richardson had heard of prisoners making weapons out of spoons, but there was no way he could envision to make one out of the spoon Moonface had forgotten, even if he had enough time. Maybe something would present itself later. He carefully put it out of sight on one of the shelves. Night was falling. He began to feel the hunger pangs, but

139

more important was dryness in his mouth heralding real thirst. No doubt this also was part of Moonface's design.

With the coming of darkness it became impossible to distinguish objects inside the storeroom. No light could enter through the solid walls and door, and very little came through the cloudy glass in the porthole. This at least could be repaired somewhat. Rich unlatched the glass port, swung it open, breathed deeply of the cool sea air. The opening was much too small for him to put his head through, but it gave him some comfort to crouch near the porthole, the better to get its full benefit. At the same time, he reflected, this would give him the opportunity of closing the port quickly and silently. He practiced the little maneuver so that he could do it in the dark without fumbling.

With the light still remaining, he could see almost straight down into the water. This resulted from the rather considerable flare of the patrol boat's bows. By the same token, one would have to lean dangerously far out over the edge of the forecastle deck to see the porthole or the side of the little ship from topside. Flared bows, of course, were common with surface ships. Even *Eel* was built with considerable flare to give her better sea-keeping ability at high speed. It was owing to this characteristic of design that years ago a cruiser had sailed from Pearl Harbor to San Francisco, unknowingly bearing the word "MADHOUSE" in huge block letters on both her bows. Her entrance into San Francisco Bay created a delighted sensation in the newspapers, and instant consternation to naval authorities. Her captain had been completely unaware that anything was out of the ordinary until after he had anchored his ship and was heading shoreward in his gig.

There was a change in the regular routine of the patrol boat. After some moments Rich realized the engine had stopped. The boat was lying to, drifting. Perhaps she had also been drifting part of the time last night. Possibly this was why *Eel* had not heard her on sonar before surfacing. It was even possible that Moonface, believing in the presence of a second submarine, was hoping to catch *Eel* unawares.

It was becoming a dark night, darker than most. After a while, peering out of his tiny porthole, Richardson was convinced that a night fog had set in. The visibility, so far as he could tell, was nearly zero. It would be a good night for someone with a radar, a bad one for anyone without. Moonface's orders might well be to lie to at night, making maximum use of whatever sonar gear he possessed. But if so, why had he gotten underway again last night? It was while he was mulling this over, wondering if the boat in which he was prisoner was capable of a sonar watch, and if so what it would use for power with the engine stopped, that a tiny noise wafted on the foggy air called him to straining attention.

Somewhere in the distance—it might be miles away, carried by the vagaries of fog and damp night atmosphere—an engine had started. He turned his head from side to side, putting first one ear and then the other to the open porthole. It *was* an engine! He had heard it starting— first rolling on compressed air and then bursting forth with power—too many times not to recognize it. It was one of *Eel*'s main diesel engines starting! There should be at least two—there were two! But the sound was so faint, so vague, that he could hardly believe he really heard it. Yet he had heard it; of this he was sure. Sonar, listening for underwater noises, probably would miss it. He wondered if any of Moonface's patrol-boat crew had also heard, and, having heard, would understand what it portended.

There could be a number of reasons why an engine might be heard in the Yellow Sea: other patrol boats, a merchant ship, even an airplane flying overhead. No Japanese could be so intimately familiar with the sound of a U.S. submarine diesel engine as the sub's own skipper. It was about the right time—a little late, perhaps—for *Eel* to surface, assuming she was back on some sort of a near-normal routine. Every sound he had heard had been a familiar one in the right order. Had he been closer, he would have heard the clank of the main induction and the clank also of the hydraulically operated engine exhaust valves. He could almost swear he had heard them, though it might have been only that he so wanted to. If true, it meant that the hydraulic system had been repaired and *Eel* was back in full commission!

It must be *Eel*. It could not be *Whitefish*. Distant and faint though it was, that sound was like a fingerprint. There was only one possible source for it! *Eel* was remaining in the vicinity, must be looking for him. She might even suspect the sampan. She would not, surely, be caught twice by the same trick of lying to with engines stopped.

If she saw the patrol boat, she would surely look it over through her periscope, would wonder whether the boat might indeed have picked up her skipper and quartermaster. . . . And then the idea which had been nagging at Richardson's mind for the past several minutes suddenly assumed full detail.

He would have to move quickly and quietly, and he must eradicate all signs of what he had done. The hull of the patrol boat was dark, probably in order to blend in better with the general low visibility at night. He would need contrasting paint; one of the sealed cans he had noted had some dried white paint around its edges. He seized it, shook the can carefully, was rewarded with the heavy gurgle of a partly full can. He laid it gently on the floor at his feet To open it—the spoon!

It would not do to commit himself too far in advance. All must be in readiness to eliminate the signs as quickly as possible, preferably as he went along. It was imperative not to betray himself by paint drippings. There must be no cause for someone to look over the side and see what he had done. He must not leave any marks on the deck, on himself, or on his clothes. He would need something to apply the paint —a rag—and something to clean his hands with afterward, another rag. One of the cans apparently contained a solvent—turpentine. He thought about using it, decided not to unless absolutely necessary. The odor might become noticeable outside his cell. Perhaps if he would wrap his hands first—better yet, his leather wool-lined mittens, still in the pocket of his jacket!

Hastily he made his preparations. He placed the can on the deck, pried up its lid carefully. With a paint-soaked rag in his left hand, he reached as far out the porthole as he could to the right, drew a single broad vertical white stroke on the black wooden hull. He could not see what he was doing, had to go by the feel of the rag against the hull planking. Three times he resoaked the rag, repeated the stroke, until he was satisfied that he had made a solid vertical smear of paint, carefully allowing for the fact that he could not reach as far at the top and bottom of the stroke as he could in its midsection. More paint on the rag. Three short horizontal strokes, not too long. Then another vertical stroke alongside the porthole. Three more horizontal strokes attached to it. Finally, with his right arm reaching as far to the left as he could, a vertical stroke and a single horizontal stroke at the bottom.

He dropped the paint-soaked rag into the water. His ruined gloves followed. Carefully he squeezed the lid down tightly on the can, placed it on the shelf where he had found it. The rag he had laid on the rim of the porthole, after some thought, also went over the side. The remaining rags went deep into the sack from which he had taken them.

The whole operation had taken perhaps an hour. It was a dangerous move. A gamble. If discovered, the retribution would be savage. Rich could feel his pulse thumping as he proceeded with his careful clean-up. Finally he was left with only the spoon. For several minutes he debated dropping it out the porthole, decided against it. He might have use for it later on. Moonface might remember it, demand it back. He wiped it off carefully. Perhaps he should place it on the floor where he had found it, but he decided against this also. In the end it was hidden again on the shelf where he had first put it.

On the side of the flared bow of the little patrol boat, around his porthole, Richardson had written in large block letters the word "EEL."

After several hours Rich decided that not only had his painting spree gone completely unnoticed, but also Moonface seemed to have forgotten all about him. Perhaps the Japanese skipper intended to let hunger and thirst weaken his resolve, in preparation for an even more thorough interrogation next day. On the other hand, every hour brought nearer the possibility that next day *Eel* might closely inspect the patrol boat through her periscope, would note the name lettered on her bow, would realize that only two persons could have written it there.

If, on the other hand, *Eel* did not see his sign, inevitably Moonface would see it. The consequences would, at their least, be most unpleasant. Among other things, it revealed at least part of what Moonface wanted to know.

Alive, now, to the possibility of other significant noises, he kept the port open and his ear to it. Nothing was to be heard except the idle lapping of the water against the patrol boat's drifting hull and the creaking of masts and gear on deck to an occasional gentle roll. The entire ship was still. Absolutely silent. He could not even hear the quiet movement of any of her crew.

After a suitable interval he cautiously put his hand out the port to sample his paint, found it satisfactorily tacky. This at least seemed to be working out, but of course everything depended upon whether or not *Eel* would choose tomorrow in daylight to look over the patrol boat. If the fog continued, the prospect of her doing so would be greatly reduced.

In his current state of mind, Richardson was not only sleepless but also acutely conscious of everything going on aboard the little ship. It must have been about midnight that he heard voices speaking in low tones in Japanese not many feet away from his prison. There was a certain furtiveness about them, as if they did not wish to be heard, as if they were worried, uneasy, perhaps in subdued fear. He shortly afterward was conscious of some other voices talking loudly, farther away. One voice, shouting in particularly violent tones, was that of Moonface. The others sounded conciliatory, placating. One clearly carried a note of justification, of exculpation, was finally reduced to frightened pleading.

Moonface's authoritarian tones increased in intensity. His denunciations grew louder. There came sounds of heavy blows. The pleading voice was crying in pain. Then several more dull thudding noises, and the pleading voice was silent. Moonface's voice continued for several minutes in a paroxysm of rage, then silence again descended upon the little ship. Richardson recognized it for what it was. It was the silence of terror.

Several more hours passed. Daylight was beginning to lighten the murk when Richardson heard purposeful footsteps coming toward his cell. Quickly he closed and latched the port, turned with foreboding as the door was unbarred and opened.

Three solemn Japanese sailors accosted Rich, tied his arms as before, led him aft.

Moonface had arrayed himself in full uniform, with samurai overtones. He had buckled a pistol belt around his ample middle. Hung from the belt, its ornamented brown scabbard secured by a length of intricately brocaded line, was a heavy curved sword about three feet in length. A shorter sword, or dirk, was stuck in the pistol belt, and from the belt also hung a leather holster and a modern automatic pistol. Richardson instantly saw that Moonface was in an evil humor and at the same time hugely pleased with himself.

"I am not ready to talk to you yet, my friend," he scowled, "but I will be soon. Have you had a good breakfast?"

Rich stared at him stonily.

"Probably not, but such are the fortunes of war. Too bad. Since I am a samurai, a two-sword man, I cannot of course eat with commoners, but it would amuse me if you attend upon me while I have my breakfast." His scowl was replaced by the unpleasant grin which, by this time, Richardson had learned to fear. He made a great show of waving his hands through the air, clapping them together. From somewhere one of the sailors brought out a white mat, unrolled it on the deck. Moonface sat on it cross-legged. "You may stand over there," he said, pointing to one side. "I do not want my faithful retainers interfered with as they serve me." Again the show of clapping his hands. An uncomfortable-looking sailor brought a tray upon which lay a dish of meat with some vegetables, several small cups, two bottles filled with colorless liquid, a pair of chopsticks.

Moonface unsheathed his dirk, inspected its keen edge, stropped it gently in the palm of his hand, and returned it to its polished wooden sheath. He picked up a sliced piece of meat with the chopsticks, stuffed it into his mouth. "You must forgive my servants," he said, smacking his lips and making sucking noises between his words; "we samurai are generally more punctilious in our requirements for proper service, but in war one must do the best one can with what one has."

Richardson shot a glance at the half-dozen crewmen standing about: the man who had unrolled the mat, the one who had brought the tray, another who seemed also to be in attendance, the three guarding him. Already, in the short time he had been aboard the ship, he felt he had gained some understanding of the Japanese character in spite of the facade of impassiveness. With the exception of Moonface, all were extremely tense. Obviously they were terrified of their big captain. "This man is insane," he said to himself, "plain crazy, and all the more dangerous because of it." He fought down the flow of saliva which had started at the sight of food, willed himself to be as impassive as the Japanese, stared woodenly at Moonface. Moonface ate the entire meal, drank ceremoniously and with satisfaction in the small cups from the more ornate of the two bottles, not at all from the other, which evidently contained only water.

Finished at last, he pushed the tray aside, lumbered to his feet, waved his arms again in a beckoning motion. "Come, my friend," he said, with the leering grin. "I have something to show you." He led Richardson to an area below decks in the after part of the ship, turned on a single light bulb in the overhead. There was a man huddled against the side of the ship. Irons were clamped on his legs. His hands were manacled to a beam over his head. Dried blood matted his hair, covered the front of his blouse. His head was hanging down, but Richardson could see that both eyes were swollen shut, and there was a deep gash across the top of his head. The skin had pulled back, exposing the bone beneath. The man was unconscious.

"This is one of my crewmen who defied my authority." The familiar titter. "My grandfather would have cut off his head immediately for such presumption. I have been kinder. I have given him a day to repent. Tomorrow you shall see me cut his head off with a single blow of this sacred sword I am wearing." He spat upon the wretched man, kicked him heavily in the side.

He turned to Richardson. "You see, my friend, what I can do. Think carefully when I send for you. Poetic, is it not? You see, my friend, what I can do. Think carefully when I send for you." He made the phrase into a little singsong chant. Still singing to himself, he turned and went back up the ladder.

His guards were looking at each other. They had evidently been given no instructions. Richardson smiled mirthlessly, pointed with his chin toward the bow. Wordlessly, they accompanied him back to his cell, walking stooped under the low overhead. When his arms were unbound and he was about to re-enter his prison, he looked the three men in the eye, tapped his forehead significantly. In a loyal crew this would have brought a reaction. It was, in a way, a test. The faces remained impassive, but there was an underlying unease as they closed the door upon him.

He did not believe any bones were broken, but every part of his body ached. The expected summons had come in midafternoon, and although feeling light-headed from lack of food and drink, he had managed to stick to his determination to give only name, rank, and serial number. The result had been a beating by several crew members who obviously hated their job but had, nevertheless, cuffed him about heartily enough to allay any suspicions Moonface might have had as to their willingness. Toward the end Moonface had himself lent a hand with a short stout piece of timber, and it was from these blows around the head and ribcage region that Richardson suffered most. Perhaps a rib had been cracked. His skull felt as if spikes had been hammered all over it. By twisting and squirming in the grasp of the men who were supposed to hold him, he had succeeded in some measure in protecting his head and soft abdominal area. His arms and legs were by consequence covered with deep bruises. His skin had been broken in several places where Moonface had struck it with his club, and finally he was bleeding quite profusely around the face and from his nose. It was perhaps this that brought the interview to a close. Doubtless the kudos for bringing in an enemy submarine captain alive would be greater than bringing him back dead.

Richardson had stopped feeling the blows as they fell upon him. Somewhere, in his remaining awareness, he realized he was only semiconscious. He perhaps actually did pass out for a moment or two. His next recollection was of being roughly carried along the deck and down the companionway into his cell. The roughness ceased as they passed through the companionway—out of sight of Moonface—and to Richardson's surprise, when after a little delay he was laid gently on the floor of the cell, someone had dumped the rags out of the bag and had spread them around into the semblance of a bed for him.

He was never clear how long he lay there. Again his state of nearunconsciousness changed imperceptibly to sleep. When he awoke, it was because of a tremendous need to urinate, almost like a surge from within his body. Moonface, of course, had given no thought to sanitary facilities. He would have to use the same stratagem as the previous night. Painfully he crawled to his knees, pulled the rags away from the lowest corner of the sloping deck, made a little pile of the most absorbent of them. His urine was full of blood and reeked with the smell of it. The thought—almost a detached observation—crossed his mind that he might have suffered permanent damage. Well, it could not be helped, and probably did not matter, for neither his kidneys nor he could stand a repetition of today's inquisition. He pitched the reeking bloody mess out the porthole.

Night was falling again, the end of his second full day aboard the Japanese patrol boat. She had not run her engines for twenty-four hours, had simply drifted all day long in the light haze, no doubt supposedly carrying out a sonar watch. With her demoralized crew and psychopathic skipper, she could be of very little benefit to the Imperial Japanese Navy. A couple of hours of lying quietly on his bed of rags had somewhat restored Richardson's strength. He was able to think clearly once again. If his hopes and assumptions had been correct, if *Eel* had indeed been keeping the patrol boat under surveillance, something was likely to happen around the end of twilight, after the dying tendrils of the day had been replaced by the secrecy of night.

He had moved again, painfully, to the porthole, was staring out of it as he had for so many hours during the past two days. He could only see out to port, more or less to the eastward, he judged. The other side of the patrol boat, the starboard side, was his blind side. If *Eel* attacked, she would probably attack from the port side, simply because that was where he had painted the name. She would realize he had painted it from the porthole, would hope he was nearby, would want to avoid damaging that part of the ship. She would probably execute a battle surface attack close alongside. She would have to keep good way on to hold herself down while she blew her tanks, therefore would approach from well astern. Then, when her ballast tanks were well emptied and she could no longer be held down by bow and stern planes, the planes would suddenly be reversed and she would pop to the surface, riding high, presenting a good gun platform for her gun crews. He regretted that the turn of the patrol boat's bows confined his view to her port forward quadrant only. He would have liked to see *Eel* as she suddenly and dramatically burst from beneath the sea. Probably he would not see her until she came abeam, already fully surfaced, guns blazing. She might sink the patrol boat, with him in it—a distinct possibility. An unlucky shot, or a ricochet, might finish what Moonface had started. What did it matter?

The scenario was fully played out in his mind, and he was therefore unprepared for a small disturbance in the water, perhaps 200 yards away, slightly forward of the patrol boat's beam. Almost, he thought, it might have been a periscope feather, but this was the wrong place for it. Perhaps it was a fish jumping. He watched the spot, saw it again. It was too early. It was in the wrong place. It was still not dark enough. This could not be the *Eel*!

But it was. Suddenly she burst out of the sea, less than fifty yards away. Bows on, her bullnose cleaving up from the depths, she reared high above the water, splashing tremendous cascades of foam from the freeing ports at the bottom of her bow buoyancy tank. He could clearly see the tightly closed torpedo tubes as they came above water. She was moving fast. There was frightened yelling on deck of the patrol boat. *Eel*'s bow lowered as her stern came up. There was already someone on her bridge. Thirty yards—twenty yards—the distance closed rapidly. Her bow had lowered to approximately four feet above the water, about half its usual fully surfaced height, as she smashed perpendicularly into the stout wooden side of the pseudo sampan.

Richardson had his face pressed to the rim of the porthole, felt the force of the blow communicated to his forehead and chin. The patrol boat heaved massively to starboard. There was a horrendous crashing of timbers, a massive pouring of water, confused shouting and yelling. *Eel*'s bow had passed from his sight, must be buried in the side of the wooden boat. Men were boiling out of her bridge, jumping out of the gun access trunk opening, which he could see on her port side. The forward torpedo room hatch flung itself open, came to rest vertically, partly shielding the area behind it. Two men leaped out, placed a machine gun in one of the mounts which had been built there. Swiftly a belt was produced, clipped in. Then one man jumped back into the hatch while the other sprawled at full length on deck, and using the open hatch as a shield, opened fire. The stuttering roar of the gun overwhelmed all other sound. On *Eel*'s bridge another group of men leaped over the wind-deflector shield to cast loose the forty-millimeter gun. Ammunition clips were appearing magically from over the bridge and up through the gun access trunk. Within seconds the forty-millimeter began to speak in a steady, monotonous pounding. Tracer bullets and solid armor-piercing shots stitched their angry message into the amidships section of the patrol boat. Rich could see several rifles on the bridge, all aimed with precision into her midship section, all of them firing rapidly.

There was yelling and confusion among the patrol boat's crew. Moonface was roaring orders. There were other voices shouting, the rapid thumps of many running feet. *Eel* had not backed clear. She was still driving ahead, holding her nose in the hole she had made. The patrol boat was in fact impaled on *Eel*'s bow. The submarine's steel bow, with its heavy bullnose casting, had driven deep into its side.

The firing increased in fury. Two more fifty-caliber machine guns opened up from *Eel*'s bridge, one on either side, and at the same time more men scrambled out on *Eel*'s deck through the gun access trunk. They were weirdly accoutered. Some carried rifles with a bandolier of ammunition slung around their shoulders. Others had pistols in their hands, the corresponding belt and holster strapped around their waists. Several carried coils of heaving line. Two men had grapnels with short pieces of chain attached to them, and additional coils of rope. Several of them carried an assortment of tools: a crowbar, sections of pipe, a fire ax. They crouched nervously on deck just forward of the bridge, only a few feet beneath the deafening banging of the forty-millimeter cannon raking the patrol boat's wooden decks. Richardson could hear the bullets striking the superstructure and hull of the patrol boat. There was a distinctly splintering impact as they shattered the thick wooden timbers.

There was the blast of a horn from the vicinity of *Eel*'s bridge. It was her compressed-air foghorn, commonly used as a signal to clear the decks of gun crews prior to an emergency dive. Instantly all guns ceased firing. Rich heard Buck Williams yell, "Come on!" The men who had been crouching on deck dashed forward, leaped past the forward torpedo-room hatch with its now quiet machine gun, passed out of view.

Some were yelling words Richardson could not understand. Others were imitating what they evidently supposed must have been the rebel battle cry during the Civil War. Still others were screaming like Indians.

There was much hoarse shouting, more splintering and smashing of wood. Richardson could distinguish the blows of the fire ax and the characteristic noise made by the crowbar as it tore apart wood panels and pried open barred doors. Obviously there was no organized resistance from the Japanese crew. If the patrol boat had had any arms she had been unable to cast them loose or use them. There were several heavy splashes, much shouting and yelling in Japanese. Then suddenly all was quiet.

Now he could hear what it was that the *Eel*'s crew was shouting, in between the rebel war yells and the Indian war whoops. It was his own name, his nickname. "Rich!" they were yelling. "Rich! Where are you, Rich?" Some of them were also shouting for Oregon.

"Here," he shouted, banging on the door of his tiny cell, but it was much too solid. He could not even rattle the door. Perhaps a paint can would do better. He grabbed one, began banging the door with it, but the resulting noise hardly seemed satisfactory. He went back to the porthole, shouted through it. "Here I am," he yelled. "Up forward."

Whether they heard him or not, he could not tell, but it seemed to make no difference. A crowd of men was heading his way. He could hear them clumping through the between-decks area, smashing lockers and scattering equipment about as they came. Buck Williams' voice was in the lead. "He must be all the way up forward," he said. "Rich, can you hear me? Can you hear me, Skipper?"

"Here I am," he yelled again.

Then Buck's voice was just outside the door to his prison. "Here we are, Skipper," he said. "Are you all right?"

"I'm fine, Buck. Get me out of this place."

149

"Stand clear of the door," said Buck. "It's got a big iron hasp and padlock over this beam. We'll have to chop it down!" A series of heavy blows rained upon it. He could hear the ax biting into the thick wood. It must have been difficult to swing the ax in the confined, low-head-room area, especially with the heavy list the patrol boat had now taken. She was slanting well over to starboard, obviously waterlogged, might even sink once *Eel* pulled her bow out of the hole she had made. In their haste and eagerness the men must be getting in each other's way. He heard Williams give instructions to some of them to stand back to give the others room to work.

A shiny ax blade bit through the heavy wood of the door, was jerked out, bit through again. Next came the edge of the crowbar, and several men must have heaved on it, for a section of the door was pulled out. He was face to face with Buck Williams.

"Hi, Skipper," said Williams. "They sure have this thing bolted down, but we'll have you out in a jiffy!"

A few more blows with the ax, and then came the tip of the crowbar again. Many men placed brawny arms on it, heaved with irresistible force. There was more splintering of wood.

"That did it," said Buck, and with the words the door fell open.

"How are you, Skipper?" said Buck again. "Are you okay? You don't look so good."

"I'm all right, Buck, but I'm sure glad to see you fellows."

"Where's Oregon?"

"They killed him yesterday," Richardson said. He could sense the effect of his announcement upon the men gathered around. Suddenly silent, they helped him from the storeroom, supported him as he painfully climbed the companionway to the open deck above. A dozen Japanese sailors were huddled in a group against the deckhouse, under the leveled rifles of half as many *Eel* men standing guard. It was difficult to stand on the slanting deck, and hard to find room, for much of the deck of the patrol boat was splintered and smashed. Timbers lay where they had been tossed by the force of the blow from *Eel*'s bow, and there was a huge hole in her wooden side. Beneath the shattered deck, framed by smashed timbers, rested the scarred forepart of the submarine, driven into the side of the patrol boat almost half its width and, like a huge wedge, splitting the wooden patrol boat virtually asunder.

Richardson's whole body hurt. His head throbbed. His leg muscles ached. His stomach felt nauseated. "Where are the rest of the Japs, Buck? Where's Moonface?"

"Moonface? Who's he?"

"I mean the Jap skipper. I'd just like to see that son of a bitch . . ." Richardson stopped. Despite the injuries he had received, his hatred of the Jap skipper, now that he had gained the upper hand, should be more dignified.

"Oh. Well, some of the Japs jumped overboard, and I guess we hit a couple of them before our boarding party got aboard. One of those in the water is a great big guy with swords and medals hung all over him. Is that the one you mean?"

"Yes, that's the one I mean. Where is he?"

"Over there." Williams pointed. There was a group of men in the water clinging to the side of the ship—its rail on the starboard side was at the water's edge—and others were floating a few feet away, holding on to various pieces of debris.

"Why don't you go back to the ship, Captain, and let Yancy look you over? We'll take care of things over here."

"I will, later. Let's get things straightened out here first. Except for Moonface, these guys were all pretty decent."

"Well, we've captured their ship, but we sure can't use it, and neither can they any more. Maybe we can help them get their boat in the water."

Richardson had not previously seen a boat, but he looked in the direction Buck pointed and saw one inverted on the roof of the deckhouse. "Have some men take it down and look it over," he said. "See that it's patched up if it needs it, and be sure it has provisions and water. Get that raft over the side also." Richardson pointed to a wooden float-like structure about ten feet square built on oil drums. Then he thought of something. "There's a prisoner in irons below. Get him out. And search this boat for any more like him."

"Right, Skipper, will do. Maybe some of these Japs will give us a hand," responded Williams, indicating the prisoners crowded against the side of the deckhouse.

The crowd of prisoners proved very willing indeed to assist with launching the boat and raft. One of them, who seemed to know what was needed, went below under guard and returned with a sack full of provisions.

"A couple of these guys are hurt, Skipper. Also, we found two more in irons, shackled to the bulkheads down there. This fellow led us to them. One's in pretty bad shape."

"Lay them out on deck and send for the pharmacist's mate. Have Yancy take a real close look at the men who were in irons." Richardson gave the orders without much thought. He had identified Moonface in the water, clinging to a piece of timber. He was separated some distance from the others. Moonface's own men were avoiding him. The expressions on their faces, once so impassive, told their own stories.

Moonface was no Bungo Pete. Richardson's revenge was already perfect. Nothing he said or did could add to or stand comparison with the obvious disgust and hatred the Japanese crewmen held for their own skipper.

"We figured you must be up forward when we saw that signboard you painted there, and the reason we didn't do a regular battle surface was that we didn't know what they might do to you before we could get to you. So we figured to come right in with the bow flooded down, smash her side, and board right over the bullnose. We blew up high after we backed clear, and Buck went down on a line to take a good look at the torpedo tubes. They work fine, and there's not even any scratches around the shutters."

Richardson was sitting at his accustomed spot in the wardroom, having just finished a delicious dinner. Yancy, Eel's tall pharmacist's mate, had put a number of bandages here and there to cover a skin injury, had applied copious quantities of liniment to the bruised areas, and categorically forbade Richardson to gorge himself on food—as he might have done had he followed his own inclination and that of Eel's cooks, who wanted to produce the most prodigious meal ever served by a submarine. Grouped around him were Keith, Blunt, and the rest of the wardroom. It was Keith who had just finished explaining the decision to ram and board as quickly as possible. There was an atmosphere of tremendous happiness. The whole ship's company partook of it, as Richardson saw from the many euphoric smiles which had greeted him when he came aboard. The only cloud in the general happiness was the story of how Oregon had been brutalized and murdered. When the details were learned, the gladness turned to rage. Several crew members proposed returning to wreak vengeance upon the Japanese lifeboat or the raft, and finally Keith had to forbid any further discussion of the topic.

The patrol boat's decks had been the scene of a second funeral, for the fusillade of automatic-weapons fire had killed two of her crew. Both were horribly shattered by fifty-caliber machine gun bullets. In addition, the Japanese crewman whom Moonface had threatened to behead was dead when Yancy reached him. Three Japanese were treated for injuries from flying wood splinters, and the other prisoner in irons was suffering from a prior beating by Moonface. Several, apparently only slightly hurt, among them Moonface, stubbornly stayed in the water and refused the proffered help of Eel's pharmacist's mate.

By contrast, there were no injuries at all among the submarine crew. No doubt the overwhelming surprise of *Eel*'s attack contributed to this. From beginning to end, the shooting had lasted less than three minutes. Bandaging the injured, requiring all the survivors who remained on board to witness the triple funeral, disengaging *Eel*'s bow, and allowing the smashed wooden boat to roll over and sink to the water's edge took an hour and a half.

After serious thought, Richardson had decided against attempting to take prisoners. Moonface was the only one he would have wanted in any case, but the man was patently a psychopath and therefore almost certainly of little value to intelligence authorities. He would, however, be a distinct and permanent nuisance, not to say a danger, to the *Eel* and her crew for the month or more that he would have to be on board. Furthermore, the only way to take him prisoner was to go into the water after him. This was less than a desirable prospect in view of the swords and knives he might still have about his person. In the end, after the wounded had been bandaged and a broken leg splinted, *Eel* simply backed clear of the wreck, leaving the boat and life raft surrounded by debris but floating safely and stocked with food, already half-loaded with survivors who were busily picking up the rest. The boat contained a simple magnetic compass, and Keith carefully handed the most self-possessed crewman (the one who had brought up the provisions and helped locate the prisoners chained below) a slip of paper on which he had written the course and distance to the nearest land: Saisho To, or Quelpart Island, seventy-five miles to the northeast.

It was not until after he had slept for several hours that Richardson was able to speak privately with his officers. The opportunity came during an inspection of the work to restore the flooded engines to operation. "Writing *Eel* on the bow of that boat was what did it, Skipper," said Keith. "After we dunked we had a lot of water in the conning tower and control room. The main induction was flooded solid up to the inboard flappers, and there was a lot of water in both enginerooms. Also we flooded these two engines here through their exhaust lines before the enginemen were able to crank the inboard exhaust valves shut. We're still checking them over pretty carefully, but I don't think we damaged them. Anyway, with all that water on board we went right down to the bottom of the Yellow Sea. Good thing the bottom was there, too! Al was shifting the main vents over to hand power and getting them shut by hand, and we'd have been able to blow soon. So even if we had been in deep water I don't think we'd have lost the ship. But it was mighty comforting all the same to feel her squash down into the mud.

"Then we had to drain all the water out and pump it over the side; so it took us several hours before we were squared away and able to come back to the surface. When we did, we found that sampan on radar right where the plot showed we had probably left you swimming. So we hung around and watched him all day.

"But"—and here Keith's voice dropped, and Buck Williams looked uneasy—"Old Man Blunt wouldn't let us plan a rescue operation. He said we couldn't be sure that you had been picked up by the sampan and that it would just be risking our lives on a hunch. There was nothing he could say, though, when that signboard of yours showed up. Matter of fact, he didn't say anything, but he still would have no part of what we were doing. So Buck and Al and I cooked up this little operation by ourselves. I hope you don't think it was too unorthodox."

Keith was obviously a little anxious, for no submarine had ever made an attack in the manner *Eel* had. Endangering the all-important torpedo tubes, however successful the outcome, was a matter for serious concern.

"It was just right," Richardson assured him. "You did exactly right. But what about the commodore? What do you mean, he took no part in your planning?"

Keith obviously had thought through what he was to say to this expected question. "We know he's your old skipper and all that, and your friend too," he said carefully, "but we're really worried about him, sir. There's something wrong with him. Not all the time, but part of the time. Sometimes he makes sense, and sometimes he doesn't." Keith's voice, already lowered in tone, had developed a flat, monotonous quality. His wide forehead bore an unaccustomed pair of vertical creases. The gray eyes, looking steadily and unblinkingly at Richardson, were troubled. "We talked about this just the night before we dunked and left you and poor old Oregon topside. We're sure now that the hydraulic accumulator suddenly bled down at just the wrong time and caused all the trouble. Lichtmann, Starberg, and Sargent were all three in the control room, about to drop through the hatch into the pump room, and they heard it bleed off. Along with Al, they've been knocking themselves out working on it ever since."

Keith instinctively moved closer, spoke even more softly. "The commodore has told just about everybody in the wardroom that Lichtmann is sabotaging the plant on the sly. No explanation how he knows. He says it's obvious, and that Lichtmann's name is even German. He says if anyone catches Lichtmann fooling around with the plant, he should shoot him on the spot! It's got so that beginning last night we set up a watch list of officers to stick with Blunt all the time. Larry relieved Buck, just now, so that all three of us could talk to you about it."

"Nobody in the crew has heard of this yet, Skipper," said Al, "but they know something peculiar is in the wind. There's nobody sabotaging the hydraulic gear—that's just the commodore's idea. We think we know where the problem is, and we think we're closing in on it. But nobody can work looking over his shoulder all the time for fear somebody will come along and shoot you!" Dugan was breathing deeply. He was obviously under heavy stress.

Richardson felt himself treading the edge of an abyss. Its depth could not be known, but the boundaries were clear, the paths that led to disaster well marked. If *Eel*'s crew were to learn of the concerns just stated, the effect would be instant. In the taut confines of a submarine on war patrol, the one all-encompassing fact, from which all others automatically flowed, was the total interdependence of all its parts, human or mechanical. The unreliability of the hydraulic system had already taken its toll in terms of effectiveness and confidence. If to this must now be added the dreadful fear of hidden disloyalty, it would be like a cancer, eating at the heart of morale. Thenceforth, no member of the crew could go about his duties in the certain knowledge, so imperative in their exposed condition, of complete support. What lookout did not already harbor the secret fear of being late to the hatch, of a miscount of persons through it, of finding it shut in his face with the boat diving? What maneuvering room electrician, receiving a signal for emergency speed, did not fear the circumstance which had caused it? What member of the crew, officer or enlisted man, upon hearing the call for battle stations did not feel a clutch of apprehension lest the enemy, this one time at last, be able to overwhelm their own best efforts?

Again, it was only their confidence in themselves and in each other, and each in all the others, that enabled this ever-present fear to be set aside. What, then, if the very basis of the tenuous fabric of cohesiveness were ripped asunder? Even if there were demonstrably no truth in the accusation against a crew member, what would be the effect of its having been voiced?

Richardson could feel himself shriveling inside as he contemplated the certain ruin that would result. No matter how carefully the thing was handled, it would be a disaster. Lichtmann might or might not have been able to create a secure position for himself during his short time with his new shipmates, but there was no way he could remain unaffected if the suspicion were to become known. Richardson must, somehow, at all costs, prevent the situation from progressing further. Certainly he must

155

get Blunt to explain the source of his suspicions and, if possible, allay them.

The greatest danger lay in the crew's becoming aware of what it was their officers were discussing so earnestly. Keith's action in ensuring that someone was with Blunt at all times had been the right move, but even this might become too obvious if continued much longer. Richardson would have to rescind the order soon, before either the crew or Blunt became aware of it. Perhaps he could take the surveillance duty himself—and then he realized he had already been doing so, up until the time of his enforced absence.

But he was undetermined, irresolute. What could he do? If the situation had continued to retrogress during his absence to the point now described, what could anyone do? Buck Williams was obviously waiting for a chance to say something. He might have some clue, suggest a direction in which movement was not yet foreclosed. "What do you think, Buck?"

"I'm out of it pretty much," said Buck Williams. "All the commodore thinks and talks about is the hydraulic system, and that's not in my department. But I sure do agree that there's something wrong with him. He doesn't sleep. Sits around most of the time in the wardroom smoking his pipe. Then, when he does start wandering around, we all wish he'd go back and be quiet again. I think if he could only get some sleep and relax a little bit, he'd be a lot better off. I know we'd all be."

The comment triggered a thought in Richardson's mind. "Keith," he said, "who succeeded to command during my absence?"

Keith looked uncomfortable. "Well, he said he would, because he was senior officer present. But then he didn't do anything. At first I tried to carry on as I had for you, but he wouldn't make any decisions, except to turn us down on everything. So finally I just had to go and take care of things myself without telling him."

"What Keith's saying is not exactly true, Skipper," said Buck, interrupting. "All of us told Keith that he just had to take over. Things were going to hell fast. It was a pretty serious situation down there on the bottom, and with you and Oregon gone. Our morale was already about zero. The commodore was no good at all, sir. Besides, I don't think he even could qualify in this submarine if he took a test right now. Lots of the orders he gave we couldn't carry out because they didn't apply to this ship."

"That's right, Skipper," said Dugan, "we just said 'Aye aye, sir,' to him, but then we'd ask Keith. He was the real skipper while you were gone."

"All right, fellows," said Rich, "I promised you I'd take care of him, and I will." But it was an empty promise. He had no plan, no notion of how to begin or what to do. He was still covered with bandages and liniment. His mind was barely functioning. He was perilously close to admitting his inadequacy when the man on telephone watch in the compartment interrupted him.

"Captain," he said, "there's an op-immediate coming in for us in the radio room."

When decoded, the message said:

INDICATIONS ARE THAT ALL YELLOW SEA TRAFFIC IS MOVING CLOSE INSHORE X MANY SMALL TO MEDIUM SIZE CARGO SHIPS CONVOYED INSHORE OF ISLANDS ON WEST COAST OF KOREA X TRAFFIC ALONG CHINESE COAST MOVING INSIDE TEN FATHOM CURVE X SPECIAL FOR BLUNTS BRUISERS X GO GET EM BOYS

"Commodore," said Richardson, "this message is a directive to get in as close to the coast of Korea, and maybe China too, as we can. This large-scale map of the area"—he tapped for emphasis a chart laid out on the wardroom table—"is an official Japanese Navy chart that we grabbed from that patrol boat. As you can see, there's a chain of small islands varying from five to ten miles off the west coast of Korea. We checked out the depth markings—it was simple; they're just in meters. There's at least two hundred feet of water all around them, all the way up to the mainland of Korea. That's almost as deep as it is anywhere in this area. The combined submarine track chart shows that most of our submarines have concentrated on the middle of the Yellow Sea. Once the Japs realized this, it made sense to stay close in to shore whenever they could. They probably do that whether or not they think there might be a submarine somewhere around, for the little they might save by heading straight across the Yellow Sea is nothing compared to the losses they would take if just one aggressive submarine got loose in a medium-sized convoy."

It was a regular wardroom conference, unchanged from any of the preceding ones except for ComSubPac's recent message, a copy of which lay on the table. Blunt sat silently puffing on one of his several pipes.

Richardson and Leone had spent considerable time preparing for this conference. "Keith," said his skipper, "show the commodore that depth-of-water overlay you worked out." Keith produced a piece of semitransparent tissue from a folder of papers. On the tissue were outlines of some of the islands and mainland sections on the larger map, and a series of carefully printed numbers in what were obviously the water areas. "Here's where it fits, sir," said Keith, spreading out the tissue, flattening it carefully. He slid it about until his land-contour lines fitted over those on the chart.

"These figures are the depth of water taken from our own best American chart of the area. They're given in fathoms, so we converted them to meters. You'll see, sir, how close the few depths on our chart correlate to the depths the Japs have on theirs. This area being so close to their home base, the Japanese Navy made a very thorough survey, and there's a lot more data on their chart than we have. But even though they have twenty soundings for our one, every sounding we show agrees with what they have. This means the charts must be accurate. Look what they show for the depth of water around some of these outlying islands. . . ."

The advocates talked on and on, each in turn picking up his thread of the argument.

"So, we've got to go here, Commodore," Richardson was saying; "the Maikotsu Suido has just got to be on the track of every one of their convoys. It must be practically like highway number one through there. The water is deep for the Yellow Sea, even though it is inside the island chains, and the strong northerly current that's supposed to be there can be used to our advantage."

Blunt took the pipe out of his mouth. "One of our best boats was in there a couple of years ago. His patrol report said this was a bad place for submarines to patrol in." They were the first words he had said for fifteen minutes.

"I know, Commodore. That was the *Wahoo*, and it was just under two years ago. Dornin took the *Trigger* in later and said the same thing. They were the only two boats to try this spot. But it doesn't make sense that an offhand comment, even by two of our best skippers, should prevent anyone else from ever trying this area. Their fish weren't dependable then, remember. Anyway, if both boats hadn't used up all their torpedoes and left the area early, they'd probably have been back in there."

The pipe was back in Blunt's mouth. His eyes closed wearily, his head nodded. Suddenly he jerked himself upright again. Rich and Keith looked at each other. Inadequate rest was undoubtedly part of his problem.

"We'll patrol submerged in there for a day or so, Commodore. We could tell the *Whitefish* to patrol outside and to the north. If we get a chance to stir things up in there, maybe the traffic will shift outside, not knowing there are two submarines, and we'll be able to give them a one-two punch."

Blunt's eyes were almost glassy. He took the pipe out of his mouth again. "Nothing doing! There's something strange going on aboard this boat, Rich! While you were working out your schemes, I've got into something a lot more important. Somebody is sabotaging the hydraulic system, and I'm going to catch him at it. When I do . . ." he looked significantly down and to the right, at his right hip, patted it with a slow deliberate motion. To his consternation, Richardson realized that under the submarine jacket he had worn all day he had buckled a gun belt, and at that very moment, in the wardroom, was armed with a holstered automatic!

A deep calm settled upon Richardson. He had hoped, by heavily involving Blunt in tactics, to divert his mind from his suspicions. The message from Admiral Small had come at just the right time. The lure of action, the necessity to concentrate upon the orders Blunt would have to give his two remaining submarines, orders which Richardson would frame for him, discuss with him, would push everything else into the background where Richardson intended the hydraulic system henceforth to remain. But obviously the scheme had failed before it had been fairly tried. Something more drastic must be done. Buck's mention of Blunt's extraordinary wakefulness had suggested another idea, a second plan which had been discarded in favor of the one he had been acting on. Now the secondary plan must be implemented. He affected not to see the gun, continued the conversation for a few minutes, excused himself temporarily. The headache resulting from the beatings he had taken on the patrol boat was returning, he said, and he needed some help for it. It was not, however, about his headaches that he was talking to the tall pharmacist's mate a few minutes later.

"Yancy," he said, "the commodore has driven himself to the point where he's completely exhausted. Can we give him something to make him sleep for a while?" Immediately thereafter he sought out Buck Williams. As he returned to the wardroom, Williams followed him, said to the exec, "Keith, I'm going to start routing our fish up forward, but first there's a change we want to make in the procedure. Can you come up there with me for a minute, so I can show it to you?"

When Keith returned, he said shortly, "It's all right, Skipper. He's got a good idea, and I told him to go ahead." He gave Richardson an imperceptible nod.

When the wardroom steward entered a few minutes later with a freshly brewed pot of coffee, Keith accepted only half a cup, announced that he intended to get some sleep for the next day's work, placed it untouched on the table. Richardson and Blunt took full cups. Rich sipped his only lightly, cradling the warm cup in his hands. His eyes stayed on Blunt as the latter drank his right down.

"That was just the right temperature this time," Blunt said. "If it weren't for coffee, none of us could function." His eyelids grew heavy, his head nodded. He jerked it upright, but again it nodded. . . . They caught him before his head struck the table. Buck Williams reappeared at the door to the wardroom, and the three officers, plus Yancy who came up from the other direction, quickly laid Blunt in his bunk.

160

"He was so tired, Captain, the sleeping pill hit him right away, just like I said," said Yancy.

"How long do you figure he'll be out?"

"Maybe twelve hours. The sedative will wear off pretty soon, but he'll sleep until his system wakes him up."

"He needs a real rest, Yancy. He ought to sleep for at least three days."

"All we gave him was a sleeping pill, Captain. He'll wake up in about twelve hours when he has to go to the head, and besides that, he'll be hungry. If you want me to keep him out for three days, he'll have to have intravenous feeding, bedpans, the whole thing."

Blunt was completely relaxed, sleeping peacefully. The tense look about his face had almost magically disappeared. Remorse at the liberty he had taken with his old friend and superior was already troubling Richardson. "No intravenous business," he said. "Yancy, you watch over him, and you be here when he's awake. No matter what's going on on board ship. You got that?"

The pharmacist's mate nodded.

"When he wakes up, you be sitting right here with something to eat—you tell the cook what to fix up, and be sure you have it ready on time—and tell him he's got to rest. If he has to go to the head, get him right back in his bunk. He's so tired, he'll sleep longer if we give him a chance."

Yancy nodded again. "Okay, sir. I'll try to keep him from getting up."

"Keith," said Rich, having moved across the narrow passageway to his own stateroom, "tell all the officers that I want their pistols locked up in their safes so that nobody can get them. Most of them are probably locked up already, but make sure. Buck is already securing all our small arms. I'll put the commodore's pistol here in my safe with my own gun." He twirled the dial on the combination to the tiny safe built into his desk, pushed aside papers and various other objects, including a holstered automatic wrapped in its gun belt, squeezed Blunt's gun in. Locking the combination, he turned back to Keith. "We've got twelve hours," he said. "How long will it take us to reach the Maikotsu Suido?"

Richardson himself was standing periscope watch in the conning tower, raising and lowering the instrument for periodic 360-degree sweeps every several minutes. Two compartments below him, in the pump room, Lichtmann, Starberg, and Sargent, supervised by Al Dugan, who normally should have had the watch, were working with vigor on the hydraulic system and had reported they were making headway. A feeling of contentment possessed Rich, not even partly dampened by the pain it caused him to go through the deep knee bends associated with raising and lowering the periscope. Strictly speaking, this particular technique was called for only during an approach, to reduce the time of periscope exposure. But the Maikotsu Suido waters were no doubt heavily covered by air as well as surface patrols. The self-flagellation of going up and down with the periscope was nothing. If anything, it would speed the cure.

The Maikotsu Suido was roughly rectangular in shape, its long axis nearly north and south. The rocky west coast of the mainland of Korea formed its eastern boundary, and a chain of relatively small islands formed the western. Its southern terminus was a group of islands extending to the mainland. To the north it was open. The Korean coast bent off in a peninsula to the west, and a group of close inshore islands around the tip of the peninsula provided a sure sanctuary for coastal traffic. It had been a sensible move to enter this body of water at its southern end, for there was a heavy current setting to the north. *Eel* could remain relatively immobile while stemming the current, and yet evacuate any particular spot rapidly by turning around to a northerly heading. Ships making a northern passage would undoubtedly favor this area because of the strong current, which, from Richardson's observations of the shoreline, must be averaging at least four knots.

Richardson's plan, communicated in the name of the wolfpack commander to Whitey Everett in the *Whitefish*, was to proceed to the eastern side of the Maikotsu Suido in hopes of picking up a target. Any action Rich could stir up would on the one hand draw local antisubmarine activity upon *Eel*, and on the other direct the Japanese supply ships farther offshore, hopefully beyond the island chain where *Whitefish* would be patrolling.

Richardson had expected to see aircraft flying about. It was understandable that none had been seen in the Yellow Sea, for Blunt had required *Eel* and *Whitefish* to patrol submerged far offshore during daylight. At night, when they were surfaced, it had up till now been uniformly hazy. Today was bright and clear, and one would expect the Japanese antisubmarine aircraft to make the most of it. Yet he had been in the conning tower for three hours, and had seen nothing. Gradually he conned *Eel* closer in to shore, taking an occasional fathometer sounding after a careful periscope search to assure there was no antisubmarine vessel in the vicinity.

Another hour passed. He turned the periscope over to Keith, went down to a hasty lunch. Blunt was still sleeping soundly. Before returning to the conning tower Rich climbed down beneath the control room into the pump room. Al Dugan was temporarily exempted from the watch list, as were his three workers, to permit them to give full time to the hydraulic mechanism.

"I think we've found the trouble," said Dugan. "It's not only the bypass valves, although they were part of it. There were all sorts of things wrong with the system—they've even got the wrong kind of hydraulic oil in it. The worst thing is that the instruction book was wrong. So when the boys in Pearl Harbor fixed it up, they set all the clearances, pressures, and sequence switches to the book values, and didn't realize that whoever got up this book must not have known what he was talking about. Lichtmann had a similar problem in the *Nerka*. Their hydraulic system was made by the same company, though it was an earlier and smaller model. We're damn lucky you got him aboard. They had to overhaul their plant the same way, just like us, on patrol.

The grease-smeared face which grinned at Richardson was only faintly reminiscent of the natty sailor in white who had driven him to the admiral's quarters on Makalapa Hill that memorable night. Part of the hydraulic plant was dismantled, strewn about the fantastically crowded compartment, and Lichtmann had obviously been sitting in the bilges, oblivious to the oil and water lying in the bottom, squeezing around and behind close-fitting piping, disassembling and reassembling parts of the mechanism. Starberg and Sargent were in the same condition. The dungarees of all three were fit only to be placed into a garbage sack and thrown overboard. Al Dugan, supposedly in a supervisory position, was hardly better off than his men.

Richardson climbed out of the pump room with the feeling that the hydraulic system at last was under control or on its way to being so. There would be time to take a walk aft to see for himself the progress of the clean-up work on the two engines which had been flooded. They were already back in full commission, but it would not hurt to let the engineroom crews know he appreciated their labors.

He was stepping over the sill of the watertight door on the after bulkhead of the control room when there was a sudden bustle and Keith's loud voice from the conning tower: "Captain to the conn!" Everyone in the control room must have heard of the reputation of the Maikotsu Suido and was, by consequence, a little keyed up. At least six voices repeated the words to him simultaneously, only a second or so behind Keith.

"Smoke on the horizon, Captain," said Keith, a dozen seconds later. "Bearing south. Looks like something coming our way!"

Through the periscope Richardson could see a tiny smudge on the horizon. He spun the periscope completely around, looking at the surface of the sea in all directions, went around a second time searching the sky. It was a clear, beautiful day topside, virtually no clouds in the sky, sea nearly calm, visibility unlimited in all directions. *Eel* had been stemming the current, heading south at slow speed submerged, close in to shore. Looming two miles away to port, rocky bluffs extended right to the water's edge. To starboard there was a clear horizon, but beyond it were the tops of an irregularly spaced group of hills, the islands on the seaward side of the Maikotsu Suido. To the north there was only the smooth horizon. To the south nothing except the smudge of smoke. As he watched it, the smoke disappeared.

"Smoke's died away, Keith," he said, lowering the periscope. He had been using the radar periscope because of its larger optical path and consequently better light-gathering capabilities.

The conning tower depth gauge read fifty-eight feet. The thirty-six-foot radar periscope would go under at keel depth of sixty-two feet. There had been four feet of it exposed. "I'll take a look through the attack scope," said Rich, stepping aft to the second shiny steel cylinder bisecting the conning tower.

The attack periscope was forty feet long. At fifty-eight feet there would be eight feet of it out of water. Its much smaller head and consequently narrower optical path gave less visual acuity, but he would risk the extra height for a short exposure in order to see from a greater height.

He squatted on his haunches behind the periscope, motioned with his hands for Keith to raise it until its handles just cleared the upper lip of the periscope well. They came up; he snapped them down into position, swung the periscope quickly dead ahead. Jabs of pain went through his knees and thigh muscles as he put his eye to the eyepiece, motioned for the periscope to be raised. He rose with it to his full height, snapped the handles upward into the stowage position, followed the periscope down until he was once again on his haunches and had to pull his head clear as it continued down into the well.

"There's at least two ships out there, Keith. I can see masts. You caught them when they blew smoke for a moment. They're probably heading this way. We'll take another look to make sure."

"Sonar, do you hear anything bearing dead ahead?" The sonar watch stander shook his head.

"Shall I send for Stafford?" asked Keith. "He's a magician on this gadget." Richardson nodded. Stafford must have been waiting for the call, was in the conning tower in less than a minute. He began tuning the sonar receiver, heavily padded earphones covering both sides of his head, an intent faraway look on his face.

164

"Two minutes since the last look," said Keith.

"Up periscope," said Rich, oblivious to the protests of his leg muscles as he resumed his squatting position.

"Several ships heading this way," he said a moment later, as the periscope descended. "Sound battle stations."

The general alarm, amplified on the ship's general announcing system, sounded like a series of low-pitched musical chimes. There was a scurrying in the control room. Richardson and Leone could sense the crew tumbling out of their bunks, breaking away from whatever work they had been doing, dashing to their stations for combat. Buck Williams jumped up the ladder from the control room, followed closely by Scott. Cornelli—he had been promoted to the helm to replace Scott, who now had Oregon's spot—took over the steering station. Behind him Rich could hear the low-pitched whir of the TDC as Buck turned it on.

"Target bearing?" said Buck in a low voice to Keith, who had moved aft alongside of him. "Due south, Buck," said Keith.

"Estimated range?"

"Beyond the horizon. Start with fifteen thousand yards, as a guess."

"That's a pretty good estimate," said Richardson, who had been listening.

"Battle stations manned and ready below," said Quin, who had taken a telephone headset out of its stowage box, put it on his head and plugged it in.

"Battle stations manned in the conning tower, Captain," said Keith. "The ship is manned for battle stations." At the beginning of the patrol Keith had pasted a little check-off list on the side of the TDC. He had already checked several items. Richardson could visualize the attentive calm throughout the submarine: the torpedo room crews at each end, the electrician's mates in the maneuvering room to whom would fall the main burden of the submerged maneuvering, the engineroom crews standing idle, ready instantly to start engines should the order come to surface. The damage-control parties, forward and aft. The extra hands in the control room and dinette, ready for whatever emergency might devolve upon them.

He crossed to the hatch leading to the control room, looked down, saw Al Dugan's sweaty, oil-streaked face looking up. "You all set down there, Al?" he asked.

"Yes, sir, Captain."

"What shape is the hydraulic system in?"

"Starberg and company are buttoning it up," said Al. "Everything but the main engine exhaust valves and the main vents is cut back in already. I'd like to leave the vents in hand power. . . ."

1 6 5

With the ship already submerged and the vents closed, there was no reason why they could not stay in hand power, for the vents did not have to be operated to surface the ship. They would, of course, have to be opened to dive. "How about diving if we need to, Al? Do you have men free of battle station assignments standing by each vent?"

"Yes, sir, Captain. No strain. We've got two on each vent, and a telephone manned by each pair. You can work your vents right now by telephone if you want to." Dugan grinned confidently.

These phones were no doubt surreptitiously manned whenever the ship went to battle stations. They were part of the interior grapevine system by which the rest of the crew would find out what was going on. "Fine," Richardson said.

"Three minutes since the last look, Skipper," said Keith. Richardson returned to the periscope station.

"I'll take a look all around this time too," he said. "Up periscope."

He repeated the squatting-and-rising ritual. "Bearing, mark," he said. "No range." He spun the periscope completely around twice, snapped the handles up. It dropped away.

"All clear all around," he said. "It's a convoy. At least three big ships, maybe a couple more. Also, there are escorts. I could see at least two masts of smaller ships on either beam of the convoy."

"Estimated range, Captain?" Buck.

"I'd still say fifteen thousand," said Rich.

"Speed?"

"No estimate. They're reasonably big ships, five- to seven-thousand-tonners."

"I'll start them at twelve knots," said Buck, twirling the dials on his instrument.

"Let's try for a radar range," said Rich. He pointed to Quin. "Control, make your depth five-two feet!" This would leave only five feet of water over the top of the periscope shears and would cause the fully extended radar periscope to reach ten feet above the surface. Height, unfortunately, was obligatory at the longer ranges. He turned to Rogers. "Are you peaked up and ready? I want this to go real fast."

"Yes, sir."

"All right. . . . Scott," he said to the quartermaster, who had now taken over the job of raising and lowering the periscopes, "when I give the word, I want the radar periscope all the way up. As soon as it hits the top, start it back down again. If Rogers gets a range before it's two-blocked, start it back down immediately. Don't worry about me, I'll get clear." Scott nodded his comprehension. This had been part of the technique developed during training with the new radar periscope. Rogers' duties were to sing out loudly as soon as he had seen a radar return indication on his A 'scope, even before measuring it.

To ensure that everyone understood, Rich rehearsed the instructions: "Rogers, set your range index at about fifteen thousand yards. As soon as you see a pip, you holler 'Range!' good and loud, so that Scott can hear it. Don't wait to match it with your range marker. You can do that afterward. I want to get the 'scope down just as soon as possible. We're going to be waving ten feet of it up in the air. It will look like a telephone pole!"

Turning to the TDC he said, "I'll get my eye on the periscope on the way up and will line it up so that it goes down exactly on the target bearing." Keith and Buck both nodded. With the periscope exposed ten feet above the surface, its tip would be out of water long before the base with the eyepiece would come out of the periscope well, long before the radar connection in the bottom of the base would engage. Hence there would be no benefit to orienting it down low, as Rich had done previously. "Everybody ready?" said Richardson. "Up periscope!"

The radar periscope started to rise. As before, Richardson squatted on his haunches facing it. He was ready for the pain, set his face so as not to show it. He snatched the handles as they came up, spread them out, lunged against the eyepiece, began to rise with it. He could hear the radar wave guide engage the trombone section at the base of the periscope, heard the snap of the radar as Rogers kicked it in to the now complete wave-guide tube. The periscope traveled all the way to the top, stopped with a bouncy jerk, started back down. Richardson followed it as far as he could, almost gasping with the pain of returning to the squatting position, snapped the handles up as they began to enter the well.

"No pip, sir," said Rogers.

"One-eight-four, true," said Keith.

"Target bearing zero-zero-four, relative," said Richardson, looking at the azimuth ring built into the bearing circle around the periscope where the tube disappeared into the top of the conning tower. "It's a convoy of four freighters, and I can see at least three escorts. Angle on the bow of the leading ship is about starboard ten. I can give you an estimate of range; let's see . . . I couldn't see the water line . . . use a fifty-foot height of mast and give them one-quarter of one division in high power."

1 6 7

Keith had seized an ivory-colored celluloid slide rule hanging by a string alongside the TDC, set the scales, read off the answer: "Twelve thousand yards!"

"Twelve thousand looks a little short to me," said Rich. "One of the escorts is out in front. Right now he bears a degree or so to the right of the bearing I gave you. One is to the left, and one farther to the right. They were all on different courses, so they must be patrolling on station. We'll soon know if the convoy itself is zigzagging. They're so close to shore that if they are, their next zig will probably be to their left. Also, I thought I could see another set of small masts astern of the last ship. There might be a fourth escort back in the clean-up spot."

"If we get a shot at them," said Keith, "that's the one we'll have to worry about."

"That one, or the left-hand escort," agreed Rich. "At least our fish are Mark Eighteens, and they won't leave a wake for him to head for."

"We still have ten fish aft, Skipper, and ten left forward. Recommend we try for a stern tube shot if we can," said Keith.

"Right. Matter of fact, we may have to shoot both bow tubes and stern tubes," said Richardson. "And besides, with these tincans moving around we'd better have a fish or two ready at each end set shallow just in case we need to take a shot at one."

Keith said, "The torpedo rooms are pretty fast on the reload, if we give them warning. Maybe we'd better have them lay out their gear now, and start reloading as we fire." Rich nodded. Keith pointed with emphasis at Quin, who had been listening with extreme attention.

Quin picked up his telephone mouthpiece, pressed the button, spoke into it. "Tubes forward and tubes aft," he said, "the skipper wants you to be ready to make a reload as fast as you can. There's four destroyers up here and four targets. Start reloading as soon as you have an empty tube. He needs some fish ready for the tincans."

Richardson shot him an approving look. "Three minutes since the last observation," said Keith. "If that optical range was any good, they ought to be just under eleven thousand yards right now."

"We'll try another radar range," said Richardson. "Same procedure as before. Everybody ready? . . . Up periscope." Up came the tube, Richardson squatting like an ancient devotee of an ageless religion in front of it, his knees spread, the tube rising almost between them, his hands waiting. The handles came out of the well. He snapped them down, jammed his forehead against the rubber guard around the eyepiece of the periscope, straightened up rapidly as the periscope continued to rise. The radar wave guide engaged the bottom of the periscope. Snap! went the radar.

"Range!" shouted Rogers.

Richardson had not yet reached the full standing position. He went back down with the periscope, snapped up its handles, backed clear at the last possible moment. Keith was standing on the opposite side of the periscope tube, looking up at the azimuth ring in the overhead. "Zero-zero-four-a-half," he said.

"Range thirteen thousand five hundred," sang out Rogers. "Good range, sir."

"Angle on the bow is still starboard ten. That was a good bearing. There are definitely four cargo ships and four escorts," said Richardson. "One of the escorts is patrolling astern, one on each flank and one ahead. No zig yet."

Turning to Rogers, he asked, "How was your radar pip? Do you think we can come down a little?"

"That was a good pip," said Rogers. "We ought to be able to come down about four feet."

"Good. Control, make your depth five-six feet!"

Eel nosed down slightly as the depth gauge began gradually to increase, steadied at the new figure. "It's nine minutes since you took a look around, Captain," said Keith.

"I'll do it next time. What's the state of charge of the torpedoes? Have you got the water injection yet?"

"All fish in the tubes got a freshening charge two days ago, Captain," said Keith. "We just took the injection temperature. It's fifty degrees. Buck has already made the temperature correction for torpedo speed on the TDC."

"Good," said Rich. "Anything else we've forgotten?"

"Well, maybe we'd better rig for silent running and rig for depth charge. Also, it wouldn't hurt to know the depth of water in case we have to go deep in a hurry."

"Stafford," said Richardson, "can you hear the escorts echo-ranging?"

Stafford didn't hear until Scott leaned over his shoulder, made him remove one earphone, and repeated the question.

"Yes, sir," said Stafford, "distant echo-ranging, bearing south."

"Quin," said Rich, "tell control to get a single ping sounding as quick as they can." He explained, turning to Keith and Buck, "If they're echo-ranging, they won't notice a single extra ping, especially at this distance."

Keith said, "We should get a bathythermograph reading, if there's time." He was going over his check-off list. The bathythermograph, which recorded water temperature against depth of submergence, gave indication of the location of temperature layers and was therefore useful for evasion.

"All right. We'll go deep after the next observation. I'll save the look around for the next time."

"Fast periscope technique again," Richardson said to Scott and Rogers—"Up periscope!"

The 'scope started up. Again Richardson went through the routine. "Range!" shouted Rogers. The 'scope started down.

"Bearing zero-zero-five-a-half," said Keith.

"Range twelve thousand," said Rogers.

"Fifteen hundred yards in three minutes gives us a speed of fifteen knots," said Richardson.

"I make it fourteen and a half by TDC," said Buck.

"Use fourteen and a half," said Richardson. "Target has zigged to his left. Angle on the bow of the leading ship is now starboard thirty. There are definitely four escorts. The leading ship is considerably bigger than the other three. It looks like a passenger cargo ship of perhaps ten thousand tons, with two stacks, and goalposts fore and aft over her cargo hatches. The other three ships are somewhat smaller, ordinary freighters. Two masts each, with booms."

"Distance to the track is six thousand yards," said Buck.

Richardson had already made the same calculation in his head. If the target continued on its present course with no further zigs, and *Eel* remained stationary, the convoy's nearest point of approach would be six thousand yards away, far outside optimum torpedo range. As yet, *Eel* had not maneuvered. It was still too early to tell how radical a zigzag plan the enemy ships were using, but they were close to the coast of Korea, and the most likely direction of their zigzagging would be toward the center of the Maikotsu Suido. The most probable next zig might even be farther to the target's left. Clearly, *Eel* would have to move over to get into position, and to do so it would be necessary to use high speed. Far better to do it now, before the escorts were close enough either to hear the submarine's propellers or to pick her up by echo-ranging on her broadside as she closed the track.

Assessment of the situation was virtually instantaneous, more a suddenly presented picture than a careful step-by-step evaluation. "Right full rudder! All ahead full! Control, make your depth one hundred feet! What was that sounding?"

"Two hundred beneath the keel," said Keith. "Two hundred sixty feet depth of water."

"Very well," said Richardson. 'Control, make your depth two hundred feet. Be careful as we near the bottom. Do not use much angle. Our sonar heads are down. If we touch, they'll be wiped off."

Six miles to the south, eight Japanese ships were moving steadily toward the same point at which *Eel* also was aiming. Four of them were targets of war, fated, if *Eel* could have her way, to find their last port of call on the bottom of the Yellow Sea. The remaining four were professional fighting ships, designed and trained to combat submarines. Perhaps a thousand men in all, about equally divided between the merchant ships and the antisub ships. Four merchant skippers, ever conscious of the possible presence of submarines, huddled unnaturally together for mutual protection, alert for any warning of danger, ready for instant flight should an enemy submarine appear. Four Japanese Navy skippers, eager for the accolade of having sunk the second U.S. sub in two weeks in the Yellow Sea. Four hundred depth charges between them, and about five hundred Japanese Navy men, no less eager than their commanders to sink an American submarine.

Opposed to these, eighty persons in *Eel*, probably better trained, certainly in a more complex ship than any of theirs. But both of *Eel*'s advantages—surprise and invisibility—stemmed from her ability to submerge. Submergence alone made it possible for eighty men to challenge a thousand, and to gain this capability the submarine had given up the ability to sustain damage. To submerge, she must be in exactly neutral buoyancy. Reserve buoyancy, which permits a surface ship to view the prospect of hull damage with some degree of equanimity, does not exist for a submerged submarine. Even a small hole in *Eel*'s pressure hull—made by a sharp enemy bow, a flailing propeller, an explosive shell from a gun, or the crushing water hammer from a near depth charge—could start a flood of water equivalent to fifty fire hydrants. A ton of water taken in—only a few hundred gallons— would be enough to send her to the bottom. If, somehow, all her ballast tanks survived whatever had caused the damage to the pressure hull (hardly likely, since they surrounded it), and if no more than one compartment had been flooded, she might, by blowing all of them dry, stagger to the surface, there to be smashed pitilessly down again by the knife-sharp bows and waiting guns of her assailants.

In the immediate future were not one contest but two, both unequal. Unequal, first, in that *Eel* would have one clear, unopposed shot at her antagonists (provided that some egregious error in approach technique, such as permitting one's periscope to be sighted, was not committed, or bad luck—sonar detection—encountered).

But once the submarine's presence became known, which it must ultimately and inevitably be by the crashing roar of her torpedoes, the inequalities would shift abruptly, and the second battle begin. From this point on, it was the submarine that would be on the defensive: slow moving, her machinery silenced save for the motors turning the propellers at minimum speed (for to run faster would make more noise), her torpedo tubes empty (reloading them would make noise), running at deep submergence, listening, always listening, for the pings of enemy sonar, for the sound of the searching propellers. Blindly twisting at excruciatingly slow speed in the desperate effort to avoid the high-speed rush of the enemy destroyer bringing the killing depth charges.

Four ships against one. Five hundred men against eighty. An alerted enemy, in their home waters, free to move swiftly in any direction, free, even, to seek help in emergency. Free to see, as well as listen. Free to make noise, to have no care for the making of noise. Free of the fear of the black water transforming itself into white at the instantaneous moment of ingress. Free of imagining, and awaiting, that tortured last view of a closely circumscribed steel world while light and power from the batteries yet remained. Free of the terror of the everlasting darkness and pressure at the bottom of the sea.

So must it have been during those last terrible moments in *Chicolar*, when awareness of the sacrifice to be exacted was replaced by the cataclysmic inrush of water which compressed the air with an ear-bursting blow, increased the temperature to unbearable height, and swept all before it into extinction.

"The normal approach course is two-seven-five," said Buck.

"Steady on course two-five-oh," snapped Richardson. He crowded over alongside Buck and Keith, looked at the TDC. "We don't have to go all the way over to the normal approach course," he said. "The range is still well open. How long will we have to run to get to two thousand yards on this course?"

"That's about a two-mile run—a little more. Let's see, at full speed, eight knots—that's two hundred-sixty-six yards a minute—it'll take us about fifteen minutes."

"Too long," said Richardson. "I've got to get a look before then. Keith, are they getting a bathythermograph reading?"

"Yep. There's a new card in the gadget."

"Okay. Tell them to take another single ping sounding when we get down to two hundred feet. We'll run about eight minutes at this speed and then come back up."

"That'll put us just about four thousand yards off the track, Skipper, a little farther maybe," said Buck.

"Fine," said Rich. "Keith, we might as well go ahead and rig for depth charge and silent running now. Get everything buttoned down tight."

172

"Okay, sir, but can we leave the hatch open and ventilation on for a while more? Besides, we might want better communication with Al. . . ."

The connng tower had only a supply ventilator. The return was through the hatch. Closing the hatch would not only isolate him from direct communication with Al Dugan—forcing reliance on telephones —it would stop the flow of air as effectively as shutting off the supply. Rigging for maximum security this far ahead of need was only a precaution. Keith's suggestion would mean a great deal for the comfort and efficiency of the fourteen men jammed into the conning tower, as well as the rest of the crew. "All right. We can hold off on the ventilation for a while."

Keith gave the necessary instructions. Suddenly Richardson had nothing to do. *Eel* tore on through the water at an unaccustomed rate. He could feel the hull trembling with the water passage. There were some small vibrations topside. A little unnecessary noise, a drumming of some portion of the bridge structure. Perhaps it was the lookouts' new platform and rails. These would have to be inspected carefully next time they had a chance, he thought.

"How much time?" he asked.

"We've been running four minutes, Skipper," said Buck. "Four minutes to wait."

Rich could feel his blood pressure gradually mounting, his pulse increasing. Below he could hear the watertight doors being closed, various men moving about. With the doors closed and dogged it was forbidden to change from one part of the ship to another except in emergency, so anticipated moves were being made now.

"How long we been running?"

"Five minutes, Captain; three minutes more to run."

His palms were itching. He had forgotten about the pain in his knees and thigh muscles. Now the aches were evident again. He waited an interminable length of time, moved over behind Buck and Keith to watch the slowly moving dials of the face of the TDC.

"We've been running seven minutes, Captain," said Keith.

"All ahead one-third," Rich called out. "Control, make your depth five-eight feet."

The annunciators clinked in the forward part of the conning tower as Cornelli executed the order. Gently *Eel*'s deck inclined upward. The drumming of the superstructure stopped.

"You get the BT card?" asked Richardson. "And what was the depth of water?"

"We got a seventy-five-foot reading at two hundred feet, Captain," said Keith, answering the last question first. "They're putting the BT card in the fixer now. We'll have it up here in a minute."

There was someone coming up the ladder from the control room. Blunt. Behind him, gesticulating helplessly, the lanky pharmacist's mate took two steps up the ladder and stopped, head framed in the opening, silently signaling his failure. Now Rich cursed the weakness which had allowed him to accede to Keith's request regarding the hatch and ventilation. Better to be sweltering in peace than cope with an erratic superior, especially during an approach! That solution was now irrevocably gone. No time to toady to the squadron commander's unpredictable states of mind. No time to consider, or evaluate, the sudden dismay communicating itself to the area just below his own diaphragm. Play the game out. Pretend his appearance had not been greeted with hastily concealed startlement. Hearty greeting. "How are you feeling, Commodore?" No sign of the deep unease awakened by his sudden appearance.

"Fine, Rich, I never slept so well in my life, but what was the pharmacist's mate doing? Why didn't you call me? He tried to keep me from turning out. Did you send him?"

"Well, frankly"—calm tone, get over this part quickly—"I told him to see what he could do for you. You've been looking a little peaked lately."

Blunt was about to say something, but Richardson went on, a little hurriedly, as if he had not noticed. "We've got a convoy of four ships up there, Commodore, with four escorts. I'm hoping to shoot bow and stern tubes. Also, we're going to be in for a depth charging, sir. It'll be pretty uncomfortable up here in the conning tower after we shut off the ventilation, so I recommend you move back to the control room when that time comes. . . ." Handling the ship in combat was Richardson's sole responsibility. Best signal his intent to exercise it.

"All right, Rich," said Blunt, "just give me a minute to get down the hatch when you give the word." There was a degree of truculence in his manner. Perhaps he felt he should have been informed as soon as the enemy ships were sighted. Surely in his state of extreme drowsiness the previous night, he had not suspected the sleeping potion which had finally enabled his body's craving for sleep to be satisfied. Probably he did not yet realize that, in contravention to his last expressed wishes, while he had been sleeping the *Eel* had entered the Maikotsu Suido, nor that coordination instructions had been sent to the *Whitefish* in his name. Hopefully, his long sleep might have restored some of his old-time equilibrium. But of this Richardson could not yet judge. There was no time to make an evaluation. The ship was about to go into mortal danger, would be under determined attack by four fully aroused escorts in half an hour. There would be one chance, only a single quick opportunity, to fire torpedoes at the convoy. Even this would exist only if prior detection could be avoided.

If all went well, the first announcement of the presence of a submarine would be the crash of lethal explosions against the steel sides of enemy cargo ships. With four ships in the convoy, and four close escorts, not to mention probable air cover, only consummate skill would make possible an attack on all. He would have only ten torpedoes to shoot. From that moment on, *Eel* would become the subject of a relentless search by at least two, and perhaps all four, vengeful tincans. If she could remain at periscope depth there was the possibility that a modicum of the initiative might yet remain with her. The probability, on the other hand, was that she would be driven deep, or as deep as the shallow Yellow Sea would permit, there reduced to a sea-mole, blind, wandering through the watery wasteland, fearing every change in enemy propeller cadence, every shift in echo-ranging scale, as the precursor of the depth charge attack that would have *Eel*'s name on it.

He would need every faculty, every capability, every intuitive sense, if he was to guide his ship and crew safely through the ordeal into which he was leading them. A querulous superior who held no responsibility for the operation of the ship, nor for the conduct of the approach and attack, could not be tolerated. He would have to be put aside even if strong methods became necessary.

Blunt was still in the forward end of the conning tower, several feet away. Richardson crowded over behind the TDC, alongside Keith and Buck Williams. "Keith," he hissed, "when I tell you, run down to the control room and get hold of Yancy. Tell him that if I send him a message to take charge I mean to take charge of Captain Blunt with as many men as he needs, and get him back in his bunk asleep in whatever way he has to do it." Keith nodded his understanding. "Don't go until I tell you to," he finished.

Keith nodded again.

"What's the distance to the track now?" Richardson said, resuming his normal voice.

"Forty-two hundred," said Buck.

"Range?"

"I'm showing—mark!—ninety-two hundred yards."

"Speed through water?"

"Own speed—three and a half knots coming down slowly."

"Depth?" demanded Richardson.

"We're at ordered depth, sir," said Keith. "Depth is five-eight feet. You haven't looked around yet. . . ."

175

"Keith, I want that bathythermograph card," said Richardson, putting special emphasis in the words. "Jump on down and see what's holding them up. Get it and bring it back up here yourself." There was an understanding look in Keith's eyes as he ran below.

"Stand by for an observation," said Richardson. "Radar periscope—we'll use the fast procedure again for our next range, Scott, but this time I want you to stop it at the deck and bring it up slowly until we break water. I want to get a look around first." Scott and Rogers nodded their comprehension.

"Up 'scope," said Richardson. The periscope came up, stopped with the handles just clear of the bottom of the well. On his knees, Rich extended them, bent over, his chin on the floor, to look through the 'scope. "Up a little," he said, motioning with his thumbs, "up a little more, that's high!" He extended his right hand palm down over the handles. Swiftly he rotated the periscope completely around, bouncing on his haunches much as a cossack sword dancer might have done, his torso and head contorted to look through the eyepiece. He made two complete circles. "All clear for now," he said, turning around to the port bow. "Here they are. Bearing, mark!" He flipped up the handles and pointed downward with his thumbs. The periscope started down into the well.

"Two-nine-six relative," said Scott, who had moved to the periscope in Keith's place to read the azimuth ring.

Richardson made a sudden horizontal cutting motion with the palms of both hands. Quin, still wearing the telephone headset, had taken Scott's place at the periscope hoist controls and stopped the periscope's descent.

"I think there's a plane up there," said Richardson. "No point in leaving the 'scope up too long. Now we'll go for the radar range. Everybody ready?" Quin and Rogers nodded.

"Bring her all the way up, Quin, until you hear Rogers sing out 'Range,' then drop it immediately. Don't worry about me. You got that?" Quin had seen the procedure many times in drill, and only moments ago again, this time for real. He nodded his understanding.

"Up periscope." The handles were up quickly this time, since the periscope had been stopped before it had reached the bottom of the well. It rose up . . .

"Range!" shouted Rogers. The 'scope started down. Richardson stepped clear.

"Eight-seven-five-oh. Good range," said Rogers.

Buck was twirling one of the control cranks on the front of the TDC. "That was down four hundred yards," he said, "but I was right on in bearing."

"Good. No zig yet. Angle on the bow is starboard thirty-five."

"Should be starboard thirty-four," said Buck. "Four hundred yards' range difference in eight minutes. That's about one and a half knots. That puts the speed up to sixteen knots." Carefully he turned a third knob on the TDC controls.

"Distance to the track?"

"Four thousand three hundred. Ten minutes since the last zig."

Another interminable wait. "Three minutes since the last look," said Williams.

"We'll make a very fast observation this time, just to check things," decided Richardson. "Fast procedure again. . . . Ready?" Nods of assent. "Up 'scope!"

The 'scope came up. "Range!" shouted Rogers.

"Zig toward!" barked Richardson. It slithered away, the hoist rod knob on the side of the periscope yoke barely grazing his forehead. He would have to be a little more agile next time, or risk a lump on his head.

"Seven thousand yards!"

"Three-zero-zero!"

"They've just zigged," said Richardson. "Only the leading ship has turned. Angle on the bow is starboard fifteen."

"Starboard fifteen," repeated Buck, cranking another one of the handles. "That was about a twenty-five-degree zig to his right. Range was down another hundred. That gives us seventeen knots. Maybe they've increased speed. These guys are really pouring on the coal!" Again, he carefully and precisely adjusted his "target speed" control knob.

"I can't see the water line yet, but it does seem to me they're making pretty good speed." Richardson turned to the radar operator. "Think we can go a little deeper, Rogers?"

"Yes, sir, that was a real good pip, that time."

"Control, make your depth six-oh feet." Quin relayed the word by telephone.

A few seconds later Al Dugan's voice came up the hatch. "We're at six-oh feet, Conn."

A good approach officer always keeps his fire control party advised of the situation topside, including the reasons for his own maneuvers and his intentions for the future. Richardson waited a few moments. Keith would be back shortly—was back, a small smoke-smudged card in his hand.

"Here's the bathythermograph card, Skipper," said Keith. "It's iso-thermal all the way down. I guess that's what it had to be with this current. It's just like the one we got this morning." He flicked his eyes briefly to the forward part of the conning tower, where Blunt stood under the closed hatch leading to the bridge, idly holding its wire lanyard. Keith turned his eyes back to Rich, nodded ever so slightly.

"I was afraid of that," said Richardson, acknowledging with his eyes the nearly imperceptible signal. He raised his voice so that Blunt could also hear. "The water is isothermal all the way, Commodore. No layer. When sighted, the target was on course approximately north, running close to the coast of Korea. It's a four-ship convoy, ships in column, with escorts ahead, astern, and on both flanks. Also, there's an aircraft patrolling overhead. I figured the convoy for a zig to his left, which he did shortly after we sighted him. Approximately twelve minutes after that he zigged again, but this time to his right, which I really didn't expect, because that keeps him really close in to the beach. If he's zigging every ten to twelve minutes, there'll probably be one more zig before we get to the firing point. Most likely away, to his left, but we can't be sure. The starboard flanking escort and the astern escort will be the ones to give us trouble. I figure to shoot right after the near escort has passed; stern tubes with a fairly large track on the leading ship, then swing around for bow tubes with a sharper track on the last three. As soon as we shoot the stern tubes, the after room will start a reload just as fast as they can, because we may need those torpedoes back there. The same with bow tubes, but the ones I'm really going to depend on immediately are the stern tubes." He was really speaking for everyone's benefit, pointed with emphasis at Quin, who, once again relieved from the periscope control by Scott, nodded his understanding that he was to relay this information to all stations.

"There are four big ships in column, and four escorts. The three leading escorts are all the same type tincan. They look new. My guess is they're the new *Mikura* class. They might be the same three that got the *Chicolar*. Anyway, they're in about the same pattern, one ahead and one on each beam of the leading ship. They're patrolling back and forth on station as well as following the zigzag. I can't make out the astern escort as well. He looks a little bigger, probably an old destroyer. I've been making all observations on the leading ship, which is a two-stack passenger-cargo ship between eight thousand and ten thousand tons. The other three ships are ordinary freighters, somewhat smaller than the leading one. We'll shoot three fish aft at the leading ship, depth set ten feet. The fourth torpedo aft we'll keep in reserve with a depth setting of four feet. Then we'll swing hard right for a quick shot, two fish each, at the last three ships. Set depth of all torpedoes forward ten feet!"

The small audience nodded its understanding. Quin pressed the button on the top of his telephone mouthpiece, spoke into it at some length.

"Quin," said Richardson when the yeoman had finished, "tell the people in the forward and after torpedo rooms there are to be no torpedoes unsecured at any time, even while they're loading them. We'll try to keep from taking sudden angles, but the chances of a quick counterattack are pretty good, and we may have to go deep in a hurry after we shoot. I want all the special securing lines rigged on the torpedoes just as though we were reloading them on surface, and if we order silent running again, they are to stop dead and hold everything right where they are."

Quin nodded his alert appreciation. "All fish to be reloaded with surface reload procedure and never to be unsecured in case we get depth charged and have to take a steep angle. Hold everything if silent running is ordered," he said. Again he pressed the button on the top of his mouthpiece, relayed the word to the torpedo rooms and, of course, simultaneously throughout the ship.

"How long since the last look?" said Rich.

"Two and a half minutes. Don't forget that aircraft!"

"Observation," said Rich. "Radar periscope; then we'll switch to number two at the deck, and I'll try for a masthead height." He glanced about the conning tower, motioned with his thumbs to Scott. "Regular procedure," he barked. The periscope came up. He grabbed the handles, rose with it, reached a fully standing position. "Mark!" he said.

"One-nine-two-a-half, true," said Keith.

"Range!" said Rogers. The periscope started down.

"Range was five-four-double-oh," said Rogers. Richardson stepped behind number two periscope, motioned with his thumbs for it to be raised. Behind him he could hear Buck Williams making the new insets in the TDC. "He might be going a bit faster yet," said Buck.

"No more than seventeen knots," said Richardson. He was again on his knees, stooped as low as he could get. The periscope handles on the attack 'scope came into view. He grabbed them, snapped them down. The periscope was facing the wrong direction. With a quick jerk he spun it quickly, sighted on the target, turned the range crank. Keith was also on his knees on the other side of it, fingers on the dial. "Mark!" said Richardson. "Down 'scope!" He banged up the handles. The periscope started down. Both he and Keith had to throw themselves out of the way of the descending yoke to avoid being struck on the head.

"I can see the water line clearly. That was a good masthead height reading. Did you get it, Keith?"

"Got it," said Keith. "Eighty-five feet. That's a good-sized ship."

"Yes, she's a beauty," agreed Richardson. "No zig yet. Angle on the bow was starboard twenty-five."

"How does twenty-seven look, Skipper?" said Buck. "That puts him on course three-four-five, using seventeen knots."

"That looks fine, use twenty-seven. How long since the last zig, Buck?"

Keith answered him, "Six minutes, Skipper."

"All right, we'll shift to the attack periscope. Control," said Richardson, "make your depth six-four feet! That will give us three feet of the attack periscope exposed," said Rich in an altered tone, addressing the members of the attack party.

"What's the weather like topside?" asked Blunt. It was a legitimate question. Richardson should have described the weather conditions earlier.

"Weather calm, clear, small waves about one or two feet in height, just enough to make our periscope hard to see. No whitecaps, however. The plane is on the far beam of the convoy. As we get closer I plan to come down at least one more foot." He turned to Keith.

"Have we completed our check-off?" he asked. Richardson would have said more, but was interrupted by the wolfpack commander.

"How do you know those new two-stack ships can't be making more than seventeen knots, Rich?" Blunt asked. "We have lots of merchant ships that can make at least twenty."

"Damn few of the older one-stackers can even make seventeen, so that's tops for this outfit," Richardson answered swiftly. Keith's look told him that his exec had caught his flash of irritation, quickly masked. By contrast with the previous one, this was not a legitimate question. Later, perhaps, during a postmortem over coffee in the wardroom. Not now, with the moment of attack nearly at hand. There had been a tinge of querulousness in Blunt's voice. Standing under the closed bridge hatch, Blunt's eyes were glittering in the deep shadows under the bushy eyebrows. Still holding to the lanyard, he leaned forward, supporting himself on it, projecting himself toward the periscopes.

"You said we're close to land. What is our position? Why wasn't I informed when we got this close in?" Blunt's voice had risen perceptibly. His bearing communicated anger. His face was flushed, his jaw hung slack, emphasizing the wattles under his chin.

"Check-off list is completed, sir," said Keith, breaking in. "We're ready to shoot bow and stern, except for opening outer doors." Keith had seen the same signs as Richardson, was loyally trying to stave off a bad situation.

"We're expecting a zig," said Richardson, taking Keith's cue and addressing his words to the fire control party. "We'll hold the outer doors closed for a bit more. The less time the fish are flooded in the tubes, the better they'll run. As soon as the enemy zigs, we'll complete preparations and be shooting almost immediately."

"Goddammit, Richardson, answer me! What have you been up to while I've been asleep?" Blunt was shouting now. His voice filled the conning tower.

"How long since the last look?" asked Richardson. His self-control was slipping. He must not show it. Even now, if he could somehow bring this extraordinary situation under control, *Eel*'s crew might not fully understand the true circumstance. In the aftermath of a successful attack, the sudden contretemps in the conning tower might be relegated to one of those strange discussions between superior officers which no one could pretend to understand. But further interference on the part of Blunt could not be borne. Within minutes, two or three at the most, *Eel* would be firing nine of her ten loaded torpedoes. Her concealment would be shattered the moment the first torpedoes found their target. She would then instantly become the hunted instead of the hunter. He would need every capability at his command to regain the initiative, to escape the sonar searchers in the four escorts—maddened because of their failure to detect *Eel* previously, now certain of her presence in the immediate vicinity.

Keith was looking at him intently. The thought in his mind was leaping at him from the wide, staring eyes.

"Richardson, I'll not be ignored like this!" The squadron commander had left his perch on the step under the hatch, was crowding past the astounded Scott, bumping Stafford's back where he still maintained his sonar vigil according to the most recent orders. Keith waited no longer, turned, crowded through the group in the opposite direction, and bolted through the still-open hatch leading to the control room.

"Two minutes since last look!" Williams, automatically picking up for the absent Leone. No doubt Buck had taken it all in, just the way Keith had, was trying to be of assistance. Not only with Captain Blunt, but also to keep the approach in hand. Blunt was standing alongside Rich. His eyes were glaring, his breath coming in short, noisy, low-pitched whistles through his partly open mouth.

The charade must be played out. At least, keep him occupied until Keith and Yancy returned. "Commodore, would you like a quick look?" With his thumb, Richardson motioned to Scott. The periscope began its ascent. Stooping—that gave him something to do for a few seconds—Rich grasped the handles. He swung the 'scope around toward Blunt, with his free hand propelled him toward it much as he might

181

one of *Eel*'s own officers, and ranged himself in Keith's position on its back side. Blunt could not prevent the intuitive, habitual move of hooking his right elbow around one handle, placing his left hand upon the other, affixing his eye to the rubber guard.

"Around this way, sir," muttered Richardson, waiting only long enough to be sure Blunt was firmly attached in the familiar position to the periscope. "This should be the bearing of the leading ship."

"Bearing, mark!" said Blunt, twitching the periscope barrel a fraction of a degree. Relief flooded through Richardson. The tone of voice and the action were those of the Blunt of old. "Range, mark!" Blunt had dropped his right hand to the range knob, was turning it.

"Four-nine-double-oh!" read Richardson, matching the just-determined enemy masthead height against the periscope range dial. Williams looked up suddenly from the TDC, jerked his head around toward the periscope. His hand flew to the range input crank of the computer, but the look on his face was one of puzzled inquiry. Clearly, the range just called out by Richardson did not agree with that generated by the Torpedo Data Computer. Rich shook his head. With relief, Buck dropped the range crank, reached to the face of the TDC, pointed to the target-bearing dial, nodded his head vigorously. Good for Buck! The bearing, at least, was right on.

"Angle on the bow, starboard twenty-five!" said Blunt. Again Buck nodded. Blunt's observation as to the attitude of the leading ship was approximately the same as that predicted by the TDC. A quick-thinking young man, that Buckley Williams. The 'scope had been up ten seconds. Now to get it down. How to cause Blunt to order it down. Leaving it up unnecessarily was not only anathema to submariners; it was, under the circumstances, dangerous. All Blunt's submarine instincts should cause him to lower it, now that a routine observation had been completed. Three more seconds passed. There was a control lever in parallel with the one Scott and Quin had been using, secreted in the dark overhead alongside the periscope—the one used by the OOD during routine submerged patrolling when there was no battle stations personnel to do it for him. Blunt showed no sign as yet of giving up his view through the instrument. Rich pulled the handle gently toward him. The periscope began to descend ever so slightly. Blunt would feel the slow movement; perhaps the thought would communicate itself to him. . . .

"Down 'scope!" Blunt stepped back, snapped up the periscope handles as Richardson jerked the lever and the long silver tube dropped away.

"Looks like a beautiful approach, Rich. You're in a perfect position to get all four of those bastards!" Blunt was rubbing his hands together with pleasure. "How I wish I were still young enough to take a boat on patrol! You young fellows are having all the fun!" The aging face was alight. The jaw muscles no longer looked flabby. In the space of a few seconds, ten years might have dropped from him. Richardson was barely able to conceal his astonishment at the precipitant right-about-face in his attitude, but temporary deliverance from a problem for which he could not, in the short time available, think of a permanent solution, supplied an even greater emotion, of relief.

Keith was coming up the ladder from the control room. Behind him was someone tall, and behind him, a third person, short, powerful, and black—Yancy and Chief Commissary Steward Woodrow, in charge of the wardroom, in charge of all the provisions on board as well, and one of the most respected men in the ship.

Yancy carried a small cardboard box in his hand. Woodrow had a rolled-up blanket under his arm and two uniform web belts over his shoulder. Keith also had picked up a pair of web belts, Richardson saw, as for the second time in half a minute he made a signal of negation. He pointed back down the hatch, saw the grateful looks of the two enlisted men as they went back below. They could not have much relished the job they had been about to carry out.

Keith's arrival in the midst of the fire control group caused a certain amount of shuffle among the tightly packed men, and in the process Richardson found the opportunity to maneuver Blunt back to his old position under the hatch—the only free space in the conning tower—while Richardson himself shouldered past Rogers on the radar console to where Stafford stood watch on the sonar. He leaned over to speak to him. Stafford, probably the only person in the conning tower to have been totally unconscious of the difficult situation just past, pulled away one earpiece to listen.

"Stafford," said Rich, "can you hear them okay?"

"Yes sir, I can hear them fine. The leading ship has twin screws, I think, and the others—I can't hear them quite as well because they're behind him—I think they're single-screw ships. I can hear three escorts, too. All the tincans have twin screws."

"The nearest escort, the one we need to worry about most, bears around two-zero-zero true. The other one that I'm worried about bears around two-four-five. He's the leading escort. I think that one will probably pass well clear ahead, but the one on two-zero-zero might come pretty close to us. Keep on that one, and let me know if you notice any change in what he's doing, either ping interval or speed, or anything." Stafford nodded, replaced the earphone over his right ear. Richardson crossed back aft to the after end of the conning tower, crowded in alongside of Keith and Buck at the TDC.

Behind both of them, facing in the opposite direction, Larry Lasche toiled at an automatic plot board. Rich heard him as he spoke over his shoulder: "Buck, I'm getting seventeen knots overall. Target course for this leg, three-four-zero."

"I've got three-four-five, seventeen knots, Larry," answered Williams. "Looks pretty good."

"What's the distance to the track?" said Richardson.

"Twenty-six hundred yards."

"We'll have to turn toward a little more," said Richardson, addressing both Leone and Williams. "We have to maneuver for this stern tube shot and at the same time not close the track too much in case they zig toward."

The face of the TDC contained a number of dials, the two most prominent of which represented the target and the *Eel*, on converging courses. Somewhere to the left of the target dial, all three men knew, there lay an escort, zigzagging back and forth irregularly as it patrolled on station to starboard of its charge. It would pass nearly overhead shortly before the time to shoot.

Rich raised his voice. "Left full rudder," he said, "make your new course one-nine-zero."

"One-nine-zero," responded Cornelli, swinging the stainless-steel steering wheel. Obediently the "own-ship" dial on the face of the TDC began to turn counterclockwise, finally settled with the bow of the miniature submarine aligned with the number 190 on a surrounding dial.

"Time since the last look?"

"Two and a half minutes," said Keith. "About nine minutes since the last zig." Keith also was ignoring the data from Blunt's observation of half a minute previous.

"Steady on one-nine-zero!" said Cornelli.

"Observation," said Richardson. "Up periscope. Number two." The periscope started up. Once again he had to ignore the muscular pain as he went through the deep knee bend ritual, motioned with his hand to Scott to stop it just before it had reached its full height. "Bearing, mark!" he said.

"One-nine-five," said Keith.

"Range"—turning the range dial on the side of the periscope—"mark! Down periscope." The periscope dropped away.

"Four-three-double-oh," said Keith.

"Angle on the bow starboard thirty," said Rich. "No zig yet. The near escort bears about ten degrees to the left of the main target, angle on the bow zero. He's patrolling on station as before. The aircraft is circling the convoy."

"Speed checks at seventeen knots," said Buck.

"Plot gets seventeen knots," said Lasche.

"Target course three-four-five," said Buck. "Distance to the track two-one-double-oh."

"This may turn out to be a long-range shot," said Richardson. "I'm concerned about this near escort. If the convoy zigs away, we'll have to close the track more, which will force us to a speed burst. We'll be broadside to him, too. If the convoy zigs toward us a little, we're in a perfect position, but if it zigs too much, it may run right over us. How long since the last zig?"

"Eleven minutes," said Keith.

"Time since last look?"

"One minute."

"Up periscope," said Rich. "I'll take a look around." He grabbed the periscope handles as soon as they came up out of the well, kept the periscope down low, spun it around rapidly. "All clear," he said. "Up!" He motioned with his thumbs. The periscope started up. "Bearing, mark!" he said. "Range, mark! Down 'scope. No zig yet."

"Checks right on," said Buck.

"How's the near escort, Skipper?" asked Keith.

"Looks like he'll pass astern," said Richardson. "Distance to the track?"

"Nineteen hundred yards," said Buck.

"We can't swing around to the right any more for our stern tubes, because there'll be a zig any minute," said Richardson. "Control," he spoke more loudly, "make your depth six-five feet." In a more normal tone he said, "That will barely let me see over the top of the small waves we've got up there. It'll also give us a little more clearance in case he runs over us—up periscope!"

"It's a zig away!" said Richardson. Through the periscope he could see the bulk of the leading ship begin to lengthen. She was riding low on the water, belching smoke again, heeling over slightly toward him in her turn. A quick turn of the periscope to the nearest escort showed it also with the starboard side in view. He had evidently turned a little sooner. Astern, three freighters were plowing along in the original path, evidently planning to turn in column as before, when they reached the knuckle in the water where the leader had put over his rudder.

"This changes everything," said Rich as the periscope descended into its housing. "Right full rudder! All ahead full!" He turned to Buck. "Starboard sixty! Give me a course for a thirty gyro, bow tubes, on the leading ship, one-twenty starboard track. We'll shoot three each at the first and second ships and try to get the stern tubes off at the third ship!"

"Course for thirty right gyros, one-twenty starboard track, bow tubes: two-two-zero!" said Buck, figuring swiftly with his fingers on the dials on the face of his TDC.

"Make your new course two-two-zero!" ordered Rich. He waited to hear Cornelli's acknowledgment from the forward end of the control room, then spoke swiftly to Keith. "So far, the near escort has shown no signs of detecting us, but he may pass very nearly overhead. The reason for not swinging farther is to give us a chance to get around for a stern tube shot afterward."

"Right! Where's the escort now?"

"He's over on our port bow with a starboard angle," answered Richardson. "But we're speeding up and closing him." Richardson turned, quickly stepped forward to the sonar again. "Stafford," he said, "keep your gear on that near escort. What's he bear now?"

"Two-one-zero," responded Stafford, obediently swinging the sonar head dial to the left.

"Very well. Keep your bearings on that fellow coming in. I want him to pass ahead."

"Aye aye," said Stafford. "Bearing two-one-zero."

"Steady on two-two-zero," sang out Cornelli.

"What's the range now?" said Richardson, stepping quickly aft again.

"Twenty-five hundred yards TDC," said Buck. "Distance to the track fifteen hundred yards. Gyros right ten, increasing."

"All ahead one-third!"

"Speed through water, four and a half knots," said Keith.

"Escort bears two-one-five," said Stafford.

"Keith, finish the rig for silent running except for the torpedo rooms. Secure the ventilation. Rig all compartments for depth charge, but leave the hatch to the control room open for the time being." He swung back to Buck. "What's the speed through water now?" he said.

"Four knots."

Still too fast to put the periscope up. The feather it would make splashing through the seas would surely be detected by the escort, now close aboard and coming nearly directly for them. He would have to wait for *Eel* to slow down a little more. On the other hand, he was nearly at the firing point. Things were moving rapidly. He cocked his head as if he could visually appraise the situation going on on the surface of the sea above. The main target would now be nearly broadside on, and in perfect position for firing. The three ships in column astern would by now have reached the turning point. Each in succession would have made its turn onto the new course. The near escort, close on the port bow, was closing in even more, but might pass ahead.

"Escort bearing two-one-five," said Stafford again.

This was bad. The escort was patrolling his own station back and forth, superimposing a random zigzag plan upon the more formal zigzag plan being carried out by the convoy. Two successive sonar bearings of the same value indicated that he was now heading directly toward *Eel*. Possibly his sonar operator had detected something suspicious in the water.

"Escort bearing two-one-four," from Stafford.

"Speed through water?" he said to Buck. He could read it almost as well himself, but it helped to have someone else do it for him.

"Three and a half knots."

"Keith, I'm going to make one more observation, and then we'll be shooting. Also, I've got to try to find that aircraft again. This is not a shooting observation, but open the outer doors forward anyway."

"Open outer doors forward, aye aye," said Keith. "We're ready to shoot in all respects, Captain, as soon as we get the outer doors open."

"Up periscope," said Richardson. The scope came up. As before, he rode it up, swung it all around rapidly, steadied it on the port bow for a second. "Bearing, mark!" he said. "Down 'scope."

"Two-three-oh," said Keith. "No range. Did you get a range?"

"No range," said Richardson. "That was the main target. The aircraft is clear to starboard. The escort is about thirty degrees to the left. He'll be passing overhead very soon."

"Escort bearing two-one-four," said Stafford.

"Outer doors are open forward, Captain," said Keith.

"Be sure all periscopes are all the way down," said Richardson. "The tincan will pass overhead in a few seconds."

All inside the conning tower could feel the tension which had suffused the air. With the securing of the blowers the noise level had dropped perceptibly. The air suddenly felt dead. The temperature rose. People spoke in lower voices simply in reaction to the atmosphere in which they moved.

"Escort bears two-one-five," said Stafford, his voice sounding unusually loud in the sudden stillness. "Still pinging the same. He's close aboard now."

He had not detected them. That was good. Everyone in the conning tower could hear the propellers resounding through the water. The *Eel* was nearly broadside to his approach. An alert sonar watch perhaps should have recognized a return echo. A change in his ping rate or his propeller speed would betray his interest.

"He's pinging steadily, long range," said Stafford. "No change in rpm."

Thum, thum, thum, thum, from the propellers. Growing louder, ever louder. This was *Eel*'s time of greatest danger. No doubt depth charges were carried at the ready, and even now, if a submarine were detected only a few hundred yards ahead, a devastating blow could be dealt her.

Thum, thum, thum, went the propellers. Louder and louder. *Thum-thum-thum!* Close aboard now. THUM-THUM-THUM-THUM-THUM-THUM-THUM-THUM!

"Tincan passing overhead!" said Stafford.

There was a swish of water through *Eel*'s superstructure. The submarine rocked gently in the destroyer's wake. The escort had passed, after all, not more than a few feet away from where they stood.

In the sudden stillness in the conning tower Blunt was staring from the forward starboard corner where he had stationed himself, still gripping the lanyard to the hatch. His face was beaded with sweat. Richardson tossed him a quick smile. Except for the fact that this was very much for real, Blunt had experienced it many times. "He's gone by," Rich said. "This is a shooting observation. Stand by forward."

"Shooting observation. Stand by forward," echoed Keith. Quin repeated the same in the telephone, giving emphasis to his voice as he transmitted the order.

"Range fifteen hundred, gyros thirty right, torpedo run eighteen-fifty," said Buck.

"Up periscope," said Richardson. He laid the vertical cross hair of the periscope directly between the stacks of his target. He was a complete automaton, and yet his mind encompassed the fact that the ship was crowded with people—soldiers, from the general olive-drab appearance —and was heavily laden. Millions of Japanese yen and untold hours of Herculean labor had gone into building her. She was obviously a new ship, probably completed after the beginning of the war. She had recently been repainted. She was a thing of pride to her skipper. She was doomed. Explosion, fire, drowning lay in the cross hair that he carefully, coldly, placed upon her.

"Mark!" he said.

"Zero-two-three-a-half," said Keith.

"Set," said Buck.

"Shoot," said Richardson. "Down periscope!"

"Fire one!" said Keith.

"Fire one!" shouted Quin into his telephone.

Keith was leaning on the firing button built into the side of *Eel*'s conning tower, just forward of the TDC. "Number one fired electrically!" announced Quin. Everyone in the conning tower had felt the jolt transmitted to the sturdy fabric of *Eel*'s hull when the torpedo had been expelled.

Keith released the firing key. "Stand by two," he said.

Lasche was counting off the seconds. "... Eight ... nine ... ten."

"Fire two" sang out Keith.

"Number two fired electrically," reported Quin.

"... Nine ... ten ..."

"Fire three!"

The jolt of the torpedo departing. Quin reporting the message from the torpedo room that the third torpedo had been fired electrically. Had this not happened, the chief in the torpedo room would instantly have fired it manually. Larry Lasche, counting out the seconds between torpedoes to ensure they were not fired too closely together.

"All torpedoes running hot, straight, and normal," announced Stafford, playing his sound head-dial back and forth over a small arc, oblivious to the fact that "hot," at least, could refer only to the old steam and compressed-air torpedoes.

"Shift targets," said Richardson. "Up periscope!" He laid the cross hair on the stack of the second ship—a neat-looking but older vessel. "Mark!" he said. Again the train of events was set in motion. He felt *Eel* jerk three more times, recognized on the one hand the death he had dealt out and on the other the fact that there could be no stopping the process, once it started, neither for himself nor anyone else.

He spun the 'scope around. The stern of the destroyer which had just passed overhead loomed huge in his magnified field of view. It had not been more than sixty seconds since it had gone over. Everything was still calm and peaceful on the surface of the sea. Nothing yet could have happened. "Right full rudder! Down periscope! All ahead full! Give me a course for stern tubes!"

Keith crowded alongside of Buck in front of the TDC, gave Rich the answer. "Recommend course three-four-zero for about a right thirty-degree gyro for tubes aft," he said.

"Starboard stop! Starboard back two-thirds!" said Rich. This would help increase the speed of the turn and at the same time keep *Eel* from gaining too much speed through the water at this crucial moment. He watched her swinging around on the dial of the TDC. It took so long for a submerged submarine to turn! She moved so slowly, had so much weight to swing around—not only her own steel structure, but also the water in her ballast tanks. She had such a huge ponderous bulk to push around through the water, so little power with which to do it.

Maneuvering on the surface was a totally different thing, even on the battery.

"Approximate bearing of the third ship is twenty degrees left of the second one," he said to Buck, "and increase his range by five hundred yards." Buck furiously cranked the dials of the TDC.

"How long before our first spread gets there, Larry?" Rich asked.

"Thirty seconds to go." He watched the bow of "own ship" on the TDC pass 300, pass 320—it was swinging a little faster now. It passed 330.

"Starboard stop," he said. "All ahead one-third." His judgment had been right, *Eel*'s speed had remained at about two and a half knots, but her swinging had perceptibly increased. Al Dugan was doing a masterful job at depth control with the speed changes, full rudder maneuvers, and six torpedoes fired forward at rapid intervals.

"Steady on three-four-zero!"

"Up periscope!" The deadly ritual again. "Shift targets. Bearing, mark! . . . Shoot!"

"Fire seven! . . . Fire eight! . . . Fire nine!"

"Three torpedoes aft fired electrically."

He spun the periscope around, saw a huge geyser of water shoot up alongside the leading ship. "A hit!" he announced. A second later the boom came in. He turned to the escort. Still no sign, still stern to. A second geyser rose alongside the forward part of the leading ship. With two torpedoes in her she was gone regardless of whether the third one, spread aft, missed or not. But as Richardson watched, the ship must have slowed down enough from the effects of the two hits to make sure the third hit also. It went off almost in the same place the first one had struck. Even as he watched her, she began to list toward him, still belching smoke and steam from her stacks, her decks boiling with startled, terrorized humanity.

The escort had evidently put his rudder left, was turning around. A cloud of steam, or vapor, burst from the stack of the second ship. The reverberations of the third boom had barely died away in *Eel*'s conning tower when a geyser of water arose alongside the forward part of the second ship and, seconds later, another in her after section. He swung to the third ship, caught the explosion there. The torpedoes had been spread to allow for variations in the solution for target speed, course, and range. If they ran as intended, one at least of each salvo should have hit each target. Six hits for nine torpedoes, fired with large gyro angles, were more than could normally be expected.

He spun the periscope around once more. A jet of steam came up from the stack of the fourth ship in column. A whistle or siren. She had turned radically to the left, was still swinging. No chance for a shot there. He swung back to the escort. Still in his turn, listing away, undoubtedly coming back to where he would assume the submarine must have been, possibly where a now-chastened sonar watch stander remembered something unusual in his echoes. The aircraft had also turned, was headed back toward the gutted convoy.

"How's the reload coming forward?" he asked.

A second's delay. Quin answered. "They got one in. The second one's going in now. Neither one ready yet."

"Let me know just as soon as they're ready to shoot forward." The destroyer was perhaps five hundred yards away, heeling over to starboard under the impetus of left rudder. It was clearly one of a new class of submarine escorts. No doubt one of the new *Mikuras*. "Frigates," they were called in the recognition pamphlet. In describing them to the wolfpack commander he had, without forethought, called up the possibility it might be this same trio which had accounted for *Chicolar* a few days ago. If *Eel* could remain at periscope depth, not be driven under, he might have a chance to exact retribution from one of them.

He spun the periscope completely around again. The aircraft might also be a problem, but the opaque Yellow Sea water was on his side. The two-stack passenger freighter was lying flat on her beam ends, stacks toward him. He could see water climbing up her deck, now vertical, which had only so recently been horizontal, pouring through deck openings into her interior. Anybody still below decks was now caught, would be unable to get out, would go down with her in the trap she had become. Her port side lay horizontal above the water. Many men were standing there, outlined against the sky. Lifeboats and life rafts hung crazily from their nests on deck, or from their davits. There had been no time to launch any of them. Her passengers and crew, the troops she carried, would be dependent for survival upon whatever wreckage broke free, of which apparently there was already a goodly amount. Land was three miles distant. They had a good chance of saving themselves if they could get free of the sinking ship, either by swimming to land or through rescue by one of the escorts. Strange. They were soldiers. He should hope they all drowned.

All this, his mind took in with instant comprehension. Number two ship had taken two hits, was down by the stern. Water was already coming up over the main deck aft. Her bow, where the upper part of a jagged hole just forward of the mast could be seen, was rising preparatory to the final plunge to the bottom.

The third ship, struck by a single torpedo, was the smallest of the three. The torpedo had hit her aft. She was stopped and also well down by the stern. Farther aft, the fourth ship, approximately similar to the last one hit, had turned course radically to the left. Belching clouds of smoke, she was obviously racing away from the carnage which had overtaken her sisters.

Farther to the left, the single escort which had been astern, an old destroyer of some kind, had apparently experienced some uncertainty but now also was turning away. Perhaps she would accompany the single undamaged ship in her flight eastward. Nothing else in sight: all was serene and calm through the remainder of the periscope's circular sweep.

Back to the escort up ahead. She was still in her turn. The aircraft was coming also, but not dead on. Evidently the pilot had no fix on *Eel*'s position. The *Mikura* frigate (if that was the correct class name) was the main concern.

"Down periscope." The tincan was a perfect shot for bow tubes, if there were but a single bow tube ready. He cursed the zig away which had forced him to change his plans at the last minute and left him without the torpedo he had planned for this eventuality.

"How much longer before we're ready to shoot forward?"

He could hear Quin repeating the question in the telephones. No answer. He knew they must be working with maximum urgency. At least one torpedo must be ready soon.

"Up periscope. Observation," he gritted. "Bearing, mark!"

"Three-four-eight," said Keith.

"Range—use forty-five feet—mark! Down periscope."

"Five hundred twenty-yards," said Keith.

"Left full rudder! New course, three-three-zero!" He needed no TDC helper for this obvious move. The less the gyro angle, the better.

Buck was frantically spinning the dials on the TDC. Keith brushed past Richardson, began spinning one of them himself.

"Angle on the bow?" said Buck.

Rich had deliberately waited, since Buck had only two hands and could only get two pieces of information into the TDC at once. Keith's help had relieved that problem.

"Port one-twenty," said Rich, "but he's turning toward. Set him up at port ninety, and I'll take another look."

The total time since the first torpedo had been fired was in the neighborhood of three minutes. Most of the time had been occupied by the necessity of turning to bring the stern tubes to bear. The Mark Eighteen torpedoes required a run of about 350 yards before the arming mechanism in the warhead rotated enough to activate the exploder. Since there were no wakes in the water, the Jap escort would not know immediately where to look for the submarine. He would instinctively reverse course, but it was possible there might be a moment or two of indecision while he searched. . . .

"Up periscope!"

"Number one tube is ready," shouted Quin.

"Observation! Bearing, mark! Range, mark! Down scope. Angle on the bow, port sixty. Turning toward." He needed the essential bits of fire control information, heard Buck set the data into the TDC.

"Set!" said Buck.

"Set depth four feet!"

"It's already set, Captain," said Keith.

"Open outer doors forward," said Rich.

"Number one outer door is open," screamed Quin, his voice pitched much higher than normal, his tenseness betraying itself in the steaming, sweating, densely packed conning tower.

"Stand by forward," said Richardson. Suddenly he felt calm. This was the time to be deliberate. This one shot must be a good one. He would leave the periscope up and aim the torpedo deliberately.

"Number two tube is loaded, Captain. Depth set four feet. You have two fish ready forward." Keith's voice.

"Bearing, mark! He's still turning. Angle on the bow, port forty-five."

"Zero-one-zero!"

"Set," said Buck. "I'm following him around."

"Short-scale pinging, bearing three-four-oh!" Stafford.

"Check fire!" roared Keith. "Correct solution light has gone out!"

"Down 'scope," said Richardson, almost wearily. The chance was gone. Obviously, with the destroyer swinging toward, the distance the torpedo would run before hitting would be too short to arm it. "Shut the outer doors," he ordered.

"He's starting a run! Shifted to short-scale pinging!" This was Stafford, repeating himself at the sound gear. His voice also was elevated a notch.

"Rig for depth charge," said Richardson, knowing well that the ship was already fully rigged for depth charge except that the control room hatch had not been closed. Torpedoes in the forward and after torpedo rooms, however, were in the process of being reloaded. "Quin," he said swiftly, "forward and after rooms! Secure for depth charging immediately."

Wide-eyed, Quin repeated his orders into the telephone.

"Shut the lower hatch," he ordered. Someone in the control room, probably Al Dugan, pulled the oblong hatch down on its lanyard. Scott leaped on it, kicked the handles shut. Unlike the hatch to the bridge, it was not fitted with a hand wheel.

Blunt's voice from the forward part of the conning tower, "Aren't we going deep, Rich?"

He had forgotten the wolfpack commander. During the entire time Blunt had stood holding on to the hatch lanyard under the bridge hatch. It was too late now to permit him to go below, even had he been willing to do so, or had Richardson been willing to spend the effort to convince him to do so.

"We'll take this one at periscope depth," announced Richardson. "He'll figure we've gone deep and will set his depth charges deep. Maybe after he passes we'll get a chance for another shot." He crowded over alongside of Stafford, just forward of number one periscope. Silently, Stafford indicated a section of the dial to which his sound head arrow was oriented.

"There he is, sir. Short-scale pinging. He's speeded up!"

"He may not have seen the periscope, but if he did, he'll figure we've gone deep now. As soon as he goes by, we'll try to line him up for a stern shot!" Richardson spoke in answer to the thought wave he felt hurled at him from everyone in the conning tower. If *Eel* could survive this first quick attack at periscope depth he might be able to get a shot off while the destroyer was getting ready for a second. All depended upon being able to get that periscope up for an observation, upon the likelihood that the tincan might have to wait a few moments for the disturbance of her depth charges to die away before she could regain contact. There might also be the necessity to do some reloading of depth charges in her launchers. He did not mention the airplane. It could not see beneath the surface. Not in the Yellow Sea. The only danger from it was a few additional bombs or depth charges dropped in the wake of the escort's barrage. Of course, if it sighted his periscope at the crucial moment when he had it up to aim the torpedo . . . He left the thought unfinished.

The sonar dial was calibrated in relative bearing, but through a connection with the submarine's gyro compass a second dial, concentric with the first, gave true bearing as well.

"True bearings!" he snapped to Stafford.

"Three-three-five, steady on three-three-five," repeated Stafford. Rich's instinctive selection of course 330 for a minimum gyro had been a good one.

"Make your course three-three-five!" ordered Richardson. "All ahead full!"

194

"What are you going to do, Rich?" Blunt again. His voice was almost squeaky.

"I'm going to run right under him at full speed! At this short range and with depth charges going off, he'll lose contact anyway. Maybe we can catch him by surprise and get through the barrage before he's able to drop them all," answered Rich, forcing himself to speak normally instead of in the clipped tones he had almost used. He must not betray his own inner tension. If only Blunt would keep quiet! "Quin!" he said, "Tubes aft, report on condition of their reload."

In a moment the report came back. "All tubes secured aft," relayed Quin. "Tube ten was not fired. Tube seven has been reloaded, but is not ready yet. All the other fish are secured in their racks."

"Very well," said Richardson. "Tell tubes aft to turn to on that fish and get it ready. We'll need it as soon as the depth charge barrage is over. Set depth on both, four feet." He looked up at Scott. "Speed through water?" he asked.

"Four knots, increasing. We're steady on three-three-five."

Rich picked up a spare set of earphones, adjusted them to his head. The penetrating, high-pitched echo-ranging was clearly audible even before he put them on. Stafford was moving the sound head dome ceaselessly back and forth over a small arc concentrated right around *Eel*'s bow. He said something which Richardson could not hear. Rich moved his left-hand earphone over to his cheek, freed the ear. "Bearing three-three-five," said Stafford. "Steady bearing. He's close aboard now. He'll be dropping any second."

Richardson could hear the whir of the screws. One of them must be bent slightly askew, for the thrashing sound of the damaged blade could plainly be distinguished. He could almost hear the rush of water past the enemy hull, visualize the concentration on her bridge as they calculated the optimum time for dropping the depth charges. Hopefully, his maneuver of turning toward and speeding up would take them unawares. Suddenly he found himself remembering the nearly identical situation years ago off New London, when, by miscalculation of one of the student officers out for a day's training, the old U.S. destroyer *Semmes* with her knifelike bow and the two huge propellers extending below her keel had come near to knocking Richardson's first command, the *S-16*, into oblivion on the bottom of Long Island Sound. *Semmes* also had had a nick in one propeller. *S-16*'s periscopes were not, however, as long as *Eel*'s. There was now a full eighteen feet of water between the surface and the highest point of *Eel*'s structure. The *Mikura* could not draw more than ten. Fifteen at the outside. As soon as he passed overhead, *Eel* would slow down again and try to catch him with a stern tube.

Funny he should think of it. That was the day Jim Bledsoe had introduced him to Laura.

Stafford had been rapidly increasing the width of the arc covered by his sound head. The pings were coming in with undiminished strength no matter in what direction it was trained. Richardson could almost hear the echo bounce off *Eel*'s steel hull, even imagined he could hear a second echo reflected off the hull of the attacking destroyer. Here it comes, he thought. Idiotically, he remembered a line from one of his favorite books about sea fights in the days of sail. "For what we are about to receive," one of the characters used to say, "O Lord, we give thanks."

Stafford ran the sound head all the way around the dial. "He's overhead," he said. Richardson did not need this information, for suddenly the entire interior of *Eel*'s conning tower reverberated with the roaring of machinery, the sibilant rush of water past a fast-moving hull, the spitting thum, thum, thum of propeller blades whirling pitilessly in the water, one of them carrying a scar which made a sort of crackling sound as it went around. There was a vibration communicated to the structure of the conning tower. Richardson could feel the submarine shudder, move bodily in the water, as the enemy ship drove by.

"He's dropped," shouted Stafford. The sonar man reached up to his receiver controls, abruptly turned down the volume. The next second or two would determine whether *Eel* sank or survived. If the depth charges were set shallow, a thunderous explosion and tremendously increased air pressure coincident with the sudden roaring influx of water—or equally serious, a sudden extraordinary heaviness as water poured in through a hole in a more remote portion of the submarine—would signal the end for everyone.

Five seconds, ten seconds. . . . *Click,* WHAM! *Click,* WHAM! *Click,* WHAM! The depth charges sounded right alongside, tremendously loud in the tense stillness inside the submarine. A slight pause, then a crashing cacophony of brutal, ear-smashing noise as a whole barrage went off almost simultaneously. A cloud of dust was thrown up in the conning tower. The deck plates under their feet were shivering. The entire submarine hull resounded, reverberated, intensified the concussions. The long thin hoist rods of the periscopes vibrated madly, almost passing out of sight. Richardson could have sworn the periscopes themselves sprang out of shape and then returned. He was shaken so violently that for a second he must have become hallucinatory. He thought he saw the steering wheel knocked loose from the forward bulkhead of the conning tower, where Cornelli stood holding it, arms rigid and muscles bulging under his sweaty dungarees. Then, just as swiftly, Rich realized the wheel was still intact, in place where it should have been.

WHAMWHAMWHAMWHAMWHAMWHAM! Six more depth charges going off almost together! Again the shivering of the steel, the bewildering effect of heavy equipment apparently disoriented, which, if it were true, would signal the destruction of the submarine. Pieces of cork flew off the sides of the conning tower. Dust rose throughout. Miraculously, the lights stayed on, dancing on their short wire pigtails. Quin, standing just forward of the opening of the deck which led to the now closed control room hatch, was knocked to his knees, fell into the cavity.

"All compartments report," said Richardson. "All stop!"

Quin painfully picked up his telephone mouthpiece, spoke into it.

Cornelli clicked the annunciators to stop. The follower pointers, actuated from the maneuvering room, clicked over also to stop. Good, thought Richardson. At least they're okay back there.

"All back two-thirds! Speed through water!"

Scott, who had been recording with a pencil on one of the pages of his quartermaster's notebook, read the dial for him. "Five knots," he said. "Twenty depth charges."

"Let me know when speed reaches three knots," said Richardson. "Tubes aft, bear a hand with number seven tube."

"All compartments report no damage," said Quin. There was relief in his voice. "Tubes aft will be ready with number seven in a minute."

"Three knots," said Scott.

"All stop," said Richardson. "All ahead one-third! Number two periscope!"

He grabbed the handles as they came out of the periscope well, savagely spun the periscope all the way around until it faced aft, put his eye to it. "There he is!" he said. "Bearing, mark!"

"One-eight-one," from Keith.

"Angle on the bow one-eight-oh," said Richardson. Range, mark!" He turned the range dial.

"Two hundred," said Keith.

"Open outer doors aft," ordered Rich. "As soon as he turns one way or the other, we'll shoot. Buck," he went on, "give him a one-seven-nine-degree port angle on the bow, speed nineteen!"

Once more, for a few seconds, *Eel* had the initiative. He spun the periscope around rapidly, flipping it to low power in order to get a larger field of view. As before, heightened with the perceptions of imminent danger and immediate combat, his mind took in everything almost photographically. His first target had sunk perceptibly lower in the water and had rolled over even farther, so that, although not quite turned turtle, it might well be on the way to doing so. Its stern had sunk beneath the water, but the bow, probably held up by an air pocket, remained partly above the surface. Crowds of men were standing on the curved plates where her side joined her bottom, and crowds of black dots, the heads of men, were in the water around her. The second freighter was straight up and down, her bow silhouetted against the western horizon. Deck equipment, displaced from its normal position, was falling from a height of a hundred feet on both sides. Most of it fell into the area where her now submerged smokestack and deckhouse lay, and where most of the survivors also must be. One of the objects moved as it fell. Perhaps he had jumped.

The third ship, still more or less on an even keel, was sinking too, but more slowly. Her stern had sunk to the water's edge, and around the bow Rich could see ten feet or more of red underwater paint. She had had time to get lifeboats out, and Rich could see two of them already in the water, apparently picking up other crew members.

Most important of all, however, was the appearance of the lead escort. The frigate which had been patrolling ahead of the two-stacked passenger cargo ship had headed over in the direction of her consort. Still some distance away, she was heading directly for *Eel*, zero angle on the bow, would be dropping her own depth charges in a couple of minutes. He swung back to the destroyer which had just depth charged him.

"He's swinging to his left. Stand by aft. Open outer doors aft. Range, mark!"

"Four-seven-five," said Keith. "Bearing one-eight-zero."

"Angle on the bow, port one-seventy. He's turning left. Crank in port one-two-oh, Buck." The TDC dials whirled.

"No spread, Keith. We'll shoot on periscope bearings as soon as you get your correct solution light."

"Tubes ready aft," announced Keith.

"Set," from Buck.

"Correct solution light aft!"

The computer in Richardson's brain was in command. His cross hair exactly bisected the bridge of the tincan. She was a war-built escort, nearly the equivalent of a destroyer. Designed particularly for anti-submarine work. Diesel-powered. Capable of at least twenty knots, maybe more. She was swinging left now, swinging a little more.

"Echo-ranging from aft. Long-scale pinging." Stafford. "Echo-ranging forward also. Long-scale pinging forward and aft." This must be the second escort.

"Stand by number ten," said Richardson again. ". . . Fire!" The jerk as the torpedo started on its way. "Stand by number seven," he said. "I think he's slowed down. Give him fifteen knots!" The probability was that the tincan had reduced speed more than this, but her initial way would carry her on. He was gratified to see that she continued to turn to the left, that her angle on the bow had now approached his advanced estimate of 120 port. "Set in angle on the bow port ninety," he said.

"Set!" from Buck.

"Light!" from Keith.

"Mark the bearing!"

"One-seven-two-a-half!"

"Set!"

"Fire!" he snapped a second time.

Maybe there would be time to do something about the other escort. He swung the periscope around. "New setup," he said. "Angle on the bow zero, bearing, mark!"

"Zero-zero-five," from Keith.

"Range, mark!"

"One thousand yards!"

"Stand by forward." There was some delay. Buck must be cranking his dials like mad. Keith's voice in his ear: "Outer doors opened forward, Captain. Ready to shoot forward. Tubes one and two. Ready with tube one."

"Set," again from Buck.

"Shooting observation!" said Richardson. "Bearing, mark! . . . Fire!" Again the jolt as the torpedo went out. Again the hiss of air, the rumble of water counterflooding the tube. One torpedo left. He aimed a little right of the onrushing escort. "Fire!" he barked for a fourth time in the space of forty seconds. He swung the periscope around once again, passed the sinking ships in a blur of kaleidoscopic disaster, settled on the escort vessel astern. He got there just in time to see a plume of water rise up amidships. At the close range, the reverberating roar of four hundred pounds of torpex arrived almost simultaneously with the sight. The torpedo must have gone off directly underneath the center of the ship, for it lifted her up amidships, irresistibly, like a huge, powerful plunger. She broke into halves. Her bow plunged downward on one side of the plume. Her stern slid down the other. In the middle of the catastrophe a mixed cloud of smoke, water, steam and debris continued to rise into the heavens. Then the water, and what had been a fine new ship, subsided, shrank swiftly down into nothingness, leaving only a pall of black smoke and huge ripples rapidly eddying from the center of the disaster. Black dust on a white disk in a mud-gray sea.

No time to play the spectator. He swung the periscope rapidly around—the other way this time (still all clear)—to the other escort coming in from ahead. She had put her rudder hard over, was already heeling far to starboard, swinging sharply to her left, in a violent emergency turn. He should never have fired at her. He should have known she would maneuver in automatic reflex to the hit on her consort. The geometry of that hastily conceived last-minute shot was totally destroyed, the torpedoes wasted. He swung the periscope farther left; as he expected, there came the third *Mikura*, hastening over to join her fellows, now reduced from two to only one.

Time to do one more thing. "Here, Keith," he said, "you have time for a quick look." He swung the periscope to the leading ship. Only a small section of her bow still protruded above the surface.

"Commodore," he called. Blunt was alongside of him. Keith swung the periscope back and forth twice, lingered for a moment in the direction of the fourth and last ship in the column, now fleeing in the distance accompanied by a single escort. He stepped away from the periscope. Blunt fixed his eye to it, eagerly duplicated Keith's maneuver.

"What's the tincan doing on our starboard bow, Commodore?" said Rich. He grabbed the handles of the periscope on the opposite side from where Blunt was looking, turned it around to the approximate bearing of the last escort.

"Angle on the bow is starboard ninety," said Blunt. "Range"—he fumbled for the dial, turned it. Rich performed Keith's function, read the dial for him. "Seven-five-oh yards," he said.

Buck, in his eagerness, could hardly keep himself from reaching for the periscope handles. Gently Richardson pulled Blunt away, propelled Buck to the periscope. Larry Lasche's eyes were also alight with hope for a view, but regretfully Richardson shook his head. He allowed Buck no more than ten seconds, time for one quick sweep past the destroyed convoy, took it back himself, spun it around twice, lowered it. "Make your depth two hundred feet," he ordered. "Pass the word to all compartments we have sunk three cargo ships and one escort, and we'll probably hear many more depth charges before this day is over."

He suddenly realized he was sweating profusely. Keith and Buck were no better. Their faces were beaded, as his must be. The temperature in the conning tower had climbed to well over 100 degrees, and the humidity, with all the vapor-producing, perspiring bodies filling it, must be 100 percent. The deck plates beneath his feet, once Scott's pride for their immaculate condition, were a quarter of an inch deep in muck. Globules of moisture were condensed on the conning tower's cold sides (anywhere the careful cork insulation was violated) or on exposed metal—the periscopes—which elsewhere was cooled by contact with sea water. Added to this was the perspiration which had dripped off their bodies and the debris which the near depth charges had discovered in the nominally clean compartment. All this had landed on the deck. They had been shuffling through it for what seemed like an age.

He was astonished to realize that from the time of initially sighting the convoy, only a little more than half an hour had passed.

At the ordered depth, two hundred feet, there was barely fifty to seventy-five feet of water beneath *Eel*. Richardson debated taking a sounding, finally decided he would risk it during a depth-charge attack, should another one eventuate. Until then the need to know whether one could go a few feet deeper was less important than the chance that taking the sounding would reveal *Eel*'s position to a now alert sonarman in one of the two remaining *Mikuras*.

But, though the screws and pinging of the two frigates could be heard for some time, *Eel* gradually crept away to the northwest, running as silently and as deep as she could. There was never any indication that the enemy antisubmarine vessels had ever regained contact, or even had tried very hard. Perhaps, as Al Dugan suggested during one of their postmortems later on, the fate that befell one of their number cooled off the ardor for battle of the other two.

8

66 Here, Nelson," said Keith, handing the tall chief radioman an encoded message. "See if you can wake up the boys at NPM with this one."

Nelson grinned as he took the paper. "There's about twenty boats trying to wake up Radio Pearl every night," he said. "It's not their sleepiness that bothers us. It's the competition."

Keith returned the humorous look. "You radio girls all stick together. Anyway, this one ought to give them a little fun back there in Com-SubPac." He took the spare set of ear phones which Nelson, in anticipation of a message to be sent after surfacing that evening, had already plugged in for him. Instantly his mind was catapulted out of the surfaced submarine into a suddenly expanded geography covering the entire Pacific Ocean. Somewhere—the signal was so clear it was perhaps only a few hundred miles away—another submarine was sending a long varying note as it tuned up its transmitter. The radioman made a grimace of disparagement. Swiftly, as Keith looked approvingly, Nelson completed a few last-minute adjustments to *Eel*'s transmitter, finally looked over to Keith for permission to make a test transmission. Keith nodded. A few swift taps on the tuning key—Nelson was well aware of the danger from Japanese direction-finding stations—he nodded readiness.

The other boat was transmitting, using a coded call sign: "NPM V W3AU K—NPM V W3AU K." Keith had developed sufficient familiarity with Morse code to be able to understand the repeated short message. Nelson waited, his hand poised over his own transmitter key. Much farther away, another boat was calling NPM and, sounding as though it must be at least a thousand miles away, the dim crackle of a distant transmitter could barely be heard: a fourth submarine calling Radio Pearl.

Nelson was gently fingering his receiver tuning control. Faintly, Keith could hear through the welter a dim but precise note. "W3AU V NPM 3," it said. Radio Pearl had answered the unknown submarine whose coded call sign was W3AU, telling it that it was third in line for receipt of a message.

Keith motioned to Nelson, but Nelson had already begun tapping out, in the smooth, effortless rhythm of a practiced radioman, *Eel*'s own call-up. "NPM V 68TC OP K," he repeated several times.

Radio Pearl seemed suddenly to have a surge of strength. "68TC V NPM K," said the signal. Keith and Nelson grinned at each other. The Japanese radio station would have to use far better techniques than this to masquerade as Radio Pearl. A sub not alert to the ploy might transmit its message at a time when Pearl Harbor could not receive it, get a routine-sounding receipt from the Japanese station, and secure its transmission thinking its message had been delivered when in fact it had not. This was the simplest of electronic warfare techniques. Once, hearing a boat being taken in, a smart NPM operator disrupted his own orderly procedure to copy the unwary submarine's message and thus foiled the Japanese station's attempt at interference. But one could not be sure of this sort of good luck. " . . . NPM 4," said the distant station.

"NPM V 68TC OP K," rapped out Nelson rapidly. The Pearl Harbor operator would very likely have heard the alien station attempting to entice *Eel* into transmitting its message at a time when Radio Pearl was not ready to receive it, would recognize that *Eel* had by consequence been unable to hear all of NPM's transmission and was asking for its repetition. He, too, transmitted more rapidly.

"68TC V NPM 4," he sent. Keith would have been unable to read it had he not known what to expect.

Nelson pushed a button alongside his transmitting key. With a *thunk*, the power hum in the transmitter standing behind them went silent. Quickly he brought his log up to date on the typewriter in the well before him. Keith noted with approval that he was preparing to copy the message from the nearby submarine.

The cryptic procedure message from the Pearl Harbor radio station had signaled the unknown nearby submarine that it was third in line to be serviced. *Eel* was fourth. Keith stared unseeingly at the radio equipment about him. Far away in the distance, he could hear the tiny dots and dashes from a distant submarine tremulously pounding out its message. Several times it had to stop and repeat, finally received the sought-for R from Radio Pearl. Then it was the turn of another submarine, perhaps a thousand miles in a different direction, also sending in its vital information to the central gathering point, finally the submarine identified as W3AU. It was not a lengthy message, and Nelson had far less difficulty in copying it, since it was so near, than the NPM operator. Keith judged the unknown sub was not more than two or three hundred miles away. Very possibly it was the *Whitefish*, an identification which would be discovered when the call was broken down and the message decoded. Nelson, no doubt, could identify not only the sub but also the operator, if it happened to be one of the many whose "hand" he knew.

The next submarine to transmit would be *Eel*. Nelson pressed his transmitter button, had it humming and fully warmed up when Radio Pearl receipted to the nearby boat.

"68TC V NMP K," said NPM.

"NPM V 68TC OP—RADIO PEARL FROM EEL PRIORITY ACTION REPORT . . ."

As Nelson pounded out the coded message, laboriously composed and then encoded while *Eel* was awaiting the time to surface, Keith could reflect that across three thousand miles of water, bouncing at least once off the ionosphere now lowered over the dark Pacific, this particular stream of rapid dots and dashes carried the news of the death of four ships and most of those on board. It told of *Eel's* own escape after minor depth charging, the possibility that some other submarine, possibly *Whitefish*, might have been in position to pick off the lone straggler which had escaped to the west. It stated that *Eel* was now down to seven torpedoes, two forward and five aft, and that ComSubPac was undoubtedly correct about ships moving north and south close in to land along the west coast of Korea. On the game board in ComSubPac's office in Hawaii, the little submarine silhouette marked "*Eel*" in the Yellow Sea would now have seven tiny Japanese flags attached to it. If w3AU was indeed the *Whitefish*, it was possible that she might have earned a second little flag added to her silhouette, if she had, as instructed, been patrolling outside the island chain directly westward of *Eel*.

The message sent and NPM's R having been received, Keith nodded his thanks to Nelson, hung up his earphones, picked up his papers and the intercepted message—Nelson was certain it was indeed from *Whitefish*—and started back to the wardroom. There, he knew, one of the interminably long conversations with the wolfpack commander was undoubtedly taking place. He had, however, hardly moved forward into the control room when it was apparent the uneventful night he had been anticipating was not to be. Dimly, through two open hatches, he heard Al Dugan's "Clear the bridge!" Simultaneously the diving alarm rang twice. Men came jumping down from above. "Dive! Dive!" shouted Al, nearer. He must now be scrambling through the hatch, latching it behind him. "Take her down! Take her down fast!"

Almost instantaneously the three red lights in the "Hull Opening Indicator Panel"—the "Christmas Tree"—for the three main engines in use winked off, to be replaced by green ones just below. Starberg, on watch on the hydraulic manifold, had already yanked open all the main vent valves. As the last engine exhaust valve went shut on the Christmas Tree, he slammed closed the main induction. Then, leaning aft a foot, he grabbed another lever and pulled it forward. This would start the bow planes rigging out to their submerged attitude. In the meantime, *Eel*'s deck tilted downward. The annunciators clicked to "ahead full" as the electricians in the maneuvering room, with hardly a pause in the rotation of *Eel*'s main motors, connected the battery to them and went to full speed ahead.

"Hatch secured!" shouted Al from the conning tower. Seconds later his sturdy legs appeared through the hatch as he jumped down into the control room. Glimpsing Keith, he hurriedly said, "Aircraft! Right up the moon streak! Close!"

"Last sounding was two hundred feet," said Keith. "That checks with our posit on the chart. Better hold her at one hundred fifty feet."

"Full dive on all planes," ordered Al. "Make your depth one-five-oh feet. Ten degrees down angle! Come on, men! Lean into those wheels!"

The lookouts, still clothed with their foul-weather gear in anticipation of a night watch on the surface, obviously needed little urging from the diving officer. Not bothering to divest themselves of any of their bridge equipment, casting worried glances at the slowly moving depth gauges, they were trying to twist the diving plane control wheels off the diving panel.

"Rig for depth charge!" shouted Al.

Keith lunged for the speaker button on the ship's announcing system, pulled it down, spoke into it, trying to give his voice a calm tone despite the surge of adrenalin he could feel running through his system. "Rig ship for depth charge," he said. "Shut all watertight doors!" He could hear the watertight doors slamming throughout the ship.

Quin appeared, picked up the battle telephone headset, adjusted it on his head. "All stations report from forward aft," he said. He listened a moment. "Ship is rigged for depth charge, Mr. Leone," he said.

"What is it, Keith?" Richardson had apparently come from the forward battery compartment into the control room just before the watertight door was closed.

Briefly Keith explained, "We're under now, sir," he said, watching the depth gauges.

"That was a fast dive, Al. How close do you think the plane was?"

"Close!" said Al. "Coming right at us! We must have been silhouetted in the moon streak. It's a good thing we had the quartermaster and two lookouts concentrating on it astern."

"Good work, Al," said Rich. "We'll know soon enough if he dropped on us."

WHAM . . . WHAM! The submarine's sturdy hull twanged with the reverberations. The tense group in the control room could feel the deck lift under them. Bits of cork flew through the air; the electric lights, hanging on short pieces of wire from their sockets, danced crazily.

"Passing seven-oh feet, Captain," said Al. "I think both of those went off astern."

Richardson said, "We'd better stay on at full speed for a little while in case he comes around for a second run. He probably dropped a flare to mark our position, but with all that juice we took out of the can today we've got to slow down as soon as possible." He thought a moment. "What course were you on when you dived, Al?"

"I was headed right up moon, nearly due south, Skipper," said Dugan. "Keith said a north or south course would give us the best radio signal to Pearl. South was against the current, and minimum silhouette across the moon streak, too. Maybe this fellow came in on our radio beam. He came right up our tail, low to the water. There were no APR signals or anything!"

There had been the usual discussion before surfacing. Perhaps Richardson should not have brought up his proposal that they move rapidly northward. Blunt had almost automatically opposed it. The lack of strong countermeasures by the convoy escorts, he said, was according to a pattern ComSubPac had observed from analysis of hundreds of patrol reports. Transmitting a lengthy radio message while making high speed would alert enemy DF stations as to their intended movements. The argument was cut short by the wolfpack commander in the manner recently more and more of a pattern of his own: having delivered his dictum, he rose and left the wardroom.

Possibly the aircraft had been sent by a vector from a shore DF station, but not likely. The coordination would have had to be too good, too swift. Most probably the immediate reaction to *Eel's* attack on the convoy had been to establish a night aircraft patrol. A combination of an accurate estimate as to the sub's later movements, plus a bit of luck, perhaps even a small direction finder in the plane, had brought it overhead. The obviously hurried nature of its depth bomb attack supported the hypothesis. Now, however, perhaps the incident could be turned to advantage. Remaining in the vicinity was out of the question. But no further discussion. Seize the opportunity.

"As soon as you're down to depth, Al, reverse course to north. Maintain full speed for ten minutes and then slow again to one-third. The current will give us a four-knot boot in the tail. The flare will of course drift with the surface current, but the wind will affect it also. It can't burn forever. The plane's navigation probably won't allow for current at all, unless he's a lot smarter than I think he is."

Quin had been listening attentively through his earphones. Now he spoke. "All compartments report no damage," he said.

"Well, Commodore," said Richardson a few minutes later, "it looks as though we've alerted this area pretty thoroughly. That fellow was obviously out looking for us, and he darned near caught us. As it was, that was one of the fastest dives this ship has ever made, about thirty seconds."

"Um," said Blunt, taking his pipe from his mouth and sipping a mug of coffee. "Who have you got working on that message you picked up just before we dived?"

"We broke out Larry to do it. He was setting it up a few minutes ago, and we should have the decode any minute."

The message said: ATTACKED TEN THOUSAND TON FREIGHTER X ONE HIT X PROBABLY SUNK X DEPTH CHARGED X WHITEFISH SERIAL TWO X SIXTEEN TORPEDOES REMAINING X

"Why didn't he report this to me?" Blunt said.

"Maybe he tried before we surfaced, Commodore," Rich said swiftly. "The best time to get the messages off to Pearl is right after surfacing, but we were late coming up tonight. Keith says he was on the circuit before we were. I'll bet he's still trying to get us on the wolfpack frequency right now."

"Um," said Blunt again, apparently at least partly convinced. "That's probably the ship that got away from you. It must have been the biggest one of the lot."

In Richardson's opinion, the freighter was nearer to five thousand than ten thousand tons, but there was no point in bringing this up.

Surfacing the *Eel* was a long and careful procedure, involving thorough sonar search before coming to periscope depth, and then a long careful search for aircraft through two periscopes before tanks were blown. Once surfaced, two main engines and the auxiliary were placed on the battery charge and the remaining two main engines, to be augmented by a third as soon as the charging rate permitted it, at full power on propulsion.

A simple one-letter signal on the wolfpack administration frequency brought an immediate response from the *Whitefish*. The message obviously was in her radio room awaiting the call: ATTACKED ESCORTED FREIGHTER COURSE WEST SPEED FIFTEEN POSITION GERTRUDE 43 TIME 1950 SUBMERGED STERN TUBES DURING TWILIGHT FOUR TORPEDOES EXPENDED SIXTEEN REMAIN X CLOSE DEPTH CHARGE ATTACK POSSIBLE DAMAGE RETIRING TO AREA CENTER FOR EVALUATION X

"Maybe we had better do the same," said the wolfpack commander in a thoughtful tone. "The Japs know there is a submarine in the Maikotsu Suido. They probably won't send anything through here for a while."

Richardson had his answer ready. "They've got to send their ships somewhere. Those they can send into port, or keep there, they will. A number are probably already en route, however, and so tomorrow they'll saturate the area with air and surface patrols. The plane that bombed us proves they've also got night air patrols out. He's probably already radioed in his report, giving our position and our course as south at slow speed, so if we're lucky they may think we're planning to stay in this vicinity. It makes sense, because that's where we found the ships. Tomorrow, when they get no sign of us, they'll think we're lying low, probably heading west."

"So why don't we head west right now, before another plane comes out and makes us dive again?"

"Because that's just what they'll expect us to do. That's where the night patrol planes will concentrate. For sure, they won't send any convoys of ships outside the Maikotsu. Don't forget, *Whitefish* got that freighter outside the island yesterday. They'll stop what ships they can, but the rest they'll run as close to the coast as possible, and under maximum protection."

"What are you figuring to do? They must by now realize there is more than one submarine here."

"They'll concentrate all available forces here, and that means there'll be less available for other areas. The chart we got from that patrol boat shows a place up to the north where, for a short distance, they have to round a point of land. At that spot there are no more inshore islands to run behind. It will take all the speed we have to get there, if we're lucky enough to stay on the surface until dawn, and we'll have to finish the run submerged in the morning. The current will be a big help. . . ." He let the sentence trail off.

Indefinably, he began to feel a surge of confidence as he spoke. Blunt was listening. There was a weariness in Blunt's face and around his eyes, combined with something else—relief; he did not have to think; the operation of a single submarine was strictly the responsibility of its captain, so long as it remained compatible with the larger responsibilities of the wolfpack. It would be easy to let Richardson have his way. To make any speed submerged—to get the most benefit from the helping current—would require remaining well below periscope depth: a morning free from worries, free for a good long sleep. Blunt's face showed the struggle for decisiveness. The normally bright lights in the wardroom had been turned down. The resulting shadows reflected the play in his sagging jowels. "All right," he said.

Carefully, Rich kept his own face expressionless. "Aye aye, sir," he replied. Too much enthusiasm might still cause Blunt to reverse the assent just given. Worse, it might jeopardize the second part of the idea he had been mulling over. Whatever convoy-control organization the enemy had would hardly permit convoys to move for the next several days, but single ships might be handled differently. They might not even be under centralized control at all. If *Eel* could get far enough away from the carnage of the previous day, she might find small-scale local traffic still moving, as yet unaware of the sinkings to the south. This would be the chance to restore Blunt. Richardson had convinced himself that the crux of Blunt's problem was lack of confidence, based on never having commanded a submarine in combat. This he could, just conceivably, do something about. The total reversal in Blunt that very day, when in desperation Rich had given him the periscope, had been the clue. It would not, after all, be much different from letting Keith Leone or Al Dugan bring *Eel* alongside a dock, or make a submerged approach during training.

It would take careful planning, the right arguments to make to the commodore, and a considerable degree of luck to bring it off. It made no demands on anyone, except himself and Blunt, and required only a little cooperation from the enemy. It was worth a try.

Eel dived before dawn, with the outline of a peninsula and the relatively large island directly to the west of it clear on the radar. Keith had not had time for his customary morning star sights, but these were unnecessary since the radar range on land provided an accurate position. There was still some distance to go before *Eel* could reach the position selected: in the center and deepest portion of a small body of water, roughly defined by the peninsula to the north, the outlying island to the northwest, the coast of Korea on the eastern side and, far to the south, the northernmost island of the chain demarking the Maikotsu Suido.

Richardson had gambled on his certainty that Blunt could not resist the bait if offered in the right way. Finally, a conditional acceptance in his grasp, he had managed to talk Blunt into turning in. In a short time he, too, would lie down and seek a couple of hours' rest. It had been an exhausting night with an exhausting day preceding. His knees and thigh muscles ached from the combined effect of the bruises inflicted by Moonface and his own rigorous stint on the periscope less than twelve hours before. There was still blood in his urine, and the yellow, blue, and purple bruises all over his body were still as vivid as ever. He gave careful instructions to Keith, Al, and Buck for running toward the selected spot and, once there, setting a periscope watch. Then at last he sat on his bunk, removed his shoes, lay back with a sigh of relaxation.

Someone was pounding on the aluminum bulkhead of his stateroom alongside the green baize curtain. "You're wanted in the conning tower, Captain," said the messenger. "Smoke on the horizon!"

He hadn't expected it this soon. He was instantly wide awake, yawning nevertheless, glanced at the clock on the bulkhead. Both hands stood straight up and down. He had been asleep—or rather, totally unconscious—for at least five hours! It was good of Keith to let him rest so long. Swiftly he pulled on his shoes, knotted the strings, stepped into the passageway, through the watertight door, around the control room table, and up the ladder into the conning tower.

"What is it, Keith?" he said, as his head came up through the hatch.

"Smoke, bearing southeast," said the executive officer. "It's coming this way, I think."

A quick look through the periscope showed a faint brown smudge in the indicated direction. Rich spun the periscope around rapidly, settled back to inspect the smoke one more time. Alongside him Keith said, "We're running at sixty-five feet, with only about a foot and a half of periscope out. It's almost a flat calm out here, as you can see. And so far this morning, we've seen the same airplane three times."

Rich lowered the periscope. "What bearing?" he asked.

"To the south. Some distance away. It's patrolling, I think."

"Good," said Rich. "If they're patrolling south of us, it means they don't think we've come this far north."

"I figure the same," said Keith. "So I let the current carry us up inshore of that outlying island. We're about eighty-five hundred yards off the tip of the point now, but there's plenty of sea room north and south, and to the west. The island bears southwest, but it's out of sight unless we come up a couple of feet."

"Good," said Rich again. "When did you see the plane last?"

"About an hour ago. He came up from the south, turned around, and flew back."

"Good," said Richardson for the third time. "If we're lucky, his coverage won't extend this far to the north. Maybe there won't even be any coverage over this ship if he comes up this way."

"That's a lot to hope for, Skipper," grinned Keith. Then, with a more sober expression, he asked, "Are you going to try that business with Captain Blunt? Isn't this rather soon after yesterday?"

"This may be the chance. Maybe it is a little soon, but that might just be the best way."

Another periscope observation confirmed that the source of the smoke was approaching. Soon, several looks later, three masts could be seen.

"Send for the commodore, Keith," said Rich, the upper part of his face still pressed into the rubber periscope eye guard. "This one is for him."

The periscope down, Richardson gravely reached over the TDC, where, around one of the knurled knobs securing its face, the white celluloid "Is-Was" hung on a string. Only a few years ago, this and the now obsolete "banjo" had been the only fire control instruments available to a submarine. The Torpedo Data Computer had replaced it in the so-called fleet boats, of which *Eel* was one of the newer representatives. By consequence, the Is-Was had become primarily a badge of office for the assistant approach officer (usually the executive officer), whose duty it was to assure that all matters relating to the approach were properly carried out, that the check-off lists were executed on time, and that the submarine commander was instantly apprised of all the information required to bring the submarine into a successful attack position. This had, of course, been Keith's function; and Richardson himself had performed it many times in drill, first for Joe Blunt and later for Jerry Watson in the *Octopus*.

As he passed the loop of the cord attached to the Is-Was around his head he felt a curious melting away of the years. Symbolically, with the donning of the badge of office, he had traveled backward in time.

The wolfpack commander was hurrying up the ladder into the conning tower. "What is it, Rich?" he said.

"Smoke on the horizon, Captain. Bearing is one-five-oh. I think we see masts of two ships down there." Richardson had deliberately used the old title of long-ago memories. "We've put the boat on course one-five-oh, so they're dead ahead. I've just taken a look around. There's nothing in sight on any other bearing. We're four miles off the beach, but there's plenty of sea room except to the east. The ship is obviously rounding this point of land. Also, we've sighted aircraft three times to the south this morning. It was last seen about an hour ago, evidently carrying out an antisub sweep. Estimated closest point of approach was about ten miles, and I think we're outside the limit of his search pattern. It looks like two ships up ahead, one smoking fairly heavily. The other one is smaller and is probably an escort of some kind."

As he spoke, Richardson had been fumbling with the dials on the Is-Was, putting the setup on it. He held it out so that Blunt could see. In the meantime Keith had slipped behind them to the rear of the conning tower, where he busied himself with setting up the situation statically on the TDC, not yet turning it on.

"The periscope is on the bearing of the target, Captain," Rich said. "It's been three minutes since the last observation."

The inference was too strong, the hint too obvious, the playing of the role too natural and direct. Almost instinctively, and obviously without giving it any analysis other than that the situation seemed to call for, Blunt gave the order which was so strongly indicated. "Up periscope," he said.

Richardson arranged himself on the opposite side of the periscope, squatting on his heels, flipped the handles down when it came out of the well, carefully kept his hands well inside the control ends of the periscope handles. Almost from reflex action, Blunt also squatted down, put his hands on the outer ends of the control handles as Rich flipped them into position, fixed his eye to the eyepiece, and rose with it to a standing position.

"Masts in line," said Blunt. "One escort. Bearing, mark! Main target!" Swiftly he spun the periscope completely around, snapped up the handles. It disappeared into the well. "Angle on the bow zero, estimated range twelve thousand," said Blunt. "I can just see the tops of his bridge. He's belching occasional clouds of black or brown smoke. A single escort patrolling ahead."

"Anything else in sight, sir?" said Rich.

"No. I took a look around. All clear. No aircraft in sight."

"Captain, we have two fish left forward, and a full set of tubes aft. Recommend we try for a stern tube shot."

Blunt's face suddenly looked younger as he curtly acknowledged the information. "At fifteen knots, how long will it take them to get here?" he asked.

A ship making fifteen knots goes 1500 yards in three minutes, or 500 yards in one minute. Rich was accustomed to making the calculation. "Twenty-four minutes, Captain," he said. "But he's probably not going that fast, and he's probably zigging besides. At twelve knots it will take him a half hour to get here. We're moving toward him at two knots, however, so if we don't maneuver, it will cut the time down by about four minutes."

Keith had started up the TDC. The familiar whirring filled the conning tower, receded into the background of their notice. Blunt and Richardson crowded into the after part of the conning tower with Keith to look at it.

"It sure was a good idea to move this thing up here," said Blunt. "I never did know what you fellows were doing with it down in the control room."

"Doing our best to keep up with you up here in the conning tower,

Skipper," said Rich. "Remember those letters you used to write recommending it be moved to where the approach officer could also see it? Well, now it's been done, and you've got one. Shall I sound the general alarm, sir?"

"Time since the last look?" rasped Blunt.

"Two minutes."

"I'll take another look first. Up 'scope."

Rich could see the habit of command returning, the practiced skill of the consummately perfect approach officer which he had been, lying dormant all these years through disuse, now, palpably, returning undiminished.

The periscope handles came up; the same routines. "Bearing, mark!" snapped Blunt. "No zig. Down scope! Angle on the bow still zero!"

Richardson had his hand on the general alarm switch box, was looking at Blunt. This was almost like one of the old drills in the *Octopus*. He had done it so many times just this way. "Sound the general alarm," said Blunt. He cranked the toggle.

As the notes of the general alarm gong resounded throughout the ship, Richardson said, "We're pretty deep, Captain. Do you think we could get a stadimeter range if we brought her up a couple of feet?"

"Let's try," said Blunt. "What's the ordered depth?"

"Six-five feet. That's only a foot and a half of periscope out of water."

"Very well," said Blunt. He crossed to the control room hatch, stood aside to let Buck Williams scramble up, peered down. Al Dugan was just arriving at his station. "Make your depth six-two feet," he said.

"Six-two feet, aye aye!"

The depth gauge needle in the conning tower began to creep upward, settled at the new depth. In the meantime men had come jumping out of their bunks, tumbling up the ladder from the control room, manning their stations. It was all so familiar to Richardson. The crews of *Eel* and *Walrus* had done it all so many times before. So had the *Octopus* crew. Though the locale was slightly different because *Octopus* was an older boat, nevertheless the action was so very much the same. "The boat is manned and ready," he reported. "One minute since the last observation. Recommend a quick look around during the next observation."

Blunt nodded. "Estimated range?" he demanded.

"Using fifteen knots I'm reading one-oh-five-double-oh yards, Captain," said Keith, "but all I've got is an estimate to start it on. Buck is taking over the TDC."

Richardson was glad to see Keith also falling into the scenario.

"I'll take a quick look around, then drop the 'scope on the bearing. When I run it up again we'll go for a stadimeter range. Are you ready, Rich?"

"Ready," said Rich and Buck almost simultaneously.

"Very well. Up periscope!"

The Old Man will have aching leg muscles tonight, thought Richardson, but he's spinning that thing around just the way he used to. The thought warmed him, reinforced him in the correctness of his decision. He centered the periscope dead ahead as Blunt snapped the handles up, squatted on his heels before it as it went down, watched Blunt's face. When he saw the command in the eyes under the shaggy eyebrows, he signaled abruptly for it to be stopped.

"I can see the top of his superstructure," said Blunt. "Use masthead height forty feet, from the tip of his mast to the top of his stack."

"Ready," said Rich.

"Up 'scope," said Blunt. "Bearing, mark! It's a zig." Swiftly he turned the range-finder wheel. "Range, mark!" Richardson followed the indicator dial with his eyes and his finger. The periscope handles were up. The 'scope was on its way down.

"Nine-six-double-oh!" said Rich.

"Left full rudder," barked Blunt. "All ahead standard! A zig to his right. Angle on the bow is port thirty."

"Distance to the track is forty-eight hundred," said Rich. "You caught him right on the point of the zig." He was turning the dials of the Is-Was as he spoke. "Normal approach course zero-six-one," he said. "Target bears one-five-one. Recommend we split the difference and steady on one-zero-six. Looks like he really means to hug the coast. We can't run long on this course. Neither can he, really!"

"Make your new course one-zero-six," ordered Blunt in a very precise tone.

"One-zero-six, aye aye," responded Cornelli, who had taken his station on the helm.

"Was that a good range, Captain?" asked Rich.

"Yes, good range."

Buck said, "He's either going faster, or the initial range was less. I've been using fifteen knots on the TDC."

"I don't think he's making as much as fifteen knots. Probably the initial range estimate was too high," Blunt said crisply. "Maybe it's a smaller ship than we figured."

"Using twelve knots then, sir. Recommend another observation at three minutes more for the first speed check."

"Can't do it," said Rich; "we're making too much speed."

"I'll take a look at six minutes," said Blunt. "When should I take the speed off her?"

"We'll have finished our turn, but we'll only have been up to speed for about three minutes, Captain. If he zigs away again, that might put us out in left field," said Rich, "but it's not likely with him already so close to shore." He had made the identical speech to Blunt many times during the practice approaches of years past.

"How long was he on the previous course?" asked Blunt.

"This was the first zig we've seen," replied Rich. "About twelve minutes after first sighting."

"Very well, I'll run for nine minutes. I want to get on the track anyhow to be in shape for a stern tube shot. We'll still be seven thousand yards off the beach. Tell the diving officer I will use a backing bell to get the way off her quickly."

Richardson crossed to the control room hatch, squatted down, relayed the instructions to Al Dugan, who had mounted partway up the ladder. "No sweat," said Al, "but don't let speed drop below two knots, okay? . . . Is the commodore making the approach all the way in?" The last portion of his speech was made in a much lower tone, intended only for Richardson's ears.

"Yes. He deserves it after all these years in the boats." Rising, Richardson strode back to the after part of the conning tower, where Blunt had crowded in behind Buck and Keith. "Dugan has the word about backing down, sir," said Rich; "he asks we not reduce speed below two knots so he won't lose depth control." Blunt, concentrating with absorbed interest upon the dials of the TDC, nodded shortly. "Should we pass the word to the ship's company what's going on, sir? Would you like to do it, or shall I?"

"You do it," Blunt said, not taking his eyes away from the face of the TDC.

"Now hear this," said Richardson into the general announcing system microphone. "We have a single ship up here with one escort. No sign of air coverage. Weather is calm, visibility excellent. Captain Blunt is making the approach, and we plan to shoot stern tubes if possible. He was my skipper on the old *Octopus*, which was lost just at the start of the war, and he was the man who qualified me in submarines. This is one for our old ship and our old shipmates." He paused a moment, was about to hang the microphone back on its hook, changed his mind. "There is a single escort patrolling ahead. We will rig for depth charge, and probably go to silent running just before making the attack." He replaced the microphone in its bracket, checked his watch as he rejoined the group behind the TDC.

"Five minutes since the last look," said Buck. "We're showing thirty-nine hundred yards to the track now."

"What should the range be after nine minutes?"

Blunt was obviously making the calculations in his own head at the same time as he asked the questions. The lightning approximation of critical distances and angles was one of the most valued of submarine approach techniques, nurtured from years of practice. At the same time, one always demanded the answers from one's approach party, partly for training and partly to guard against any possible error or misunderstanding. The two requirements had evolved into a habit cultivated by all submariners. Richardson could almost see the wheels turning inside the minds of both Buck and Keith as he also made the calculation. Nine minutes at six knots would be 1,800 yards for *Eel*, but since part of the time had been spent turning and speeding up, 1,400 yards would be a better estimate. *Eel* was making seven-tenths of that distance good toward the target: a thousand yards. At twelve knots the target had time to cover 3,600 yards, about 85 percent of it effective toward shortening the range. Say 3,100 yards, plus the thousand *Eel* would be traveling toward her. After nine minutes the range would be reduced by about 4,100 yards.

"About fifty-five hundred if he's making twelve knots," said Buck.

Keith nodded. "About the same," he said.

"Fifty-six hundred by plot," said Lasche.

A gratified look played about the corners of Blunt's mouth. Richardson nodded also. "I'd make it fifty-seven hundred, Captain, allowing a little more for our maneuvers," he said. "But not many old Jap freighters make twelve knots."

"Well, the big ones can," said Blunt, "and that convoy yesterday made seventeen. But you're right. This fellow is medium size, and he's sending up a lot of smoke. What will the range be if he's making ten knots?"

It was almost like one of the old drills with Blunt, the skipper and at the same time the training officer, examining his younger trainees. The speed difference—two knots, or 200 yards every three minutes for nine minutes. "About sixty-two hundred yards," said three voices at once.

"Seven minutes since last look," said Buck, reading the timer dial on his TDC.

"All stop." The annunciators clicked. "All back one-third." They clicked again.

Keith was checking the "own-ship" speed dial on the TDC. "We were right on seven knots," he said after a moment. "It's dropping slowly now." There was a long wait. "Six knots," said Keith. Another long wait. Richardson could feel tension mounting. The approach was being made by the book. The tactics were exactly right, but a long run toward the track without observation was risky in case the target maneuvered in the meantime. On the other hand, they had caught her just at the turn of the zig. Most zigs lasted at least six minutes, generally longer, and the target had been observed to be on the previous leg of the zig for a much longer period than this. But one never knew what might happen up above. "Five knots," said Keith.

"All back two-thirds."

"Eight minutes since last look."

The range, according to the TDC, was approaching 5,800 yards. It would, of course, be far more accurate than the mental calculations, since *Eel*'s own course and speed were automatically integrated into the solution. The information as to target speed and course were, by contrast, derived from observation. They were the critical factors. The machine would only solve according to the information put into it.

The drumming of water through the superstructure, of which Richardson had been only subconsciously aware, was reducing. This was always the hardest moment: to make the decisions, to be confident they were the right decisions, and yet to have to wait for them to work out; to know that while judgments were right they could easily be overturned by unanticipated events. For the second time he ran over the check-off list pasted to the side of the TDC. Keith, he noticed, had been doing the same thing. The torpedoes were ready, the depth was set, all necessary data for the patrol report was being recorded. The fathometer had been turned on for a moment, barely long enough to confirm that the depth of water was as shown on the chart. It was not yet time to fire; consequently the outer doors on the torpedo tubes were still closed. The ship had not maneuvered into the firing position, was still on the approach phase. There was much to be done before they could shoot, and a lot would depend upon what the target, unseen for nine minutes, and not yet seen at all (except the masts) by Rich or anyone except Blunt, would do.

"Four knots," said Keith.

"Eight and a half minutes," said Buck. "Range by TDC five-six-double-oh."

Eel's speed through the water was dropping rapidly now.

"Eight minutes forty-five seconds," from Buck.

"Speed three knots."

"All stop!" barked Blunt. He waited a moment, then ordered, "All ahead one-third."

There were two sets of clinks from the annunciators at the forward end of the conning tower, then Cornelli's voice, "Answered all ahead one-third."

From below, up through the conning tower hatch, came Al Dugan calling, "Steady on ordered depth, six-two feet."

"Up periscope," said Blunt.

"Nine minutes," said Buck. "Right on."

"Speed two and a quarter knots," said Keith.

"What should the target bear?" asked Blunt. He had arranged himself so that when the periscope came up he would be facing about twenty degrees to the right of dead ahead.

"Should bear one-four-three true, zero-three-seven relative."

"Put me on it," rasped Blunt. The 'scope was coming up. Rich grabbed the handles, swung them around to the indicated bearing as Blunt applied his forehead to the rubber buffer, rode it up.

"There they are—no zig, bearing, mark!"

"Zero-three-nine," said Keith, peering at the azimuth circle at the top of the periscope.

"Range—use seventy feet—mark! Down 'scope." Blunt slapped up the handles, stepped back.

Rich rode the periscope down on the opposite side, reading the dials as it went, pulling his head clear just in time to avoid being struck by the heavy yoke as it descended into the well. "Six-three-double-oh," he said.

"That was a good range," said Blunt. "He hasn't zigged yet. Angle on the bow still port thirty. . . ."

"Should be thirty-three," said Buck from his TDC.

"Good," said Blunt. "What speed does that give us?"

"That checks at eleven knots," said Buck.

"I make it ten and a half knots," said Larry Lasche from his plot.

"Was that a good range, sir?" asked Rich. "Could you see his water-line?

"Excellent range," said Blunt. "I could see his waterline clearly. He's riding low on the water. There's just a little of his red boot topping showing. It's an old freighter, probably coal-burning."

"Can we run a little deeper, sir?"

"Yes, make your depth six-four feet," commented Blunt. "I want to catch him on the zig. He should be zigging any minute now. How long since we looked?"

"Mark—one minute. Ten minutes since last zig."

The short clipped sentences must have been musical to Blunt's once finely tuned ears. They were to Richardson's. Everything was clicking into place. This was just the way it should be.

"Recommend another look around, Captain," said Rich. "Also take a look for aircraft over the target."

"I want to catch him on the zig," worried Blunt. "Right, I'll take a quick look around for aircraft. Stand by for an observation. Time?"

"Coming up two minutes!"

"Up periscope." He grabbed it, spun it around quickly, steadied on the target. "Bearing, mark!" he said. The 'scope slithered away.

"Zero-three-six," said Rich.

"No zig yet," said Blunt. "Nothing in sight except land to the east."

"Did you check for aircraft, sir?"

"Yes. No aircraft in sight."

"How about the escort?"

"Escort is patrolling ahead and is well clear on the target's far bow. It's a small ship, about like one of our PC sub chasers."

"Not one of those we saw yesterday?" asked Rich.

"No. Smaller. He's patrolling on station. I'll keep my eye on him."

"One minute since the last look," said Buck.

"Up periscope! Observation," barked Blunt.

"Bearing, mark!"

"Zero-three-five."

"No zig yet. Range"—he turned the range knob—"mark!"

"Five thousand!" said Rich as the periscope dropped away.

"How long now since the zig?" asked Blunt.

"Twelve minutes."

"Distance to the track?"

"Two-seven-double-oh yards."

"I've got to get in there," said Blunt, "but I don't dare run over there right now with a zig due to come any minute. Besides we've got to get pretty much on the track in order to swing for a decent stern tube shot."

"There's still plenty of time, Captain," said Rich. "A zig must be about due. As soon as he steadies up on his new course we can put our head down and run for a firing position."

"Right," said Blunt. "But it will be just our luck to have an airplane show up just when I want to increase speed."

"No need to worry about a plane seeing us under water, Captain. The sea is too dirty. All we have to be careful of is kicking up a wake at the wrong time. Dropping down to a hundred feet or so before speeding up might be a good idea if the patrol plane comes back." Richardson wanted badly to ask for a look himself, but refrained. Such a request, a natural one from a sub skipper supervising a junior officer's approach during training, would in this case be interpreted as an assertion of his prerogative as the real captain of the submarine. It might destroy the atmosphere he had been so successful in creating up to now. Instead, he must content himself with formation of a mental picture and with insinuating into Blunt's consciousness, as any proper assistant approach officer should, such maneuvers as he might think necessary.

"Thirteen minutes since the zig," said Buck. "Larry and I are getting ten knots." No one had directed him to report the minutes, but he as well as anyone was aware of the importance of catching the exact moment of the zig. The next zig would be critical.

Blunt called for the periscope, put it down again. Another range and bearing were fed into the TDC. Richardson noted approvingly that Blunt's periscope exposures were extremely short, as short as his own, nearly as short as they had been when Commander Joe Blunt of the *Octopus*, nine years ago, had so prided himself upon his ability to get a complete and accurate periscope observation in seven seconds. Intentionally, Rich had not suggested using the radar periscope. Blunt had been a past master on the attack 'scope. This approach was to be as near as he could make it to the techniques Blunt had been so good at.

At Blunt's direction, Al Dugan increased depth another foot, to sixty-five feet. In the calm water even two and a half feet of periscope might be spotted by an alert lookout as the ships drew nearer. Stafford on the sonar had been monotonously reporting the bearings of two sets of screws with no change in their steady beat. *Eel*'s sonar equipment was far more acute than the older one fitted in *Octopus*. Perhaps Blunt had failed to realize that the first sign of a zig might be indicated by some variation in Stafford's reports. Perhaps a subtle hint was in order.

"Keep the sound bearings coming, Stafford," Rich ordered, crossing over to the sonar equipment and speaking loudly so that Stafford could hear him through his heavily padded earphones. "We're expecting a zig any minute."

Stafford nodded his comprehension, pointed to his bearing dial, shook his head to indicate no change. He answered rather loudly because of his artificial deafness, "Watch for zig, aye aye. No zig yet, sir."

Blunt seemed not to have heard. "We'll wait another minute," he said. He put his hand to his forehead, shut his eyes, and spanned across the bones of his temples with his thumb and fingers. The gesture, which took only a moment, startled Richardson. The fleeting hand motion was out of character. But Blunt's next words were the right ones, the ones Richardson had been willing him to say: "How have the sound bearings been checking?" he asked.

"Right on, Captain," said Buck. "Lagging about a quarter degree, no more."

Blunt appeared pensive. Rich looked at him carefully, trying at the same time not to seem overly interested in his appearance. The crowded conditions in the conning tower made this, at least, fairly easy. Blunt's brow was furrowed, but this was certainly normal. Perhaps Richardson had only fancied that there had been an instant of weakness. The wolfpack commander crowded closer to the TDC, peering between the heads of Buck and Keith and effectively cutting off further inspection of his face.

In the best submarine fire control parties, few words are spoken except those absolutely necessary. Silence reigns, broken only by the ship noises conveying their own messages, the background whirring of the selsyn motors in the TDC, the muted murmur from the likewise silent control room. As far as possible, hand signals take the place of verbal communication. Words spoken take on added significance in consequence.

Suddenly, in *Eel*'s conning tower, there was nothing to do, nothing to say, nothing to check. Only the slowly creeping dials on the face of the TDC to watch, or the equally slow movement of the tiny dot of light indicating *Eel*'s barely perceptible progress across Larry Lasche's plotting sheet. Despite his determination, Richardson felt himself becoming nervous. It was always like this, as the target approached, but he always had in mind, also, what he would do for each of its possible maneuvers—including the possibility of no maneuver at all. But now he could not know what Blunt was thinking.

The old Blunt of *Octopus* days would have seized the opportunity to describe what he intended if the target zigged in either direction or not at all. He might even have indulged in a short discussion of the various possibilities and the likelihood of each. But that was eight years ago, during peacetime training exercises, when the only actual danger was collision with escort or target. Today, with conditions so much a carbon copy of the simplest exercise approach, there were depth charges in the escort, depth bombs in the aircraft, and men trained to use them. There was a hostile shore close at hand. Collision no longer would be solely the result of stupidity and clumsiness on the part of the submarine, and inability to avoid on the part of the target. Now it was something avidly sought by all surface ships.

The enemy freighter's zigzag pattern was such that another zig was probable any moment. Sonar would discover it by some change in the drift of the bearings or in the regular cadence of the propellers. A radical zig away, to the target's right, might produce an impossibly long range shot, or, at least, make bow tubes mandatory. A big left zig would run the target through a perfect firing position, requiring little or no maneuvering on *Eel*'s part. A small zig in either direction would still allow the submarine to achieve a firing position, though a small right zig might present the greater problem. No zig at all was probably the worst of all the possibilities. Any zig carried with it at least the likelihood that there would be no further zigs for several minutes, long enough for the submarine to get in firing position and her torpedoes to complete their lethal runs.

On the other hand, if there was no zig soon, *Eel* would be forced nevertheless to begin the slow maneuver necessary to bring her stern tubes to bear. Nearly a complete course reversal would be necessary. But once additional speed was put on the boat and her rudder placed hard over, a zig would be harder to detect on sonar. Canceling the submarine's maneuver and replacing it with another would be difficult if not impossible in the time remaining. Hence the waiting, the quick, rapidly repeated observations, the rising tension.

Rich could hear the sibilant sound of water as *Eel* patiently drove through it, the hum of the ventilation blowers down below, the gentle hiss of air coming in through the vent in the overhead of the conning tower. The ship had long since been rigged for silent running and for depth charge, but the blowers had not yet been shut off. Even so, everyone in the conning tower was perspiring freely. With the crush of people—fourteen men jammed into a horizontal steel cylinder eight feet in diameter and sixteen feet long—there was nothing that could be done about it. When the ventilation blowers were finally secured and the hatch shut to the control room, the temperature in the conning tower would shoot to 120. The perspiration would increase, and so would the moisture in the air.

"Bearing one-two-eight," announced Stafford.

"That's half a degree to the right, Captain," said Keith. "It might be a zig to his left."

"Up 'scope," said Blunt. "Zig to his left," he announced. "He's still turning. Down 'scope." He stopped the periscope before it descended very far into the well, just far enough to get its upper extremity under water, waited about fifteen seconds, motioned for it to go back up. "Bearing, mark!" he said. "Range"—he fumbled for the range knob (strange: one's hand simply dropped to it, under the handle;

Richardson had never before noticed anyone having trouble finding it), grasped the knob, turned it—"mark!"

"Three-eight-double-oh!" read Rich from the back of the periscope as it dropped away. He was suddenly conscious of beads of perspiration on his face. The range was becoming short.

"Angle on the bow is zero," announced Blunt.

Buck said, "That puts him on course three-one-nine. Course to head for him, one-three-nine!"

"Right full rudder! Come right to new course one-three-nine!" ordered Blunt.

"No time, Captain," said Richardson, speaking rapidly. "He'll be here in eleven minutes. Recommend come left to zero-five-zero and pull across his track. That will set him up for a straight stern shot."

"Guess you're right," muttered Blunt. There was something in his voice. Some slight hesitation. Perhaps it was embarrassment.

"Rudder is right full, sir!" Cornelli sang out loudly from the other end of the conning tower.

"How's your speed check, Buck?" Blunt had moved over behind the TDC again.

"Ten knots, sir. Good speed check."

"Captain," said Richardson, speaking in a hoarse whisper, "rudder is right full!" For the second time there was the hand clutching the forehead, spanning over the momentarily closed eyes.

"I'm getting a turn count," said Stafford. "One hundred ten rpm. Single screw."

"That checks out, Captain," said Rich, still speaking almost under his breath. "Ten turns per knot is about right." Then, desperately, still in a loud whisper, "Don't you want to put the rudder left?" His last few words were spoken in a rush, with increased emphasis, yet a deliberate downplay of the intensity he felt rising within him.

Blunt looked puzzled, but he did not answer. That hand-to-forehead gesture again. The submarine had barely begun to swing. No time to argue the misunderstanding. "Shift the rudder!" barked Rich. "Rudder should be full left! New course, zero-five-zero!" He looked sharply at Blunt, mustering in his mind the words he would use to explain his action, to convince Blunt of the need for it. To his surprise, they were not necessary. The wolfpack commander continued his grave inspection of the dials on the face of the TDC. Not a line on his face indicated concern over any matter other than the slowly developing tactical problem there displayed. He could not be unaware of the change in the intended maneuver. Yet, by every evidence available to Richardson, the incident was as if it had never occurred.

223

Something unreal, unexplainable, lay just beneath the surface. Rich felt he could sense it, could perhaps understand it too, if only he could have a clue. Blunt had momentarily lost the picture; Rich, as assistant approach officer, had quite properly corrected the situation. In a training approach, things would now merely continue to the normal firing point. True, had it been an approach for submarine command qualification, the observing officers might not have passed the candidate. Richardson, acting as Blunt's assistant but actually in command, still held full responsibility for the conduct of the approach and the safety of his submarine. By correcting Blunt's error he had asserted himself as the real commander of the *Eel*. He had done it with sorrow, with hesitation. He could not understand how Joe Blunt, the man with a TDC-like mind, could possibly have lost the picture so completely. Yet, he had, indisputably. More, he had somehow failed to grasp the simple solution offered by Rich until, in perplexity, it had had to be done almost by subterfuge.

Over it all lay the appreciation that the action Richardson had to take probably had ruined his effort to rehabilitate Blunt.

But instead of an explosive misunderstanding or a petulant acceptance of what Rich had done, there was no reaction at all. There was not even any change in the expression on Blunt's face. It was as if nothing untoward had happened.

Carefully, Rich inspected his superior's face for the second time within a very few minutes. Nothing. The oldtime zest he thought he had noticed when Blunt first took over the periscope was no longer evident—the jowls were again sagging—but nothing more. Perhaps Blunt was merely covering up. After the attack was completed there would be a postmortem. There would be private discussions. That must be it. There was no time to bandy about now in argument. Blunt was sticking to the business at hand, as he should, as Richardson also should.

Eel had barely begun to turn to starboard; now, her rudder shifted to full left, she corrected herself and was beginning, according to the TDC dials, slowly to turn to port. At this speed she would hardly get far enough off the target's track to give the torpedoes time to arm. Surely, Blunt would increase speed. Two-thirds speed would do it. Perhaps Blunt was waiting until *Eel* was more nearly around to the new course, but that made little sense because the length of time wasted in turning at slow speed would still further reduce the distance the sub would be able to attain off the track. Irresolutely, Rich waited. The "own ship" dial on the TDC showed *Eel* had turned about ten degrees; there were forty-five degrees more to turn. No move by Blunt. Strange.

224

Something had to be done. After all, Rich was supposed to be his assistant. He could no longer contain himself. Maybe a hint would do it. "Where's the escort, Captain?"

"Escort is still patrolling on station about one thousand yards ahead of the target. Right now he's still on the target's starboard bow, but he's beginning a swing over to the other side. He's well clear for now."

"At this speed he'll be going by in about six minutes." Rich was deliberately understating the time by a small fraction. "With this setup we could put sonar on him instead of the target. . . . Was that a hint of a nod from Blunt? He still stood where he had been for the past half-minute—did he mean for Rich to give the order? Abruptly, Rich swung away from the TDC, jostled his way past the crowded bodies in the conning tower to its forward end, where Stafford sat crouched before his sonar console. He lifted one of Stafford's earphones, spoke briefly, pointed to a sector of his bearing dial. The sonarman nodded his comprehension.

"Sonar's on the escort, Captain," reported Rich as he made his way back to the TDC. "Escort is already to the right of the target and seems to be passing well clear."

Another imperceptible nod from the wolfpack commander. With the momentum achieved, the obvious step was easy. "Recommend two-thirds speed to get us around and clear the track, sir." This time Rich did not wait, gave the order. The clink of the annunciators and Cornelli's report. Within seconds the "own ship" dial seemed to have taken on a bit more of life. *Eel* was turning faster. The slowly changing geometry of the creeping dials was now clearly becoming favorable.

"We're all ready to shoot aft, Captain, except for the outer doors on the torpedo tubes. Three fish. Tubes seven, eight, and nine. Depth is set at fifteen. Number ten is set at five feet. Recommend we proceed at this speed for five minutes and then slow to one-third again for an observation."

"Very well," said Blunt.

Again the hiatus, waiting, while the dials on the TDC face slowly turned, registering what the target would be doing if its course and speed were indeed those set into the instrument, and provided there had been no undetected change. At Rich's instruction, Stafford was giving regular reports on the doings of the escort and occasionally switching over to the main target, whose heavy single-screw beat was easily distinguishable from the higher speed twin propellers of her protector. If there were anything unexpected happening while *Eel*, because of her increased speed, could not use her periscope, it did not show on the sonar bearings of either vessel. The continually confirmed fact added confidence, although Richardson could not recall when he had perspired so during an approach and attack.

"Five minutes since we speeded up. Five and a half since the zig!" Williams was reading the timer built into his computer face.

"All ahead one-third," said Blunt.

Perhaps the bad moment was over. Rich felt like cheering. "When we get down below three knots," he said, "recommend a quick check of the target and escort, then search all around for aircraft. It's just possible they'll have that patrol plane up here for when the ship rounds the point."

Blunt was looking at him. It was the first time he had done so for several minutes, since before Rich had changed the helm order. His mouth formed words, but for a moment nothing came out. Finally he spoke. "What should the target bear?"

Again there was that feeling of unreality. There had definitely been a slight hesitation in Blunt's voice. Yet his question was eminently logical. It was what an approach officer should be asking, except that Buck Williams, at the TDC, or Keith Leone, backing him up, were those most likely to have the information at their fingertips. Furthermore, Blunt himself had just been looking at the instrument.

Richardson, simply because there was not room for more at the face of the TDC, had been standing one rank back. "About one-three-five relative," he said. From where he stood he could not read the numbers on the dials, but from their relative positions this would be not far off. "We're coming up on the firing bearing, Captain. We can hurry it up and shoot with a left gyro angle on a sharp track; but the longer we wait, now, the nearer it will be to a straight stern shot on a ninety track."

Blunt nodded thoughtfully. His face also was beaded with sweat. His bushy brows veiled the deep gray eyes.

"Seven minutes since the zig. Speed three knots." Buck, reading his TDC.

Time to put up the periscope. For a dreadful second Rich thought he might have to initiate the action as before, felt flooded with relief when Blunt gave the order.

The periscope technique was perfection. Blunt rose with the base of the tube, stopped it a foot short of full extension, took a quick range and bearing of the target, then dropped it until its base was slightly below the top of the periscope well. He remained squatting before it for a few seconds, in the meantime directing the ship's depth increased by another foot, then motioned for the instrument to be raised again. This time he allowed it to go to its full elevation, swiftly spun through two complete circuits—the second time Rich, watching closely, could see that he had turned the motorcycle-type control handle so that he was searching the sky—he suddenly stopped spinning the periscope. "Plane!" he said. "Bearing, mark!"

"One-seven-five," read Rich from the azimuth circle through which the periscope tube passed out the top of the conning tower. "Two-two-five true," said Keith, swiftly converting by adding the submarine's course to the relative bearing.

"He's well clear for now," growled Blunt as the periscope descended. "Looks like a patrol plane, all right, coming up from the south. He's still pretty distant. It will all be over by the time he can get here."

"Open outer doors?" asked Keith, once more going through his check-off card.

"Open the outer doors aft!" said Blunt. "What's the gyro angle now? How long before he comes on to a straight stern shot?"

"What's the escort doing, Captain?" Richardson's question was interrupted by a loud report from Stafford. "Echo-ranging has speeded up!" In a bound, Richardson was alongside the sonarman, looking at his dials. He put on the spare earphones, listened intently for a long quarter minute. Then he rose, replaced the earphones, was back alongside Blunt. "The escort's almost dead astern, Captain," he said seriously, "and he's speeded up his pinging. He may have become suspicious. He's pinging right up our wake—I'm sure he can't be getting a good echo!"

"Gyros left twenty. Decreasing. Seventy starboard track. Range, twelve hundred!" Buck's concentration on the information showing on the TDC was reflected in his staccato report. "Correct solution light aft," more quietly reported Keith. "About one minute until the gyro angles are zero."

"Target bearing one-four-eight!" shouted Stafford. "Moving right, fast! Escort on one-eight-four, shifted to short scale! I think he has contact on us!"

Damn Stafford anyway! Why did he have to pick exactly this instant to become excited? Richardson swore to himself, forgetting that Stafford spoke loudly because of his earphones, and was doing his duty. Only the approach officer—certainly not the sonarman—could accurately evaluate the immediate significance of this information.

"Tubes seven, eight and nine ready aft," reported Quin. "Outer doors are open, depth set fifteen feet."

Keith was whispering something into his ear. "We've not yet finished the rig for depth charge," he was saying. Richardson was grateful to him for having had the good sense not to add this item to the plethora of information and reports Blunt was receiving. "Do it quietly, by phone," he answered.

Blunt was standing with hands at his side, head bent forward, eyes staring at the floor. Afterward Rich would recall this moment as the moment of truth, the decisive one of the entire patrol, the instant of time which, ever after, in his mind was the watershed between the past and what was to come. "Recommend final bearing and shoot, Captain," Rich said. "Gyros are approaching ten left. Range is twelve hundred."

Blunt raised his head, stared at Rich. "Very well," he said. Again, there was that hint of hesitation. "Up periscope!" The incisive manner of less than a minute past was gone. His hand was at his temples again. He did not stoop to ride the 'scope out of the well, merely stood before it, let it rise to him.

"Should bear one-six-six," read Buck from the TDC. Rich twisted the periscope around to the bearing, at the same time noted that, in accordance with Blunt's long habit, he had left the previous range observation still cranked in on the periscope's range finder. Hardly anyone bothered to crank the observed range off the stadimeter after using the 'scope. This took time, required the periscope to stay up a trifle longer. The experienced approach officer was not bothered by the resulting split image at near ranges; in fact, it provided an instant visual reference as to whether the target was farther or nearer, even before the range was taken, and it made it easier and quicker to measure the range when desired. The procedure was part of Blunt's periscope technique which Richardson had adopted and in his turn had passed on to Jim Bledsoe, Keith, Buck and Al.

What was unusual was Blunt's reaction when he put his eyes to the rubber guards. "Dammit, Richardson, who's been fooling with the 'scope? Someone's got the wrong range on it!"

The range on the stadimeter was what Blunt had put on it last time the 'scope was up. No one else could have reached it in the bottom of the periscope well. It was off, but only because the range had lessened. Moreover, it must be very nearly correct, even though a minute or so had passed. With the target nearly broadside to, the range could not have changed much. On a ninety track—torpedoes due to strike at ninety degrees on the target's beam—it didn't matter anyway. Cautiously, Rich turned the range wheel, reduced the range another hundred yards. This ought to bring the tip of the target's mast about back to her waterline.

"Neh-mind . . . I'll do it." It was the first time Rich had ever heard

Blunt slur his words in this way. "Range, mark!" The range dial at the base of the periscope opposite the eyepiece had not moved.

"Eleven hundred," snapped Rich instinctively, reading the numbers opposite the pointer.

But then dismay gripped him, for Blunt, his hand still on the range stadimeter wheel, began turning it back and forth, moving the pointer over a range variation exceeding a thousand yards!

Time, which had been passing so slowly for the final minutes of the approach, now was moving with frantic speed. "Angle on the bow!" hissed Rich imperatively. "Are you on in bearing?"

"Starboard ninety. I'm on his stack. . . . What's wrong with this damn periscope? . . ."

No one had noticed anything. Keith was watching the angle solver section of the TDC, his right hand hovering over the firing key. Buck, beside him, was poised to set in the slightest change in the final bearing of the target. The proper thing to do was to push Blunt aside and take the firing ranges himself, but on a ninety track, range made no difference. The resulting bustle would only add confusion. "Mark the bearing," Rich said loudly. "One-seven-two!" he read off the azimuth ring.

"Right on! Set!" Buck had not had to touch the TDC.

"Shoot," muttered Rich into Blunt's ear. "It's perfect! Shoot now!"

Blunt's hand was still on the range wheel, still twisting it. He said nothing. In the split rangefinder view, the target's masthead must be moving from his deck to an equal distance below the waterline and back.

"Shoot!" barked Richardson. Keith leaned on the firing key. Larry Lasche began to count. In the after torpedo room there was the snap of the firing valve, the air-and-water roar as the impulse bottle emptied into the torpedo tube, the starting whine of the torpedo motor, the tiny jolt—less than it would have been from a forward tube—as the suddenly started torpedo was ejected. Then the additional slap as the poppet valve opened to swallow the air before it escaped, and the burbling snore as water, flooding into the now empty tube, jammed the air back into the tube and through the now opened poppet line into the torpedo room. A heavy splash as a cascade of water followed the air and landed in the bilges.

The chief torpedoman had not needed to follow through with the hand firing key. "Number seven tube fired electrically," the torpedoman wearing the phones reported, pushing the button on his mouthpiece.

"Number seven tube fired electrically," said Quin in the conning tower.

Three fish would be enough, had been already decided upon. "Eight fired electrically . . . nine fired electrically," reported Quin as the sequential reports arrived in his earphones.

"Shoot!" said Blunt, still looking through the periscope. Keith looked back, startled, inquiring. Richardson made a motion of negation.

"Down periscope!" said Rich. Gently he pushed Blunt back, folded up the handles so they would not strike the edge of the well as the 'scope dropped into it.

"How long until the first fish gets there?" asked Rich.

"Twenty-five seconds more," responded Lasche.

"Let me know at ten seconds," said Blunt.

Again there was silence in the conning tower. The deed had been done. His face bubbling with sweat, Blunt stood in the pose so characteristic of him, hands on hips, waiting. Richardson, equally covered with perspiration, trickles of moisture running down inside his shirt, recalled his own habit of so many years before, in *Octopus*' conning tower. He picked up the Is-Was which had been hanging forgotten on its string around his neck, began setting it up for a collision course between the torpedoes and the target.

"Ten seconds to go."

"Up periscope," said Blunt. "She's a beautiful ship. Take a range—mark!"

"One-oh-five-oh," read Richardson.

"Angle on the bow is port ninety. She's got a single tall stack, a large deckhouse, cargo wells forward and aft. Not more than six inches of her waterline is showing—probably loaded with cargo for the Kwantung Army." Blunt had hardly finished saying the words when suddenly a thunderous roar shook the conning tower. "It's a hit," he shouted. "A beautiful hit! Right under the stack! Smoke and junk is blown sky high! Oh, it's beautiful! He's a goner for sure! He's already listing over toward us! His back is broken!" Mesmerized, Blunt was staring at the damage. Again he had changed. The catatonic reflex had disappeared.

"What happened to the second torpedo?" he asked. Then he answered his own question. "She slowed down so suddenly with the first hit that the second fish must have missed ahead."

A second explosion. Cheers from the men in the conning tower. On the other side of the now closed control room hatch, throughout the submarine, more cheers.

"Another hit aft!" shouted Blunt. "That was our third torpedo! Our first fish slowed him down so much that the third torpedo came in and hit him halfway between the stack and the stern! He's broken in half! The deckhouse is already half under water, the bow is high in the air. It's bent backward as though it might fall over on top of the stack! The stern is blown nearly off! Boy, those guys never knew what hit them!"

"What's the escort doing, Captain?" asked Richardson. His eagerness to see the target had vanished. There was death on the sea. The grave of a tired old ship that had never had a chance. A few survivors swimming. Chunks of debris and great globules of coal dust on the sea to mark the place where she had been.

"He's way out ahead and well clear," responded Blunt.

"How about a look around and see if you can spot that aircraft, Skipper."

"Oh, all right, Rich. You sure have a fixation on that airplane!" So saying, Captain Blunt began to turn the periscope in a clockwise direction, the elbow of his right arm hooked over the right handle, his left hand pushing the other. Suddenly he stopped. "By God, Rich, you're right. I never figured he could get here this fast!"

"Bearing two-zero-two," snapped Richardson from the azimuth circle overhead. Keith would take the hint and translate it to true bearing.

"True bearing is two-five-one," announced Keith, reading it off the dials of the TDC.

"Well, he's sure got something to look at this time," chuckled Blunt, "but I guess we'd better not stick around with the periscope up." He snapped up the handles of the periscope, motioned down with his thumbs. Its base sank swiftly out of sight. "Make your depth one-eight-oh feet," he ordered. "What's the best course to get out of this place?" He was wiping his sweaty hands on the hip pockets of his uniform trousers in the characteristic gesture Rich remembered so well. "That plane was a good two miles away, maybe more. There's nothing he can do about us now. What's the bearing of the PC-boat?"

"Escort is bearing due west, shifted back to long-scale pinging and closing the target," responded Stafford. "Sinking ship is at two-two-four."

"Right full rudder," ordered Blunt. "Make your new course one-five-oh. All ahead two-thirds. . . . Rich," he said, clapping him on the shoulder, "what do you say we secure from battle stations and send for two cups of coffee, one for you and one for me? These guys can't lay a finger on us, and I'm just in the mood for a cup of that good java your boys make up forward."

Rich forced a smile back at him. "You're giving the orders," he said. "Right now you're still running this boat. That was the most beautifully executed approach I've ever seen!" It sounded pompous, even patronizing. He himself would have resented the word "beautiful" in a similar circumstance. But these thoughts barely touched the fringes of his mind. A deep despair had settled upon him. He would have to talk with Keith soon. Keith alone of all the persons in the conning tower had noticed something. He had a head on him. The burden was too big, anyway, for Rich to bear alone. Keith would have some good ideas.

9

"**W**e have only four torpedoes left, Commodore, but *White-fish* has sixteen. We know where the enemy is sending his ships now, but only *Whitefish* is fully effective. What we need to do now is to position her in the middle of the most likely place, and then do everything we can to make the enemy come by."

Another evening conference over coffee in the wardroom was in prog_ress. It differed from its interminably long predecessors, however, in one salient feature: the ebullient spirits of the wolfpack commander. The physical reaction to his strenuous athletic exertions on the periscope, and the mental ones of conducting the approach and attack, had expressed themselves in extreme fatigue. He had announced he would nap for an hour, but instead slept so soundly that it had been necessary to shake him to announce the evening meal. In the meantime, *Eel* had surfaced and was now well clear of land in the broader reaches of the Yellow Sea to the west.

Euphoria was evident in Blunt's animation and appearance. A decade had again dropped off his face. His eyes were bright and alert. The near-catatonic paralysis which had twice seemed to possess his thought processes was no longer evident. He was, Rich felt with a peculiar foreboding, again like the much-admired skipper of old. Instead of merely listening almost noncommittally to the arguments placed before him by Rich and Keith and, less frequently, one of the others, this night he joined eagerly in the discussion.

"The thing to do, Rich, is to put *Whitefish* in the Maikotsu Suido where we were, maybe all the way down at the southern end again. But how do we know the Japs will continue to run ships through it?"

"That's the main part of the problem, Commodore," said Richardson. "They won't, if they think there's a submarine there. So far, there's still a chance they may not realize there's two of us around. If they're as confused as our headquarters sometimes seems to be, they might think a single boat got those four cargo ships the other day.

"After *Chicolar* was sunk we lay pretty low, remember, for several days. There was no reason for them to suspect more subs around, especially if they didn't get their times well coordinated. That would explain their lack of air-patrol activity, and it might even explain

Moonface. It would have been a great coup if he could have come in with proof positive of another boat in the area. Since we hit into that big convoy in the Maikotsu Suido, however, we've seen a number of aircraft. They're obviously out looking for us. If they figure they've pinpointed our location they will probably feel other areas are fairly safe. We know one thing for sure: these ships moving up the coast of Korea are vitally important to Japan's occupying forces in China. Remember the briefing we got just before getting underway."

"What are you proposing, Rich?"

Keith's eyes were fixed upon Richardson. This had already been discussed, and Rich knew he had the wholehearted support of his executive officer. "If we send the *Whitefish* in there, Commodore," he said slowly, "and get detected ourselves some distance away, they might think the area is clear. . . ."

"You mean deliberately get spotted by aircraft out in the middle of the Yellow Sea? They'll have their best patrol craft out looking for us, and they'll be carrying more than just the two bombs we heard the other day! When they spot us they'll keep the air saturated with aircraft! They'll prevent us from surfacing, just as we did the Nazi subs in the Atlantic! Once we zeroed in on one we stayed there till it ran out of battery, and when it had to come up, we killed it!"

A long appraising look passed between them. Blunt was now again his old self, else there would have been no chance at all for Richardson's scheme. As Keith had remarked, it made no difference whether he really had conducted a good approach or only thought he had. The effect would be the same. But though his confidence had returned, at least for the time being, his prewar submarine experience could not have prepared him to cope with the realities of aircraft. They were there, and they had to be feared, but one had a job to do regardless. Rich and Keith had realized this would be the point upon which the decision would turn. They would be pitting the vigilance of their lookouts against the speed of an airplane and an enemy pilot's ability to deliver his airborne depth charges accurately.

"Yes sir," Richardson said, "that's just what I mean."

The storm must have come straight down from the Gulf of Pohai, also known as the Gulf of Chihli, which was an extraordinarily apt name, thought Al Dugan. Swathed in foul-weather gear and oilskins, he, four lookouts and a quartermaster strove to keep an alert watch on *Eel*'s heaving, ice-covered bridge. This was a hell of a way to fight a war. Even though he knew the scheme was to decoy Japanese antisubmarine effort away from *Whitefish*, it was just *Eel*'s luck to have to do it in a freezing norther. His own immediate misfortune was to have to spend three more hours on the bridge sticking his nose in it. This was the second day out in the middle of the Yellow Sea, and nearly all the time had been on the surface in this cursed storm. The bad weather had probably kept enemy aircraft more or less closed in also, for *Eel* had seen only half a dozen planes during the entire two-day period and, although she had deliberately dived late, the planes had never approached closely enough to drop depth charges. It was even possible the submarine wallowing in the frothy sea had escaped detection amid all the whitecapped waves. For that matter, no shipping had showed up in front of *Whitefish*'s torpedo tubes either. At least, she had sent no messages. By agreement, while in the Maikotsu Suido *Whitefish* was to remain under radio silence unless her presence was revealed by an attack upon a Japanese ship.

Very likely the five cargo ships sunk during the past several days had represented a pretty fair percentage of Japan's available shipping for the supply runs to China. This alone might explain *Whitefish*'s lack of contact; it was also likely that the Japanese convoy shipping officials were awaiting more certain evidence that the coast was clear before sending additional ships on the suddenly perilous voyage to the north. In the meantime, Dugan was thoroughly miserable. He hunched his shoulders inside his heavy garments, checked again to see that the hood of his parka was as tightly knotted around his face as possible. Even so, water was sneaking in, running down his neck, soaking the front of his shirt inside the fur-lined jacket which was under the waterproof parka. His mittens—he had worn a pair of woolen mittens inside a pair of leather ones—were soaked through. A thin sheeting of ice crystals had formed on the outside of the outer leather mittens, and they had lost all ability to keep out the cold. His mistake had been in thinking to warm his hands by shoving them in the pockets of his parka trousers. Water had somehow already found its way there, and it was not until he felt the wetness around his fingers inside the inner mittens that he had realized it.

The submarine was barely moving through the water, barely maintaining steerageway, keeping herself head on into the seas so that, should a sudden submergence be necessary, there would be minimal impedance by wave action. Also, to improve the diving time, *Eel* was riding well flooded down, her ballast tanks only partly emptied. She was consequently low in the water and logy in her motion, rising slowly to meet the white-crested waves as the sea thrust them relentlessly down upon her in monotonous procession. Always she rose a little, but never enough. The sea would burst through her bullnose and over her bow in a solid mass of green icy water which would then travel aft, draining swiftly away through her slatted foredeck as she struggled to rise beneath it. It inundated the forward five-inch gun and reached the base of the bridge with sufficient force to send another shower of spray and roiled white water solidly over the forty-milli-meter platform to burst against the steel bulwark behind which Dugan and his bridge crew were huddled. The lookouts had been brought down from their perches high on the periscope shears, instructed to re-main close together behind the bridge bulwarks. Watching the sky was the important thing, Al had told them, repeating the instructions that all previous Officers of the Deck had told the lookouts in their turns.

"Stay especially alert for aircraft coming in low to the water," Richardson had emphasized. There was no use to caution the lookouts about planes diving out of the sun. Until the past hour, there had been no sun. It was also unnecessary to stress to the lookouts—as all OODs had—that there was plenty of recent cause for the Japanese to be angry at any U.S. submarine they might come upon. Hopefully, they might still be willing to believe a single sub was responsible for the sinkings in the Yellow Sea, and without doubt upon finding one they would bring it under the heaviest attack they could muster. Cornelli, quartermaster of the watch, had responsibility for the after section of the sky and horizon, backing up the two lookouts assigned the port and starboard quarter. Dugan himself served that same function in the forward sector. Cornelli was also responsible for regular inspection of all six pairs of binoculars on the bridge, and for providing new dry lens paper to take the place of the wadded-up hunks of wet tissue which, after a few minutes of use, were no longer able to keep the binocular lenses clear.

It was late afternoon. The sun was low in the southwest, would be setting in another hour or so. Back aft, the feeble sputters of a single engine exhaust, constantly drowned as the sea rose above it, were a reminder that the battery was fully charged and the propellers turn-ing over at minimum speed. It was a reminder also that, beneath them, the people inside the submarine were warm and dry. Even the men in the operating engineroom, though they might be glad for a heavy jacket, would have no difficulty avoiding the blast of cold air coming in. They could have a sandwich or a cup or coffee anytime. In the meantime, Dugan was cold, hungry, and wet.

Eel was rising and falling slowly, alternately bow and stern, rolling slightly—not much. This was because of the large free surface effect of her only partly emptied ballast tanks. American submarines in the old days were considered to be unstable in this condition, and somehow the idea had persisted, but Dugan had never found it to be so. His only worries were the weather: the cold and freezing, the ice crunching about on the slatted bridge deck which made footing uncertain. Because of the cold he and his bridge crew moved more slowly, were more apt to slip or stumble, or interfere with each other. The railings around the hatch were slippery with frozen moisture. Getting six men below with bulky, frozen clothing would inevitably take longer than the eight seconds they had established as a standard in the sunny Hawaiian training areas. An occasional larger-than-usual sea would frequently come entirely over the bridge windscreen, drenching everyone. Were they forced to dive into such a sea, it was just possible the ship might go down more rapidly than usual, while at the same time the bridge personnel would be that much slower in getting below. This was one of the reasons why they had been brought down from their daylight perches on the periscope shears. All were no doubt very much aware of the problem, and their concern must have been increased by reflection upon the accident which had left Richardson and Oregon on the bridge a week ago.

It had been decided that the next time an airplane was sighted it would be the signal for *Eel* to submerge and remain submerged as if she really were intent upon evasion. Otherwise the Japanese might realize she was acting out of character and suspect she was decoying them. So far as Al Dugan and his bridge watch squad were concerned, this could not happen too soon.

The deeps of the ocean are always inviting to a submariner. It is only the surface of the sea that is sometimes harsh.

Heavy winds from the north had finally, only within the hour, blown away the leaden overcast. Visibility was excellent, the sky a brilliant blue in all directions without hint of a cloud. The sun, a low cheerless orb to the southwest, now approaching the horizon, had not been able to penetrate the intense cold. Even its usual radiant warmth had hardly been noticeable to Al Dugan's benumbed cheeks. With visibility like this, any aircraft should be spotted long before it came close enough to catch the *Eel* on the surface with a bomb or depth charge.

On the other hand, the Japanese must be aware of this also. They would come in close to the water, as low as they dared to fly, having started their attack runs from beyond the visible horizon. Perhaps this was what was going on, for no aircraft had been seen for several hours. In this event, of course, or at night, when visibility was reduced, the airplanes would come in on radar. *Eel* had had a new radar-signal-detection apparatus installed during the previous refit at Pearl Harbor, and this gadget, known as the APR, had already been useful to warn them of radar surveillance. More than once during the past two days it had enabled them to be safely submerged when the Japanese aircraft arrived. Were an aircraft to make a radar approach from over the horizon, the man on watch at the APR would be the first person in the ship to become aware of it. Dugan felt a measure of confidence as he ceaselessly searched the air above the horizon through his dampened binoculars. He would see the Japanese aircraft before it came, or get warning of it from the APR set in the control room. He was tired of waiting, wished the enemy would come. It would be a favor.

"Bridge!" It was the bridge speaker on the underside of the bridge overhang. "Bridge, APR signal! Strength one!"

A steady signal at strength three, according to ComSubPac, was the time to dive. "Strength one" meant only that an aircraft radar was in the vicinity, probably many miles away. Al pushed the "press to talk" button alongside the bridge speaker twice by way of acknowledgment.

"Bridge! APR signal coming in and out. Maximum strength one. Looks like an aircraft radar searching back and forth."

Dugan again pressed the bridge speaker button twice, using the heel of his mittened hand, for his fingers felt too numb to function.

There was a patrol plane in the air, probably carrying on a routine search in the Yellow Sea. The fluctuations in strength resulted from variations in the plane's own heading as it patrolled back and forth on its search line. If it ever remained steady, particularly if it gradually increased in strength while remaining steady, this would be definite indication that the plane had detected the submarine—a steel mass in a watery one—and was beginning a run in. Even before it reached strength three, in this case, Dugan silently promised himself, he would pull the plug.

"Lookouts, look alive now!" he sang out. "There's a plane in the area looking for us. He's pretty far away, but he might come closer!" Everyone on the bridge was already well aware of the situation, he knew, for they also had heard the report from the man on watch at the radar detector set.

Long seconds crawled by in slow procession. Finally Dugan pushed the button again. "Control, bridge. What's with that APR contact?"

"Still the same, Bridge. Getting stronger and weaker. Maximum strength one."

A bell tinkled in Dugan's mind. "Coming in and out," the man had said. One of the stratagems the Japanese had used, he remembered, as had U.S. aircraft in the Atlantic war, was to vary the strength of the radar beam to give the impression of searching while actually homing on a firm contact.

"Control, bridge. Ask Mr. Leone to take a look at that contact."

Keith's voice came back almost immediately through the speaker. "Bridge, control. Al, I'm here on the set. Just got here. It looks like two radars to me, both on the same frequency and both of them are cutting in and out rather rapidly."

"Control, bridge," said Dugan into the speaker, "does it look like they're on another contact?"

"That's what it looks like, Al," said Keith from below, his voice distinctly recognizable despite the bridge speaker's less than optimum reproduction quality. "But so far as we know, we're the only thing out here. Better stay on your toes up there. Maybe they're playing games with us."

"Double-sharp lookout, all hands!" shouted Dugan, carefully wiping up his binocular lenses again and swinging a careful search through the entire forward section of the horizon. The two forward lookouts would be doing the same, he knew, as would Cornelli and the two after lookouts in the other direction.

"Bridge, control," Keith again. "Definitely two radars. Both patrolling, but they're getting fainter now. APR strength one-half."

Dugan pushed the speaker button twice in relief and at the same time mild disappointment. If they had only steadied up for a while, he thought, we could be submerging where it's warm and comfortable. As he let go of the button the second time he realized he had momentarily cut off another transmission from Keith.

". . . maybe up to their regular stunt, Al. They've already spotted us six times out here. They must know where to look for us."

Dugan was about to reach for the speaker button to make another acknowledgment, had been leaning on the bridge windbreak with his binoculars over the edge, staring dead ahead at the horizon, when suddenly he noticed something. A tiny discontinuity, a thin dark line seemingly on the horizon, which suddenly disappeared. Instantly he knew what it was. "Clear the bridge!" he bellowed. He reached for the diving alarm, pressed it twice with his entire mittened hand, heard the reassuring sound of the diving alarm reproduced over the ship's general announcing system. "Dive! Dive!" he shouted into the bridge speaker.

He stood aside to permit the heavily bundled lookouts and quartermaster to get down the hatch. As they did so, he heard Cornelli screaming, "Aircraft! Coming in from astern!"

239

Two planes! One ahead and one astern. They *had* been working a game! They had been coordinating their attacks! One coming in from ahead, and now one coming in from astern. Both flying low to the water. How far away were they? How quick could the submarine dive? The lookouts were clear. Cornelli, waiting, jumped into the yawning hatch. His bulky, heavily clothed figure completely filled the hole.

Dugan had not heard the vents opening or the diesel engine shut off, but he was aware of the main induction slamming home behind him. A sea traveled up over *Eel*'s bow, broke over the forward forty-milli-meter platform, boiled up over the windscreen. She wasn't diving yet—couldn't be—but she was half-submerged anyway with this sea coming aboard. Water was pouring down the hatch all over Cornelli, who had less than a second before found the ladder and was descending as rapidly as he could. No time to waste. Dugan simply leaped onto Cornelli's back, knocking him down the ladder, falling down himself, grabbing the braided copper hatch lanyard in his hand as he descended. The wire rope slipped through his hands, but he expected this, felt the toggle slam into his wrist. His feet touched only a single rung of the ladder as his weight on the lanyard pulled the hatch down with him. A deluge of water was pouring into the ship through the hatch. It stopped sharply as the hatch slammed home. He held down hard on the lanyard, almost in a sitting position, while Cornelli picked him-self up, crowded past him, scrambled partway up the rungs of the ladder, and spun the dogging hand wheel shut.

"Hatch secured!" shouted Cornelli, through chattering lips.

There was half an inch of cold water sloshing around on the conning tower deck plates. No matter, it would quickly drain through into the bilges. "Take her down fast!" shouted Dugan. "Two aircraft making a run on us!" He released the lanyard, took two quick steps to the control room hatch, was gladdened to see Keith standing beneath him. The executive officer had evidently moved over from the radar detector and was now superintending the diving operation. He had himself grabbed the bow plane control wheel and was holding it on full dive. The lookout who would normally have taken the bow plane was standing beside him hastily pulling off his wet parka. Another lookout had the stern planes, was moving them to full dive as Dugan watched.

Dugan scrambled down the ladder to the control room, whispered hoarsely to Keith, "Two planes coming in, one ahead and one dead astern. They're right on the water and coming in fast. Get her down as fast as you can!"

"Right," said Keith. "I'll take the dive for now. You rig for depth charge. Get the watertight doors shut!"

Without answering, Dugan reached for the announcing system microphone, "All hands rig ship for depth charge!" he said into it urgently. "Shut all watertight doors! Two planes coming in for attack!" Approximately twenty seconds had passed since the diving alarm had sounded.

Richardson had joined the tense group in the control room, had heard the last few words of the colloquy between Leone and Dugan. "How far away would you say they were, Al?" he asked.

"Two or three miles, maybe a little more for the one I saw," responded Dugan. "I didn't see the other one, but I guess it was about the same. Cornelli saw it just as I sounded the diving alarm. They were making a coordinated attack on us."

"Down on the deck like that they probably aren't going more than a hundred eighty knots That's three miles a minute," said Richardson. "About half a minute more before they get here."

Dugan was feverishly divesting himself of his foul-weather gear, pulled the parka over his head, threw it on the chart table over the gyro compass in the center of the control room. A river of water ran from it over the linoleum top of the table, dripped to the deck beneath.

"What's the depth of water here, Keith?" asked Richardson.

"No more than two hundred fifty feet, Skipper," answered Keith, not taking his eyes away from the diving control panel. "We're under now. Depth five-oh feet."

"Go on over to a fifteen-degree down angle, Keith. We've got to get as deep as we can as quick as we can. Al, see that the sound heads are rigged in. We may hit bottom with this steep angle."

"Aye!" said Dugan as he reached again for the announcing microphone. "Rig in the sound heads," he ordered. "Forward torpedo room, bear a hand! Rig in the sound heads immediately. We may hit bottom. Report by telephone when they are rigged in."

Instead of easing off on the stern planes to level the ship after her initial dive, as was the ordinary procedure, the stern planesman under Keith's direction grimly held the stern planes in the "full dive" position. *Eel*'s deck continued to tilt down even more.

"All ahead emergency!" barked Richardson, vectoring his voice up the hatch to the conning tower. They could feel the increased bite of the electric motors as the electrician's mates opened their rheostats wide.

"We'll lose the bubble in the small-angle indicators, Captain," said Dugan. "It goes out at ten degrees."

"Let it," said Rich. "Shift to the large-angle indicators. Pass the word to all hands to rig ship for steep angle. The planes will figure to catch us within a few seconds after we've completely submerged, and they'll expect that we won't be very deep by that time. We've got to get just as deep as we can—left full rudder!" He explained the order tersely. "Got to get off the track. Coming in from ahead and astern that way means they're geared to drop their eggs right on line and ahead of our diving point. Can't help it if it slows up our dive a little."

The water which had recently fallen upon the control room deck had mixed with the carefully applied wax of a previous, less strenuous period. The linoleum deck had become slippery. The fifteen-degree dive angle, relatively shallow when drawn on a sheet of paper, assumed a strenuous, perceptibly out-of-horizontal attitude. Al Dugan braced himself against the corner of the table, still trying to peel off his outer clothing. Keith and Rich gripped the steep steel ladder, now leaning well past the perpendicular, which led from the control room to the conning tower. At its top the watertight hatch had been closed in response to the order to rig for depth charge. The two tool benches with padded tops, normally located on the deck just before the diving panel to provide seats for the men operating the bow and stern planes, had begun to slide on the deck. One of the lookouts, not immediately occupied, ranged himself forward of them, one hand gripping the side of the control room table, braced the other against the forward-most bench, kept them from slipping farther. Keith cast him a grateful glance.

"Seven-oh feet," said Keith. "Fifteen degrees down bubble. Forty-five seconds since we dived." The lookout whose place he had taken had by now removed his parka and foul-weather jacket, moved silently into position on the bow planes. Keith stepped back a foot.

"Fifty seconds," he said. "She's going down fast now."

"Make your depth two hundred feet, Keith," said Rich. "Hold your angle for a while, though, until passing about one hundred fifty feet."

All watched the depth gauges as, with excruciating slowness, they moved onward to the safe haven of the depths.

Richardson was doing some rapid mental calculations. "At fifteen degrees down bubble, the stern of the boat is about seventy-five feet higher than the bow, or roughly fifty feet higher than the control room, where the depth gauge is. That means our stern has only been out of sight for about ten seconds. We put the rudder over just about the right moment—there won't have been time for any noticeable change of course to be noted by the attacking aircraft. Since then we've changed course about thirty degrees to the left, which means we're about one hundred yards off the track already, except that the stern is probably only about fifty yards off the track."

There was a metallic thud followed by a clatter of loose objects from somewhere below. Muffled oaths came up through the hatch grating in the control room deck. A toolbox had slipped its moorings and had fallen to the deck in the pump room, no doubt bursting open and strewing its contents all about. Rich could imagine the cooks in their galley, one compartment aft, bracing themselves to hold dinner on the stoves. In the torpedo rooms, at least, the four torpedoes remaining were secured in the torpedo tubes, with tail buffers up tight. There was consequently no chance that a torpedo, poorly secured in a rack, perhaps with a faulty securing strap (a number had broken just in normal use), might get loose. He found himself thinking that the initial kick of the rudder would of course have been to starboard, and the propeller wash, no doubt visible on the surface, would probably have first indicated an apparent change of course to the right. A trained naval pilot, however, would not have been fooled. The propeller wash must still be coming to the surface. Sixty seconds had passed. The depth bombs must have been released into the water.

"Passing one-five-zero feet," said Keith.

"Take the angle off the boat, Keith. Zero bubble."

"Stern planes on full rise," ordered Keith. Obediently the stern planesman, still swathed in his heavy rainclothes and submarine jacket, his face now covered with large globules of sweat, reversed the direction in which he was holding his control wheel.

"Ease the rudder," ordered Rich. "Rudder amidships!" *Eel* was now some forty-five degrees away from her initial heading, and with her rudder amidships and her unusual down-by-the-nose attitude coming off rapidly, her speed went up another notch, to nearly nine knots. Nine knots to outrun an airplane coming twenty times as fast!

"Sixty-five seconds," someone said. If they were dropping, they had already done so. Sonar, which might have heard the charges hitting the water, was of course blind, because the retractable heads below the keel had been housed. At this speed they could hear nothing anyhow. The acoustic frequency head mounted topside had been manned when the submarine dived, but its operator could hear only the wild roar of water through which the submarine was tearing at maximum submerged speed. It would not be long—it could not be long—they must have dropped. . . .

WHAM! A tremendous, side-splitting, careening blow! The fifteen-degree down angle which *Eel* had assumed had already perceptibly lessened, and it was no longer necessary to hold on to the steel ladder which they had previously been holding so tightly. Rich and Keith were, however, still gripping it, and they could feel it buckle within their grasp and then spring back to its original shape. The full shock of the depth charge seemed thus to have been communicated directly into their own bodies. Al Dugan, less securely braced, had perhaps felt the shock less but was nevertheless thrown to the floor. Something had gone wrong in the pump room. The sound of an electric motor increasing rapidly in speed, the normally inconspicuous whir of its running rising violently in pitch until it nearly resembled a police siren. This could be disastrous. Through the cloud of dust raised by the explosion and the confusion occasioned by the shock of its nearness, Rich was conscious of Keith and the planesmen standing steadily to their posts, rocked though they were, yet desperately fighting to maintain control of their leaping, quivering equipment. Throughout the ship the men on watch must be going through the same thing, silently and desperately, pitting their wits and their training against the blow of the enemy.

WHAM! A second explosion, louder even than the first. Then, almost coming on top of each other, WHAM! WHAM! Two more, slightly less loud.

"Stern planes jammed on full rise!" The stern planesman's desperate shout instantly brought Keith and Richardson to his side.

"All stop!" shouted Richardson. This would at least eliminate the wash of the emergency ahead propellers against the stern planes immediately behind them, would reduce their upward thrust, which would otherwise have *Eel* on the surface within seconds.

"Shift to hand power!" snapped Keith. Releasing his control wheel, the stern planesman grabbed the shift lever, tried to pull it out of its socket in order to place it in the hand-power position. It would not move. Keith and Richardson placed their hands over his on the handle, braced their feet on the diving panel, pulled with the combined strength of three men. It snapped loose, and together the three shoved it into the hand-power position. Swiftly Keith reached for the folded-in cranking handle on the periphery of the four-foot-diameter stern plane wheel, pulled it out against its spring, set it into its socket. He and the stern planesman each placed both hands upon it, leaned their entire weight into the wheel, began laboriously, wordlessly, and with frantic speed, to crank it against heavy resistance toward the zero position.

Al Dugan, having picked himself up from the floor, joined Richardson. Keith and the stern planesman were cranking furiously. The stern plane angle indicator *was* moving, though very much more slowly than under hydraulic power.

WHAM! Another depth charge, and a few seconds later, WHAM! A sixth. No one paid any attention. The emergency was in the stern planes. They must be leveled before the boat took the up angle which could spell disaster. Already the fifteen-degree down angle had been reduced to zero. Now it was going the other way. Rich noticed with approval that the bow planesman, very much aware of the desperate struggle taking place immediately to his left and watching it with an intent look of dismay, had instinctively and without orders turned his bow plane wheel to "dive" to counteract the effect of the stern planes. At least, he still had control in hydraulic power, and since the propellers had been stopped, the immense effect of the stern planes upon the attitude of the submarine would be lessened. Normally, the submerged maneuvering convention was that bow planes control the depth of the submarine and stern planes its angle. Richardson put his hand on the man's shoulder. "Good work, Smitty," he said. Under the stress of the moment, unhabitual use of the man's nickname came naturally. He turned his attention back to the stern plane wheel. The indicator was now nearing zero, indicating that the vital control surface had been restored to its neutral position.

"Good going, Keith," said Richardson. "And the same for you, Blackwood," addressing the perspiring and panting stern planesman. He was still dressed in the heavy clothing he had worn for his lookout stint on the bridge, and must obviously be pouring with sweat inside. It was hot in the control room. With all the doors and hatches shut and all bulkhead valves closed in the ventilation lines, there was no circulation of air. Less than two minutes before, Blackwood had been near to freezing on the bridge. Now he was roasting down below.

"All ahead one-third," said Rich. "Do you want to see if you can put the stern planes back in hydraulic power?"

"We'll try it," said Keith. "What do you think the trouble was, Al?"

"My guess is that the depth charge went off pretty near to the stern planes while they were on hard rise, and jammed them into the stops. Didn't you find it pretty hard to crank them clear in hand?" said Al.

"Right," said Keith, while Blackwood nodded. "They went much easier once we started them moving."

Richardson crossed to the general-announcing-system control station, punched the call button for the after torpedo room. "Stern room," he said into the microphone, "is there any visible damage to the stern plane ram or hydraulic system?"

"Negative, Control," said a voice immediately. "One of those depth charges sounded like it was right alongside, and it really gave them a jolt, but everything looks okay."

"All right," said Keith. "Go ahead and shift, Blackwood, but stand by to shift right back into hand power if you don't have control in hydraulic."

Gravely Blackwood operated the shift mechanism, tested his plane, nodded, reported to Keith, "Stern planes look okay, sir. I have control in hydraulic power."

"Good," said Rich. Then, addressing Keith, "Make your depth two-zero-zero feet. I daresay those planes will stick around awhile, so we'll just stay down here until they've had a chance to get tired. Have all compartments check for damage and report."

As was to be expected, the close shave with the two aircraft was the main topic of conversation throughout the ship. There had, however, been no damage. A fuse had been knocked out of the field circuit of one of the air compressor motors, causing it nearly to run away, but Lichtmann, on watch in the pump room, had been on the point of cutting off the air compressors anyway, as was routine on a dive. He had managed to cut the armature current before any serious damage had been done. It would be well, however, to check it carefully, Dugan reported, before using that particular air compressor again. Fortunately, the pump room harbored two of the vital mechanisms.

"At least, Commodore," said Richardson, trying to make as light as he could of the incident, "they obviously had located us earlier, and carefully planned this attack. That means our decoy plan is working."

"Too damn well, if you ask me," responded Blunt. "Whitey Everett better have something to show for this, is all I can say!"

The wolfpack commander's words were not a witticism. The two were having coffee alone in the wardroom. Clearly, Richardson's scheme had gone too far for Blunt's peace of mind. He must move carefully to avoid driving him back into the unrealistic state he had been in. Obviously, something serious, either psychological or physical, was happening to him. Keith had stated the obvious fact: stress of any kind was destructive to him.

Indeed, Richardson had already decided that the ComSubPac directive not to dive until the APR contact strength had reached three was obviously not applicable if an aircraft had previous knowledge of the submarine's presence. During an attack run it would naturally reduce the strength of its radar signals to avoid alerting a radar detector aboard the target submarine. Henceforth, *Eel* would dive at strength one, or upon any persistent APR contact, whatever the strength. . . . He hoped there would be a message from *Whitefish* that night indi-

cating that the stratagem carried out at so much risk had been successful.

But *Whitefish* sent no message. Instead was a message from Com-
SubPac:

RECENT BIG FUSS IN YELLOW SEA MUST BE DUE TO EFFECTIVE AREA COVER-
AGE AND SINKINGS BY BLUNTS BRUISERS X INDICATIONS INTENSIFIED ANTI-
SUBMARINE ACTIVITY BY AIR PATROLS X CONVOYS STILL MOVING ON WEST
COAST OF KOREA ALSO CHINA COAST CLOSE INSHORE X GREAT WORK JOE
COMSUBPAC SENDS X

"They must be going around Whitey, Commodore," said Richardson. "He's in the Maikotsu Suido, all right, probably right in the middle
of it. But this message says the ships are running close inshore, and my
guess is they're staying just as close to shore as they can get. They're
probably moving at night also, which could be another reason he's not
picking them up." Rich had strenuously protested against requiring
Whitefish to send radio messages. Japanese direction-finding stations
had doubtless been alerted to locate the submarine in the Yellow Sea.
If they should now recognize that there were two subs to worry about
instead of only one, the risk to both would be intensified and the chance
of targets for either greatly reduced. *Eel* could send messages for the
time being, he had argued, for the presence of one submarine in the
Yellow Sea was known; doing so, in fact, was desirable to draw attention away from the location of her wolfpack mate.

"I recommend we send *Whitefish* a message tonight that we're coming in to join her in the Maikotsu Suido," announced Richardson
soberly. "We can send the message while we're still out here, and tell
her not to receipt for it or open up her radio in any way. We have
four fish left, and if we're lucky, we might be able to bag another
ship. If we can get one out of a convoy running along the coast, that
will divert the rest of them offshore into the middle of the Maikotsu
Suido, and that's where *Whitefish* will be waiting for them." Rich
could see that Blunt was somewhat less than enthusiastic.

"Why don't we just tell *Whitefish* to go into shallow water?" said
Blunt.

Richardson could feel his eyes narrowing. If Blunt could not see
the obvious, somebody had to tell him. "Listen to me," he said; then
suddenly he realized that his voice had taken on much the same timbre
as when he had protested Blunt's callous comments about Joan
and Cordelia Woods. "Listen: Les Hartly lost his ass and his ship because he didn't know his business! It was our job to square him away,
and we didn't do it. He thought he knew all the answers because he'd

been a skipper a long time, but a lot of things have changed since he made war patrols. He ran into a bear trap without even knowing what was going on, and they nailed him. It's just the opposite with Whitey Everett. This is his first command. He's not sure of himself. He's good at the periscope, but he's never made a surface attack at night, and you know he won't. He'll never go after those ships in shallow water, either, and we'll just waste the rest of our time out here in the area. Dammit, Commodore, we've got to back in there! We know where the enemy is, and that's where we've got to go!" The intensity of Richardson's words clearly surprised the squadron commander. A lot depended upon Blunt's reaction to Richardson's harsh words. His mention of Les Hartly had been just right. Blunt hesitated. Rich moved in for the kill.

"Commodore, Les was away from the war too long. Things changed a great deal while he was in Mare Island getting the *Chicolar* ready. In a different way, the same thing is the problem with Whitey. Hardly anybody has figured everything out on his first patrol in command. Even you, sir. This is your first war patrol. You get to have a feel for the enemy after you've been fighting them. You can't get it by reading patrol reports. Keith and I are the experienced ones. This is the sixth war patrol for me and the ninth for Keith. We know what we can do, and we know what the enemy can do. ComSubPac has some experienced skippers on his staff. He knows, too. He is practically ordering us to go into the shallow water after them, and he's right."

The squadron commander said nothing. His eyes flickered twice as he listened. Richardson realized he had carried the day. In a very real sense, command of the wolfpack had now passed to him. The patrol had already cost something in terms of mutual respect and friendship— this would merely add a little more to the price—but the way was clear for him to put his scheme into execution.

Shortly before dawn, having run at maximum speed to the east all night, *Eel* slipped between two of the islands at the southern edge of the western side of the Maikotsu Suido. Immediately she felt the current set to the north. Relentlessly Rich drove her toward the coast of Korea, intending to get as near as possible before it became necessary to dive. Perhaps all the aircraft patrols were far to the west into the Yellow Sea. Morning twilight was well advanced before the need to remain undetected caused him reluctantly to submerge.

By ten o'clock *Eel* was patrolling 2,000 yards off a point of land around which any ships heading up or down the coast would have to pass. It was an ideal spot for submarine patrol, provided one was acclimated to shallow water. There was no way traffic hugging the coast could avoid a submarine stationing herself here. Shortly after noon a single freighter, unescorted, chugged slowly up the coast, zigzagging perfunctorily, puffing a cloud of black smoke from obviously ancient boilers, secure in the information that ships had been passing daily, that no submarines were close in to shore. The approach was almost like a dance, simple in its execution, flawless in its performance, strenuous only in some of the details. With a slight stretch of the imagination, the maneuvers, the periscope work, the macabre ritual before the sacrifice, could be compared to the high leaps and entrechats of a dancer acting out the denouement of a tragic ballet. Shortly before *Eel* achieved the firing position, more smoke appeared to the south. The situation was exactly as Rich had hoped it might be. One last pirouette, a rising crescendo of music, a final leap before the graceful submission to the inevitable outcome—only the ending was barbaric because it was real, not fanciful, its artistry shattered in the thunderous roar of two torpedoes striking ten seconds apart, a cloud of smoke, debris, and steam rising from the vitals of the doomed ship—this too was real—and it was death, and murder, and war, and no longer artistic, but only dreadful.

And then the ship was gone, leaving wreckage floating about on the water, a matted slick of coal dust, junk and life rafts, and a single damaged lifeboat into which a dozen men climbed. More men were on the life raft, and more clung to pieces of wreckage. But some of them clung to nothing, merely floated motionless, scalded to death in the engine room or boiler rooms, broken by the shock of the earthquake which had overwhelmed them, converted suddenly from living sensate beings into the pitiless flotsam of war.

Far to the south, three columns of smoke turned sharply westward. They would move well out into the Maikotsu Suido before heading north again, knowing that the submarine so catastrophically revealed in their path could not possibly follow submerged. An aircraft would soon appear, did appear, circling the area of devastation off the little point of land. Richardson watched it all through the tiny tip of the attack periscope, barely exposed above the placid surface.

Four hours later Stafford reported distant explosions to the northward. Some of them, he said, sounded like torpedoes, but this must have been his imagination willfully embroidering upon the situation. No one at that distance could tell a torpedo from a depth charge.

He had, however, counted twenty-five or more explosions. Six of them, or perhaps as many as ten, judging by their timing, could certainly have been torpedoes. *Whitefish* must have got into action.

ATTACKED THREE SHIP CONVOY POSITION MIKE XRAY FORTY TWO X SANK ONE FREIGHTER X DEPTH CHARGED X TEN TORPEDOES REMAINING ALL TUBES LOADED X CLEARING AREA TO INSPECT FOR DAMAGE X. The message was sent in the wolfpack code and therefore required no identification as to addressee or sender.

"He fired six fish and probably missed with his second salvo," commented Blunt. "At least he equalized his expenditure of torpedoes and has six forward and four aft ready to go. That was good planning."

It was, of course, exactly what every submarine skipper should endeavor to do. Although considerable design effort had been expended, no workable scheme had ever been developed to permit torpedoes to be transferred from one end of a submarine to the other without taking them out of the ship. Even though dismantled into its three main components—air flask, warhead, and afterbody—the air flask was too long to be maneuvered around the bends in the congested fore-and-aft passageway, even if there were equipment to do it with. Obviously, a prudent submarine captain would do his best to equalize torpedo expenditures between the forward and after torpedo rooms so that the undesirable condition of having a surplus of torpedoes in one end and empty tubes in the other would not occur.

"Commodore," said Rich, "I think we'd better follow Whitey and clear the area too. We've raised so much hell here in the Maikotsu Suido that they'll have all of their available ASW forces out looking for us. By now they've got to know for sure that there are two submarines involved."

"What do you suggest, Rich?" asked Blunt. There was a querulous note in his voice.

"This is the first time any submarine has gone into the Maikotsu Suido since the *Trigger*, more than a year ago. Before her it was the *Wahoo*, but they were the only two. Both were topnotch subs, with top skippers, and both reported this area as being difficult for submarines because of the high current and confined waters. No subs have come here since the *Trigger*, and the Japanese have had a clear run through here. No doubt they figured for some reason we simply were not up to sending any more boats here. Now, all of a sudden, they have lost six ships in the Maikotsu, and two more just beyond its borders. They've already saturated the area with antisub air patrols. They've got to know, now, there are two submarines here. They've got to stop all traffic, at least in this vicinity, until they find them."

Blunt seemed to accept this analysis.

"So, all we're going to find around here for the next few days are air and surface patrols. We have about a week left in the area, and I think we ought to try to get rid of at least some of those ten fish Whitey has remaining. If we move right away and catch a convoy running along the Chinese coast, the Japs might even think there are four subs in the Yellow Sea. That will likely make them shut down all their traffic for a while, and that alone will hurt them."

Blunt appeared to agree, yet he remained irresolute. "There's no reason for *Eel* to go over there," he said. "Those two fish you have left aft won't be much use." The unstated portion of the argument, the important part of it, Blunt still could not see: without the presence of the *Eel* to drive her, *Whitefish* would find no more targets.

The discussion would have gone on longer. Richardson had not expected an easy victory. The degree to which he could push for his own point of view had to be balanced against the resultant stiffening, the psychological resistance which Rich had by now come to expect. Admiral Small, in Pearl Harbor, made it all academic. For the second time, his message was most complimentary: DEPREDATIONS OUR BOATS CLOSE INSHORE KOREA HAVE CAUSED JAPANESE FITS X WELL DONE BRUISERS, it said. Then it went on to the meat of the communication:

KWANTUNG ARMY EMBARKING TWO DIVISIONS THREE LARGE TRANSPORTS TSINGTAO X DEPARTURE IMMINENT X ESCORTED BY TOP ASW TEAM RPT TOP ASW TEAM NOW REDUCED FROM THREE TO TWO MIKURAS PLUS DAY-LIGHT AIR COVER X INDICATIONS CONVOY BOUND FOR ICEBERG X WILL SORTIE DURING DARKNESS FOR HIGH SPEED DAYLIGHT DASH ACROSS YELLOW SEA TO COAST KOREA X MUST NOT RPT MUST NOT ARRIVE X COMSUBPAC SENDS X TERMINATE ALL OTHER OPERATIONS CMA MAKE MAXIMUM EFFORT X

On a moonless night in a cold but musty sea, *Eel* arrowed at maximum sustained speed to the northwest. The storm of the past week had blown away the customary overcast, but this could not last long in the Yellow Sea, and the cloud cover with its atmosphere of sea dust had returned. Somewhere to starboard, *Whitefish* was also running for the same destination. Now, the decision made, Richardson found himself unable to remain in the warmth and comfort of *Eel*'s below-deck spaces, or to participate in the interminable strategy sessions in the wardroom. Nor was there solace in the bellowing roar of four powerful diesel engines, the purposeful routine of the control room, or the quiet readiness of the conning tower. There was no interest left in the torpedo rooms; only two useless fish remained, both aft—well, not quite useless. If *Eel* could engage the escorts, take them away from the convoy, *Whitefish* had ten torpedoes with which to deal with the three troop transports. *Eel*'s two fish might give her some capability, should an opportunity develop, of handling at least one of the two remaining *Mikuras*. As to the other, he would simply have to take what came and do what he could. The important thing was to make it possible for Whitey Everett to carry on, for only *Whitefish* could do the job that had to be done.

Restlessly, Richardson wandered from forward torpedo room to after torpedo room. The supreme test of his career, of his command of *Eel*, was about to come. He must be ready for it, must meet it, without adequate weapons. Only once before, in his youth, had he been faced with a similar situation. On a camping trip with three other boys, all of them Eagle Scouts, they had come upon a female grizzly bear with young. The bear attacked, the boys ran, and she caught one of them. Rich had saved his life by making a huge show of attacking the cub, striking it with a stick until it bawled, with result that its mother left her victim and made for him instead. He had by consequence spent the night in a tree, from where he had continued to occupy the bear's attention while the other scouts took their injured companion to safety. The totally unexpected conclusion to the affair was that the Senator from his state, learning of it from a newspaper account, had offered him a vacant appointment to the Naval Academy for the following year.

That had been nearly fourteen years ago, and there were some analogies to his present situation. The wolfpack commander had been quite right in his observation that the two torpedoes remaining, both in stern tubes, would be of little use. Perhaps they could sink one of the transports—indeed, if the chance offered, he would seize it. But *Eel*'s job clearly was to help *Whitefish* get into action with her ten torpedoes, and if necessary she must be prepared to take the required risk. If Richardson could divert the attention of the escorts, Everett would be able to make an unopposed approach. With the transports in close formation, as they would be, he ought to be able to hit at least two of them.

In the ensuing confusion *Eel* would have her best chance to evade the escorts. Then, if she could somehow get on the surface unobserved, and providing she had not been forced to expend her two now doubly precious torpedoes—how fortunate that he had insisted on taking the two extra fish!—there might yet be an opportunity to pick off the third troopship. Even if *Eel*'s torpedoes were all gone by then, there were still the deck guns. Or, by re-engaging the escorts (for they would have raced to rejoin their injured charges) *Eel* might still be able to provide the ingredient which would enable Whitey Everett to make one final effort.

252

The dangers of the course he was setting for *Eel* were, however, also very clear. With only two torpedoes remaining, and both of them in stern tubes, she was not in a good defensive position. There were, of course, the deck guns, and a single unescorted troopship might be attacked with surface gunfire; but the transport, too, would have guns. Furthermore, she would be calling for aircraft on her radio. A long fight would undoubtedly ensue, and the longer it lasted, the more the probability that an airplane would abruptly terminate it. A fight with the two escorts was even more out of the question; and should there be only one, whatever the outcome of such a battle, *Eel* would almost certainly be in no condition to pursue and attack anything.

The only place in the ship which seemed to offer what he sought— the silence, the solitude, the contemplative peace—was the alert quiet of *Eel*'s darkened bridge. Here he could come closest to the privacy his troubled thoughts craved. It was cold, but he had protected himself with foul-weather clothing. The air was calm and relatively dry. The cold did not seem to penetrate, even though *Eel* was surging through the quiet waters at maximum speed.

There must be a following wind. The exhaust from four main engines, spewing their diesel defiance into the dark Japanese-controlled sea, proved him right. With *Eel* fully surfaced and the sea quiet, the exhaust pipes were a good six inches or more clear of the water. The water spray and smoke were directed downward, but the smoke reversed itself, rose lazily in four tiny plumes which hung suspended above the ship as they continually rose and were continually fed from beneath, until they disappeared above into the dark night.

He stood silently against the after rail, bracing himself in the corner it made with the forty-millimeter gun cradled there. A few feet forward of him, two lookouts and a quartermaster, maintaining their vigil, paid him no attention. Farther forward loomed the bulky after portion of the periscope standards, and beyond them the bulletproof bridge bulwarks and windscreen in which he could dimly make out the round heads of the Officer of the Deck and two more lookouts. He had forgotten to notice who had the deck—no, he hadn't forgotten; it was Al Dugan, who had reported as Rich came on the bridge that the most recent survey of the hydraulic system indicated it was performing as well as could be expected, but would require another thorough overhaul upon return to Pearl Harbor.

Bungo Pete had not been in his mind of recent days, had been pretty well driven out of it by the emergency over Joe Blunt. Moonface had also helped him forget for a time. It occurred to him that he might have happened upon the motivations behind the pseudo samurai. Ambitious he undoubtedly was. He was also imbued with the idea of re-discovering an ancestral culture, which, in California, must have been ridiculed. Had he been able to bring in the broken commanding officer of a second submarine, after the destruction of *Chicolar*, his status among his fellows would have risen high indeed; but it would have risen highest in his own recently repatriated mind.

Now, in a moment of understanding, Richardson could see why his occasional images of Bungo Pete, in reverie or nightmare, almost always were a composition of persons he knew and admired. Sammy Sams, from *Walrus'* training days in Balboa; funny that he should have so stuck in his mind. Joe Blunt, naturally—before the present patrol. Jerry Watson, occasionally. Admiral Small. But never Moonface. Moonface was the antithesis of Nakame, of all he admired in his su-periors, all he could admire and appreciate in an enemy. Yet even though Rich could admire such an enemy as Nakame, he could at the same time set in motion the events which, because there was a war, might result in Nakame's death no less surely than that of an enemy despised.

Or his own death. That was never far from the equation.

In the effort to restore Blunt there had been another motive, of course: that of regard for a once-adored superior. He had done all he could, all he knew to do. And he had failed—that he now recognized. The occasional strangeness, the lack of sensitivity, even Blunt's new habit of speaking in a series of tired clichés, were evident at Pearl before the patrol began. The wonder was that Admiral Small had noticed nothing. Perhaps more accurately, the admiral had not realized that what he had seen was deeper than mere staleness at a desk job. Otherwise Small would never have permitted Blunt to go to sea.

Lately Rich had begun to feel Blunt's difficulty was more than psychological. The mind which only a few months ago had been so precise, so capable, so courageous, now could not stand stress or re-sponsibility. Keith must be right: while some sort of psychological breakdown could not be ruled out, the signs pointed to something physical. His shifts of mood, even of capabilities, were too sudden, too extreme, to be merely a state of mind or emotion. Keith had suggested taking Yancy, the pharmacist's mate, into their confidence, but Rich refused, agreeing finally only to Keith's borrowing, without explana-tion, some of the texts Yancy had stowed in his medical locker. But the books, which both Keith and Richardson studied surreptitiously, gave little enlightenment beyond appreciation that a number of obscure influences could be at work.

Bungo Pete and Moonface were both now in the past. He had killed

Nakame. This was something that had to be done. But he had refrained from killing Moonface when he had the chance. And of the two, Moonface unquestionably deserved destruction far more than Bungo Pete. But the destruction of Moonface would have had no meaning. Bungo had been an honorable opponent, a respected—if feared—enemy. Moonface was a sadistic maniac. Why had he stayed his hand with Moonface? Why had he not taken him prisoner when he had the opportunity? Was his failure to do so an indication of an unexplained weakness within himself that responded in some peculiar inverted way to the stresses of war? Or was he losing his sense of proprieties under the stresses of war and combat? Was he, somehow, equating the mercy shown Moonface as, in some strange way, expiation of the blood sin he had committed against Nakame?

But in a larger sense, what was sin? In a disordered world, could one hold to any fundamental of order, or must one's basic sanity, one's sense of right or wrong, also be laid upon the altar of conflict? The war had been begun by evil men controlled by ambition and greed, but even they had ceaselessly announced the holiness of their aims, the legitimacy and rightness of what they sought to accomplish. Did they believe their own propaganda? Of this, of course, he had no way of knowing, but it was at least possible that they did believe it. Furthermore, millions of good men, not involved in the high political machinations which had resulted in the war, believed it because they had to. They had no other choice. Yet, in so doing, they sacrificed their own individuality, their own clearness of perception, their own birthright of humanity.

He, Edward Richardson, Commander, U.S. Navy, encased in his steel prison which was also his instrument, his pride, and his weapon, his submarine *Eel*, his samurai sword, was only a tiny piece of flotsam amid the jetsam of the world. Yet he was master of the destiny of eighty men on board, in a way controller of the destiny of eighty more men in another submarine a few miles away. He had set them once again hurrying through the night on an errand at the end of which, if all went as he planned it, lay death and destruction for hundreds, possibly thousands, of human beings who had neither done him offense nor could do so even if they were aware of his existence.

Joan and Laura. The second his ideal (he now admitted this to himself), but for a hundred reasons forever unattainable. The other real, warm flesh and blood, greatly giving, yet somehow soiled by the war that had blemished him too. They also were flotsam among the jetsam of the world, drifting helplessly down the path fate had allotted to them. Just as he was.

Eel dipped gently in the slowly rolling sea, speeding forward into the darkness. Destination: the coast of China, her four diesel engines roaring at flank speed, carrying fate within her bowels. But fate, real enough in so many ways, had little to do with the two torpedoes she had remaining of her original armament.

Deep under the surface of the Yellow Sea, a single shielded light had burned long in an otherwise darkened compartment. Two men had sat hunched in their seats, the corner of the table between them, staring at the chart spread upon it, measuring distances and dimensions with navigator's dividers, studying every feature. Committing it to memory, as though it had not been before them nearly every night, in one form or another. Conversation was low, sparse, and in quiet tones. It would not be right to awaken those who needed their rest. It was against the unspoken code of the combat submariner to disturb anyone's sleep except to call him for a watch, or because of some emergency. But this was not the reason for the deep quiet in which Keith and Richardson had conducted their private conference.

Elsewhere in the submarine, the regular ordered bustle of one-third of the crew standing watch prevailed as usual. The men on telephone watch in each torpedo room; the enginerooms with their great, indomitable diesels; the electrician's mates with their extraordinary, complex, switching cubicles; the cooks in their tiny, efficient galley; the quiet, methodical nerve center in the control room; the silent, ominous conning tower. Here, in the empty wardroom, with the others busy elsewhere or snatching a few hours' rest in their bunks against the next day's trials, skipper and exec spoke in lower than normal voices in intuitive recognition that they were planning to force action upon another man, and the eighty men of his crew, whom the fortunes of war had placed temporarily under their control.

Whitey would not run his ship close in to shore. He could be efficient only where he had sufficient depth of water to be comfortable, though no submariner could really be comfortable in the Yellow Sea. But he would not run into shallow water. Yet the coastline of China, particularly in the area around Tsingtao, was virtually all shallow water. And it went without saying that the enemy ships were choosing the shallowest water of all, barely deep enough to avoid running aground in the ageless muck the rivers of China had been carrying down since the beginning of history.

It was up to Richardson to bring the *Whitefish* into combat, to pass the rapier of action from his own spent hand to that of Whitey Everett, and, in the name of Blunt, cause Whitey to fulfill the mission on which so much depended.

- 10 -

The United States Ship *Eel* lay to quietly off Tsingtao. Her diesels were silent, their customary mutter stilled. Less than a mile away to starboard, the bulky outline of land brooded over the placid water. There was no moon. Darkness was complete. The only sense that could really be said to be receiving stimulation was the sense of smell. Reaching across a small stretch of shallow water, permeating everything, was the sweet-sour odor of land. It was the same smell so frequently referred to as "the smell of the sea," but the seaman knows it as the smell where sea and land join.

Below decks, the highly structured life of a submarine on war patrol in enemy-controlled waters was going on as usual, except for one important difference—an extreme, unnatural quietness. Only the absolutely necessary machinery was running: the ventilation blowers and the air-conditioning sets. In every compartment men went about their routine duties with a special softness about all their movements. Some had removed their shoes. All were walking about very quietly, avoiding all unnecessary noise, speaking to each other in low, somber tones. What work was necessary was performed slowly, carefully. Tools involved were carefully wrapped in rags, so that there would be no inadvertent noise of the striking of steel upon steel to be transmitted through the hull to the water and to unfriendly ears.

It would not be correct to infer that *Eel*'s crew was at battle stations, for no such signal had been given. In fact, it had been announced that the general alarm would not be rung. If needed, the call to action would be transmitted by telephone to all compartments. Everyone was enjoined to remain in the vicinity of his battle station—not a difficult order to comply with in view of the submarine custom of doing this without orders when action was believed imminent. Even those on watch, required by the ship's organization to tend certain machinery or remain in certain areas, were, by Keith's careful design, on their battle stations as well.

On the bridge the silence was oppressive. There was almost a crowd there, for in addition to the regular watch, consisting of Buck Williams, Scott, four lookouts, and Ensign Johnny Cargill, assistant OOD, there were also the executive officer, the captain, and the wolfpack commander. All kept their binoculars ceaselessly to their eyes, and each, had he been asked, would have confessed nervousness over the excruciatingly loud hum of the few pieces of machinery still running. Surely this could be heard many yards away, perhaps as far as several hundred yards! It could awake a trained ear to the fact that the unusual silhouette floating so quietly in the shallows was actually the upper part of a nearly submerged submarine, full of tense, foreign-looking men.

Eel had been trimmed so that her main deck was virtually at the water's edge. Anyone approaching from a little distance would see only the submarine's bridge, dominated by the closely spaced periscope supports and, lower down, apparently standing in the water, two bulky structures from each of which protruded a stubby, evil-looking gun barrel. The submarine's main deck, 300 feet of it lying flat on the water, would not be visible until one came right upon it. The only evidence of its presence would be a strange continuity of flatness superimposed on the gently undulating, uneasy sea.

Two vitally important objects had been achieved by flooding down. First was a great reduction in silhouette, a change in the entire outward configuration of the ship. The second was that should *Eel* unexpectedly drift upon a mud flat, it would be a simple matter, by blowing tanks, to decrease her draft as much as six feet aft and ten feet forward, thus freeing her of the bottom and permitting her to be driven immediately into deeper water without even the necessity of starting engines. The instant power of her batteries, always available, was something no surface ship could match.

It was 1 o'clock in the morning of a moonless night, and the Yellow Sea was overcast with its customary haze. *Eel* had surfaced close in to shore and crammed a rapid charge into her batteries. Then, with every sense alert, the fathometer taking occasional "single ping" soundings of the bottom, she had slowly moved in to shallow water. Conversation on the bridge was desultory, in low voices clipped short, as though someone might hear them from the shore if they talked too loudly or too long.

"This is the third night in a row we've been here. I wonder what's holding up those transports?"

"Maybe the Kwantung Army is slower embarking its troops than ComSubPac figures. They must be bringing a lot of equipment with them."

"Maybe they know we're here. Maybe they mean to wait till we have to leave station."

"Then they'll have a long wait, Commodore. The second message said to remain here until further orders, or until the ships come out. Before we left Pearl, Admiral Small told us this was the main reason for the wolfpack. It's up to us to stop them, no matter how long we have to stay. If we need to, we can stretch our provisions for another month."

Blunt, Leone, and Richardson had congregated by themselves around the starboard TBT, were leaning their elbows on the bridge bulwarks, holding their binoculars to their eyes, speaking softly so their voices would not carry to the others on the bridge. Williams and Scott, sensing their exclusion, had taken the other corner, near the port TBT. The lookouts, several feet above on their platforms, were likewise out of earshot.

"Dammit, Rich, I shouldn't have let you shoot off all your fish the way you did. Those two you have left aft aren't enough for this sort of a donnybrook!"

"When he briefed us, the admiral didn't know when the Kwantung Army would move these divisions, or even if they would at all. This is the first word about them he's sent us, and we're the only U.S. forces within five hundred miles. There's twelve torpedoes between us and the *Whitefish*, and he expects us to make good use of them." Richardson's reply was direct because the whole topic had already been covered in detail.

"A week ago the radio skeds had a message saying the *Sawfish* and *Piper* were en route to patrol stations off Iwo Jima," said Keith, "and the *Pike* and *Whale* are off Okinawa. They're the nearest boats."

"That's right, Commodore, and that makes four new patrol stations ComSubPac has to fill. That could be why he never sent a replacement for *Chicolar*." It was perhaps unnecessary to bring up the lost submarine again, but Blunt must be headed off before he suddenly reversed his previous approval of Richardson's scheme.

He wondered whether the latest message also might have been originated by Joan—most likely by the entire team of which Mrs. Elliott and Cordelia Wood were also a part. The essential data must have been translated from intercepted Japanese messages. He also puzzled why the transports intended to exit Tsingtao during darkness; this was directly contrary to the habit of years. Ordinarily Japanese convoys sortied from harbor during daylight, when any submarines blockading the port would have to be submerged and could be immobilized by aircraft and antisub craft. The only explanation must be that this particular convoy, because of its enormous value, intended to change the pattern. Obviously it wished to get well clear of the harbor before dawn, before a ubiquitous Chinese coast watcher could report it. At top speed, the Yellow Sea could be crossed in less than twenty-four hours, involving a single daylight period. A high-speed run, begun an hour before daybreak, would bring the ships to the sheltered coast of Korea shortly after nightfall. Only one day would be spent exposed to submarines submerged in the middle of the sea; with any luck at all, none would have been able to position themselves in their path.

Unfortunately, there had been no information as to which direction the ships would go once they left Tsingtao. Rich and Keith had theorized that they would turn sharply left and proceed to the northeast along the coast of the Shantung Peninsula. At dawn, they argued, the Japanese would turn east or even southeast. Remaining close to the shore line would render them immune to radar detection from any submarine patrolling off the harbor entrance and thus prevent, or reduce, the opportunity for such a sub to position itself along their daylight track later on.

But there was no assurance this was correct. The convoy might head directly east upon clearing the harbor—this was, after all, the quickest way across the Yellow Sea. If so, they would be detected by Whitey Everett's surface search radar as soon as the ships were clear from land return. From his patrol station seven miles out, Whitey would have the option of making a night surface attack or following them from ahead to attack submerged after daybreak.

Eel's inshore position had been chosen because she was virtually out of torpedoes. Unable directly to damage the enemy, she could at least track them, so stationing herself that the large troop ships, drawing twenty-five feet or more, would have to pass to seaward of her. With land only a mile away, no enemy radar could detect *Eel* against the clutter. The convoy's escorts logically would patrol on its seaward side during this initial phase of the passage.

Eel's presence very close to shore would be least anticipated by the enemy, and at the same time safest from detection. But Richardson could not help noticing his own quickened pulse, and he knew his must not be the only one. A submarine's sole protection—her entire capability of surviving in enemy waters—was her ability to dive when detected or attacked. This he had given up. More, he had argued the wolfpack commander into reluctant acquiescence. Were his calculations to be wrong, were his estimate of enemy intentions and capabilities incorrect, *Eel* might be caught on the surface with no way out except a running gun battle while she dashed for deep water.

This was the reason for preparing the forty-millimeter guns for action, and for the warning given to the rest of the ship's company. The bridge twenty-millimeters and fifty-caliber machine guns also had been rousted out of their stowages and mounted. Ammunition for all guns had been brought up and placed in readiness near each.

Below, ammunition for both five-inch guns had been taken out of the magazines and laid out on deck in the crew's dinette and in the control room under the gun access trunk. The two men detailed to the fifty-caliber machine gun from the forward torpedo room hatch were standing by, probably sitting on a bunk immediately beneath the lower trunk hatch. A third man with a telephone plugged into a phone jack inside the trunk—its wire led upward past the lower hatch—would be waiting with them. On orders from the bridge, all three would enter the trunk, pull up the loop of the telephone wire, and shut the lower hatch. On further orders they would fling open the top hatch and open fire in any ordered direction except astern. They had, however, been rigorously briefed that they were not to open the hatch until direct orders had been received from the bridge, which would not be given if an immediate dash toward deeper water was contemplated. In *Eel*'s present condition, even with bow planes rigged out and given a slight upward inclination, there was still entirely too much chance that a burst of speed might drive the submarine's bow under.

Time was passing extraordinarily slowly, thought Richardson, for the third day in a row and the tenth time this particular night. As 2 o'clock approached, another fruitless vigil was becoming increasingly probable. Blunt had gone below. He, at least, was now sleeping regularly. Strange; his hypertension had been replaced by the opposite: almost a lethargy. After a while Richardson had sent Keith down also to try to get some rest. Morning twilight would begin about 6 o'clock. It was approximately an hour's run at high speed to seaward to reach water deep enough for diving. To allow a little margin, it had been decided to move out at 4:30, shortly after the change of the watch section.

If Japanese ships came out of harbor and turned up the coast line, as appeared their most likely course, it would be *Eel*'s duty to provide sufficient information to permit *Whitefish* to parallel the Japanese ships from off shore, in deep water. When they turned to the east or southeast, as ultimately they would have to do, *Whitefish* would have been positioned to the best possible advantage for a submerged attack at daylight.

It had taken a great deal of persuasion to cause Captain Blunt to believe that he had given the final approval and the implementing order. Much effort had been expended in planting the idea and disposing of all others. The clinching argument, as it turned out, concerned the idea that *Eel*, with only two torpedoes remaining, both of them aft, might possibly be directed to return to base. In view of this, Richardson suggested, Blunt might consider shifting over to the *Whitefish*. As wolf-pack commander, with primary responsibility for the blockade of Tsingtao, he would of course wish to remain on the scene. The idea agitated Blunt, as Rich knew it would, and he vehemently refused to consider it. He also refused to entertain the proposal which Buck Williams, by prearrangement, then put forward: that the two submarines rendezvous and transfer some of *Whitefish*'s torpedoes to *Eel*. The maneuver would of course require opening deck hatches, rigging booms, laboriously hoisting torpedoes out of *Whitefish*, dropping them in the water and then hoisting them aboard *Eel*. As Buck pointed out, the operation had been carried out innumerable times in peacetime exercises, and both *Whitefish* and *Eel* had the necessary equipment.

But it had never been done under wartime conditions, for a boat caught by aircraft with hatches open would be unable to submerge. Blunt had vetoed it on this ground, and also—Richardson had to admit this argument had some validity—that to deprive Whitey Everett of some of his ten torpedoes remaining would leave him also with empty torpedo tubes should he need to defend himself against antisubmarine craft.

The impasse had the effect of submerging the primary issue under two others of lesser substance. By the time the manner of *Eel*'s employment came under discussion, Blunt interposed little further objection. After that it was only a matter of preventing him from again dwelling on his flagship's apparently vulnerable position.

"Permission to come on the bridge to relieve a lookout?" Every fifteen minutes one of the lookouts was relieved to go below to warm himself, drink a cup of coffee, and do a stint as a control-room messenger. This meant it must now be fifteen minutes after two.

For the past forty-five seconds Rich had been staring through his binoculars at the shadowy promontory which marked the entrance to the bay of Tsingtao. He opened his eyes wider, tried to will his pupils to expand even farther. Something had excited his interest in the shadows to the west. He tried all the tricks he had practiced since his first night watch, years ago, on the bridge of the *Octopus*: looking above the shadowy outline of the land, looking below it, swinging his glasses gently back and forth so as to notice any unusual discontinuity.

"Buck," he said, "take a look over here on the starboard bow, just to the left of that point of land!" The point of land to which he referred was nearly invisible—it was the near side of the entrance to the bay—but for three days of periscope observation close in, and night surface operations closer yet, it had been one of their principal points of reference.

"I'm looking at it, Captain," said Williams. "What do you see?"

"Don't know. Nothing, maybe."

"Me too. It's awful dark over there." Abruptly Williams thrust his head beneath the bridge overhang, extended it over the hatch to the conning tower. He spoke in a low, carrying tone, suited to the muted situation into which they had placed themselves. "Radar, take a real good check at the harbor entrance. Do you see anything moving?"

Close in to land, the shore return or "grass" on both radar scopes generally blotted out any pips on the land side, though not to seaward. It was this fact which alone made possible *Eel's* otherwise untenable position, and indeed had caused that position to be selected. During three nights of experimentation, Rogers had discovered, however, that by beaming the radar parallel to the coast and greatly reducing his receiver gain it was possible he might get some impression of a large object once it cleared the shore. He was already operating in this mode, concentrating of course on the Tsingtao harbor entrance. But it was far from a precise thing, and it would be easy to miss something.

"Radar, aye aye," came Rogers' voice. A few moments later he sang out again, "I think I see something there. Might be a ship. Range about four thousand. Looks like two ships."

"Do you see anything, Buck?"

"No, sir. What do you see?"

"I think I can see something. It's all so dark. The point seemed a little bit longer all of a sudden. Now it's shorter again—there it is again."

"Yes, I see it too, now. It must be ships."

"That makes three I've seen. Ask radar what they're getting."

Williams had no opportunity to ask the question, for suddenly Rogers' voice came up through the conning tower hatch, "Bridge, radar has three big ships and two little ones. Looks like they're moving out of harbor."

"Shall I call the crew to battle stations, Skipper?"

"Affirmative, but don't use the general alarm. Pass the word by telephone." This had already been prescribed, but it would not hurt to re-emphasize the instruction. "Gun crews stand by in the control room and crew's dinette." Williams leaned over the hatch and gave the orders.

"Tell radio to send the first of those messages to the *Whitefish*." The first of a set of prearranged messages in Keith's wolfpack code, only a single letter in length, would alert the other submarine to the fact that ships were leaving the harbor. Later, depending upon which way they went, one of the others would be sent. *Whitefish's* radio operator would answer by exactly repeating the signal he had heard.

"Bridge!" Rogers' voice, pitched higher, betraying some of his tension and excitement. "Bridge, radar has three ships and two escorts. Range is decreasing. I think they've started to head this way, sir!"

"What's the range?" bellowed Buck, forgetting the injunction for quietness.

"Four thousand! But I've got a column of ships on the PPI 'scope now, and the range to the leading one is getting less!"

"I'm in the conning tower, Bridge." Keith's voice. "It looks like they're coming out, all right. Whitey has the alert message. Three big ships in column. The lead one has turned to his left and is coming up the coast, just as we figured."

"What are the escorts doing?"

"Can't tell yet. One is out ahead, but it looks like he's favoring the seaward side. The other one, we can't tell at all. The convoy looks like three real big ships!"

The message had said two divisions of the Kwantung Army, and had specified three troop transports. Its information was right on the mark.

"Buck, get your gun crews up here on the bridge; I'll take over the deck. Have them load and train out, but nobody is to open fire until I give the word."

"Aye aye, sir—you don't need a turn-over do you, Captain?"

"No. I have all the dope."

Rich fixed his binoculars in the direction where he knew the ships should be. Nothing. The dark shadows of the blacked-out ships must be there, but the total absence of any light whatever, the lowering overcast so common to this area, the lack of any moon or star illumination, all combined to create a stygian emptiness that the human eye could not pierce. He had, as a matter of fact, figured on exactly this. It was part of his plan, for it would be even harder to see *Eel*'s much reduced silhouette, particularly since lookouts from any surface ship would be many feet higher above the water and would have to look down into the dark sea. The only danger lay in the possibility that one of the escorts might elect to run inshore of the convoy and thus, by mischance, blunder upon the flooded-down submarine. Indeed, the escort would probably draw much less water than *Eel* required in her nearly submerged condition. This, too, had been considered. Merchant ships would not dare move so close in to shore as to suck mud into their condensers and cooling-water lines. They would require probably a minimum of fifteen feet of water under their keels, whereas *Eel*, with all machinery stopped, ready to move on the battery, would need no large water intake and could afford to be in water so shallow that her keel nearly touched. The enemy convoy should pass by at least a mile to seaward.

The four lookouts on the bridge and the one who had just gone below had been selected for their night vision and steadiness under stress, and specially trained to handle the forty-millimeter cannon at either end of the bridge. Augmented by six more men who came up from below, they quietly busied themselves with getting the guns ready.

"If we have to shoot, it will be port side first, Buck." If it came to a gun action, Richardson intended to begin it on opposite courses, so that the enemy would have to turn completely around in the shallows to pursue the submarine. In the meantime, *Eel* would have a start in the run to deep water.

"Bridge, range three thousand. Three ships in column on a north-easterly course. Passing up the coast. Our plot shows them two miles off the beach. Both escorts have taken station on their seaward flank. They're real big ships, Bridge!"

That was Keith, standing under the conning tower hatch, speaking quietly up into the blackness above him. A dim red glow suffused his strained features as he stood framed in the hatch opening. Richardson had not remembered noticing strain on him before, although it was clear that the war had burned something out of him as it had of every-one. He wondered whether he also showed strain, surmised that he probably did.

There was virtually no wind. As usual, the sea was almost glassy smooth, its placidity accentuated by the shallow water effect. The land smell, once pungent, was now no longer noticeable. *Eel*'s position had not changed. Perhaps the wind had shifted. The most likely explanation, however, was simply that they had become accustomed to the odor. Besides, the heightened pulse and increased flow of adrenalin associated with the approach of danger would concentrate perceptions in a dif-ferent direction.

Had *Eel* a salvo of torpedoes remaining in her tubes, her torpedomen would be making them ready at this very moment. This would have also required a totally different plan of action, for torpedoes almost invariably went deep before reaching their running depth. They would strike bottom if fired from *Eel*'s present position. The torpedo situation, in fact, had been the determining argument in getting Blunt's approval to place *Whitefish* offshore, in deeper water, and *Eel* inshore in the shallows. Even so, Whitey Everett would be uneasy at the limited depth of water available to him.

Richardson had never approached this close to enemy ships without being able to see at least some outline of their shapes, no matter how dark it was. The absence of light this night, however, was profound.

At range 3,000 yards, even though he was looking right at them, exactly on the bearings both sonar and radar were giving him, before his eyes was only fathomless blackness, a dull, porous, velvet curtain he could not pierce. Strange that he could make out the loom of land on the starboard quarter, extending forward to the starboard beam, and yet could not see the ships to seaward! Somehow he had got an indication of them as they passed out the harbor entrance, but up ahead, where the sea stretched black to join the black night and the black sky, there was not even a hint of shadowy discontinuity which might outline a ship less than a mile and a half away! Almost continuously, he tried his old trick, looking above and below where he judged the horizon to be.

Wait. There was something, something lighter than the darkness. It was bigger than he expected, and, surprisingly, elevated well above where he had thought the horizon was. Suddenly he could see it, a huge shadowy shape, dark gray sides looming a faint, ghostly white, moving ponderously and irresistibly across *Eel*'s bow from starboard to port.

"Bridge, range two thousand five hundred. Leading ship should be dead ahead. *Whitefish* has our second message." That was Keith calling quietly up from the conning tower.

"I see them, Keith. Angle on the bow is about forty-five port."

"That's the way it looks on plot, Bridge. Three ships in column. We're tracking them at nine knots, and their closest point of approach to us will be about a mile, broad on our port bow."

Now Rich could see the second ship in column, following in the wake of the first—and in a moment, the third. Having started up the coast, no doubt they would continue following the line of the Shantung Peninsula, in the shallowest water possible, until daybreak. Then they would turn directly across the Yellow Sea in a high speed zigzag run to gain the shelter of the shallow water on the Korean side. Once the convoy had passed, *Eel* would follow from astern and radio to *Whitefish* the vital particulars of enemy position, course, and speed, which would permit her sister submarine to submerge ahead of the convoy's daylight track.

Already two such messages, consisting of only a single letter each, had been sent. The chance of their interception by the enemy ships was remote. But it would be necessary to be sparing of messages, even extremely short ones.

"Leading ship at closest point of approach, Bridge. Range at CPA, two-one-double-oh, beginning to open."

The three ships were now clearly visible. Great, silent, crowded giants, grinding forward on the silent sea. In a moment more he could hear them as well as see them, for in the quiet on *Eel*'s bridge the calm water carried their machinery noise distinctly to his ears. Big ships, but single-screw, he thought. He could hear their propellers thunking steadily, their machinery clanking, an air blower shrieking with a dry bearing. In the second ship, someone was beating on something with a hammer. The sound of metal on metal must be projected directly through the ship's structure into the sea surrounding it. The steady, systematic pounding was occasionally interrupted for brief intervals as the man first plied his hammer, then paused, probably to inspect his work, then resumed hammering again. Perhaps the ship had a black-smith's shop, but more likely, mused Richardson, someone was repairing something by the time-honored sledgehammer method.

"Second ship at CPA, Bridge," from Keith. "Formation is still the same, but the rear escort is moving over a little, and dropping aft."

"Bridge, aye," said Richardson in a low, carrying tone. Probably he could have used a normal tone of voice—no doubt the Japanese crews a mile away were doing so—but the stillness of night and the quietness that enveloped the *Eel* held their own requirements, even if only psychological. "Keep a careful watch on him. We're manned and ready for surface action up here if he becomes suspicious." He need have said nothing, of course. Keith did not need to be told to do or not to do anything about that astern escort. Rich had merely accommodated a compulsive requirement of his own. It was indicative of his own nervousness. He must take a grip on himself, not permit his own inner tension to show through.

The need to lie to quietly was an onerous one. Everyone in the ship would rather be underway, even on the surface—best of all, submerged clear of the shallow water. Lying still, partly submerged on the mud flats, hiding in the sea and yet so horribly exposed, produced a feeling of helplessness, of vulnerability. Yet it had all been argued out, thought through, explained carefully to the entire ship's company. Clearly it made sense, in this instance, to behave contrary to the normal sub-marine pattern. *Eel* was taking maximum advantage of all passive alertness equipment. Her sound heads were rigged out (with instructions for instant raising if any orders were given to the motors); her radar detector was continuously manned; all her radio receivers (except the one tuned to the wolfpack frequency) were being constantly tuned throughout their ranges to pick up any nearby transmissions. Her search radar, which normally did emit a signal, was being operated inter-mittently, its transmitter keyed only at sporadic intervals for quick sweeps, its receiver continuously watched for signs of any other radar interference.

Were danger to threaten, *Eel* could get underway instantly, silently, on her main motors and battery. At the maximum discharge rate, once her main ballast tanks were blown fully dry, she could reach a speed of eighteen knots, though only for a very short time. But the ship would be running in eerie quiet, with no plume of diesel exhaust to assist pursuit, no thunder of main engines drifting over the quiet waters, which, by their sudden cessation, might betray the moment of dive. A dive would be ridiculously simple once adequate depth of water was reached, for there would be no engines to stop, no main induction to shut, no switching from generators to battery. All that was necessary was to open the main vents, shut the bridge hatch, and drive her bodily under.

She could even make a respectable speed in the flooded-down condition. Nothing like eighteen knots, of course. But it would be necessary to keep bow planes and stern planes manned, and Al Dugan would have to give careful attention to the diving station; for in this condition *Eel* had practically no buoyancy at all and would submerge without warning upon the slightest wrong movement of the planes.

"Third ship is nearing CPA, Bridge. Still twenty-one hundred yards. Leading two ships are opening out. Range to leading ship three thousand. The rear escort has moved over and is now dead astern of the third ship."

This could spell trouble. *Eel*'s purpose was to trail the convoy from astern. Detection by one of the escorts would of course ruin this scheme. Far worse, detection would subject *Eel* to a surface attack in a spot where she could not submerge. Enemy gunfire would spell disaster. Or one of the escorts, lighter and far more maneuverable than the half-submerged submarine, might try to ram. Its sharp bow would easily cut through superstructure, ballast tank, and pressure hull to transform *Eel* forever into a sunken, rusting, mud-filled hulk, slowly disappearing into the aeons-old estuarial flats of an ageless shore.

Richardson was searching for the escort astern of the last ship, finally saw her gliding along, ghostlike, suspended in the darkness. The destroyer, or destroyer escort, was broadside-to, low in the water, a tiny superstructure forward, the barest suggestion of something aft. Strange how small she looked! The ComSubPac message had said the escorts were *Mikuras*. This tincan did not by any means look as big as the escorts *Eel* had already encountered. The blackness of the sea and the sky, the total absence of illumination or any indication of a horizon, the dwarfing comparison with the high-sided troop transports, must have robbed him of his ability to judge size. She was much smaller, indubitably, than the ships which had preceded her. In one way, the smaller she was the more dangerous; for a shallow-draft ship would have less hesitancy in entering shoal water. If she did not fear mud in

268

her engine cooling system, she could nimbly run well inshore of *Eel*. Such a vessel could attack from any direction she wished, whereas the deep-lying submarine had only one choice open to her: an emergency burst of speed toward the deep sea. On the plus side, it was probable that a small escort would not carry heavy armament.

"I see him," said Rich. He waited. Apparently no one else could. He kept his binoculars trained on the enemy ship. If her silhouette shortened, it would probably mean that she was changing position again, most probably moving over to the inshore side of the convoy. Were she to do this, her chances of detecting *Eel*'s disembodied bridge, floating with such agonized quiet, would be greatly increased.

There! The silhouette *had* shortened. The escort was now presenting a port angle of approximately forty-five degrees. If she turned all the way, to an end-on situation, it must be assumed that she had seen something suspicious and was coming to investigate. Considering the difficulty Richardson had had himself in seeing the escort after the radar told him she was there, he could hardly believe this was possible. She might be pursuing merely a routine zigzag plan, or be crossing over to the other side for some other reason. . . . A long, careful look convinced Rich that the escort was not turning all the way, had settled on a new course, which, at the moment, gave her somewhere between a thirty- and a forty-five-degree port angle on the bow. She would pass about a thousand yards away.

For the first time Rich spoke loudly. "Men, remember your instructions. No gun is to shoot until I give the order. He's heading over this way, but he's not coming right at us, and I don't think he's suspicious. If he does see us, I'll give the word to start shooting as soon as we can see him clearly. Do not shoot until I tell you. And remember, every shot is to go into his bridge!" Rich sensed rather than heard the murmur of agreement from the gun crews.

"I see him!" said one of the men standing forward of the bridge overhang on the platform serving the forward forty-millimeter cannon. He was one of the regular battle lookouts. Now that the gun was completely ready, he was using his binoculars again.

"Good. Keep your eye on him. Everyone else let me know when you see the target. . . . Buck, tell them down below what's going on."

As Buck Williams leaned under the bridge overhang to call the information down the hatch, the other forward lookout spoke up. "I see him too, sir."

"Follow him with your gun. Do not shoot!" Subconsciously, Rich realized that the possibility of some overly tense sailor opening fire prematurely must constantly be guarded against. He had decided in his own mind not to open fire until there was no longer any doubt *Eel* had been detected. Initial detection would be followed by a period of curiosity, during which the enemy would continue to approach. *Eel* had an inestimable advantage, to be exploited to the limit. Not until the range had closed to the point where every shot could virtually be counted on to hit the target would *Eel* open fire. Once the enemy's initial attack had been blunted, her bridge knocked out, the rapid-fire guns would be freed to rake the entire hull. Enough holes, even small-sized ones, at the waterline would sink her. Roughly half the rounds loaded in the fifty-caliber belts, the twenty-millimeter cans, and the forty-millimeter racks were armor-piercing. They could be depended upon to penetrate anything a tincan would be likely to carry.

"Range to escort," one thousand." Keith's voice from the conning tower hatch. The escort was now clearly in view just forward of *Eel*'s port beam. For a few minutes Rich had been wondering whether she might indeed be one of the *Mikura*-class frigates. In this case, he would again have to revise his estimates as to her size, armament, and draft—upward this time. He could see her clearly now. Her silhouette had broadened. She was nearly broadside-to again. She was a twin of the first escort *Eel* had sunk, might well be one of the two survivors of that attack. All three had been identical.

The ASW ship was not quite as long as *Eel* and probably was smaller in displacement. No doubt she was designed to outrun the submarine in a fair chase. She was big enough to carry a heavy gun of some sort, at least one four-inch (the briefing had specified such a gun), plus various rapid-fire weapons of her own. *Eel* would have to fire first, and effectively, immediately following the moment of surprised recognition to knock her out before she got her own guns going.

It had been about five minutes since the escort had come into view. She still gave no indication she had seen the ungainly silhouette off to her port side. Freed of the hurried pace of the periscope observations, Richardson could look her over carefully. She was a handsome ship, low to the water, her long clean side unbroken by any hint of portholes or other penetrations. Her forecastle was sharply raked, with a rather large square bridge set at least a third of the way aft from the bow. Amidships a single fat smokestack squatted incongruously, its height not quite equal to that of the bridge structure. There was some kind of a gun forward on the forecastle, but it was trained fore and aft, with no sign of anyone preparing it for combat. Abaft the bridge, around the stack and all the way to the square flat stern, was an indistinguishable jumble of top hamper and deck gear. He thought he could distinguish depth charge racks on the very stern, but of this he could not be sure.

Detail after detail stood out. Strange that he could see clearly, and yet there was no indication *Eel* had been seen. Doubtless the much smaller size of *Eel*'s silhouette, the fact that it was obscured by the dark hills behind it, that the enemy escort was outlined against the nothingness of the sea and the heavy sky, must be the determining factors. That and the matter of initiative. The Japanese had had no indication there was an enemy submarine waiting outside their harbor, no doubt were still settling down to their sea routine. *Eel*, on the other hand, had been primed for desperate action for three days, her every sensing capability at maximum alertness. Clearly audible was the gentle slap of waves splashing under the wooden slats of *Eel*'s main deck. *Eel*'s ventilation sets had never seemed louder. Her air-conditioning machinery sounded as if all its gears were stripped, and he could hear the rhythmic beat of the compressors. Likewise, he could hear the enemy escort's engines, diesels from the sound of them, their loud stutter borne in over the water, intensified by the acuteness of his senses.

"Bridge," said Keith through the hatch, "target is at new CPA, range nine-five-oh, steady course."

There was still a very real danger that *Eel* would be seen as the destroyer swept past. Perhaps an after lookout would be more alert than those forward. Nevertheless, the likelihood from now on would diminish. Richardson had been holding his breath for nearly a minute. Three fifty-caliber, two twenty-millimeter and two forty-millimeter guns were still trained on her, were silently following her. They would continue to do so for a few minutes longer, but already the extraordinarily black night was beginning to close around the little ship. In a few minutes she would be swallowed by darkness again. Her outlines were growing hazy. He expelled a second long-held breath. Now she was gone.

"Range to escort one-four-five-oh, Bridge, opening. No change in course."

Richardson again twice clicked the bearing buzzer built into the handle of the port TBT. This would let Keith know that he had heard and acknowledged the report. He would, however, keep his gun crews on the alert for a few minutes longer, for insurance. . . .

"Range to leading ship four-six-five-oh, Bridge. Plot still shows him on the same course. The near escort is now at two thousand yards, still going away. He's drawn up abeam of the last ship in column."

The danger had not materialized. Suddenly, unaccountably, Richardson almost wished it had. Nothing could have withstood the surprise fusillade of automatic fire *Eel* had been ready to lay upon her—he caught himself up short. Was this after all so very different from the fate he had dealt Bungo Pete? Or was it the old death wish in another guise? There was an ebbing of feeling within him, a wearying. The adrenalin flow was dissipating, and with it his sense of mission and combat. A deep yawn forced his jaws agape. Sleep would be delicious.

But there was work yet to be done. He moved to the bridge microphone, pressed the button. "Keith," he said, "give me a course and speed to trail. I'd like to stay about seven thousand yards astern of the last ship, but close enough to have a good radar return on all of them."

Dawn was breaking. About an hour previously, *Eel* had slowed nearly to a halt to permit the convoy to gain distance. Two more messages had been sent to Whitey Everett in the *Whitefish*. Now it was approaching the time for the critically important message. Everyone expected the convoy would make a radical course change at dawn and head at maximum speed on a southeasterly course, but it was still possible that the ships would instead continue along the coast of the Shantung Peninsula to its farthest extremity or even around it, ultimately to turn left into the Gulf of Po Hai. *Eel* must inform *Whitefish* just as soon as the evidence was clear.

Two special messages had been made up in anticipation of the two possible situations. One, a single long dash, would indicate that the convoy was continuing to hug the coast. The second consisted of a short dash followed by the wolfpack letter code for course and speed.

Richardson had been on the bridge all night and had begun to realize how cold it could be in the northern reaches of the Yellow Sea in early winter. He had taken the precaution of once again ordering Keith to get some sleep. It would be important for Keith to be well rested for the daylight pursuit anticipated. Blunt, of course, he could not control, but Blunt was not concerned with *Eel*'s proper functioning. Since the attack on the freighter north of the Maikotsu Suido, Blunt had changed. He made no further reference to sabotage of the hydraulic system and was no longer taciturn. He had become, if anything, at times loquacious. He slept frequently. Except for sporadic interest, as in the discussion preliminary to the present operation, he took no further part in what went on about him. With occasional exceptions which had to be anticipated and handled carefully, for the past several days he had acquiesced in whatever instructions were given, in his name, to the other submarine under his command.

Eel had dropped so far astern that, with growing daylight, the only thing visible of the convoy was a faint cloud of smoke beyond the horizon. She had at the same time moved off the track to starboard in order to gain distance away from the land. The Japanese as well as the Chinese might be employing coast watchers, and it would be well to have sufficient water for diving in case of attack from the air.

Now, within a few minutes, would be time for the convoy to change course, if it was intending to. The blackness of night had long since turned to a gray haze, and this, too, was burning off. The sun, not yet over the horizon, would burst in full splendor upon the scene in about half an hour. Richardson was mentally prepared for the report, when it came: "Bridge, radar reports convoy has changed course to the right."

"Very well, Conn," responded Richardson, pushing the bridge microphone button. "Can you give me a course? Is there any indication of increased speed?"

"Not yet, sir. Plot and TDC are working on it." He wished Keith were coordinating radar, TDC, and plot, but determined that he would not call him. The others surely should be able to operate the various components satisfactorily. But Richardson need not have worried. The next report from the conning tower was in Keith's voice. He had evidently left word to be called when the situation changed.

"Bridge, conn. Target has increased speed. Plot and TDC are tracking him on course one-three-oh, speed thirteen. All three ships have changed course to the right in a column movement. The last one is just completing her turn now."

"Good work, Keith," said Richardson on the speaker. "Are you sure enough of your information to send the message to *Whitefish?*"

"Affirmative, Skipper. Got it ready to go."

"Send it as soon as you can. Let me know when you get a receipt."

The bridge speaker blared again with Keith's voice in a slightly different timbre. He was speaking from the radio room. "Message sent and receipted for by *Whitefish*, Bridge," he said.

A moment later Keith stood beside him on the bridge. "That's about it, Skipper," he said. "The last radar fix we had on Whitey shows him dead ahead of the convoy about twelve miles out. There should be some action over there in less than an hour."

"Do we still have radar contact on them?"

"Yes, sure. Why?"

"Because . . . I don't think we ought to dive yet. We'd better stay up as long as we can and see what happens."

"We might get spotted and driven down by a plane. Besides, you've been up all night, and all day before that. You rate some rest, Skipper."

"Sleep can wait. If a plane spots us, that might help *Whitefish* by drawing those two escorts in our direction. What I'm really thinking about, though, is that we've got to keep those three transports from getting to Okinawa. After Whitey attacks, they'll scatter—and it will be up to us to put him back in contact for a second attack."

"That is, if he'll try a surface end-around with planes up there," observed Keith, uneasily.

The sun, driving up over the horizon, transmitted little warmth to the frigid group bundled up on *Eel*'s bridge, but it did have the effect of burning off the night's overcast and producing a clear blue sky. The visibility in all directions was phenomenal, totally the reverse of the situation of only a few hours before. Fully surfaced, *Eel* now plowed along easily in the moderate sea associated with deeper water. With enough depth for diving beneath her keel, the more familiar circumstances induced a feeling of comfort among her entire complement, only slightly lessened by the fact that any aircraft patrol worthy of the name could pick her up by sight alone at a distance of many miles. But unless the plane were flying extremely close to the water, *Eel* would sight it also in plenty of time to dive. She would not again be caught by any tricks with the plane's radar transmitter power.

If aircraft came out to escort the convoy, which was inevitable because of its importance, they would concentrate ahead of it, where a submarine in attack position would be. On the other hand, if they could be induced to attack the wrong submarine, every depth bomb dropped on *Eel* was one less that could be used on *Whitefish*, one less that could be effective in protecting the convoy.

"Convoy's been on this course one-half hour, Bridge."

"Did you get a fix on *Whitefish* when she dived? When should she be getting in?"

"We figure the convoy will be running over the *Whitefish* in about fifteen more minutes."

One of the after lookouts was screaming. Richardson did not need to hear the words clearly to understand what he was saying. "Plane! Starboard quarter!" the man was shouting.

"Clear the bridge!" shouted Richardson. He swung a quick look aft through his binoculars. The plane was still some distance away, but obviously coming directly toward the *Eel*. There would be plenty of time to get her down. He stood aside, allowed the lookouts, the quartermaster, and Keith to precede him, and then Al Dugan, whose watch it now was. Two blasts on the diving alarm. "Take her down!" He straightened up, put his binoculars back to his eyes. The plane, a two-engine bomber, was still coming, still four to five miles away. The main vents were popping. The air was whistling out of them. *Eel*'s bow was already settling toward the sea. Richardson stooped under the bridge overhang, felt for the hand rail over the hatch, swung down into the hole, grabbed the lanyard, and pulled the hatch to. It gave a satisfying click as the latch snapped home, and Cornelli leaped past him to dog it tightly.

"One-five-oh feet," Rich said. "How does that check with the chart, Keith?"

Leone was in the after part of the conning tower, bent over the chart of the area spread upon the table in the far corner. "One-five-oh looks okay, Captain," he said. "Not much deeper than that, though, or we'll drive her nose into the mud."

A deep feeling of weariness pervaded Richardson's body. The cold air on the bridge had been bracing, but inside the submarine the warmth of the interior was instantly stupefying. "Control, make your depth one-five-oh feet," he repeated. "Ease your angle when you pass one hundred feet."

He yawned hugely as he spoke. Suddenly it was all he could do to concentrate on giving the necessary orders. The boat was under, her bow was tilted down at a satisfactory angle, and there should be no trace of her left on the surface except the wake of her passage.

"Left full rudder," he ordered. He would not, at least, blunder blindly into a bomb or depth charge dropped ahead of the diving point.

Eel had been submerged just ten minutes and had already returned to periscope depth. There was nothing in sight. The plane must have had orders not to waste its time over a submarine diving where it could not possibly attack the all-important convoy. Its instructions would be to proceed ahead of the troopships, against the possibility of a submarine in attack position—against *Whitefish*, in fact. How long had it been since *Whitefish* had dived, anyway? And if successful, when might Whitey's torpedo explosions be heard?

"Any time now," said Keith.

Richardson was spinning the periscope around. Nothing in sight. Several quick, careful looks, then up a little higher. Still nothing. No plane, no ships, no smoke, just brilliant blue sky and a yellow-brown, mud-colored sea with a small chop: waves about two feet high. Around again, more slowly, several times, dropping the periscope occasionally just beneath the surface in order to break up the continuity of exposure. Still nothing in sight. How long now?

It was only five minutes since he had asked the question, reassured Keith. According to Larry Lasche's plot, something could be happening any minute, but on the other hand, a delay of even ten or fifteen minutes ought not to be surprising. Buck had roused himself—he could not have had more than an hour or so in his bunk—and had taken over the TDC. It was not running, for he had no information to set into the instrument. Stafford, searching carefully all around on the sonar, concentrating in the estimated direction of the convoy, could hear nothing. The ships were much too far away to hear screws. Blunt also was in the conning tower; nearly the whole of *Eel's* battle stations control party was there. Something must happen. *Whitefish* simply must not fail now.

A distant boom filled the confined space.

"Torpedo explosion," reported Stafford, unnecessarily.

Ten seconds later there should be another. He looked at his watch. His eyes, accustomed by the periscope to the brilliant sunlight on the surface, had difficulty in focusing on the tiny second hand. Ten seconds must have passed—fifteen seconds at least, now. Thirty seconds. Only a single hit. Perhaps Whitey Everett had conservatively fired only at the leading troopship. Undoubtedly there would be depth charges, if only to keep him submerged below periscope depth while the uninjured ships made their getaway.

Whitefish was one of the thin-skinned submarines, as *Walrus* had been. There was no definite proof that the "heavy hull" submarines were better able to stand depth charging than the "thin-skinners," but this was nevertheless generally believed to be the case. So far, Everett had retreated to an inactive portion of the area to inspect for damages after every depth charge attack. A heavy barrage at this point, which the escorts might very likely drop simply as a face-saving measure, whether or not they had any idea of *Whitefish's* location, might have the same effect again.

"Stand by to surface," croaked Richardson. "Up periscope." As he swiftly spun the instrument around, he felt the querying glances of the conning tower crew. He went around carefully three times. Nothing in sight. He clicked up the handles of the periscope. It dropped away.

"Ready to surface," said Keith. Here at least was someone who understood that targets of this importance, so laboriously set up, must not be abandoned.

"Surface the boat!" The sound of air blowing in the ballast tanks, the sudden lifting effect as they expelled water from the flooding holes at their bottoms, were almost like personal reflexes of his own.

"Four main engines on propulsion," Richardson said.

The bridge was still cascading water from all of its parts. The main induction banged open behind him. *Eel* drove ahead on her battery, thrusting her nearly submerged bulk through the seas and into the teeth of a strong cold breeze, while back aft four mufflers spit white water and groaned as the engines rolled over.

"Lookouts to the bridge!" They came piling up in their foul-weather gear, well protected against the cold and the wet. Rich had not been so provident. His already rumpled khakis had been heavily splattered across the back as he came up the hatch, and the chilled wind was already biting into him.

"Here, Captain," said Cornelli coming up the hatch, handing him a foul-weather jacket. "Mr. Keith . . . I mean, Mr. Leone, said to give you this." Gratefully Richardson put it on while Cornelli moved aft to take up his watch station.

Williams and Leone were beside him. "We're running down the bearing of the convoy," said Richardson. "I'll keep the deck. Buck, you handle the routine. Allow no extra people on the bridge. Keith, you stand by in the conning tower. Pass the word to all hands to look alive. We may have to dive suddenly. Keep a continuous high periscope and radar watch on. The convoy may have split up. It sounds like one ship was hit, and if so, the other two will be getting away from the attack position as fast as they can."

"Bridge, conn." This was Stafford's voice. "Sonar has distant depth charging dead ahead."

"One more thing, Keith," as his second-in-command swung on to the ladder leading to the conning tower. "I may hold up the dive for a bit, even if we do see a plane." The puzzled look on Keith's face gave way to comprehension as Richardson went on. "If we weren't down to only two torpedoes, we could end-around ourselves. As it is, the best we can do is try to take some of the heat off of *Whitefish*."

Dormant in his brain was the thought that if *Eel* should be sighted reasonably near the torpedoed ship before a firm sonar contact had been obtained on *Whitefish*, surface and air escorts, now feverishly looking for the submarine responsible, might assume that *Eel* was the culprit. If, in the meantime, the direction in which the remainder of the convoy had fled could be determined, there might be a chance to put *Whitefish* back into contact for a second attack.

"Bridge, radar contact! A little on the port bow!"

Eel had been fully surfaced for some minutes, was now pounding along at nearly full speed, throwing spray from under her bows as she plunged into the freshening sea, spattering a continuous pattern of salt droplets on her main deck. The wind, already strong and very cold, was now screeching over the top of the windscreen with the added component of the submarine's velocity in the opposite direction. Several minutes ago the lookouts had been called down from their exposed perches on the sides of the periscope shears and directed to huddle together behind the chariot bridge bulwarks. There they still maintained vigil over the same arc of sky and sea, each to his own quadrant. Their function, of course, was to guard against approach of an aircraft. It was upon the elevated periscope, nearly nineteen feet above the uppermost tip of the periscope shears, that Richardson was depending for the first sight of the enemy.

"We have two big ships and two little ships on the PPI 'scope. Looks like they're on course about southwest. Range is twelve miles. They're on our starboard bow, Bridge. A couple of miles astern of this outfit and a little nearer—about eleven miles—there's another ship. It looks like it's alone. Plot is showing it as stopped, but we can't be sure yet." Keith from the conning tower.

"Anything in sight through the periscope?"

"Negative, Bridge—we're checking the bearing carefully. . . . Correction! The periscope sees masts a little on the port bow. That's the single ship!"

Richardson debated the advisability of using one of his last torpedoes to finish off the injured ship, but as *Eel* approached, she was already being abandoned, her listing sides covered with tiny antlike creatures climbing down the steel plates, sliding down ropes into the water. The sea was black around her with round black dots, each one the head of a man struggling for his life. Only three lifeboats could be seen. Perhaps there were a few more life rafts—not many. The periscope could count only five, overloaded, teeming with people, surrounded by more hanging to their sides. The boats were in little better shape. He fought down the revulsion. This was what he had come for. He could not, would not, help. The men were doomed. The winter sea would be pitiless. Another torpedo was not needed.

Richardson decided to drive between the damaged ship and the convoy, abandoning the damaged one in order to track the fleeing convoy remnant from the east. It was a near certainty that after having put sufficient distance between themselves and the scene of the torpedoing they would again change course to the east. Later, he or Whitey might return to give the coup de grace to the damaged transport, if it had not sunk.

The damaged transport was well in sight through the naked eye from *Eel*'s bridge, well inside the horizon, the angle of its masts increasing perceptibly from the vertical as the doomed ship listed, when suddenly a column of water sprang up alongside. The leaning masts, jolted by the torpedo hit (for this it must be), slowly straightened up, then continued on past the vertical, to list in the other direction. As he watched, they leaned farther and farther, until they disappeared from sight, to be replaced by the dark red wedge of the underpart of a ship's bows.

Damn Whitey anyway! The ship was already sinking! Even a single additional torpedo in her was a waste! Not only would that torpedo far better have been saved for one of the other two transports, he was also wasting valuable time remaining submerged in the vicinity. The proper thing for *Whitefish* to do was to get up on the surface and join *Eel* in pursuing the two undamaged troopships. Two subs on the surface, widely separated, would make air cover all the more difficult. Working in coordination, they could cover all possible routes the enemy might take. Together, they could make it impossible for them to get away. Soldiers still in the States, soon to land upon Iwo Jima and Okinawa, would die if those two troopships, with their efficient, trained soldiers, were not sent to the bottom!

In the meantime, no aircraft had been sighted in the cloudless sky. Perhaps the plane which had forced *Eel* to dive early in the morning had reached the limits of its endurance and headed back to base. More likely, it was flying in autisubmarine patrol orbit around the surviving transports. In that event, the second torpedo attack on the damaged ship might cause it to swing in that direction for a closer look, with consequent greater chances of sighting *Eel*.

"Keep a sharp lookout for aircraft," growled Richardson. "They'll come from any direction, but most likely from the starboard bow." Perhaps it would have been better to have said nothing, for the lookouts were already sufficiently keyed up. Not more than five minutes had passed before the forward starboard lookout suddenly yelled, "Plane!" pointing with his arm at the horizon.

In the distance a tiny silhouette floated in the sky, wings motionless. The lookout, a new man, very young, on his first patrol, held his binoculars a tiny distance from his face so that he could swivel his eyes nervously at Richardson. Obviously he expected a moment later to be climbing down the ladder into the conning tower.

Without taking his binoculars down from his eyes, Richardson spoke in a loud tone, endeavoring at the same time to project a note of calmness. "Where's the plane?" he said. "I don't see any."

"There, sir! Coming right at us! . . . Oh." The lookout, pointing, became visibly deflated as the bird, now obviously much nearer than the horizon, turned lazily and gave a single lusty flap with its wings.

An encouraging word was necessary for sake of the boy's self-esteem. In a kindly voice Richardson said, "That's all right. We'd far rather have you call one wrong once in a while than miss one you should see. With visibility like today, we'll have plenty of time to look it over before diving." As he spoke, he recognized an unusual pedantic quality to his expression. He had forced the words out almost with a sigh. They had taken an inexpressible effort. He must guard against this.

He had been up all night, true, but that was no excuse. The men trusted him, must think him infallible. He was the best surety they had for their own safety.

Far in the distance, well to starboard now and out of sight, was the remainder of the convoy, with two-thirds of the soldiers who had left Tsingtao. Somewhere off to port, now resting on the bottom of the Yellow Sea, her position marked in a general way by a tiny cluster of white lifeboats on the horizon, and an already reduced mass of black dots representing humanity around them, lay the ship just sunk by the *Whitefish*. Somewhere in that vicinity also must be *Whitefish* herself, probably still at periscope depth because of the lack of aircraft or surface escorts, possibly close enough to recognize her sister submarine plowing along at flank speed through the gathering sea and the freshening wind. She should be able to hear *Eel* by sonar even if she could not see her through the periscope, and just possibly her sonar operator would be sufficiently experienced to recognize the high-speed propeller beat and the two-cycle high-speed diesels characteristic of an American submarine. If *Whitefish* were aware of her wolfpack mate's urgent passage, she should surface, if for no other reason than emulation.

Whitey Everett was obligated to continue to pursue the convoy as soon as countermeasures against him had ceased. But he, too, had probably been up most of the night, and so, no doubt, had most of his crew. The mental strain required to return to periscope depth shortly after a depth charging and in the face of possibly waiting countermeasures must have been great. It was all to his credit that he had done so, even though by Rich's estimate a second torpedo was wasted on the already sinking troopship. Following this effort, by normal standards Whitey could be excused if he had decided to return to the sheltering depths to rest himself and his crew. Possibly, if *Eel* were to head in that direction, calling *Whitefish* on the sonar, contact could be made with him. But if so, contact with the fleeing convoy would be lost.

Richardson was not aware of weighing the alternatives. Perhaps his mind was already too clouded to consider them properly. Stafford was directed to call *Whitefish* continuously on the sonar, sending the code signal for surface chase. But *Eel* pounded on without slowing through the rising sea, throwing an ever-increasing cloud of spray on deck, periodically changing course in obedience to Keith's recommendations as the tracking party combined periscope sightings of masts with radar information. Sooner or later the troopships must change course to the east, and *Eel* would then be directly ahead of them. But what could

Eel do with only two torpedoes against two escorts and two huge transports? Richardson now regretted, with the intensity borne of inability to remedy the situation, that he had not insisted upon taking some of *Whitefish*'s torpedoes. The thing could have been done in a few hours of intense work, even if it had never been done before in the war zone. If Blunt had ordered Whitey Everett to do it, he would have had to comply.

But where was Blunt? Richardson had been on the bridge for hours now and had heard not a word from him. He had not asked for him, for there was nothing in the way of combined operations that could be done, now that *Whitefish* had successfully attacked and was out of communication. As soon as *Whitefish* surfaced and checked in by radio, Blunt would of course be informed, even though it would be Richardson's proposals that would be sent to her as directives in Blunt's name.

And what about that airplane that had caused the *Eel* to dive? It must have been assigned to the protection of this convoy. Perhaps there were other ships traversing the Yellow Sea also, and it was no doubt true that both aircraft fuel and aircraft themselves were in short supply to Japan. But where was it? That plane, or another one, could not be far away. *Eel* must not be sighted once she got ahead of the convoy.

Al Dugan had relieved Buck Williams as OOD. "I got a couple of hours' sleep, Skipper—was out like a light, too—so I feel pretty good. Keith says he wishes you could get some rest." He had brought with him a mug of black coffee and three huge sandwiches, which Richardson gulped gratefully. Obviously, despite their words, no one expected him to go below.

"Where's the commodore?" he asked.

"He's been asleep. Turned in after we surfaced, and just woke up for lunch. He's probably in the conning tower now, or will be as soon as he finishes eating. I hurried up so Buck could eat." Dugan paused, then spoke again with a different note in his voice. "Captain, I've got to tell you, we have trouble again with the hydraulic system. It's really going to need a total overhaul to find out what the matter is. Something isn't acting right."

Richardson put his binoculars down from his eyes, looked around seriously. The cold wind had burned a deep redness into his face. The collar of his foul-weather jacket was turned up and buttoned, so that the artificial fur protected the back of his neck and caressed his cheeks, and he had procured a blue knit sailor's watch cap from the conning tower, which he had jammed on over his head as far as it would go, covering his ears. The face which looked at Dugan was puffy, a mottled mahogany covered with a stubble of whiskers. Above it the skin around his eyes and across the bridge of his nose was white where the binoculars had protected it, but the eyes themselves, seemingly deeper set than usual in their sockets, were red with strain and fatigue. "What's the trouble now?" he said, his numb lips and tongue having difficulty with the words.

"She's recycling again too fast. I've got Lichtmann down there in the pump room watching it. He'll stay there, and if we need to relieve him, I'll send Starberg or Sargent down. Bow planes, stern planes, and steering are set for hand operation, and so is the main induction. The cooks are checked out on the induction, and there's extra people in the enginerooms to handle the exhaust valves by hand. The main vents are all shifted over to hand power again, too, with telephones and people standing by."

Richardson nodded. "What's Lichtmann doing?"

"He's got the main plant turned off, with the rams full and the bypass valve shut. The accumulator is full, with air pressure on top. He'll turn the plant on when we need it, and then secure it again. You know we can refill the accumulator by bleeding off the air on top and then using the hand pump. So that's all rigged and ready to go. We've been testing it, and Lichtmann can give us another full accumulator, after the first one is discharged, in a couple minutes of hard pumping. So we can handle everything, although we can't do all the things all at once, the way we used to. That's why I put everything we can in hand power. . . . That fellow Lichtmann is sure a jewel. Where in the world did you find him?"

"He's a legacy from Stocker Kane," said Richardson, quietly, and Dugan knew that the slight hesitation in Richardson's words was not entirely from the cold weather on the bridge.

"Bridge, conn. Convoy has changed course to the left again. New course one-eight-oh. Recommend we come left to one-eight-oh." This was the third course change the convoy had made in the past hour and a half. The ships were now well abaft *Eel*'s starboard beam, running on parallel course. To head for what had been estimated to be their original destination point on the coast of Korea, they would have to come around left at least fifty degrees more.

"Bridge, control. APR contact. Strength two." The first indication of the presence of an aircraft.

"Look sharp, lookouts! There's an aircraft around here somewhere!" With the beautiful visibility, there should be no trouble in seeing the aircraft. The seas themselves were still small, although perceptibly building up, and the plane would be sighted the moment it came over the horizon should it try the same gambit that had so nearly caught the *Eel* a week or so before. For hours Richardson had been pondering his tactic in the event of an airplane contact. To dive on APR contact, which had been his latest determination, would eliminate any further chance of catching the convoy, but to be detected by the airplane would have almost the same effect. In that case . . . Suddenly it was clear what he must do.

"Al," he said, "I'll take over the entire deck. You go down and stand by the dive in the control room. If this plane shows up, I want to go down fast, even if we are in hand power. We've got to avoid detection, but we can't dive until the last minute. I want to go deep so as to get clear, and if we have to, we'll change course on the way. But then I'll want to come back to periscope depth immediately and surface as soon as we can. We mustn't lose any more time submerged than we can possibly help."

"Aye aye, sir," said Al. But still he looked puzzled. "What are we going to do with the convoy, Skipper?" he began. But then he stopped. There was something in Richardson's face, some look of fixed purpose mounted on the thin edge of exhaustion, which dissuaded him from adding the additional requirement of an explanation. With a final "Going below!" he ducked under the bridge overhang and stepped on the ladder rungs.

"Tell Keith on your way down, Al," said Richardson, as Dugan's head passed below the level of the bridge deck, "and keep me fully informed about that APR contact. That's going to be the key to the whole thing!"

The convoy had swung around another twenty degrees, to course 160 degrees true, and the APR contact had remained steady. The plane was probably circling in front of the convoy and would inevitably soon detect *Eel*, particularly when further course changes would put the submarine more nearly ahead also. Richardson was about to issue another cautionary warning to the lookouts, but refrained. They were already as alert as they could be. Nervousness might only cause another mistaken identification of a bird as an aircraft.

"APR contact fading slightly. Strength one." Al was making the reports himself from the control room. The radar signal was steady, not rising and falling as had been the case previously, and having reached its closest point of approach, the plane was now getting farther away. Soon it would turn back.

Time passed. The *Whitefish* had surfaced at last, was a number of miles astern. The convoy was changing course every half hour, Richardson decided. Plot now gave their course as 140, and *Eel* had altered her course accordingly, putting the ships well on her starboard quarter. One more similar change to the left would bring them within ten degrees of the predicted course, and they might well choose to come all the way around. *Whitefish*, in the meantime, diverging from *Eel*'s track, would be in a position to attack again if they reversed course to the west.

Richardson had been on the bridge for hours, sustained by sandwiches handed up from below and countless mugs of black coffee. There was a rising need within him which could no longer be kept below the level of severe, if not disabling, distraction, bordering on growing torment. A quick trip below ordinarily would take care of the business, and had several times already. But this was no longer possible. He could not leave the bridge now, even for the two or three minutes the mission would require. Not with the prospect of imminent air attack. The lookouts, all of them new members of the crew, youngsters whose only submarine experience was in *Eel*, would be caught by surprise. They might even be a bit shocked, but it didn't matter what they thought. The old submarine solution would have to do. The old N-boats and O-boats had only a covered bucket for use submerged, which the most junior member of the crew would have to carry topside and dump at appropriate times. In their ability to dive, submarines possessed one tremendous asset other ships did not have: when you dived, you flushed the whole outside surface of the ship.

Of course, you always did it to leeward. Thought of doing it made the need imperative, the torture unbearable. A wad of lens paper. A muttered excuse to Buck Williams, now OOD again. The starboard side, just abaft the fifty-caliber stowage. Half a dozen quick steps aft to the cigarette deck. His hands fumbled ridiculously, cold-stiffened fingers tearing at the zipper of his parka trousers, then at his belt and the oversize buttons in the fly of his woolen pants. A deep sigh of relief. He could not have stood it much longer. A long moment of slowly ebbing pain.

"APR contact, strength one and a half!" The plane was coming closer.

"APR contact! Strength two!" The question: to be detected or not detected.

Blunt was on the bridge. "What are you planning to do, Rich?"

"Get below, Commodore," Richardson said testily. "There's a plane coming in. We've got to be clear to dive in a hurry. I'll tell you about it as soon as I can!"

The look under Blunt's shaggy brows seemed less sure of itself than it had in previous years or even during the early stages of the current war patrol. There was almost a respectful note in his voice, along with the recently acquired querulousness, as he replied, "Okay, Rich, I'll be in the conning tower."

Richardson punched the bridge microphone. "Plot, any sign of a convoy change to the left?"

"Negative, Bridge. Convoy course one-four-zero base course, zig-zagging."

"Bridge, control. APR contact strength three!" It was at this signal strength that ComSubPac had advised all submarines should dive. And it was adherence to this directive that had placed *Eel* under severe risk not long ago. Almost without volition, he voiced his concern.

"Lookouts, there's a plane coming in on us. We don't know what direction, most likely from aft. Keep a sharp lookout!" If the convoy would only make its last change of course now, *Eel* could submerge on its track, undetected, and might have a chance for an attack with her last precious torpedoes. If he waited too long, detection by the aircraft might cause an unpremeditated radical change in the convoy course and thus throw away all the day's work in reaching position.

Yet, if the escorts cooperated, detection of *Eel* might possibly work to Whitey Everett's advantage. Richardson had to hope both escorts, supported by the plane, would attack, not knowing there were two subs to contend with, thinking that by working together they might eliminate the single submarine pursuing them. Once *Eel* was located and under attack, the troopships would make another radical swing away from the vicinity. Doubtless they would run southwest again, possibly even nearly due west. All depended on *Eel* being detected at the right time, and *Whitefish* not; so that Whitey could submerge undisturbed in the path of the transports, now hopefully denuded of escorts or air coverage.

"APR contact! Strength three and a half!"

"Convoy course one-four-zero, no change." Al and Keith were anticipating his requirements for information.

"Aircraft dead astern!" Cornelli shouting from the after part of the bridge. He swung aft quickly. The aircraft was well above the horizon, still at a great distance, flying relatively high. Perhaps they had already been detected. Richardson felt almost a sense of relief. This part, at least, was now out of his hands. "All right, I have him in sight," he said.

The plane seemed hung in the heavens, almost stationary. It was approaching directly toward them. Well, if the convoy would not change course toward him, he would at least try to get on its path.

The maneuver would drive the transports more to the west, make things that much easier for *Whitefish*.

"Right full rudder," he bawled down the hatch. "Come right to two-three-zero!" This would put *Eel* on a course perpendicular to the estimated convoy course, and it would permit her most quickly to gain position dead ahead. When the plane saw this maneuver it would evaluate it as meaning but one thing: that *Eel* was running in for an attack position on the convoy. Only a few minutes would be needed. The convoy should reverse course. But how would the plane signal to the convoy? Perhaps there was a common radio frequency, but most likely, to give *Eel*'s position accurately, specifically to give it to the escorts, the plane would have to drop at least a smoke float, and probably a bomb as well.

Well, so be it. There was no doubt the plane had seen them now. It had turned slightly to compensate for *Eel*'s own course change. It was the same plane which had flushed *Eel* that morning, or one exactly like it. He could see the glint of the whirling blades in the early afternoon sun and the two engine nacelles under the wings. It might be able to increase speed to four miles a minute on a run in. He estimated the range right now to be about six miles, but it would not do to run this one too close.

"Clear the bridge!" he called. Might as well get the lookouts and Cornelli below ahead of time. Thirty seconds. Yes, the plane was probably now about four miles away. With a fast dive *Eel* could get completely submerged in thirty seconds, probably even faster at the speed with which she was still racing ahead. The wind was now coming over the port bow and was considerably less unpleasant, since he could keep his back to it as he watched the airplane.

Fifteen seconds more. It would be touch and go, but this was the way it had to be. "Clear the bridge!" he shouted. "Take her down!" There was no one on the bridge but himself, but all dives should be done as nearly as possible with the customary routine. He fumbled for the diving alarm, placed his mittened hand on it, pressed twice. The vents popped. One more quick look at the airplane. It was beginning its dive, coming in at a shallow angle. Estimated range three to four miles. This would be good. *Eel* was due to catch a bomb, but except by the greatest of misfortune she would survive it unscathed. The important point was that it would give at least one of the convoy escorts a point of aim, a datum point to investigate. The involved scheme which Richardson had laboriously composed while conducting the end-around run depended upon separating the convoy from the escorts. His gloved hands fumbled for the hand rail. He dropped down the hatch, grabbed the lanyard toggle, heard the hatch click shut.

Eel was already perceptibly angling downward in a swift, sure-footed dive. "Hatch secured," shouted Cornelli, too loudly, thought Richardson.

"Depth of water is two-five-oh feet, Skipper," said Al from below. "I'll start taking the angle off after we pass one-hundred-seventy-five feet."

The conning tower annunciators, both of which should have been at the "ahead flank" position, had been moved over to "ahead emergency." Obviously Al's doing. With the full voltage of the battery discharging current almost as if there were a short circuit, the propellers for a few minutes would be turning even faster than under the drive of *Eel*'s four diesels. *Eel*'s deck tilted down even more. He heard Al speak imperatively to the planesmen. "Full dive on bow planes. Stern planes keep the angle at fifteen degrees. Yes, I said fifteen degrees!" *Eel* leaned even more steeply into the dive.

"Mark! Four-six feet," said Cornelli. But he held out his hand to show that he had no stop watch. In the back of the conning tower Keith was grinning, exhibited the stopwatch with his thumb on the winding stem. "Twenty-three seconds," he said, consulting it. "Fastest dive in the books. I almost didn't get the periscope down. When the water hit it, I thought we were going to break it right off!"

Rich nodded, crossed to the control room hatch, squatted on his heels to talk to Dugan. "We've stopped our watch up here, Al," he said. "Did you get a watch started on the dive?"

"You bet, Skipper." Al had one in his hand, the short white lanyard looped around his thumb. "We're passing seventy feet now. It's forty-five seconds since the diving alarm, and we're just reaching fifteen degrees down bubble."

"What's your speed through water?"

"Still showing twelve knots. It dropped fast as soon as we opened the vents, but it's dropping a lot slower now." There was indeed a furious rush of water around the conning tower, perceptibly shaking it, vibrating all topside equipment.

"Passing one hundred feet, Skipper," said Al. "Do you want to change course?"

"Good. Left full rudder," he ordered, raising his voice to the helmsman standing with his back to him alongside Cornelli. "Come left to one-four-zero." The plane would be approaching the diving point now, would be adjusting for time late, computing the lead angle. Probably it had already dropped, since the release point for the speed and altitude would no doubt be passed long before the airplane arrived over the diving point.

"Taking the angle off now," said Al. "The rudder helps."

Richardson could feel the submarine's attitude returning to the normal horizontal.

"Steady on one-four-zero," said the helmsman. Just as he said the words they were swallowed up by the roar of a tremendous explosion in the water near at hand. *Eel*'s tough frame shook like a tuning fork, its component members vibrating in their own discordant cacophony, as the shock wave was converted into the innumerable frequency ranges to which the parts of it resonated.

"That was good and close," Keith started to say, when his words likewise were engulfed in a second explosion, a ringing, high-pitched metallic WHAM, as though some giant outside *Eel*'s hull were striking her side with a tremendous sledgehammer.

"All compartments report," said Cornelli, grabbing a hand telephone set from its rack. He held the phone to his ear for several minutes, nodding his head briefly from time to time. "I figured they'd all be on the line, sir," he said. "All compartments report no damage."

"Al," said Richardson, "you still have speed control. Get us up to periscope depth as soon as you can."

"Periscope depth, aye aye. All ahead one-third," called out Dugan. The annunciators clicked as the helmsman carried out the order, and *Eel* began to climb back to sixty-foot keel depth in a much less dramatic fashion than she had initially gone the other way.

Richardson had forgotten Blunt in the conning tower. Now the latter spoke. "What are you up to, Rich?" he said.

"We've got two torpedoes left, Commodore, and I want to try to turn the convoy around to give *Whitefish* a chance to get into action one more time."

"How are you going to do that with only two fish? And even if you do get one of the ships, the escorts will keep you from surfacing. . . ."

"Yes, sir, but what if we knock off the escorts?" Richardson stared hard at Blunt. He did not want to reveal his entire scheme, for the discussion which would inevitably follow would arouse concern in the well-knit submarine crew which could only be to its disadvantage. Again Blunt looked unsure of himself. He almost replied, then evidently changed his mind, said nothing.

Several minutes later, through *Eel*'s periscope, barely projecting above the tops of the waves, splashed over by some of them, Richardson had two things in view: the Japanese patrol bomber, now minus two of its limited supply of bombs, orbiting over the general area and obviously looking for his periscope; and a single escort which had appeared over the western horizon. Upon seeing it, he had directed that a white smoke candle be broken out and made ready near the submerged signal ejector. If the bomber was not thoughtful enough to fire a smoke float for the tincan, it might be necessary for *Eel* to do it. It was a disappointment, however, that only a single escort had taken the bait.

The frigate's lookouts must all be blind, thought Richardson, as for the fourth time in three hours he elevated *Eel*'s periscope well above the wave tops to give them every possible opportunity to see it. Sonar conditions must be abominable. The tincan swept on heedlessly, pinging loudly, surely getting a good return echo, but giving no sign of having any contact whatsoever. His intention to be discovered only while *Eel*'s stern with its two loaded torpedoes was directed toward the enemy had caused him to forgo an equal number of other opportunities, when a depth charge attack might have developed from a disadvantageous bearing. Also, he had been forced to keep a close eye on the patrol bomber, which was swinging in wide circles around the general vicinty. The plane had never, however, given *Eel* an opportunity to use the smoke float; for this, it must approach close enough to the submarine's position to have plausibly dropped it. At some point the plane would turn low on fuel, having been in the air since before dawn.

It was now late afternoon. The convoy must have headed west again, and, with a four-hour head start, it was lengthening its distance every moment. Probably it had soon changed to the south once more, and would again follow the same pattern as previously, giving the latest area of contact a wide berth before finally settling down to an easterly course toward the coast of Korea.

The patrol bomber was coming in low, the first time it had come in so low. *Eel*'s stern pointed nearly toward the destroyer. Distance, perhaps five miles away. He had the periscope low again, so low that every other wave either blocked his view entirely or covered the periscope with yellow water. The plane was passing fairly close, though not overhead. Its pilot could not have seen the periscope. Since it would be sunset in an hour, perhaps this was to be the aircraft's last pass through the area before heading for base.

'Stand by with the smoke candle!"

If he could be sure the patrol plane had no more depth bombs, he might risk letting him see the periscope and drop a smoke candle of his own. But of this he could not be sure. *Eel* would be forced to go deep when evidence of a real attack run developed. Once forced deep by the plane and under persistent depth charge attack from the *Mikura*, there might never be a chance to return to periscope depth. *Eel*'s own smoke candle would simulate one from the plane, but the pilot would know he had not dropped it and—just possibly—might be able to communicate the fact to the escort skipper. The thing to do was to fire it just after the plane had passed, but without the pilot being able to see it. Richardson cursed his indecision. Twice he had run through the same debate and passed up a possible opportunity, fearing it would be too obvious. Again he watched the plane pass by, low to the water, a mile and a half or two miles away. This was the closest it had come yet. Then, gradually gaining in altitude, it flew off to the west. He waited a few seconds. This might be the moment, but there would still be time for the plane to reverse course and return to the scene if he acted prematurely. When it had diminished to a relatively small silhouette in the cloudless sky, he ordered the smoke float loaded into the ejector and fired. A feeling of almost detached curiosity as to what the results would be took possession of him.

It was almost a minute before the smoke functioned. Richardson was about to write it off as a dud, when suddenly there was a tiny cloud of white smoke blossoming on the water some distance astern.

"Sixty feet," he ordered. This would give nearly seven feet of periscope for the destroyer to look at. He would need it, for the lengthening shadows of growing twilight were drawing near.

Signs of incipient activity on the escort. He had seen the smoke. Slowly, almost leisurely, he approached it. No doubt the destroyer's skipper was puzzled how it came to be there. He would think the plane had dropped it after all, and that perhaps it was merely delayed in going off. It would be hard to imagine it deliberately being placed there by the submarine he was looking for. Richardson could feel the tenseness of his own state of mind, his own fatigue (which he must not show), the dependence which he was placing upon this stratagem. Carefully he maneuvered so that *Eel*'s stern pointed directly at the tincan's bow.

"Destroyer screws have speeded up," said Stafford. "He's shifted to short-scale pinging! Starting a run!" Stafford's voice, as usual, betrayed his rising excitement. Veteran though he was, he would never—nor would Richardson—be able to discount the potential lethality of a well-delivered depth charge salvo.

"Make your depth six-five feet, Control." He could hear the whine of the TDC behind him as Buck Williams set in the information, relayed from Stafford, from Keith, from himself, at the periscope.

"Gyros are three left," said Keith. "Torpedo run is nine hundred yards. We still have to flood the tubes and open the outer doors— what's the matter, Captain?"

"We can't shoot," said Richardson in a weary, exasperated tone.

290

"He's zigzagging." With only two torpedoes left, *Eel* must fire only when there was certainty of hitting. This meant a "down-the-throat" shot with all data static: bow to bow or, as in this case, stern to bow. A sinuating, weaving course, such as the escort was now using, made the chance of missing too great. Rich motioned with his thumbs for the periscope to be dropped a foot. He squatted down with it, continuing to look through it from a stooped position. "He thinks we've gone deep," he said. "He's coming in so slow he can't have set his charges shallow. They'd blow his own stern off. So we'll cross him up by staying at periscope depth. Range, mark!" He turned the range knob on the side of the periscope.

"Range nine-two-oh yards," said Keith. "Torpedo run seven-five-oh."

"Shut all watertight doors," said Richardson. "Here he comes!" He had in the meantime directed Al Dugan to run one foot lower in the water, at sixty-six-foot keel depth instead of sixty-five. This permitted Richardson to stand with less of a stoop as he kept the periscope at the lowest possible height from which, between toppling waves, he could still see his adversary. "He's going to pass astern close aboard, but a clean miss if I ever saw one—there he goes! He's dropping now!" It was unprecedented for a submarine captain to observe his own depth charging, although it had been done (at much greater range) during depth charge indoctrination drills at Pearl Harbor. The thought did not at all occur to Richardson until much later. "This chap must be an absolute amateur. He's attacking our wake instead of a solid contact. He's made a clean miss by at least fifty yards!"

The periscope was under more than it was out of water. Richardson's view of the enemy ship was a series of fleeting glimpses rather than a steady inspection. At this close range, better perspective was provided by the periscope in low power. The tincan was new-looking—war-construction obviously—painted overall a dull gray. Her most outstanding feature was the characteristically Japanese undulating deck line—extra design and construction effort with no apparent operational payoff. The deck curved sharply upward at the bow, which was widely flared for seakeeping ability, and upon the forecastle was mounted a large, long-barreled, destroyer-type deck gun. Her hull was metal—the welding seams and characteristic "oil-canning" of the thin steel were clear to be seen—but the heavy, squat bridge structure and mast appeared to be of wood. Between waves rolling over the periscope, Richardson could see the bridge personnel, all staring aft, some with binoculars. Men on deck and around the now empty depth charge racks were also staring over the stern into the water, obviously waiting for the depth charges to detonate. Abaft the mast was a single, exaggeratedly fat, stubby stack projecting from a low deckhouse, but no smoke or exhaust gases could be seen issuing from it. On the contrary, an exhaust of some kind was coming out from a large black opening in the side of the ship under the after portion of the main deck.

There was a sudden appearance of instantaneous immobility in the sea, and almost simultaneously a crashing roar filled the submarine. Several tremendous shocks in succession were transmitted to *Eel*'s stout hide. The giant outside was wielding his sledgehammer with gusto. The periscope quivered, vibrated strongly against his eyes. Fortunately, the eyepiece was surrounded with a heavy rubber buffer, shaped partly to protect the user's eyes from stray light and partly to give him a firm ridge against which to press the soft flesh between his eyes and their bony sockets. The story would later be told how Richardson had stood at his periscope in the midst of a depth charge attack which had *Eel* resounding throughout like a tremendous steel drum, her sturdy body whipped and tortured, her machinery damaged from the heavy shocks. The fact was he had the advantage, possessed by no one else in the submarine, of seeing the depth charges dropped and knowing they were clear astern. Noisy they might be, but dangerous they were not—at least not much. And once they began to explode, the ice broken, as it were, they were only an annoyance.

But there must be some way to bring this sea dance to an end. Those depth charge racks would take some time to refill. Maybe now was the time. The tincan skipper would try to ram if he saw the submarine. Perhaps he should have a point of aim.

"All ahead two-thirds! Left full rudder—ease your rudder—amidships—meet her—steady as you go!"

"Steady on two-six-eight-a-half," from Cornelli at the helm.

"Steer two-seven-zero." That would make it easier on the plot and everyone concerned.

Eel and the escort were now on nearly opposite courses. Soon the escort would turn, come back to the scene of the depth charge attack, try to regain sonar contact, look hopefully for signs of success. Range by periscope stadimeter was 1,000 yards . . . 1,400 yards. She must turn soon, was turning, with rudder hard over, listing to starboard. Increased exhaust smoke was coming out of her sides; her engines had speeded up. She came all the way around. *Eel* was making five knots; her periscope must be throwing up a perceptible feather.

"Angle on the bow, starboard ten." The periscope was leaking. Perhaps the vibration during the depth charging had loosened the seal rings through which it passed at the top of the conning tower. A rivulet of water trickled down on Richardson's forehead, between his eyes. Another splatted on the top of his head and down the back of his neck. "Range—mark!" he said. "Down 'scope. Get me a rain hat!"

"One-seven-five-oh." Someone handed him a towel. Blunt. He had been standing silently in the conning tower for minutes, perhaps hours. Not a word was said. Scott passed over one of the baseball hats which a number of the crew had been wearing. It had a long broad bill— just right. He put it on backward.

The TDC was whining. "Need an observation," said Buck Williams.

"Up 'scope—angle on the bow, port five."

"Range one-six-five-oh," said Keith.

"Set," said Buck. "He must still be zigzagging. That changed the gyro from right four and a half to left three."

Not good enough. The escort had to be on a steady course to ensure the torpedo would hit. Mush Morton in the *Wahoo* had once faced such a situation, although with more torpedoes. So had Roy Benson in an early patrol in *Trigger*. Both reported that the destroyer needed a point of aim to steady on, and they had held their periscopes up to provide one with the result that the destroyer had rushed directly at them, and was met by a salvo of torpedoes. The "down-the-throat" shot had not been at all popular with submarine skippers, however. It was undeniably risky, downright hairy. Only one of *Wahoo*'s torpedoes had hit out of six fired. *Trigger*'s had exploded prematurely. But torpedo performance was now vastly improved.

"We have to get this over with," said Richardson. "This periscope has been up for a long time, and we must be making a big feather, but he doesn't act as if he sees it. . . . Control, make your depth four-two feet!" He felt water running off the cap and down the sides of his face, salt trickling into his mouth. *Eel*'s deck tilted upward slightly, and he had to rotate the hand grip in his left hand to stay on the escort. He had not looked around recently. This would be the time to do it. The pressure of water against the periscope at five knots, which made it more difficult to turn, would be eliminated with the top of the shears five feet above the surface. The little rivulet of water running down the side of the periscope seemed diabolically to follow him no matter on what bearing he looked. He made two swift circles, settled back on the escort. The exercise of walking it around had brought an added dividend, a tiny modicum of relief from the overpowering weariness.

"Four-two feet, Conn," said Al Dugan.

He felt high out of water. His eye—the tip of the periscope—was now nearly twenty-five feet above the water. Five feet of the conical periscope shears would also be exposed. The escort would see this, would

293

assume the submarine had been damaged, had perhaps lost control, broached, and was either trying to surface or struggling to get back down again.

"Bearing, mark!" he snapped. "What's the course for a zero gyro angle, zero angle on the bow?"

"Bearing zero-nine-three. Recommend course two-seven-three, Skipper." Keith.

"Come right to course two-seven-three!"

"Right to course two-seven-three—steady on two-seven-three." Cornelli spoke loudly from the forward part of the conning tower.

Shadows were lengthening. There was a flash—orange mixed with red—from the forecastle of the escort. A gun. There was another flash. They must be shooting at the periscope. Hastily Richardson swung the periscope all the way around, searching for splashes, saw none. "They've seen us now," he said. "Control, make your depth six-oh feet. Down periscope!" In a moment he would raise the periscope again, but it was a relief to wipe his streaming face. The conning tower had been darkened, all white lights extinguished. His right eye, accustomed to the much brighter, though waning, light topside, was virtually blind. The pupil of his left eye had no doubt narrowed sympathetically, for he found himself fumbling among the familiar objects and people.

"Six-oh feet, Conn."

"Up 'scope." He would leave it up, provide a point of aim which would irresistibly draw the escort directly for it in an attempt to ram. If the escort would stop zigzagging, the result would be a perfect down-the-throat shot. He would have to take a chance with his periscope, pray that a lucky shot would not strike it.

"We're ready aft," said Keith. "Torpedo run is one thousand yards. Gyro is exactly one-eight-oh. Are you on the bearing?"

The periscope vertical cross hair was bisecting the escort's bridge, lay exactly in line with her stem and stick-mast. She looked disproportionately—ridiculously—broad. There was another orange flash on the forecastle, hidden partially by the high raked bow, now that Richardson's periscope-eye view had returned to a more normal six feet. She had not wavered for several seconds, no doubt had ceased zigzagging, probably had increased speed.

"Make her speed fifteen knots," he said. "Bearing, mark!"

"One-eight-oh-a-half."

"Cornelli"—he raised his voice so the helmsman could hear clearly—"steer two-seven-three-a-half." He watched as his periscope cross hair drifted slowly to the right, until it was just clear of the escort's port side. He brought it back until it lined up once again with stem and mast.

"Bearing, mark!" he said again. He could feel the pressure mounting, the taut stillness in the conning tower, the unblinking eyes staring at him, the dry throats and nervous lips which must go with their alacrity in carrying out his orders. The electric torpedoes would show no wakes. Not knowing it had been shot at, the escort would not try to avoid. If they missed, she would come relentlessly on and pass directly overhead in her attempt to ram. In any case, recognizing that the sub must be at or very near periscope depth, she would know exactly what depth setting to use on the inevitable barrage of depth charges. There had not been time for an entire salvo of charges to be made ready, but undoubtedly several of them had already been wrestled into the racks for an immediate re-attack.

"Torpedo run, seven-fifty yards!" Buck Williams' clipped voice was not that of the irreverent youth who had disobeyed him when the Kona wave had been about to strike.

"Shoot!"

"Fire nine!" shouted Keith, Buck, and Quin almost simultaneously, the last into his telephone mouthpiece. He barely felt the jolt as a burst of high pressure air ejected the torpedo. With any speed on, ejection aft was always facilitated. He must leave the periscope up for another few seconds to keep the escort running true, headed for it, not zigzagging.

"Can't hear the torpedo aft in the screws," said Stafford.

"Torpedo fired electrically," said Quin.

"Running time thirty-three seconds," said Lasche.

"Steady on two-seven-three-a-half," said Cornelli.

"That looked like a beautiful shot, Skipper," said Keith quietly. "Fifteen seconds to go."

Someone was counting the seconds in a loud voice. Larry. The escort had grown perceptibly larger. There was another flash from the forecastle. This time Rich saw the splash as the periscope went through it, a vertical column of water high enough to hide the frigate momentarily from his view. The shell must have missed the periscope barrel by only a few inches. It was fortunate that on a moving ship the gunner's aim was probably being thrown off just a little.

"Twenty-five," said Larry, counting from his plotting table.

Richardson could feel the perspiration on his forehead, around his eyes, on the palms of his hands. *Eel* was still making two-thirds speed, and the periscope vibrated gently against his right eye. Surprisingly, it was painful.

The escort was now filling the entire field of the periscope in high power, the slope of its sides barely discernible on either side. It looked curiously flat. The single eyepiece of the periscope gave no depth.

295

Seemingly a very short distance behind its bow, although he knew it to be a full third of the tincan's length, the square-windowed bridge of the little ship filled what was left of the field of view.

"Thirty-three," said Lasche. "Thirty-four."

"It must have missed," said Keith. How could he speak so calmly!

Nothing else to do. Richardson had not intended to use both of his remaining torpedoes on a single ordinary escort. He had hoped to occupy both of the antisubmarine craft, but had failed in that as well. Now he had no choice. It was even unlikely *Eel* could go deep enough in the short time remaining to clear the escort's sharp bow. No doubt it had been specially strengthened for ramming, as had the bows of American escorts. "Stand by number ten!"

Richardson lined the periscope exactly on the target's bow. "One-eight-oh," said Keith.

"Shoot!" He uttered the word with finality. It carried with it a sense of being the last cast of the die. *Eel* had nothing left to fight with. If this torpedo missed, it was a certainty that in a few more seconds her periscopes would be knocked over, the shears bent or broken off, perhaps even the conning tower ruptured.

". . . Fired electrically," said Quin.

"Run, four-five-oh yards." Keith. "Running time, twenty-three seconds."

He should start to go deep, but it would do no good. No matter what, the stern would remain near the surface for a while. Better take the blow on the periscope shears than the rudder and propellers. Ten seconds more to go. Five seconds.

Something was happening to the tincan's bow. It shook perceptibly. The bridge structure, which had seemed so close behind the stem, had been replaced by a solid column of white water, stained by a vertical streak of blackness in its center. Simultaneously, the shock of the explosion slammed into the submarine's conning tower, and an instant later the noise—a bellowing cataclysmic thunderclap—came in.

The escort's stem shivered again, more slowly, then began to twist to the left and at the same time sag deeper in the water. Before Richardson's eyes it leaned to starboard and quickly slid under water. The last thing he saw was a relatively large unbroken expense of forecastle deck, on which some kind of capstan and anchor equipment was clearly visible, as the shattered bow, torn completely loose from the remainder of the ship by the force of the explosion, swiftly disappeared.

He flipped the periscope to low power. The explosion must have taken place under the keel and just forward of the bridge, for the bridge structure could still be seen, horribly shattered, all its windows smashed, the neat square outline now buckled and twisted. The rest of the ship, too, was sinking fast. He could see her stern elevated above the top of the bridge structure, and the base of the bridge itself was already well under water. He swung the periscope around twice, swiftly. Nothing else in sight. "Surface!" he ordered. "Four engines! Here, Keith, you take the periscope!"

Men were cheering in the conning tower and below in the control room. Someone thrust a towel at him to wipe his face. Several of the conning tower crew, completely forgetting naval protocol, were pounding him on the back, shouting words in his face, grasping at him to touch him, almost caress him. Dimly he was aware of air blasts from the control room, the lifting strain of the ballast tanks. Scott handed him a foul-weather jacket, followed it with his binoculars.

"Thirty feet," someone called. "Twenty-six feet and holding."

"Bow's out! Stern's out. All clear all around," shouted Keith.

"Open the hatch!"

Scott spun the hand wheel. It banged open with a crash. A torrent of air blasted out of it, lifting him. Richardson leaped to the bridge, ignoring the cascade of water still pouring from the periscope shears and bridge overhang. Swiftly he scanned the skies with his binoculars. Nothing in sight. "Lookouts!" he shouted. "Open the induction!" Clank of the induction valve. Gouts of black exhaust mixed with water from four main engine mufflers.

"I'll take the deck, Captain," said Al Dugan. "Keith gave me the course. He's laying out the search for the convoy right now. You need some rest, sir; why don't you go below and sack out for a while?"

Gratefully Richardson turned over the details of the bridge watch to Dugan. Perhaps he would take his advice, but for the moment he could not feel weary. His binoculars settled for a long lingering minute on the destroyed escort. She was now vertical in the water, almost fully submerged except for a small section of the stern. Men were bobbing in the water around her. Someone was standing on top of the stern itself, and as Richardson watched, made a headlong dive into the sea. Among the debris that floated around the swiftly submerging hulk were two life rafts and what looked like an overturned lifeboat. On her new course, *Eel* would pass within half a mile of the spot. There was nothing he could do to help. He must pursue the remaining ships, endeavor to turn them back somehow, somehow bring *Whitefish* back into contact.

The stern of the escort had disappeared. A plume of white water burst from the spot where she had sunk. A great white mushroom boiled up, covered the entire area. The crash of the exploding depth charges stunned his ears. When the white, watery mushroom, fifty feet in height and a hundred feet in diameter, had disappeared, there was not even debris left in sight. No doubt much would rise to the surface to mark the grave of the little ship, but there could not possibly be any survivors.

All the lookouts, Scott, and even Al Dugan were mesmerized, awe-stricken at what they had seen.

"Mind your business, all of you," shouted Richardson. "You lookouts get on your sectors! If there's a plane around, he'll be coming over to see what happened!" His own guilt at having overlong inspected the result of his handiwork was expressing itself in unnecessary railing at his crew for the all-too-human fault of doing the same thing. Guiltily, they all swung back into their proper search arcs.

"Sorry, Skipper," muttered Dugan, with his binoculars to his eyes ostentatiously surveying another portion of the horizon. Richardson as swiftly felt remorse at his outburst. He could not bring himself to talk, squeezed Dugan's arm by way of acknowledgment.

Al Dugan dared to put down his binoculars, turned squarely to face Richardson. "Skipper," he said, "you're beat to a frazzle. You've got to get some rest. Besides, you ought to look at yourself in a mirror. Do you realize you have a black eye?"

This too would be added to the legend. The vibration of the peri-scope against his eye during the depth charging, even though it had been protected by a rubber buffer, had been sufficiently strong and prolonged to bruise the tender skin. The result was a perfect black eye, a regulation "shiner" in all respects save the manner in which it was acquired. Little he could do about it, he reflected, as he washed his face at last at the fold-up wash basin beneath his medicine cabinet. He plunged his face deep into the dripping washcloth, bathed it first with hot water and then with cold, rubbed it vigorously. The fatigue lines stood out clearly. His bunk beckoned. It would be so restful to lie there, if only for half an hour! But he dared not. Another cup of coffee, a hasty sandwich, and Richardson was back in the conning tower. He must be alert the moment a message arrived from *Whitefish*, must supervise the search for the fleeing convoy, must show Blunt where to station *Whitefish* for one final effort.

- 11 -

By midnight *Eel* had covered all the possible positions of the flee-ing ships, had they turned eastward anytime before 10 o'clock. Definitely the convoy had not done so. It was Richardson's second night up in a row, and somehow he had found a new source of energy, for the terrible lassitude of the early evening was less evident. Probably he should have turned in, as his officers urged. But the knowledge that part of the Kwantung Army was loose in the Yellow Sea only a few miles distant, bound for Okinawa and inadequately escorted, was a driving force which took the place of any will of his own. By Blunt's order, which he had drafted, *Whitefish* was heading south to intercept. Twice, Richardson had sent her messages reflecting what he had learned of the enemy movements. It was *Eel*'s responsibility, as the submarine last in contact, to find the convoy and position her wolfpack mate most advantageously.

He spent most of the time in the conning tower poring over the charts, alternating this with periods on the bridge—it was not so dark as the previous night—and once, as he had made his custom, walking through the ship to visit every compartment to talk with as many of the crew as possible. He would have been hard put to define why this simple habit had grown so important to him, would have said it "gave him a feel" for his crew, would have totally disavowed any suggestion that it had become an important ritual to him, or that the crew also, confined to their stations in the submarine's compartments, had come to look forward to these visits on the eve of battle.

The only sour note in *Eel*'s readiness, outside of her complete expenditure of all torpedoes, was her hydraulic system. The situation had been accurately described by Al Dugan. Richardson found Licht-mann nodding on his station in the tiny, crowded pump room, where he had been valiantly trying to match Richardson's sleepless vigil, had replaced him with Starberg, and sent him up to his bunk with a clap on the shoulder and warm words of gratitude. It was hot in the pump room, and the atmosphere was heavy with oil. Immobility made drowsiness inevitable; yet, in emergency, instant alertness was manda-tory. Gravely, he elicited a promise from both men that they would exchange positions every six hours and include Sargent in the vigil as well.

All seven sets of vent valves he found alertly manned. Like Licht-mann, the men had nothing to do unless the diving alarm were to sound, but there was a man with a telephone headset at each station, and many others around in each compartment. Everyone in the ship was acutely aware of the importance of instant operation of the main vents, should the diving alarm be sounded. The pin in each mechanism was in the correct place for hand operation. Richardson was vocifer-ously assured by all that each valve had been operated many times al-ready, was free and easy to pull by hand. In the enginerooms, the four roaring diesels were, as always, a source of comfort and admiration. He grinned when he noted the rpm dial on each registering 760 instead of the rated maximum of 720 rpm's. A little operation on the governor linkages had been all that was necessary, and their added speed was reflected in higher propeller rpm's and the extra knot *Eel* was logging on her pitometer speed indicator.

Richardson had slipped on a pair of dark red goggles prior to leaving the dimly lighted conning tower, and for this reason no one noticed the black eye until, in the maneuvering room, the chief on watch, egged on by his watch mates, diffidently asked him about it. First carefully shutting his eyes against the light, he lifted the goggles, was rewarded by a chorus of delighted chuckles. Instantly he wished he had not done it, however, for his eyes stayed shut of their own accord when he put the goggles back in place. His head nodded. Had he not stumbled with a small movement of the ship he would have fallen asleep on his feet. He had to force himself to visit the last compartment, talk with the crew in the after torpedo room. This visit was obligatory, for it was here that that last supremely important torpedo had been watched over, made ready, and fired. But it was too hot in the submarine. The noise in the enginerooms was stupefying. Hastily he walked forward to the control room, climbed the ladder to the conning tower and then to the bridge.

It was about an hour past midnight. Radar contact had at last been made. The convoy still consisted of two troopships and a single escort. They had made a large diversion to the west and had indeed passed close to the *Whitefish*. But nothing happened. *Whitefish* had dived but been unable to close for an attack; now she too was on the surface again, driving southeast in obedience to more orders sent in the name of the wolfpack commander.

The convoy had finally once again swung to an easterly course, and *Eel*, under cover of the night, was maneuvering to cut the corner and get into position directly ahead. Keeping the convoy under surveillance from ahead instead of astern, Richardson had decided, would provide a better opportunity of holding or regaining contact after *Whitefish* had made the dawn attack which by this time he knew would be the most he could hope for. The likelihood of a night air-craft patrol was remote. The two submarines had added the better part of a day to the transports' Yellow Sea transit, and robbed them of the intended all-daylight passage. The two remaining troopships were exposed to the night surface attack they had tried to avoid.

But tonight they were completely safe. *Eel* had no torpedoes, and *Whitefish* would not attack at night. He sat on Stafford's vacant stool, folded his arms on his knees, leaned his head on them.

He could not have been totally asleep, for he remained aware of the muted comings and goings of the conning tower crew, Keith's occasional advice to the Officer of the Deck, the radar reports to plot, and even the request to dump a sack of garbage. But the brownout of fatigue was claiming its due. His senses dulled, his perceptions began to drift. He was back aboard the *Walrus*, had just felt the depth charges of Bungo Pete for the first time, was in love with Laura, despised Joan because (he assumed) she was causing Jim to be unfaithful to Laura. But this could not be entirely Joan's fault, for Jim had been unfaithful in Australia as well, and Rich, in his turn, had also found relief from reality in Joan's arms. Now Rich had killed Bungo Pete, and he had been disloyal to his idealized thoughts of Laura. Bungo had returned in the person of Moonface, to claim his vengeance. He hated Moonface, but not Bungo Pete.

Joe Blunt too. He was Tateo Nakame—Bungo Pete—in American guise. The idea of the older warriors supporting the younger ones whom they had trained, who now carried the load of the combat. Now it was reversed. Now Blunt needed help, needed the support of those who had once looked to him for wisdom, skill, and judgment. Ships were everywhere, some sinking, some flying. Bungo's *Akikaze*, with Blunt in command, had opened fire on *Eel* from the bottom of the sea. *Eel* could not hit her with torpedoes, for she was too deep. And now there was the escort destroyer he had just sunk, the one that had given him the black eye.

"Morning twilight, Captain. Morning twilight, Captain. Morning twilight, Captain. . . ." There was a hand on his shoulder shaking him. A disembodied hand. "Morning twilight, Captain." Someone had lifted his head gently, was slapping his cheeks. "Here, drink this." It was a mug of coffee. The steam warmed his nose and cheeks, reflected from his eyelids. Keith was in command of the *Eel* and he was in love with Joan and he was holding the cup of coffee and slapping his face.

Slow dawning. Understanding. "What is it? Did I doze off?"

"You sure did, Skipper. We don't see how you stood it so long, as it was. Here, drink this coffee. It's morning twilight, and the *Whitefish* has just dived to attack."

"Where's the convoy?"

"Twelve miles astern. We're tracking them at fourteen knots, and I've slowed to maintain the range constant."

Groggily Richardson wrenched to his feet. *Eel* lurched. He stumbled, put out his hand to steady himself. It slipped on the slick steel periscope barrel. He nearly fell, grabbed one of its hoist rods. He gulped down the coffee, then the fried egg sandwich which Keith suddenly produced from a hidden corner. It was still hot. So! His sleep, and now his awakening, had been part of a prearranged operation! Damn them all anyway! They needn't think they could control him! His mind cleared slowly as he studied the radar 'scope. Three ships in column, the smallest the escort, leading.

"They haven't been zigzagging," said Keith. "Maybe they'll start at dawn. Anyway, it looks like they'll pass right over *Whitefish*. We had her right here when she dived." He laid a pencil on a spot about halfway between the center of the 'scope and the small pip indicating the escort. "He should be shooting in about twenty minutes more."

"Any aircraft contacts?"

"Negative. We're watching the APR, though. Maybe somebody will come out at dawn."

Richardson nodded. The pieces were falling into place. *Whitefish* had reported six torpedoes remaining, three forward and three aft. She would get only one salvo off, would have another salvo left in the other end of the ship. At best, only one of the three ships would be hit. Whatever else, it had better be one of the troopships! His efforts of the day before had largely been wasted, except that now there was only a single escort. It would have been far better had *Eel* somehow pressed home herself into the convoy to put her last two fish into a primary target! He had forgotten the aircraft patrol, that the plane had prevented him from submerging in an attack position, that had not *Eel* forced the convoy to head again to the westward it would at this moment be within the shelter of the Korean archipelago, with no further opportunity for any submarine to attack.

Richardson and Leone were still watching the radar when they realized the formation had lost its cohesiveness. The distance between the last two ships began to increase. Then the small pip which was the escort pulled aside, dropped back with the lagging large pip.

"*Whitefish* has attacked," observed Blunt. He had come to the conning tower without their being aware of it.

"Yes, and the escort is looking for him. We may hear some depth charging soon."

"The second ship in column is still heading this way," said Keith.

"We'll have to turn him around." Richardson's numbed brain was working with the details. "What's the weather like topside?" he asked.

"Same as yesterday: cold, with a light chop."

"Good. Call all hands, Keith. Pass the word to stand by for surface action."

"What are you going to do, Rich?" asked Blunt.

"This transport skipper may still think the only submarine around is behind him. If the remaining escort stays with the ship Whitey has just torpedoed and the undamaged troopship comes on alone, we might have a chance to sink him with gunfire. If the tincan is with him, the tincan will head for us and the transport will reverse course. That may give Whitey a fourth crack at him."

Richardson spoke rapidly. His voice was not normal. The weariness was showing through, even though the few hours of near-sleep in the conning tower had mightily rejuvenated him. He yawned rapidly several times. The adrenalin was beginning to pop through his veins, but his system needed extra oxygen to make up for accumulated fatigue. Deliberately he forced himself to take several deep breaths. He began to explain to Keith that it was vital he be kept informed of any change in the disposition of the three ships, then broke off. Keith knew this. No point in wasting the effort. Carrying a second mug of coffee, he made his way to the bridge.

The destroyer escort skipper must have been discouraged at losing his consort and two of his convoy, but that didn't stop him from doing his duty. Very soon, Eel's radar showed only two ships, one large and one small. Plot quickly confirmed that they were continuing their course to the east. And as the brilliant edge of the sun came over the eastern horizon, burning away the remaining shadows with long streamers of light leaping from wave crest to wave crest, to the consternation of the two Japanese skippers a surfaced submarine lay limned exactly against the crescent-shaped, rapidly growing orb. Moments before, there had been nothing there. Both Japanese captains had thought their erstwhile attacker to be by this time several miles astern, but the new apparition, clearly a submarine, revealed unmistakable hostile intent by opening fire with two large guns, landing one solid hit on the troopship's forecastle and several near-misses in the water alongside.

The Mikura-class frigate dashed toward the submarine, which dived, and the merchant skipper, frantically reversing course, was happy to hear several loud depth charges astern. These signified that the escort

303

at last had contact and was working over their antagonist. Under such conditions, he had been thoroughly and frequently briefed, a sub's ability to assume the offensive was nil; so, as he came again in sight of the crowded lifeboats and rafts from his companion, well aware both of the risk he took and of the importance of the soldiers in the water, he disobeyed his orders by slowing to pick up the survivors. For an hour he remained in the vicinity, not without trepidation, in case the submarine being depth charged should fight its way clear and come back, while the surviving troops climbed up his cargo nets. Finally, his ship seriously overcrowded, he took up a northerly course, gave a wide berth to the area where depth charging was continuing, and once again, this time without incident, turned eastward.

The Japanese skipper would have been far less courageous had he had any way of knowing that almost directly beneath him, as he hove to, lay the submarine which had actually fired the torpedoes which had sunk his two companions. One of the depth charges dropped almost at random in the immediately ensuing counterattack had been uncomfortably close, starting a gasket in one of the internal risers of number seven main ballast tank in the after torpedo room. The result was a slight leak, and Whitey Everett had therefore set *Whitefish* gently on the muddy bottom of the Yellow Sea while the damage was surveyed and repaired. When heavy screws, approaching, slowing, circling, and finally stopping were reported, Everett had suspected some new and unusual tactic on the part of the enemy. He had forthwith directed cessation of all repair work and stopping of all running machinery. Not until about two hours after the heavy screws restarted and all noises on the surface had faded away did he resume normal activities.

For his first patrol in command, Whitey Everett had done well; he had sunk five ships and would bring back but three torpedoes, all in stern tubes. His officers and crew applauded his decision not to push his luck.

It was the worst of bad fortune, Richardson decided, for *Eel* to have this time dived in an area of the Yellow Sea where the sonar conditions were the best he had ever experienced. More, by its own good fortune—or perhaps a combination of excellent sonar equipment and an unusually alert operator—the tincan had come directly upon *Eel* with a firm, solid contact and an apparently unlimited supply of depth charges. Perhaps Richardson should have remained at periscope depth. He might have, had there been any torpedoes remaining in *Eel*'s tubes, or had not the signs of deep fatigue, discernible in the entire ship's company as well as himself, impelled him otherwise. Perhaps, too, there was a psychological compulsion, a realization that fate could not load the dice of war entirely on one side indefinitely, that *Eel* had had more than her share of success recently, that the enemy too had some capability and must have his innings. In any event, *Eel* lost the initiative when she went deep. The depth charge attack she was now enduring was the most severe and the most deliberate of Richardson's experience.

Were the water deeper, there would have been a greater range of uncertainty as to what setting to place on the depth charges. As it was, *Eel* could go no deeper than two hundred feet, and her Japanese antagonist easily remained in contact. The sound of his screws came in alternately from one side or the other, ahead or astern, but always remaining at close range. The initial flurry of charges was small in number, only six, but extremely well placed. Thereafter the tincan contented itself with dropping only one, or perhaps two, at the optimum point of each deliberate, careful approach. All were close, and all had done some damage.

Perhaps there was an unknown oil leak, or an air leak, to betray *Eel*'s position to the surface. Perhaps the water was clear enough in this particular area for the submarine's outline to be hazily visible to a masthead lookout. In the Yellow Sea this hardly seemed possible. But the enemy's ability to hold contact was uncanny. Perhaps an aircraft had come out to help him. Maybe it could see through the mud-yellow water. At 200 feet, after all, the highest point of the submarine would be only 154 feet—exactly half her length—beneath the surface.

All machinery, with the exception of the main motors, had long since been secured. The humidity of the atmosphere inside the boat had instantly gone to 100 percent and remained there, with the constant addition of moisture from the bodies of *Eel*'s sweating crew, as the air temperature crept steadily upward. Never again, Richardson decided, would *Eel*'s linoleum decks be waxed. The moisture settled upon them, lifted the wax, and the whole was stirred into a disgusting ooze as men shuffled through it. In the meantime, an accumulation of small leaks was gradually filling the bilges of the enginerooms and the motor room. *Eel* was slowly losing trim. To pump bilges would require running the drain pump. To pump out an equivalent amount of water from one of the trimming tanks would require use of the trim pump. Both would make noise, and Richardson refused to permit them to be run. Little by little the amount of lift required on bow planes and stern planes increased, until finally they reached their limits. It was then necessary for *Eel* herself to run with an up angle so that some of the thrust of her slow-moving propellers, turning at minimum speed, could be directly converted to an upward component. Precarious footing on a steeply sloping deck was thenceforth added to her crew's discomfort.

It was the waiting, however, that was the hardest. Waiting while Stafford reported occasionally, hopefully, "Shifted to long scale"—which might indicate uncertainty as to the exact location of the submarine—and then with something like a note of despair, "Shifted to short-scale pinging." Most difficult of all was when Stafford would announce, "She's starting a run!" Then there would be the waiting while Richardson and Stafford, both wearing earphones at the sonar receiver console, tried to determine whether the enemy was most likely to miss ahead or astern, so that Richardson could give the order to the rudder at the best moment to increase the amount of the error. Then the escort would move off a few hundred yards and listen for betraying noises while the reverberations of her depth charges died away. Finally she would resume echo-ranging, sometimes with the successive pings in quick succession on short scale, sometimes, perhaps only for the sake of variety, more widely spaced on the long-range scale.

Late in the afternoon, following a particularly accurate attack in which a depth charge had exploded close aboard on either side, filling the interior of the submarine with dust only just settled, shaking her insides as if the various structural components were made of some flexible plastic material, Blunt climbed heavily into the conning tower.

"We can't go on like this much longer, Rich. Lichtmann has just reported to Dugan that the last depth charging has wrecked one of the air compressors. Maybe we should just stop all machinery and lie doggo on the bottom for a while." Blunt's face was pale, covered with perspiration, smudged with dirt and oil. His khaki shirt was soaked through, with hardly a dry spot on it. His trousers were the same. He had thrown a towel around his neck, mopped his face and the top of his head ceaselessly as he talked. The towel, too, was dirty and wringing wet. Most noticeable about him, however, were his eyes. They were streaked with red, and they darted ceaselessly this way and that as he spoke. His face worked, his jaws and lips hung slack. His head wobbled on his neck as he spoke.

Removing his earphone, wiping the perspiration off his ears and both sides of his head with his own towel, Richardson turned two deep red coals instead of eyes—one set in a puffy black swelling—upon his superior. "No!" he said. "Once we set her on the bottom, we'll never get her off! As soon as they find out . . ." He let the sentence trail off. Blunt would know as well as anyone what would happen once the enemy knew the submarine had stopped moving, must therefore be lying on the bottom. "All hands not actively employed have been ordered to their bunks to conserve oxygen, Commodore," he said after a moment. "You should try to lie down and get some rest, too." His own system had long since ceased crying for sleep. It was numb; but the near horizons of his view, the brittleness of his thought processes, presented their own warnings. Regardless of his will, his body—or parts of it—was sleeping anyway.

"You're the one who needs some rest," said Blunt.

It was an unrealistic comment to be addressed to a submarine skipper in the midst of a depth charging. No doubt Blunt meant it only in the complimentary sense.

Rich waved a hand in deprecation. "Where's Keith?"

"I meant to tell you. He was in the after engineroom when the depth charges went off. He was knocked out somehow. Yancy is back with him."

This was a blow. Keith Leone was not only his right-hand man, upon whom he had come to depend more than anyone else, he had also become his closest friend. "How bad is he hurt?"

"Don't know yet. Several others were shaken up too, and somebody in the after room must have flipped, because he began running forward shouting to surface the boat and let the married men out. They stopped him with a wrench on the head. He and Keith are laid out together in the engineroom."

"Shifted to short scale! She's starting a run!" As Richardson swung around to the sonar receiving console and adjusted his earphones, he noticed that Stafford's hands were shaking. So, nearly, were his own. He could see the pulse jumping in his wrists. Through the earphones Rich could hear the malevolent propeller beats coming closer. The rapid pings of the Japanese sonar sounded triumphant. They were exactly like those of a U.S. destroyer. He could pay no further attention to Blunt, who was standing irresolutely on the top rung of the ladder leading to the control room. The hatch was normally closed upon rigging for depth charge. Blunt had opened it to mount to the conning tower.

"She's coming in on our port bow," whispered Stafford tensely. The pointer indicator for the sound heads indicated the same. "No bearing drift at all! She's coming right in on top of us!"

This was going to be a good run. The pings seemed to come right through the machine, and right through *Eel*'s pressure hull as well. Richardson could hear them without the earphones.

Perhaps a slight change in tactics would be in order. The tincan must be within a thousand yards. The cone of its sonar beam must have a limiting angle of depression, like American sonars. There would be a conical space beneath it where it was deaf. "Left full rudder," he ordered.

Cornelli, at the steering wheel where he had been for twelve hours, spelled occasionally by Scott, began cranking the large steel wheel. Like all the other hydraulically controlled mechanisms, it had been shifted to hand power and now operated as a pump by which oil could slowly be pushed through the hydraulic lines and gradually move the heavy rudder rams. Cornelli had stripped to the waist. His muscular torso gleamed with sweat under the light of the emergency battle lantern above him. The wheel was four feet in diameter, with a handle which could be snapped out against a spring on its rim. With both hands on the handle, Cornelli was jackknifing himself at the waist rapidly. Drops of sweat flew off his arms and shoulders as he furiously pumped the heavy steel wheel. The rudder angle indicator moved left with agonizing slowness.

"That's well, Cornelli," said Richardson. The rudder had not quite reached full left, but it was far enough. Cornelli was panting heavily. The oxygen content in *Eel*'s atmosphere was low. He was heaving deep breaths, alternately inflating and contracting his chest and stomach muscles.

"Rudder is twenty left. Thanks, sir," he puffed.

Through the gyro repeater built into the sonar dials Richardson could see *Eel* slowly move left, bringing the pinging escort more nearly dead ahead. "All right, Cornelli, start bringing the rudder back to zero. Scott, you help him." The air inside the submarine had become considerably more foul than was normal for an all-day submergence. The exertions of the crew, despite the enforced inactivity of some of them, resulted in greatly increased oxygen consumption. Cornelli was still heaving great, nearly sobbing, pants. Richardson felt that he himself was ready to do the same even without physical exertion. Blunt had been panting merely from having climbed up the ladder from the control room. After a few turns of the wheel Cornelli gratefully turned it over to Scott. "Just bring it back slow and stop on zero," said Richardson. "We've got her swinging now."

He turned, called past Blunt to Al Dugan at the diving station, "Al, we're going to speed up. When we do, bring her up to a hundred fifty feet."

Al Dugan also had a towel wrapped around his neck. Perspiration glinted on the ends of his close-cropped hair. He leaned back, looked up the hatch. "One-five-oh feet," he said.

"All ahead full," ordered Richardson. The rudder was nearing zero as he gave the command. "Commodore," he continued, "she's about to drop again! Please go below and shut the hatch!"

"I figure we've just entered the cone," said Stafford. "We're going to pass right under her on the opposite course."

"I know," said Richardson. He might have gone on to explain his reasoning, which was that once inside the cone of silence there was less chance the enemy ship would hear the sudden increase in speed of *Eel*'s propellers, and also a fairly good chance that she would not be able to react quickly enough to change the settings on her depth charges. Additionally, there was the factor that with the two ships proceeding on opposite courses, once *Eel* had passed beneath her adversary her propeller wash would thrust an increased amount of water directly toward the other ship. There might be an appreciable delay before the frigate could regain contact, since her sonar would also have to contend with her own propeller wash, as well as the water turbulence from her depth charges. Richardson said nothing, however, for suddenly it would have been too great an effort. A huge yawn racked his being. Almost with a sigh, really a deep pant by which his system subconsciously strove for more oxygen to keep it going, he asked, "Scott, when is sunset?"

"Half an hour ago," said Scott.

"How about evening twilight?"

"About an hour altogether. It will be dark in half an hour more."

"She's dropped!" screamed Stafford in Richardson's ear. Stafford was an oldtime submariner, a sonar man from way back, with many years of experience. He had been invaluable on the patrol thus far, as on the previous one. But even good men had their limits. Perhaps this was the last patrol Stafford should have to make—that is, if this were not to be the last one for other reasons.

"How many?"

"Don't know. Two at least! Maybe more this time!"

WHAM! A tremendous, all-encompassing explosion . . . WHAM! Another, equally loud. There was a sound of rushing water. WHAM! WHAM! Two more, even louder, almost simultaneous. Something struck the side of the submarine, skidded or scraped for a moment, fell clear. Richardson felt momentarily disoriented. Stafford had been knocked off his stool in front of the sonar equipment. Richardson saved himself from falling by gripping the handrail alongside the control room hatch. Blunt, however, still standing in the hatch, had been knocked backward off the ladder and had disappeared below into the control room just as the hatch itself, sprung loose from its latch, slammed shut with a resounding clap and then bounced open again.

Quin was prone on the floor, under Scott, who had fallen upon him. Unaccountably, the light in the conning tower was suddenly dim. The main lighting circuit had gone out. Only the emergency battle lights were still burning. The cloud of dust was so great that Richardson could hardly see to the after end of the cylindrical compartment, to the TDC and plotting table, normally the battle stations of Buck Williams and Larry Lasche. In the control room, through the reopened hatch, there was a haze of dust through the likewise dimmed light. There was confusion down there too. Blunt, in falling, must have landed upon Dugan, although Richardson could not see the situation clearly enough to discern who was who in the scramble. Relief flooded through him when Dugan's bulky figure arose from the tangle, the top of his head assumed something like its normal position. There was blood smeared on it, Richardson noted. Whether Dugan's or someone else's was not clear, but at least he was back on his feet.

"All compartments report!" Rich shouted down the hatch.

Quin, with his earphones, would have been the normal channel for the order, but he was still temporarily out of commission. He could see him trying to listen, however.

Suddenly Dugan leaned back. "After engineroom reports damage!" he said, speaking swiftly.

"Are they taking water?"

It could not be serious. Al Dugan had yet to feel the weight in his diving controls. There was, however, that sound of rushing water, which he could still hear. It sounded like something changed in the superstructure. There was a quality to the noise which Richardson had never heard before.

He grabbed the telephone handset. Through it Richardson could hear compartments still reporting, as they had been trained, from forward aft.

"Silence on the line!" he bellowed into the telephone mouthpiece. "After engineroom report!"

The voice at the other end of the line seemed extremely distant, weak. It stated its message of horror, baldly, matter-of-factly, without embellishment or inflection of voice. It was almost as though the speaker were too tired, or too much under shock, to place any personal feeling into what he had to say: "After engineroom is flooding!"

Richardson had been expecting something like this. Neither strong steel hull nor human flesh and blood could continue to stand up under the crushing pounding so deliberately delivered for the past several hours. Nor could vital internal machinery. This was the end. This the solution to the problems. Now he could abandon himself to the inevitable. He was so tired—so tired. WHAM! WHAM! Two more depth charges. God, would they never stop? The last two depth charges, however, seemed not quite so close as the previous ones. The destroyer had finished its pass and was now dead astern. Had not *Eel* speeded up, the two middle depth charges in the pattern would have fallen neatly around the conning tower instead of farther aft. Now the frigate would be turning around, beaming its sonar where its plot would indicate *Eel* should be. But the escort would be pinging straight up *Eel*'s wake, through the disturbed water of her thrashing screws, the inline disturbance of six closely spaced depth charges. Richardson could increase its difficulty by maneuvering to keep the disturbance between them. Even with full speed, however, the rapidly accumulating weight of water in *Eel*'s after engineroom would soon be too much to carry. He could hasten the end by ordering "all stop" and letting her sink quietly to the bottom. The men in the after engineroom could prolong their lives a little by evacuating the compartment, dogging it down tightly after them. Then everyone could rest.

The alternative was to fight it. *Eel* must have gained some distance on her attacker. There would be a period of some peace, some opportunity to see if it might not yet be possible to salvage the situation. What was it that old Joe Blunt used to say so many years ago when he was still the much-admired skipper of the *Octopus*? "When you get into firing position, take your time and do it right." That was one of them. The other was something to the effect that no matter what happened, there would be time to do what had to be done. Only the coward gave up and let circumstances rule him.

Richardson was aware of Quin staring at him with great wide-open eyes. Al Dugan in the control room below was taking a step up the ladder to bring Richardson into clearer view.

"All compartments, this is the captain. Stand firm to your stations! I'm going aft!" Deliberately he forced himself calmly to replace the handset in its cradle. "Buck," he called, "I'm going to the after engineroom. You're in charge up here. You can reach me by telephone. Keep the speed on, and keep that tincan astern. I'll be back in three minutes!"

He stepped into the hatch, placed his heels on the ladder leading to the control room. It would do the control room gang good to see him coming down in his accustomed way, back to the ladder, hands on the skirt below the hatch rim opposite. "Gangway, Al," he said. The diving officer, standing on the bottom rung of the ladder, swung clear. "Is she getting heavy aft?" he asked Dugan in a low tone.

"A little, but we're still holding her at this speed. I don't think we can if we slow down, though."

The steps he must take had almost instantaneously become clear in Richardson's mind. First, at all costs keep off the bottom. Second, stop or reduce the flooding. Third, get Keith and all other injured persons to a place of comparative safety, leaving only able-bodied men to do what could be done in the after engineroom. "Al," he said, speaking swiftly, "line up your air manifold for blowing number seven main ballast tank alone. If you find yourself getting out of trim, or if we have to slow down, put a bubble in it big enough to balance the weight of the water in the after engineroom. Be careful and don't put too much air in the tank." Dugan nodded.

"Line up the drain pump on the drain line and be ready to start it. If we can still reach the after engineroom bilge suction, I'll open it and give you the word to start pumping. And remember, if you get too much air in number seven tank, the only way to get rid of it will be through the vent valve, and it will go right to the surface for them to see!"

As Richardson swiftly made his way through the successive compartments, opening the watertight doors, seeing they were redogged behind him, he was acutely conscious of the haggard looks with which everyone regarded him. His was the responsibility for the situation, and it was to him alone they had to look for survival.

There were two or three men peering through the heavy glass viewing port in the closed watertight door between the forward and after enginerooms. One of them had his hand on the compartment air-salvage valve above the door. They moved quickly aside for him. No water was yet visible in the compartment.

"Open the door," he ordered. Instantly the dogging mechanism handle was spun, the door swung open. He stepped through. "Dog it and keep a watch on me," he said crisply. "Stand by to put pressure on the compartment, but don't do it unless I signal, or unless you see water." Air pressure in the engineroom, a last resort to reduce intake of water, would thereafter prevent opening either door to the compartment until an airlock system was devised.

Water was coming in from somewhere. He could hear the hydrant-like spurt of it beneath the deck plates. The upper level was deserted except for Yancy, the pharmacist's mate.

"Where's Leone?" asked Richardson.

"He's down below with Mr. Cargill and Chief Frank. He's okay, sir. The other man is all right, too. He just couldn't take any more. So I gave him a sedative, and I think he'll be okay when he wakes up. He's over there lying on the generator flat." Yancy indicated the area aft of the starboard main engine.

"Good. Get some help and get him through the door forward right away, and roll him into a bunk." He indicated the watertight door through which he had just entered, then swiftly dropped through the open hatch in the deck plates, climbed down the thin steel rungs in the ladder. He was nearly to his knees in water in an incredibly confined space between the two huge engines.

Keith, a large abrasion on the side of his head, sloshed toward him. "Looks like the sea line to this freshwater cooler is ruptured right at the hull valve," he said. "We've got the hull valve shut, but it's the valve body itself that's broken. There's no way of stopping the water coming in unless we can take the sea pressure off."

"We're getting the drain pump lined up. How fast is the water coming in? Can we reach the drain pump suction?"

"Pretty fast. It's up nearly to the lower generator flats, but so far I don't think any has got into the main generators. Good thing we were able to take the angle off when we speeded up. We'll get the bilge suction open, but the drain pump won't be able to handle it. It's coming in too fast. We'll have to put a pressure on the compartment."

"Not a hundred and fifty feet worth. We've got to reduce external pressure too. Tell off the engineers you'll need down here. Send forward everybody not required here or in the compartments aft. You can start pressurizing whenever you're ready, but let me know first, and come out yourself. A few pounds will be enough, and I'm going to need you back in conn."

Suddenly it was clear what he had to do. From the look in Keith's eyes he understood, and agreed. "That last salvo makes sixty-five depth charges he's dropped on us," Richardson said quietly. "He probably has at least that many more in his locker, and sonar conditions are phenomenal. He'll figure to keep us down here either until our battery gives out or he gets one of those blockbusters right on target. It's time to see if those five-inchers are as good as we think they are!"

There was a hissing of air through hidden pipes. Al Dugan had begun to put air into the aftermost ballast tank to counteract the growing weight of water in the after part of the boat. With a final word to Keith, Richardson started up the ladder. He had reached the upper level of the engineroom, had just motioned to the men watching through the viewing port of the watertight door, when a change in *Eel* communicated itself to him. Perhaps it was the lessening of the sensation of speed through the water. Perhaps it was a gradual squashing down aft. His sixth sense—a faculty developed by all submarine skippers—told him all. The main motors had stopped!

A telephone handset was nearby for the convenience of the engine throttlemen. He grabbed it. "This is the captain! What's happened?"

It must be the maneuvering room which answered. "Ordered all stop, sir." There was lethargy, acceptance, in the voice. To stop the screws meant sinking to the bottom. There could be only one possible result of such a move, and only a single reason could be the cause. Some catastrophe had taken place in the nerve center of the submarine!

"Conn! Are you still on the line?"

"Yessir, Captain." Quin's voice. It, too, carried a hidden message. "The commodore ordered all stop, sir."

"*Who* ordered?"

"The commodore, sir!"

The watertight door had been undogged. The men were swinging it open. Rich slammed the phone in its place, jackknifed through the door, ran the length of the forward engineroom. Here they had not seen him coming because the door was behind an exhaust trunk and out of the line of sight. Several seconds were needed to get it open. In the crew's dinette, however, someone had been listening surreptitiously on the phones. The watertight door was already being undogged as Richardson raced for it.

He was panting heavily when he reached the diving station. Al Dugan's face was working. "As soon as you went aft, the commodore went back up the ladder and had the hatch shut. A minute ago he sent word you had been injured, and he was taking command and putting the ship on the bottom. He's flipped, sir! You can tell by looking at him" The oval-shaped hatch to the conning tower was closed. Both dogs had been hammered home.

Consternation. A knot in the gut. Neither must be allowed to show. "All right, Al. I'll take care of this. Is your air manifold still rigged to blow number seven tank?"

"Just through the after group. The forward group blow is as was."

"Fine. Keep her balanced, and keep her off the bottom. Use safety tank if you have to." There was grateful relief in Dugan's acknowledgment. Rich could guess at the quandary he had been in.

"Sargent!" The auxiliaryman responded with alacrity. "Yessir!"

Richardson spoke slowly and distinctly, so that everyone in the control room would hear and understand. "Shift steering and annunciators from the conning tower to the control room!" Sargent jumped to the forward bulkhead, rapidly began to make the shift.

"Al, get a quartermaster out of the damage-repair gang and put him on the steering station. Report when he has steering control." To the man wearing the telephone headset Rich said, "Inform all stations that I have the conn in the control room."

"Blow safety!" suddenly called out Dugan. The diving officer raised his right hand, palm open. Lichtmann, appearing from nowhere in Sargent's place, knocked the air valve open. "Secure!" Dugan clenched his fist. Lichtmann spun the handle shut.

314

"Steering and annuciators shifted to the control room, Captain!" Sargent was reporting.

"I have steering control, sir. Annunciators too." The new helmsman was Sodermalm, a lithe young sailor with several patrols under his belt.

"All ahead full!" Richardson still spoke portentously. This was the test, the resolution of the most immediate emergency. Sodermalm clicked over the annunciators.

"Captain says all ahead full from the control room," he heard the phoneman say into his mouthpiece. The electricians in the maneuvering room must have been waiting for the order, for the answering signals on the two instruments were instant and simultaneous. Richardson could feel *Eel* responding to the additional power. Grins of approbation from Dugan and the men in the control room.

There was still more to be done. "Conn, control," he said to the man wearing the phones—it was Livingston, the young seaman who only yesterday had mistaken a bird for a plane—"What is the latest bearing of the enemy?"

Under the steady gaze of his skipper, Livingston was intent on redeeming his spurious warning. He carefully repeated the message, afterward treasured the fleeting smile of gratitude from his superior's strained, stubbled face when he reported, "Two-three-seven, true, sir."

The enemy was still dead astern. The total time elapsed since the most recent salvo of depth charges had been less than five minutes. There was still a little breathing space. This would be the moment to relieve some of the tension. If the new helmsman behaved true to form, he might be the means. "Sodermalm, you don't look big enough to steer the ship in hand power. Get some others to help you, and see if you can ease the course right to zero-five-seven."

"Ease right to zero-five-seven, aye aye. I can handle this better than those conning tower jockeys anytime. This is no sweat. Just tell me what you want and leave it to me, sir!" Sody, as Rich knew the crew called the irrepressible little Swede, was nothing if not a self-confident sailor. Smiles appeared on several faces. Rich also grinned inwardly, and then decided to let some of it show.

Now for the most difficult problem. Access to the sonar gear and Stafford's expertise was imperative. The tincan would be getting ready for another run soon. "Livingston, tell conn to open the hatch. I'm coming up." Control had been wrested from Blunt with ridiculous ease. It was important for morale that it be absolutely clear there had never been a threat to Richardson's command of the submarine. He swung himself onto the rungs of the ladder. Quin would repeat the instruction from Livingston loudly enough for all in the conning tower to hear. Blunt would realize he had been bested, would give in as gracefully as he could.

The hatch dogs moved a trifle, but then they returned to the engaged position. The hatch remained closed. Livingston gave the clue. "Quin says the commodore is standing on the hatch!" But the words were no sooner out than the dogs precipitantly turned free. The hatch sprang open. He leaped up the ladder rungs.

A scuffle was going on. Blunt, Williams, and Lasche were struggling between the periscopes. Quin staring aghast. Scott—it must have been he who had kicked open the hatch—the same. Cornelli, still braced at his useless steering wheel, rigidly keeping his eyes front. Only Stafford, padded earphones covering half his face, seemed oblivious. "Stop!" roared Richardson. "Stop it! All three of you!" The three were breathing with tremendous heaves. Rich, too, had hardly recovered from his run from the after engineroom, and was panting again from his swift ascent to the conning tower.

The wolfpack commander was the first to speak. He was sputtering with rage, the querulous note in his voice never more evident. His eyes were unnaturally wide, staring. His whole face was loose. Even his words were loose, poorly pronounced. His breath came in great, fetid wheezes. "Richardson, I took command of this ship when you left your station! Somebody has to take care of things around here! I'm charging these two officers with assault on a superior in the performance of his duty, and I want them transferred as soon as we reach port!"

"He wouldn't get off the hatch when you wanted to come up," said Williams, "so Larry and I pulled him off. We knew you weren't hurt. He made that up. Maybe he was thinking of Keith—is he all right? What about the flooding aft?"

Ignoring the questions, Richardson spoke rapidly. "We've got to surface. Get the gun crews ready!" He turned to Blunt. "Commodore," he began, spacing his words but speaking gently, "you're not yourself. Please go below. The pharmacist's mate will report to you. . . ."

"No! You can't make me! I've taken charge here!" Blunt's voice trembled.

He would have said more, but Stafford interrupted. There was excitement in his tone, combined with dread. "I think she's shifted to short scale and started a run! She's dead aft in the baffles! Our screws are making so much noise I can't tell for sure!"

Were *Eel* to turn to clear the sonar for better hearing, her partial broadside would return a far more definite echo than the *Mikura* could get by pinging up her wake, as she was at the moment forced to do. For some time Rich had been considering another idea, born of what he had read of German submarine tactics. "Control," he called down the hatch, "Al, open the forward group vents. Get ready to blow a big bubble through forward group tanks!"

"Control, aye!" A moment later Dugan leaned his head back again. "Forward group vents are open. We're ready to blow!"

"All stop," ordered Richardson. Cornelli reached for his annunciator controls, but the order had been called down to the control room. Cornelli had forgotten he was disconnected. He dropped his hands, helplessly looked backward.

The follower pointers still functioned, however, and clicked over to "stop" just as Al Dugan called from below, "All stop, answered."

"Blow forward group, Al. Full blow! Half a minute!" The noise of air blowing. A different sound in the water rushing past, because full of bubbles. *Eel* coasted through them as they rose from her open vents and broke up into millions of tiny, sonar-stopping granules of air. A long bubble streak would form on the surface as well, but in the rapidly growing darkness this might not immediately be noticed. When it was, the tincan skipper would very likely think he had delivered a lethal blow at last. Whatever else, for a time his sonar would never penetrate the double barrier of *Eel*'s wake, thrown directly into his receiver, and the cloud of diffused air immediately following. He would have to proceed through the entire mess before his sonar conditions would be back to normal, and might well assume, temporarily at least, that the air bubble marked the rupture of *Eel*'s pressure hull; that the now flooded submarine, dead at last, was lying on the bottom under it.

Rich was looking at his watch. *Eel*'s speed had only begun to drop. He ordered emergency speed a few seconds before the half-minute expired, and the needle on the pitometer log indicator again began to rise. It was hardly possible the enemy tincan would recognize the change through the reverberations in the water and the blanket of air now astern. Very deliberately, Rich put on the spare set of sonar earphones. In the depleted condition of her battery, *Eel* could not run long at full battery discharge, but a long run was not in his mind. Depth charges were; and after a lengthy silence, during which the roaring of water rushing past and the vibration of whatever it was that had been damaged topside seemed to grow ever louder, he suddenly relaxed.

Stafford was also grinning, for the first time that day. Through the earphones, dim in the distance and masked by the tumultuous wash of *Eel*'s thrashing screws, there could clearly be heard the thunder of many depth charges. The tincan was depth charging the air bubble! It would be long minutes before the enemy skipper realized he had not driven *Eel* to earth at last.

This would be the opportunity. Richardson had given Blunt no attention for several minutes, was on the point of forgetting him when he realized he was still in the conning tower. The wolfpack commander was still breathing hard, still slack-jawed, his eyes still glaring under the bunched, bushy brows. Obviously he was still confused, still antagonistic. He would be terribly in the way. It was not possible to stop the sharpness in Richardson's voice. "Commodore, please! I asked you to go below! We're going to have to do a battle surface!"

"No! You can't make me!" The identical words as before. Unreal. Manic.

"Quin, pass the word for Yancy to come up here." Richardson waited until the pharmacist's mate appeared on the ladder. "Commodore, unless you go below with Yancy by yourself, we'll have to have you carried down. I really mean it, sir!" Not until later did Richardson recall his next words, wrenched from the depths of his private grief. They were expressive of all that had happened between them, all Rich had tried to do for his onetime idol; symbolic, too, of the change in their relationship, and of the onslaught of time which casts one up and at the same moment must cast another down. "I've come to the end of my rope, Joe," he said. It was the first time ever that he had used Blunt's given name.

There was something juvenile, something pitifully childish, in the stubborn refusal, the retreat into the accustomed corner under the bridge hatch. But there was neither time nor any more emotion to waste.

Quin was trying to get Richardson's attention. "Mr. Leone is on the phone. He says the engineroom is lined up to pump, and he's beginning to pressurize the compartment. He says he'll have to use a lot of air if we stay down."

Once air pressure in the after engineroom became equal to the sea pressure at the depth, water would cease coming in. When air pressure exceeded sea pressure, water would begin flowing back through the same hole through which it had entered. This would be true, of course, only so long as the water level in the engineroom covered the hole; and anyone remaining in the compartment would be subjected to the same pressure, with consequent danger of the bends if prolonged. But there was no longer any need for that worry.

He picked up the handset. "Keith? . . . Go ahead. We'll be coming up in a very few minutes, so hold it down to ten pounds' pressure."

It must be quite dark topside. *Eel* would slow down and come to periscope depth immediately. This would greatly reduce the necessary air pressure in the after engineroom. The bubble in number seven tank would expand as the ship rose nearer to the surface, giving additional buoyancy, but of course additional buoyancy would be needed as she slowed down. Exactly how much was the problem. As the lifting effect of the stern planes became less pronounced, the whole business of balancing weights and buoyancy submerged would become more ticklish. The risk of emitting another bubble, if the buoyancy aft became too great, would have to be accepted.

Richardson paced around the periscope in the darkened conning tower, becoming readjusted to the reduced light. He could hear the repeated orders to "blow" and "secure the air"—and once or twice a quickly telephoned order to the after torpedo room to "crack the vent," then shut it tightly again—as Dugan fought to maintain submerged trim.

There were other noises too. The bustle of breaking out ammunition, the preparation of the gun crews, the setting up of the ammunition supply parties. At one point, Richardson got on the telephone to all compartments and quietly announced his instructions to the gun crews. The gun captains and the pointers and trainers of the two five-inch guns were summoned to the conning tower for specific instructions. Their first move would be to check the bore-sight of their guns, for their telescopes might well have been damaged or knocked out of alignment. They could do this swiftly by sighting on the previously laid-out marks on deck forward and aft, using Buck Williams' improvised bore-sight telescope jammed into the open breech. Then they were free to swing on the target, but they were not to open fire until ordered.

The six men, goggled and garbed in heavy clothing, listened gravely. This was very near to the situation for which they had trained and planned two months ago, and for which periodically, whenever they had the opportunity, they had checked out the guns. Their only chance to fire them since leaving Pearl had come briefly, some twelve hours previously, at the last troopship. Combined with awareness of the emergency, it was also clear there was a certain relish at the prospect of vengeance against their tormentor. The gun captains would wear telephones and would receive range settings from Buck Williams, who would be manning another set in the conning tower. Buck, in turn, would receive ranges from the radar and firing bearings from the bridge TBTs.

Final instructions were for Keith alone. "If anything happens to me on the bridge," Richardson said, "do not dive under any circumstances. We'll have to hope that water hasn't gotten into number three and four generators—Johnny Cargill and Frank will be checking on that. The first thing to do is to damage this tincan so that he won't be able to follow, or anyway, keep up with us." It was characteristic of Keith that he should merely nod.

Time for all the preparations could not have taken ten minutes. The crew was working in desperate haste, well aware of the danger that the destroyer might come upon them before they were ready. In the dim visibility through the periscope, the tincan could barely be seen in the darkness. *Eel*'s high-speed run had gained considerable distance. Now the enemy was slowly and methodically moving up her wake. He had probably finally realized his mistake with the air bubble, but was still beset by confused echoes from his own recent depth charges and from the turbulent water left behind by the submarine's propellers. Nevertheless, the sonar conditions would clear, and at the end of the disturbed water he must find the submarine.

The conning tower was crowded with men, nearly all wearing red goggles. All wore heavy clothing, for it would be cold topside in contrast to the atmosphere inside the submarine, which was hot, smelly, and humid. The profuse perspiration pouring down Richardson's skin inside his own heavy jacket bothered him not at all, but the perspiration around his eyes as he looked through the periscope was more annoying than the drip landing on his forehead. Ceaselessly he wiped his face on a towel, frequently was forced to use a piece of lens paper on the glass objective lens of the periscope as it clouded up with the moisture exuding from his face.

"We're ready below!" Dugan's report sailed up through the control room hatch. For some minutes Richardson had been debating with himself once again whether it would be better to execute a traditional battle surface close aboard his adversary in hopes of overwhelming him with gunfire before he was able to respond. Again he put aside this alternative, although it ran counter to traditional submarine training before the war. Sonar conditions were simply too good. *Eel* would be detected before she was able to get close enough to execute the standard drill, and once this happened, the enemy would instantly renew the depth charging, or try to ram. Far better to surface without warning, at a greater range. This would give *Eel* time for several precious minutes of gunfire.

Opposed to the submarine's assemblage of guns—two short-barrel five-inchers plus automatic weapons ranging from the lethal forty-millimeter on down—the enemy escort vessel could muster a single four-inch, backed up by an unknown number of rapid-fire guns of various calibers. It was upon his five-inchers that Richardson was depending to get in some quick, vital, damaging blows, most importantly in the vicinity of the four-inch on the tincan's forecastle. A single hit from this gun could penetrate *Eel*'s pressure hull and totally eliminate her ability to dive. The Jap's bow had undoubtedly been designed for ramming, and a single blow from it, struck fair, would surely rupture *Eel*'s hull and drive her under as well. Better to retain the advantage of surprise and begin the action from afar.

"Shut the lower hatch! All ahead standard!" The slam of the hatch between conning tower and control room. The clink of the annunciators, now, like steering, returned to the conning tower. "Left fifteen degrees rudder. Come left to one-eight-oh!" Richardson intended to surface broadside to the enemy so that both five-inchers could be gotten into action immediately. Too much rudder, however, might give Al Dugan trouble with depth control, riding as he was with a bubble in the aftermost ballast tank. On the other hand, the increased speed would give the bow planes and stern planes greater bite.

"Four knots, Captain." Buck Williams, wearing a telephone headset, was reading the ship's speed from the face of the TDC. The TDC would be used like a gunfire range computer, with radar ranges and TBT bearings set into it. Output, compensating for enemy movement, would be read off from it directly to the gun captains at each of the guns.

"Steady on course south." Cornelli at the helm.

"Quin, tell the diving officer to start blowing!" Quin repeated the order. Instantly the sound of high pressure air flowing into the ballast tanks could be heard. Richardson could feel the lift of the emptying tanks, but there was no answering rising sensation. Al would operate the bow and stern planes to hold the submarine down as long as possible. The blowing increased in volume. "Depth six-oh feet." Keith was reading the conning tower depth gauge for him. "Speed through water five-a-half knots."

"Stadimeter range," said Richardson, "mark!"

"Two-eight-double-oh," read Keith. Angle on the bow and bearing had already been fed into the TDC. "Checking right in there!" from Williams.

The blowing continued. There was a moment of tense stillness. The next move would be Dugan's.

"Can't hold her! Reversing planes!" Dugan's voice boomed loud on the general announcing speaker in the conning tower. Suddenly the submarine began to rise beneath them. Al had been directed to bring her up all flat, partly to get the main deck clear as soon as possible, partly to keep water in the after engineroom bilges from collecting in the after end and possibly, at that last moment, damaging the all-important generators.

"All back full!" ordered Richardson.

"Four-five feet," said Keith. "Four-oh feet." Water could be heard pouring through the superstructure, sluicing off the bridge. "Three-oh feet. Two-eight feet. Two-four feet . . . Two-four feet and holding!"

"All stop! Open the hatch!" bellowed Richardson. "Open the gun access trunk! Gun crews on deck!" The hatch banged open. There was a slight lift of air through the hatch, instantly dissipated because only the conning tower volume was involved. Richardson scrambled up the ladder, stepped clear of the horde of men following him. Instantly he was glad he had picked the port side to begin the action. The starboard side of the bridge—a large section of the bulletproof steel plating—was missing, evidently blown off by that last, closest, depth charging. Perhaps it was this which he had heard striking the side of the submarine and clattering on down into the depths. Luckily there was no further damage. No doubt the heavy plating had warded off the depth charge explosion. If so, to this everyone in the conning tower, and perhaps *Eel* herself, owed their lives.

Richardson was conscious of the bang of the gun access trunk hatch, the scurrying feet of many men running aft and forward. The men who had come up the hatch immediately after him had already cast loose the two forty-millimeter guns. Others pulled out the twin twenty-millimeters and hurriedly mounted them on their little stand just aft of the periscope shears, and still others mounted the three fifty-caliber machine guns in their mounting sockets on the undamaged port side of the bridge. On the forecastle he could see the round forward torpedo room hatch being lifted to the vertical and the shadowy forms of two men lifting their machine gun out, setting it in its socket to the left of the open hatch circle.

Keith's voice from the conning tower. "Diving officer reports securing high pressure air. Shifting to low pressure blowers. Ship is riding at twenty-two-foot keel depth. Bridge speaker system is out!"

Richardson had expected this report from Dugan by loudspeaker. It was evident he had tried to make it, and that the bridge speaker system was one more casualty of the recent depth charging.

"Captain, I'm sending Quin up to relay your orders by telephone. We'll have to take a chance on a wire through the hatch. We have wire cutters in the conning tower if we need them, and he has another in his pocket."

Seconds later Quin was standing beside Richardson alongside the port TBT.

"I have communications with the forward and after five-inch guns, Captain," said Quin. "They're bore-sighting them now. Mr. Williams is giving them range: twenty-four hundred yards."

"Good," said Richardson. He raised his voice. "Hold fast, men!" he shouted. They had all been thoroughly briefed, but it was well to repeat the order. "Hold fast until I give the order!"

"Five-inchers and the forward-torpedo-room hatch have the word," said Quin. A mutter of comprehension reached Richardson from all the bridge personnel.

"Bore-sight completed, forward five-inch," said Quin. "Just a minute on the after gun—after gun bore-sight completed, Captain. Both guns, bore-sight completed. Training out on the port beam."

"Ask them if they can see the target through their telescopes." He heard Quin repeating the question, a moment later the reassuring reply, "Number one and two five-inch both can see the target clearly."

Richardson was looking at the enemy ship through the TBT binoculars, never once removing his eyes from it. He thumbed the button built into the handle. The enemy must have just become aware of *Eel*'s sudden appearance on the surface.

"Have we got a second radar range on them yet, Quin?" he asked.

"Getting it right now, sir. Mr. Williams is getting radar range two-two-double-oh. He's having the guns set in two-one-five-oh on their range dial."

"Very well. All guns load." He could hear the disciplined clatter as the five-inch shells were slammed into the breeches and the locks slammed home behind them. The forties had their clips of four rounds each already in place. One jerk back on the arming lever and a round was rammed to the firing chamber. The same with the twenties with their canned ammunition and the fifty calibers with their belts. The months of training were paying off. The first time this had been tried in drill there had been much clutter and confusion. Not this time. He had strenuously impressed upon all hands the importance of getting off this first broadside, these first few salvos, suddenly, with precision, and if possible with complete surprise.

Through his binoculars the enemy ship had been presenting a slight starboard angle on the bow, perhaps ten degrees. Now its already truncated silhouette shortened, became symmetrical. Richardson realized he was looking dead on at the enemy ship. The bridge command circuit had been rigged up. Miraculously, its permanent topside parts had not been damaged—it was a much simpler system and entirely separate from the ship's announcing system. He spoke into the microphone hanging from its cord which he had placed between the twin eyepieces of the TBT binoculars. "Angle on the bow zero," he said. "He's seen us. Heading this way. Bearing, mark!" He pushed the button again.

"Williams says Mr. Leone can see him through the periscope," said

Quin. "They're checking his speed now. They had him on five knots, but he's speeding up, they think. They're setting a new range at the guns, two thousand yards."

Eel lay quietly in the water, all her way having drifted off. Fully surfaced, she rocked gently in the two-foot waves. Evening twilight had long since disappeared. Deliberately, Richardson had not ordered the main engines started. Despite the partial depletion of *Eel*'s battery, it was still good for about half an hour of full speed. He would rather continue to give the impression of being disabled, and at the same time retain the sudden rapid mobility afforded by the battery.

"Forties, twenties, and fifties will not shoot until specially ordered," said Richardson, avoiding use of the word, "fire." This too had already been thoroughly explained. The forties would be permitted to open up at fifteen hundred yards' range. The twenties and fifties not until one thousand yards.

There was a flash from the forward deck of the approaching escort vessel. He had opened fire with his four-inch gun. This had been anticipated. The risk of a lucky hit would have to be taken. The enemy would, at least, have to shoot directly over its own high bow. Aiming would be difficult. Richardson did not even bother to search for the fall of shot.

"Buck has sent range two thousand to both guns," said Quin hurriedly, forgetting the more formal appellation he should have used for the torpedo officer. "Range is twenty-one-fifty, closing. Speed ten knots, tracking right on."

"Tell Mr. Leone to shoot when the hitting range is two thousand," said Richardson. He raised his voice. "Stand by on the bridge. The main battery will be opening up in a moment." He did not want an overly tense member of the bridge crew to waste his ammunition prematurely.

"Range two-one-double-oh," said Quin. Richardson could visualize the two dozen rounds of ammunition laid out by each gun, the second and third shells cradled in arms of the loaders ready to be slammed into the breeches. There was another gout of flame from the foredeck of the approaching destroyer escort.

"Range is two-oh-five-oh, commence firing," reported Quin breathlessly.

BAM BAM! The two five-inch guns went off almost simultaneously. Two brilliant flashes of orange-yellow flame on the main deck. A few seconds' delay, then BAM BAM once more, and then for a third time the twin salvo roared out. The two guns gradually diverged in time as the gun crews vied with each other in ejecting the expended shell cases, slamming the new shells into the breeches, clearing away the hot brass

324

from around the guns, keeping the ammunition train going. The forward gun was firing a split-second faster than the after gun, but it had a longer ammunition train and no ammunition supply scuttle through the main deck. For prolonged firing the after gun would be able to maintain a more rapid pace. At the moment, however, the two guns were firing ammunition laid out on deck. It was an outburst of frenzied action.

For a few seconds, Richardson could abandon himself to the role of spectator, watching the fall of shot, observing the enemy reaction. He could even watch the trajectory of his own five-inch projectiles by the faint glow put in the base of each to assist in spotting. The first two must have landed simultaneously; one, or perhaps both, in the water only yards in front of the approaching destroyer. The resulting splash—almost a vertical column of water—was as high as the top of her mast. It must have deluged the crew on deck around her gun. The second and third he could not see, nor the fourth and fifth, but then he began to see splashes in the water beyond, half concealed by the bulk of the approaching ship.

"Down two hundred!" he shouted to Quin. He heard Quin repeat the message to Keith. First shots were almost always short in range because of the cold gun effect. It was quite possible that one or two had hit the enemy already. With no range correction, the next shots might be over. At the short range, any splashes immediately beyond the target, as long as they were in line, must however have been from shells which had torn their way through her superstructure. He lined up the TBT, pressed the button. That would send down a deflection correction, if one was needed.

"Mr. Keith says periscope agrees with down two hundred," said Quin. "Range is now fifteen hundred, TDC."

Richardson seized a moment of silence while both deck guns were loading, yelled, "Forties, open fire on target's bridge!"

This too had been rehearsed. Instantaneously the monotonous, sharp WHACK, WHACK, WHACK of the forties began, their crews racing about, jerking the quadruple clips from their racks, slamming them into their loading slides. The forties were fitted with tracers and had almost a flat trajectory. He could see them, arching only slightly, reaching toward the enemy ship. Some were exploding on contact. The others, armor-piercing, were going into the dark hull. An unearthly glow suffused the escort's angular silhouette as they struck, or as the tracers illuminated it briefly on passing, leaving its dark bulk even blacker on the black sea. There was another flash of flame on her foredeck, only the fourth or fifth. She was not making nearly so good practice (as the old gunnery saying went) as *Eel*. A critical factor, of course, was that the submarine had more than double the heavy armament. Furthermore, the forties had aircraft proximity fuses. Some of their bursts were not on impact but in the air, over the deck. They must be inflicting terrible casualties on exposed personnel. So far, the enemy tincan had not opened up with any automatic weapons—undoubtedly because, coming end-on as she was, her own bridge and superstructure masked at least some of them. But now there came a series of red flashes from the top of her bridge structure. Someone had got a machine gun going up there. It was small, however, probably no larger than fifty-caliber, hardly able to reach effectively across the intervening half-mile or more to the submarine.

So far *Eel* had received no hits, and at the same time Richardson was certain that his five-inchers must have struck the enemy several times. Clearly, the forty-millimeters were hitting repeatedly. Several times he had heard a whistling, tearing sound, knew it to be the passage of a large-caliber shell overhead. The closest must have passed a good ten feet above the bridge. The enemy was shooting over. That was a good sign. *Eel*'s own five-inchers must have pumped out ten shots each by now. Surely they had already dealt significant damage.

"Range one thousand yards!" shouted Quin in his ear, screaming to be heard above the monotonous regular pounding of the forties.

"All right, men!" yelled Richardson, pounding the shoulders of the group huddled with the fifty-calibers alongside him on the bridge. His gesture took in the twenty-millimeter crew. "Commence fire! All weapons!"

It was like a jet of fire spurting from *Eel*'s bridge. Three thin arcs of fifty-caliber tracer ammunition, arching fairly high, dropped upon the enemy ship, as did a pair of twin tracers arching slightly less high from the twenty-millimeter mount immediately aft. Up forward, from the forward torpedo room trunk, another single arc of fifty-caliber tracers streamed out toward the enemy.

The five-inchers were methodically continuing their destructive pounding. Their pace was slower now, having used up the ready ammunition laid out in advance. The pointers by consequence were aiming each shot with careful deliberation.

"Enemy speed has slowed to eight knots," shouted Quin. They had hurt her. If the damage was to her main propulsion plant, while *Eel*'s was still in full commission—assuming the men in the after engineroom had been able to get the leak under control—*Eel* could probably outrun her. If the damage were to her hull, so that the tincan's skipper had been forced to reduce speed because she was taking water, so much the better. But, of course, slowing might have been for some other reason, not related to damage.

Richardson had only to give the order for the full power of *Eel*'s two batteries, quickly followed by the hastily started diesels, to begin escape and evasion. He could head the ship southwest. Perhaps regain contact with the last fleeing transport if *Whitefish* had not sunk her. Possibly, somehow, he might one more time find the means to bring *Whitefish* into contact for one last attack with her remaining torpedoes. Perhaps, now that the troopship was bereft of escorts, *Eel* might be able to sink her by gunfire in a night action. If his brain was still able to function to plan the search. If he could find her, after all these hours. Provided there was still no air cover, or that the tincan did not get to her first.

But running would only hand the initiative over to the enemy. Once the tincan skipper was released from the pressure of *Eel*'s fire, he could more easily cope with whatever damage he had sustained, reorganize his gun crews, and resume the pursuit. Logically, he would put his major effort into getting his biggest weapon, the four-inch gun on his forecastle, back in commission. On the other hand, *Eel*'s five-inch guns would have to be silenced. It would be too risky to keep gun crews on the submarine's low, wave-swept deck at high speed, and even more hazardous to keep hatches open and ammunition trains functioning. The tincan would have unopposed target practice with his four-incher as long as he could keep the sub in range. A single chance hit could easily turn the tables a second time.

Richardson would always say he had not yet made up his mind which course to follow, when he saw the silhouette of the enemy ship broaden. There was a moment of exultation as he watched the tincan swing away, and then he realized what the enemy skipper was doing. He was unmasking his guns aft, presenting his broadside. Coming in bows-on had prevented effective use of his own gun battery. Perhaps he had also needed a little time to get it organized. *Eel*, after all, had had ten minutes of precious preparation time before she surfaced, and since that moment less than three minutes had yet elapsed.

But the enemy ship must have been badly hurt. The rate of fire of her four-inch gun on the forecastle had reduced greatly. It had not fired at all for nearly a minute. At 500 yards, announced by radar at about the time Richardson saw the enemy ship come around broadside-to, *Eel*'s automatic weapons were hitting all over her, searching out every unprotected space topside, no doubt penetrating the thin metal of her hull to seek out some unfortunates below.

There was another tearing sound overhead, higher-pitched, lighter-weight than before—and then another—and another. Some kind of heavy automatic weapon had opened up. Steady, repetitive blossoms of orange were showing amid the top hamper on deck abaft the enemy's squat stack. In seconds they would be bringing those screaming shells down on *Eel*'s bridge. The hammering of *Eel*'s own weapons made impossible any but the most basic of communications. The three bridge-mounted fifty-caliber machine guns, clattering away alongside Richardson, had been directed to concentrate their fire on the enemy's bridge. Best not to disturb them. This was a job for the twin twenties on their stand aft of the periscope shears, and perhaps the after forty. Abruptly, Richardson left his post alongside the port TBT, dashed around behind the periscope supports to the starboard side of the bridge, arrived amid the gun crew of the twenty. They were changing ammunition canisters. The gunner was a man named Wyatt, picked for his imperturbability and his rock-steadiness in pointing the gun. Richardson grabbed him by the shoulders, began to shout into his ear, suddenly felt the gunner's body jerk. There was the sickening sound of a heavy, blunt object tearing through flesh, shattering bone, exploding. Wyatt's head dropped. There was no struggle, no reflex action. The man had been there one moment, was gone the next. There was the ricochet of something striking the periscope shears, the scream of a bullet glancing off and spinning sidewise, misshapen, through the air. Richardson was conscious of several resounding smashes against the heavy side plating of *Eel*'s bridge.

There was no protection around the twenty-millimeter, nor the two forties. Three or four other men were down—he could not tell for sure in the darkness and the hurry. Two twenty-millimeter ammunition canisters had been replaced on the two guns. Hastily he let Wyatt slump to the deck, grabbed the charging-handles of the guns, pulled them toward him. He could feel the first shell in each gun slide home. He pressed his shoulders into the shoulder rests, grabbed for the combined triggers. Despite the heavy mount, the shock of the twenty-millimeter recoil slammed against him, driving its hard vibrations into the upper part of his body.

He was part of the fierce rhythm of the moment. The dance of death. By raising and lowering his entire trunk, swiveling from side to side, he could aim the tracer bullets. He could see them landing in the water. Too close. He stooped down a little. That elevated the trajectory. The water splashes—the Valkyries arriving—marched up to the hull of the enemy ship. The curved red trail of the tracers now terminated on the dark low-lying hull. There were no more splashes. He was hitting the side of the ship. Elevate just a touch more. On to Gehenna! Reap the vengeance of battle!

He dropped the tracers directly into the center of the orange flashes. Twitch slightly to right and left, raise up a trifle—yes, that brought some splashes into the water—bend at the waist a little more, march them up into the area where the enemy gun is shooting from. Back and forth, back and forth. Kill them! Kill them! Kill them! A mere movement of his shoulders marched the beserk arc of screaming bullets half the length of the after part of the tincan. Berserk. The demoniacal ejaculation! Suddenly he realized that he was no longer watching a tracer arc. He had fired off both canisters of ammunition. The guns were empty. With a savage motion he released the triggers, stepped back from the shoulder rests. "Reload!" he shrieked.

"We're getting them from the dinette!" someone shouted. "The ammunition locker on deck is empty!"

That would take too long. They were probably frantically reloading empty cans in the dinette. Whatever gun had opened up on the main deck aft of the tincan, it had been silenced, but the fifty-caliber on the top of her bridge structure was still spitting. Through his binoculars he could see a group of men struggling with the four-inch gun on the forecastle. He had not noticed it firing recently, and in fact he could see—now that there was no gun firing in his immediate vicinity to blind him with its flashes—that the four-inch gun was not even trained in *Eel*'s direction. It must be out of commission. As he watched it, however, the length of its barrel shortened. A new crew was bringing it back into action. *Eel*'s own two five-inch guns were still firing away, considerably slower than their initial flurry of shots, but with telling effect. Despite the lack of visibility, there were some changes evident in the dark hull now only 500 yards away. It seemed lower in the water. The deckhouse was askew, not square; its originally angular shape was now marred. Probably splinters had played havoc in that general area.

But the tincan was still capable of doing damage. That four-inch gun needed only a single lucky hit. So far, he was morally sure it had not struck home. *Eel*'s after forty-millimeter gun was still spewing forth its flat trajectory tracers, slower now, in groups of four as the ammunition train raced to hand up more ammunition from the open hatch on deck immediately aft of the bridge. Two steps aft to the forty. He created an oasis of silence around him by putting his hand across the magazine loading slot. "The gun!" he shouted hoarsely. "The gun on the forecastle!" He jerked the strap of his binoculars from around his neck, handed the glasses to the gun-pointer. The man nodded nervously. In the momentary lull, six four-round clips of forty-millimeter ammunition had arrived, were being held by the anxious gun crew. "Resume fire!" he shouted.

There was a flash—orange and red—from the enemy's four-inch gun. *Eel*'s own forty-millimeter tracers were striking just at its base. Another flash, and then a sharp concussion forward of *Eel*'s bridge. A third— another concussion. The enemy had scored at least two hits, maybe three. But then the fiery stream of tracers walked up the side of the enemy forecastle, impacted directly upon the gun and the crowded men around it. In the explosion as the bullets hit, Richardson had the impression of crumpled, shattered bodies, and in their midst the outline of the gun itself, somehow changed, not normal. Some part of it was bent, perhaps torn away. A gesture to the forty-millimeter pointer, and four screaming tracers searched out the top of the enemy bridge, putting an end to that valiant effort.

The tincan's hull was becoming shorter again. It was turning, all silent, dark and massive, turning as a wounded animal at bay might turn, blinded, dying, yet still dangerous, still seeking vengeance, still hero- ically fighting. Richardson was back at the port TBT. "Quin!" he shouted. No answer. Quin was not there. The three fifty-caliber ma- chine guns were still being served, but on the starboard side of the bridge there were two prone bodies. He felt around the hatch for the tel- ephone cord, followed it to the crumpled, still form wearing the headset. No time to tell if Quin was dead or still living. Hastily Richardson unbuckled the telephone, slammed the earphones over his head, buckled the mouthpiece around his neck. He pressed the micro- phone button. "Conn, do you hear me?"

In the earphones, which felt warm and slippery, he heard Keith's answering voice. "Conn, aye aye."

"He's turning toward us, Keith. He's trying to ram!"

"Range four-five-oh yards. We're tracking him on radar. What's the angle on the bow?"

"Starboard ten—now it's zero. He's coming in!"

Richardson was holding the telephone speaker button down with his left hand, steadying the TBT binoculars with his right, as he watched the enemy bow swing, ominous and deadly, toward him. Perhaps it would not be necessary for the enemy ship to ram. The four-inch hits forward might already have done their business. An explosive, armor- piercing shell could shatter a huge hole through which the sea would pour in an impossible torrent. He half expected to feel *Eel*'s deck in- cline under his feet, her hull grow logy and slowly sink beneath him. But it had only been a few seconds since the double impact, although there might also have been one or two other hits of which he was not aware. The pressure hull, however, was well below the main deck. Much of it—nearly all of it—was below the waterline. In all likelihood it would be protected by the sea. If a shell did strike home, however, water would instantly follow.

"Main deck fore and aft. Number one and number two five-inch, are you still in commission?" He had not heard them firing in the last several seconds. To his relief, both gun captains answered, but his relief turned to despair when he heard their reports.

"Number one gun out of commission. Jammed in train. Several men hurt!"

"Number two gun out of ammunition. They can't seem to get it up from below!"

"How many rounds you got, number one gun?"

"Four on deck."

"Run them back to number two gun! Use the starboard side! Number two gun, set your range at zero and aim at the enemy's waterline. Open fire as soon as you can!

"Maneuvering, are you on the line?"

"Maneuvering, aye aye!" He could imagine the avid attention with which the idle maneuvering room crew must have been following the telephone conversation which was their only link to the action topside.

"Shift your sticks into reverse. When I give the order to back emergency, put everything you can put to the screws. Give it all you've got, but watch your circuit breakers! Don't blow them!" Richardson visualized the control sticks of the electric-control cubicle being placed in the position for backing, the battery readied to be thrown on the motor buses at full voltage and maximum current. It would be virtually a dead short through the main motors, and he would have to trust the good judgment of the electrician's mates not to throw the current on so fast they burned out something.

Then Richardson had another idea. "Control, are you on the line? . . . Tell Mr. Dugan . . ."

"Al Dugan right here, Captain," said the familiar voice in his earphones.

"Secure sending ammunition to number one gun! It's jammed. See what you can do about breaking up the problem back aft. We need ammunition to number two five-inch!"

"I've already stopped ammunition forward. We're checking on number two right now."

"Get those wounded men on the forecastle below. As soon as everyone's clear around number one gun, secure the gun access trunk!"

And then another thought. "Foxhole, if he hits us it'll probably be up forward. Don't take any chances. Get down inside and shut that hatch tight before he hits!" The enemy captain would expect *Eel* to try to escape by going ahead instead of astern. Astern was clearly the way to go. If there were a collision, it would be forward. Again Richardson was glad of the rigorous drill, and the careful communication setup so laboriously checked out by Keith and Buck. The enemy ship was coming in at dead slow speed, no doubt guided by some extraordinary individual still alive on the bridge, or possibly steering from an emergency steering station aft. The fifties were playing an absolute tattoo all over the large square bridge structure. No one could live under that hail of destruction. She was perceptibly lower in the water, much closer now, perhaps losing speed a trifle. Richardson could now see holes where the five-inch had entered. She was undoubtedly a shambles inside. No one could be alive in the forward part of the ship, except if well below the waterline. Only those people fortunate enough to be stationed aft of the large superstructure—which was stopping most of the automatic-weapon fire—could possibly be surviving. She must be steered from aft.

"Range two hundred yards. Speed five." Keith's voice steady, as always. He must be looking through the periscope at the same time he was relaying radar ranges and observed angles to Buck Williams. Amazing that he could see anything through it. Somewhere Keith must have picked up a telephone headset, for it was not in the original scheme that he also should wear one. Five knots. There had been just a shade of emphasis on the range. One hundred sixty six yards a minute. Perhaps this was why Keith had specified range two hundred yards. Rich had made all his dispositions but one. *Eel*'s bridge structure must not be permitted to mask her remaining five-inch gun as she backed clear.

"All back emergency!" yelled Richardson down the hatch and into the telephone mouthpiece as well. Surprisingly, he heard the click of the annunciators. There must have been a momentary hiatus in the noise level at precisely that instant. "Left full rudder!" he shouted. "Port TBT staying on target!" That would keep the gun firing on the beam, keep *Eel*'s bridge from getting in the way of the gun pointers. Cornelli had not had much to do for the last several minutes. He would put his full energy into getting the rudder left as fast as it ever had been done by hand. Buck would use the TBT bearings to keep his TDC lined up—though deflection angles would be of little use and even less importance at close range.

There was a burst of white water on either quarter, burbling up alongside with extraordinary speed. He could feel the acceleration jerk of 252 volts at full amperage suddenly thrown across the main motor armatures. *Eel*'s stern sagged downward slightly, then bobbed up as the racing propellers bit into the water. The wash thrown up by the straining screws swept high along the rounded belly of her ballast tanks on both sides, even splashed up onto the main deck opposite the silent mufflers of the after engineroom.

"Number two five-inch has ammunition, Bridge. We're opening fire!" The announcement by telephone was almost blotted out by the roar of the five-inch gun, all the louder for having been awaited so long. At point-blank range the effect was tremendous. The shell struck the water just upon entry into the enemy bow a few feet on the starboard side of her stem, must have traveled nearly the entire length of the enemy ship before exploding somewhere in its after portion. Richardson could see water pouring through the neat round hole it had made in the bow shell plating. The fifty-caliber machine guns were coming into their own at the close range. The "foxhole," particularly, maintained an enfilading crossfire that swept the enemy decks from a totally different direction. In the meantime, *Eel*'s surprise movement astern was carrying her to starboard of the enemy, curving to her own port. The second shot of the five-inch gun consequently entered the tincan's side somewhere in the vicinity of the bridge, traveled on an angular course entirely through the ship, and detonated in the water beyond it. The splash of the underwater explosion threw up a column of spray behind the tortured hulk. It was clear now that the enemy ship would miss in its desperate charge, was, in fact, no longer manageable.

Richardson was suddenly conscious of Keith's presence alongside of him on the bridge as the third and then the fourth devastating blows from the five-inch were dealt. *Eel*, in her curving reverse course, had in effect maneuvered so that the enemy remained constantly on her port beam as he staggered the last hundred yards of his final, hopeless effort. Now the *Mikura*-class frigate lay on the water, tired, prostrate, visibly sinking.

"All stop!" shouted Richardson. "Cease fire! Cease fire!"

The silence was unbelievable. Richardson's eardrums felt as if they had closed up in self-protection and now were having difficulty readjusting to the normal noises at sea. Gradually he became aware of a whistling sound, combined with a gurgling and a pouring of water. *Eel*'s own sternward motion, diminishing, was responsible for some of it; but more, he realized, particularly the whistling noise, must come from the enemy ship. Of course she had closed all her watertight doors and hatches, but she had been riddled by so many small holes, as well as the large ones made by the five-inch guns, that there was no capability left in her shattered hull to hold an air bubble. The noise was air whistling out of the holes throughout her body.

She lay flat on the water, her deck at the water's edge, her squat bridge-deckhouse combination, splintered and shattered, standing vertically like a lighthouse in a quiet sea. Air still bubbled from within her, making a dozen ridiculous little geysers as it escaped from the now submerged hull. *Eel*, her sternway petering out, had traced a semicircle in the astern direction. He could see it all, though it was a dark night. The ruined bridge began leaning to starboard, and simultaneously the forward part of the little ship sank lower so that the square structure never fell into the sea, but instead seemingly quartered into it. As the steel hull which supported it slowly upended, bow first, its stern momentarily reappeared above the surface. Then the whole thing was gone.

Richardson waited a moment. The next move should be to pick up survivors, but if any depth charges had been made ready in anticipation of another attack, they would go off soon, probably about the time they reached the bottom of the sea. The wait, which seemed interminable, could not have been long. Once again, as had happened the previous day, the ocean erupted around the grave of the sunken ship. When all was quiet once more, there was no life left. Only a few shattered timbers tossing helplessly in a white canopy of foam on a suddenly uneasy sea, and tiny pieces of debris speckling it all, like pepper from a grinder on whipped cream.

As Richardson gave orders to secure all guns, ammunition, and personnel topside, and to proceed into the center of the wreckage to search for any possible survivors, he heard Yancy asking permission to speak to him.

"I've got bad news, Captain," he said. Richardson waited numbly. This was bound to be the final result of his decision to fight on the surface, but there had been no other choice. The gods of war must be given their sacrifice. Doubtless all had died aboard his adversary—probably as many as a hundred men. *Eel* carried eighty—eighty-one, counting the wolfpack commander—and it was too much to hope that they would all escape scot-free.

"We have three men killed, sir. Wyatt, Quin, and Johnson; and ten wounded. Two fairly seriously—Thompson and Webber, and . . ." Yancy seemed to be in doubt as to how to phrase the next item. He hesitated a long moment. "The commodore is dead."

"What!" The startled cry was the antithesis of Yancy's carefully studied, bold statement of fact. Blunt had not even been topside during the battle. He had spoken to him only a few hours before, just before surfacing; automatically he looked at his watch, saw to his astonishment that from surfacing until this moment had been less than fifteen minutes.

"You don't look so good yourself, Captain," said the pharmacist's mate. "You have blood all over your face and head."

Still overwhelmed by Yancy's surprise news, Richardson removed the telephone earphones and mouthpiece. "I'm all right," he said, "I took these from Quin. This must be his blood that's on me." Unaccountably, Quin's death seemed far more personal than that of Blunt, more like that of Oregon. Quin and Oregon had both followed him from the *Walrus* to the *Eel*. Quin, in fact, had been with him even before, in *S-16*.

Still, Blunt's death was the big surprise, the greatest shock, because there was no reason for it. "What happened to the commodore? What do you mean, he's dead!"

Yancy swiveled away his eyes. "We brought him to the wardroom, the way you told us, and that's where we found him. His head was down on his arms on the table as if he was asleep. Sometimes he used to catnap that way. We were bringing some of the hurt men in there, and when he didn't move, I looked at him and saw he was dead."

"But my God, man! A man doesn't just die. . . . What happened? . . . Are you sure . . ." The sentence went uncompleted, the question lost. It made no difference. Suddenly all Richardson's exhilaration over the successful outcome of the battle evaporated. All was gall in his mouth. His eyes ached, wanted to close. He forced them open. He was so stupefied with exhaustion that he could feel nothing beyond the burning in his eyes and the overpowering need to lie down. His mind told him his body ached as much as his eyes, and would ache more after a few hours' rest. He had proved a nemesis to so many people. Jim Bledsoe and the entire crew of the *Walrus*. Bungo Pete. Oregon. Quin, Wyatt, Johnson, and now old Joe Blunt, whose own dolphins, given him so many years ago, he still wore on his best uniforms.

He looked up, saw Yancy staring at him gravely. "Where is he, Yancy?"

"I got some men laying him out in his bunk, Captain. Like I said, he looks okay. There's not a mark on him except his neck is all swelled up."

"What do you think could have happened?"

"I haven't really had a chance to check him. Don't know. Maybe a heart attack. Maybe a stroke. Most likely he hurt himself falling down the hatch. He could have broke his neck and not know it. Then, maybe, walking around, bending over and all, he might have pinched the spinal cord." Yancy hesitated. He wanted to say something more. "He hasn't been acting normal, sir. Not for a long time. I knew when you and Mr. Leone were reading my books, and I read them too. There was something else wrong with him, sir. I'm no doctor, and it's just a guess, but I think there was something wrong in his head. He would

335

blow hot and cold, like, and he could never take any pressure. Maybe there was something wrong with the blood to his brain. That and a broken neck could have finished him easy."

"Any chance that he's just conked out and will come to a little later? . . ."

"No, sir. He's dead." There was a note of finality in Yancy's voice which Richardson recognized he would have to accept.

But he could not go below just yet, and Al Dugan was waiting to make his report. There was the damage to be checked. The submarine to make seaworthy again. The rig for dive to be rigorously gone over once more. Numbers three and four main engines to be checked out, and the situation in the after engineroom itself to be considered. Could a plug be placed in the cooler intake line? If not, how could *Eel* submerge—or could the drain pump handle the leak so she could submerge safely to shallow depths for a short time?

What about the hydraulic system and the air compressors? Al Dugan would report on those. The periscopes. They would have to be checked carefully, not only because of the depth charging but also because something, perhaps only a small-caliber projectile, had struck the periscope shears. It might have distorted the alignment of the bearings.

Those concussions when the four-inch shells hit. Was *Eel*'s pressure hull still sound? Number one five-inch gun, jammed in train: that was where at least one of the enemy's large-caliber projectiles had struck. Any shell holes in the hull would have to have temporary plugs. The gun should, if possible, be trained back fore and aft before the ship dived again.

If she could dive. If *Eel* could not dive, then what about enemy aircraft in the morning?

There was so much to consider, so many decisions to be made. He was so tired, and the night had just begun. The loss of life, the damage, might be worth it—could only be worth it—if *Whitefish* reported destruction of the last troopship. He must send Whitey a message, ask about the transport, announce that Everett was now in command of the wolfpack. . . .

"Put one and two main engines on a battery charge," he said.

- 12 -

Letting down from the high excitement of personal combat was like dying. There was no bottom to the toboggan slide of consciousness, no limit to the trancelike sluggishness that gradually, but so surely, engulfed him. Despite the myriad problems which now insisted on his personal attention, each stumbling over the heels of the one preceding, despite his consciousness of the responsibility which rested upon him, for the first time in his life Richardson found himself totally unable to make even the simplest decisions. Agonizingly, viciously, he flogged himself to stay awake, stay alert, deal with them. Nothing else to do, except attend to the hundred or so details needed to make *Eel* seaworthy again, fit to submerge. Nothing to think about, except how to keep from sleeping. But he could feel the juices of his faculties ebbing away, draining out of him. A sluice valve had been opened. He was an empty vessel. The brownout of fatigue was turning into a blackout.

He was totally unaware of the stratagem by which Keith inveigled him to sit on his bunk, and then, without a word, lifted his feet and placed them also upon it. There was not even anything to dream about, not even the dead, who once were alive and vital and quick, and now were so quiet, so rested, so evermore sealed in their shattered bodies.

Sleep was deep, dreamless, forever, and its restorative powers worked their magic. When he began to see living, sensate beings: Laura, Admiral Small, Keith, *Eel* herself—though she was sensate in a different way—he managed to will himself awake. Even while asleep he somehow was normally always aware of any change in *Eel's* condition, but not this time. She had been surfaced at his last recollection, and now was submerged, riding quietly.

There must have been someone watching him, for in a moment Keith came in with a cup of steaming coffee, a sandwich, and some papers. A quick glance at the clock on the bulkhead—how long had he been sleeping? It must be only a couple of hours past midnight; he could not believe the hands of the clock had not somehow become interchanged, that it was late morning, that he had been more than eight hours unconscious.

Webber, the most seriously injured of the wounded men, had died

337

in the night without regaining consciousness, Keith reported. Yancy had told Richardson that there was nothing he could do for him except ease his suffering if he regained consciousness (none of this could Rich recall), and his death had occurred only a few hours later. His body had been placed in its zippered leatherette bunk cover like the others, and stowed in one of the two unoccupied torpedo tubes in the forward torpedo room.

It had taken nearly until dawn to make emergency repairs so that they could submerge, Keith went on to relate, but there had been no complications and no need to call him. No additional holes had been found in the pressure hull, other than those Richardson had already seen, and an air test before diving had been satisfactory. Keith exhibited the message he had sent to Whitey Everett informing him that as next senior he had succeeded to command of the wolfpack. Another of the papers was Everett's acknowledging message directing return to base through the least frequented part of the Yellow Sea, with all daylight hours spent submerged until clear of the Ryukyus.

Then came the bad moment. Keith silently handed him the intercepted report by *Whitefish* to ComSubPac of her engagement with the convoy, the sinking of two of the troopships, the rupture of a vent riser gasket from a close depth charge, and the unusual actions of an unknown set of heavy merchant-type propellers about two hours later. Richardson could feel the bitterness rise up in him as he read the message. It was for this they had sacrificed Quin, Wyatt, Johnson, Webber, and—yes—Joe Blunt! And there had not even been an attempt to attack the last transport! Keith, he saw, mirrored his feelings.

"Who knows of this message?" he asked, taking a deep sip of coffee to quiet himself.

"Nobody, sir. The decode, I mean. Everyone was so busy, I just decoded it myself. I figured you would want to see it first. . . ."

Richardson thought a minute. His mind was beginning to function clearly again. "Let's leave it that way. This won't go down well with anybody in this ship. There's no need to have it talked about. ComSubPac will get our log and patrol report, and he'll have to decide what more, if anything, ought to be done about it. After all, Whitey has sunk five ships in his first command patrol."

"I know, Skipper, but you set him up for every one of them, and there should have been six! That last troopship was a perfect sitting duck for anyone with the guts to come up to periscope depth to see what was going on! It cost us five of our shipmates for nothing, and now at least one of those two Kwantung Army divisions will be shooting at our Army and Marines on Iwo and Okinawa!" Keith's repressed passion suddenly blazed through. "Why don't we send our own message to ComSubPac and tell him what really went on!" Abruptly, Keith became aware that the red-rimmed eyes seemed deeper sunk, the half-buried black eye in the haggard face so close to his own more covered than before by the swollen, darkened flesh.

Richardson must have been more at odds with himself than anyone knew. More tired than anyone could have thought. He felt a surge of anger welling within him, directed not at Whitey Everett, but at the bearer of the unpleasant tidings. It was not logical. He should not blame Keith. Keith, of all people, had a right to feel this way. Barely he contained himself, trembling with the effort, tried to answer in an even tone. After all, Keith was the most loyal one aboard. He, too, had been through a lot. "No!" he barked. "Absolutely not!"

Richardson should not have sounded so peremptory. Keith was only doing his duty. The shock of hearing his own flash of anger enabled him to continue more normally: "Neither would I have gotten anywhere if I hadn't had Joe Blunt to teach me all he knew about submarining, and you and Jim Bledsoe and some of the others to help me when I needed it. The only thing I'm sorry about is that five good men died trying to do something important, and it didn't work."

Keith looked abashed. The emotions of both were near the surface. Impulsively Richardson reached out, gripped him on the shoulder, squeezed with all the strength in his hand. It was the right thing to do. The gesture made it all right again. Richardson felt as though a weight had been partially lifted from him also. Later, after everyone had had a chance to pull himself together, he would arrange a memorial service in front of the torpedo tubes in the forward torpedo room.

The decision as to disposition of the dead, although he could hardly remember having made it, was the only one he had been able to concentrate on before Keith lifted his feet onto his bunk and put out the light. It must have been the trauma of having to view his destroyed shipmates which had enabled him to retain his self-control long enough to consider what to do, but even so it had required great effort to stem the dropping tide of coherent thought. Had Captain Blunt not been one of the dead, they would all have been given a sailor's burial at sea in the time-honored tradition of a flag-covered corpse gently dropped over the side. But Yancy could give no further information as to the cause of Blunt's death, despite a second examination. The body of Captain Blunt would have to be brought back to Pearl Harbor for autopsy. He could not bury Quin and the others at sea when the wolfpack commander would be brought home. In the end, each of the four bodies was quietly encased in its own zippered bunk cover. Then

—this Richardson insisted upon supervising personally—each was loaded into one of the six torpedo tubes in *Eel*'s forward torpedo room, after which the tubes were placed out of commission so that they could not be fired, even accidentally. Now, with addition of Webber, there was only a single torpedo tube forward not so labeled. But that was of no consequence. There were no torpedoes left anyway.

The greatest repair problem revolved around being able to submerge. *Eel* had been struck six times in all by the enemy's four-inch gun, and a dozen times or more by the smaller calibers. None of the small automatic weapons had been able to penetrate the pressure hull, but the large-size projectiles had done so twice: in the gun access trunk and the forward engineroom. Major repair effort had gone to the engineroom, for the access trunk could be sealed off from below merely by shutting the hatch connecting it to the control room. The hole in the engineroom, a slash some six inches long and four wide with jagged edges bent inside the ship, required ingenuity.

There had been some talk with Al Dugan about the best means of plugging it, though Rich could not remember any of the details they had discussed. Now it was the first thing he inspected. There were two huge bolts down through the hole, passing through heavy bars across its short dimension, each of them capped with a heavy hexagonal nut. Thick gasket material bulging down through the gash concealed what was evidently a heavy plate spanning it on the outside.

"It was easy when we found the right thing to cannibalize," Al Dugan told him with professional pride. "One of the air compressors is out of commission anyway with a cracked foundation, so we just cut a section of the foundation, bent it to fit the curve of the hull, and slapped her on the outside. Covers the hole with a lot to spare all around. We put Glyptal all over everything, and so far she doesn't even leak. There's a watch on it anyhow, with a bucket, just in case. But I hope you're not planning on any more depth charges till after Pearl Harbor gets a whack at it!"

Rich gravely assured him he would henceforth do his utmost to avoid depth charges, at least until a proper welded patch had been installed. In the after engineroom, things were also cheerful. Through a great deal of hard work, temporary repairs had been effected to the damaged seawater discharge line. A certain amount of steady leakage could not be prevented, and this would increase, of course, at the deeper depths. But unless the situation worsened considerably, the drain pump could take care of it by running fifteen minutes out of every hour. As a precautionary move, a special watch had been set on the cooler also, with a telephone, to give instant warning should the

340

leak increase. Richardson left the engineroom convinced the repair had been handled as well as could be.

Despite Dugan's pessimistic report during the height of the surface pursuit, the hydraulic plant had again been returned to a semblance of running condition. With everything possible switched over to hand power, it could, if carefully monitored, continue to perform the few basic operations for which there was no hand-powered alternative. The insoluble problem in the pump room was a new one. One of *Eel*'s pair of air compressors, as Dugan had said, was permanently out of commission with its bearings out of line and its foundations cracked right across. Even without the section removed from the base, it would need a major repair job in port. The other compressor had also been thrown out of alignment by the same depth charge, but to a lesser degree. It could run and had in fact been running, but after only three hours, long before *Eel*'s nearly depleted air banks had been recharged, it ceased to jam air. Inspection showed, as suspected, that the misalignment had caused failure of the just-replaced third and fourth stage discharge valves, necessitating their replacement a second time. As Al explained it, the single air compressor remaining could not be relied on for more than a few hours before the new valve disks would also break, or be scored beyond use, and only two additional spare sets were on board besides those he would remove from the other compressor. He did not need to tell Richardson what this meant. Compressed air was vital to a submarine for many small purposes, but its major functions were to start main engines, fire torpedoes, and blow tanks. The mere acts of submerging and surfacing again were now nearly prohibitively costly. *Eel*'s status as an operational submarine was by consequence greatly reduced. She would have had to leave station in any case, short of emergency.

In midafternoon a call from the conning tower reached Richardson during his second visit to the after engineroom. In a moment he was at the periscope.

"What is it?" he asked Larry Lasche, now promoted to standing his first "top watch" alone.

"Don't know, Captain. Just this white thing on the horizon, on the port bow. Also, I've seen three patrolling aircraft on my watch."

Through the periscope Richardson inspected the object. It seemed totally innocuous in the distance, floating quietly on the calm sea. A fifteen-degree course alteration put it more nearly dead ahead for a closer passage and a more careful inspection.

"It's a raft," he finally said. "There's birds flying around and pecking at something on it."

It was as though a vague intuition were tugging at Richardson's memory, calling to him. The raft drew nearer. He was paying entirely too much attention to it. Nervously he spun the periscope around several times, dunked it, raised it again. There was nothing else in sight. The sky was clear in all directions, and so was the horizon. Always he returned to the raft. Always its outlines grew more clear, more familiar.

Suddenly Richardson whirled to Lasche. "Larry, do you have our position on the chart?"

"Yes, sir. Over here on the chart table."

"And where was it we had that tangle with Moonface and that fake fishing trawler of his?"

"I don't remember exactly, sir, but the log will have the position. . . ."

In a moment the general location of Richardson's short imprisonment in Moonface's patrol boat was marked off on the chart. His skipper's next words brought a strange sensation to Larry Lasche's scalp. Nervously he rubbed his hand across the top of his head.

"Call Keith and Buck," Richardson said in a repressed, tight voice. "We're not twenty miles away from our position when you fellows had that fight with Moonface's patrol boat and got me back aboard. That's their raft out there, and Moonface is still on it!"

Keith, Buck, and Al Dugan, who had insisted upon joining the excited group in the conning tower, all took turns looking through the periscope.

"But how can it be?" said Keith. "He wasn't badly injured so far as we could see, and he had his whole crew with him and a good-sized boat in the water. It had a mast and sails, and plenty of water and food. They should have been able to reach land in a couple of days. If the boat could carry all the people, it probably made sense to abandon the raft, but . . ."

"When they abandoned the raft, they didn't take their skipper with them," said Rich in the same repressed tone.

"You mean, they deserted him?" burst out Lasche. A meaningful silence took possession of the conning tower.

It was Richardson who had the closest view when *Eel* passed by less than twenty-five yards away. Suddenly he lowered the periscope.

"What's the matter, Skipper?" asked Buck, who happened to catch the fleeting look of disgust on his face.

"It's pretty nauseating," he replied. "Moonface has been dead a long time and lying on that raft in the sun."

The moment of silence was the second of those uncomfortable stillnesses everyone expects someone else to break. Richardson could visualize the scene: the bellowed orders, the imprecations, the denunciations, finally the shouted pleas. The stolid silence which must have been its own answer. The pitiless sun, cold nights, and lack of water, combined with the effects of his wound, could end only one agonizing way. For a time Moonface might have hoped for a change of heart among the crewmen, and after he was alone, perhaps, he must have hoped someone else—some other ship—would happen upon him. Toward the end he must even have hoped that an American submarine, possibly the *Eel* herself, might turn up. All the while, until delirium began, he must have tasted in full measure the bitterness of being contemptuously cast aside, spurned, condemned not only by his fellow men but by his own crew. No degradation, no deserved retribution, could have been greater.

And now Moonface lay spread-eagled on his raft, his tremendous body burned black by the sun, bloated by the swelling of the gases within, the facial tissues of his cheeks drawn tight in a ghastly grimace showing his large, stained teeth. His eyes had been already gouged out by the birds gathered around him. The inside of his mouth, his tongue, the tender tissues of his lips, the softest skin of his neck, even his private parts, now exposed and distended, had been prey for days to an obscene flock of feathered sea-vultures.

The periscope, with its magnification of six, brought Richardson within a few feet of the horrible spectacle, and it was from this he recoiled in disgust and dismay.

"Well," said Buck Williams, breaking the hush, "I can't say I feel too terribly sorry for him. It couldn't have happened to a more deserving fellow."

"I sure agree," simultaneously said both Dugan and Lasche. Cornelli and Scott, who had unobtrusively mounted to the conning tower, showed by the looks on their faces that they, too, shared the sentiment. Only Keith put a different shape on it.

"One thing we have to remember, though—he was sick. Considering what he said about going to school in California, and his ability to speak English, he must have lived there quite awhile. Probably Japan and the Jap Navy didn't accept him very well because of all that, too. He must have been a tormented man. Still, he was trying to serve his country. Just as we are. The commodore gave us a lot of trouble, but that's what he was trying to do, too."

"And so was Bungo Pete," observed Richardson unwarily. Again, there was silence. No one in the conning tower spoke in response. With a start, Richardson realized he had broken a taboo. There had been a conspiracy of silence on board the *Eel*. It was the first time, in his own hearing at least, that the name "Bungo Pete" had been voiced aloud. The looks in the eyes of the others, even of the normally impassive Scott and Cornelli, told him they had understood his inner turmoil. From the beginning they had understood. They knew he had done it for them, and for their contemporaries, living and dead, in other submarines; though he could not excuse himself, must always suffer for what he had had to do, which they also understood—yet he would have had to do it all over again. Although this continuous self-immolation must be his personal and private sacrifice, they had tried to help in the only way they could.

The circumstances in which war sometimes places men, their prior training, the decisions they have to make and the time they have to make them—all are mixed, intertwined, involved in the mammoth conflict between ideals of which war is the ultimate expression. The human being, caught in such circumstances, may find hidden elements of his character of which until then he had been unaware, which he would never know except through the eyes of others.

Mirrored in the faces of the small company in the conning tower, Richardson for the first time sensed that they had supported him not only as their titular leader, but for his own sake. The U.S. Navy had made him their commander, but the intuitive alchemy of men, their personalities interacting with his—or what they were able to see of his—created a bond far stronger than that of simple discipline. They would follow him, had followed him, not because the organization and the system demanded it, but through a higher order of loyalty, regard, appreciation of the man they thought him to be.

And then he knew that he had once felt that way about Joe Blunt. But Blunt had not measured up to the trust and confidence his junior, Richardson, had placed in him. He had failed the standard he had set for himself, the standard to which Richardson, by consequence, had held him. It was a high standard, but not unattainable; it was the one to which Richardson also aspired. Blunt had taught it to him. He must never betray it. It was for this reason, he now saw, that he had felt Blunt's failure so personally and so deeply.

Eel's crew had not known Blunt as the man he had been, but only as he was at the last. Vainly, Richardson had been telling them the old Blunt was the real one. But the real Blunt, to them, could only be the man they had all known. It was he, the man they had seen and felt, whom they would always remember. They had supported Richardson willingly in what he had been trying to do for Blunt, but they had done it for him, not for the wolfpack commander. The subconscious reason behind his heightened reaction to Keith's criticism of Whitey Everett now also stood clear and tall: man must stand by man, by the higher qualities of man implicit in the meaning of humanity. Even enemies must learn to recognize their ultimate brotherhood. Most important of all, man must stand by himself, must never betray the image he has created of himself, for that image is the only reality.

He knew, then, what he must do. There was one thing he could do for the memory of Moonface, but really it was not for him at all but for Tateo Nakame, an enemy he had been forced to destroy without opportunity for thought; and for Joe Blunt, a friend and superior who had destroyed himself. It was in the nature of the expiation of a blood debt, a debt brought about by forces beyond his own control but for which, nevertheless, he must make what restitution lay in his power. It was the debt of the decent man.

Not everyone would understand, but some would. *Eel* would not surface, should not surface. Not only had Everett's order forbidden it; he could not expose his crew to yet another hazardous hand power dive to avoid a fast-approaching aircraft.

He put it into as few words as he could. Someday, if the moment of truth fell on them, they would remember. It would be like that other time when he had sent everyone below, and alone on *Eel*'s bridge had made the dreadful decisions. He would again act alone, bearing the full responsibility. It would be a moment of religion. He allowed himself only one comment, to allay any possible fears. "We ourselves put that raft in the water," he said. "We know there aren't any booby traps on it."

The others listened as he gave his instructions. "I'll take the conn," he said. "Cornelli, take over the helm. Al, I'll need your fine hand on the dive. Alert the pump room that the hydraulic system is likely to be exercised a little. Also, it may cost us a little of your air." He started to order Keith and Buck below as well, hesitated at the silent plea in Keith's eyes. Buck, not waiting for any word, purposefully stepped to the after end of the conning tower and started up the TDC. The whine of its synchros filled the tiny cylindrical compartment.

The order to go below unfinished, Richardson turned to Keith with a brief, quizzical smile. It was a shaky smile, he instantly realized, and then one final point came home. This, after all, was exactly as it had been during that final fight with Nakame. For it had been Leone, in the conning tower, who had loyally supported his every move and had backed him up at the radar and the periscope; Scott, whose perfect steering in that crucial encounter, well knowing what he was doing, had enabled him to hit the lifeboats; Dugan, with his inspired

345

handling of *Eel*'s semisubmergence in the sudden tiny typhoon which had enveloped them, who had enabled him to get the attack off perfectly. Williams, who had set up the torpedoes and fired them at his order. All of them, who had shared everything then, and had shared everything since.

Although he relived the episode in his mind many times afterward, Richardson was never able to explain to himself or anyone on board the *Eel* that day just how it was that he made all the unfamiliar maneuvers exactly correctly. Through some intuitive sense he made all the calculations, added all the factors, did everything exactly right.

As *Eel* approached the bobbing life raft on which lay the putrefying form of Moonface, the man he had once hated more than anyone else in the world, he called down to Dugan, "Stand by bow buoyancy! Stand by forward group blow!" He gave a couple of tiny course corrections to Cornelli. *Eel*'s speed was set at two knots, sixty-seven yards per minute. Scott, with a stopwatch, was counting the seconds aloud. Buck Williams had set up the TDC with a target speed of zero. From a range of 1,000 yards on, Rogers on the radar gave him continuous information as to precisely the distance to the life raft.

At the critical moment, when Scott called, "Mark!" he shouted the expected orders down the hatch to Al Dugan.

"Blow bow buoyancy! Blow forward group! Full rise on bow planes!"

He stood looking through the periscope at the raft and the bloated body on it, now sweeping rapidly toward him. If the raft struck the periscope, it might damage it. He must be quick to lower it in time, if he missed.

The conning tower deck tilted sharply upward under his feet. He could feel the lifting strain of the forward tanks as Dugan lavishly expended high pressure air. The periscope seemed to lean back as it rose swiftly out of the water. Suddenly he was looking down from a great height. He had to shift to low power and tilt the periscope exit pupil lens down to its bottom limit of depression to keep the raft in sight.

Rising from the depths, *Eel*'s bow struck the under side of the raft, splintered the timbers which held it together, knocked apart the metal drums on which it was built. Impaled on the submarine's bow, it rose out of the water and tipped to starboard. The startled sea birds went flying. The raft slid crazily aft along the top of *Eel*'s steel bow buoyancy tank until some underportion of it caught against a cleat welded on the tank's surface. There it hung momentarily. It tilted even farther, still hooked, tipped more to starboard. Finally, as the carrion sea creatures flapped and shrieked their displeasure, the decaying flesh of what had been Moonface became dislodged from its position on the slatted boards to which it had stuck, rolled over once as it slid off the raft—a stiffened arm waved thanks and farewell—and fell into the sea.

The body drifted nearer, passed within the inner circle of periscope view. He gave Dugan orders to vent the air from the tanks, return *Eel* to her normal submerged condition. Swiftly he spun the periscope around, saw Moonface floating aft.

It was all Richardson could do for him. The corpse might float for a few hours, but it would soon disintegrate and disappear, one at last with the sea. At least, Moonface would have a sailor's grave. The Japanese Navy, far better served by officers of the stripe of Tateo Nakame, need never know of the disgrace Moonface had brought upon it.

Nor, for that matter (and the unbidden thought almost brought a smile to Richardson's face), was there any longer a chance that another Japanese patrol boat, coming upon the raft, might cause embarassing questions to be asked of Moonface's crew, wherever they might now be.

Extract from A. H. Small, Vice Admiral, USN, Commander Submarine Force, Pacific Fleet, Third Endorsement to *Eel* Report of Second War Patrol

1.   The second war patrol of the EEL was conducted as a member of a coordinated submarine attack group in the Yellow and East China seas under the overall command of Captain Joseph K. Blunt, until Captain Blunt's death in action during the final engagement of the patrol. The commanding officer of the EEL during this patrol, as for her first patrol, was Commander Edward G. Richardson, USN.

2.   This is, without question, one of the outstanding patrols of the war, marked by cool calculation, daring, and skill. It was marred only by materiel troubles and the unfortunate loss of life from enemy gunfire. The force commander joins the officers and crew of EEL in deep personal regret at the loss of their shipmates. Particularly noteworthy was the manner in which EEL, though out of torpedoes, cooperated with the remaining submarine in the group to bring the enemy ships to action. The commanding officer is congratulated for his persistence in repeatedly forcing the extremely valuable troop transports contacted off Tsingtao to reverse course, thus subjecting themselves to further attack. To this inspired and aggressive performance in carrying out the operational orders of the wolfpack commander is due the sinking of two of three heavily loaded troop transports headed for the home islands of Japan. The loss of these prime troops must have been a severe blow to the enemy war effort, and it is only regretted that one of the ships made good her escape.

3. The death of Captain Blunt has been made the subject of a special medical report. While the injury suffered during a heavy depth charge attack and the subsequent strain of a viciously fought surface gun action were contributory causes, the primary cause of his death has been established as a deep, fast-growing right parietal tumor of the brain which was not detected prior to departure. Commander Submarine Force, Pacific Fleet, wishes publicly to express his personal sorrow that the services of so outstanding a submarine officer should thus have been lost to the navy, and to extend his offical condolences to Captain Blunt's shipmates and the commanding officer of the EEL.

4. EEL's commanding officer, officers, and crew are deserving of the highest praise upon the completion of a second most aggressive, smartly conducted, and outstandingly successful patrol, and for extensive damage to the enemy in confined waters close to a hostile shoreline.

A. H. Small

ABOUT THE AUTHOR

Edward Beach was graduated from the United States Naval Academy in 1939. He saw duty aboard three submarines during World War II, and from 1953 to 1957 he served as Naval Aide to President Eisenhower. In 1960 he commanded the nuclear-powered USS *Triton* in her underwater circumnavigation of the earth, and from this voyage came his book *Around the World Submerged*. Prior to that he wrote two books, *Submarine!* and the novel *Run Silent, Run Deep*, the latter a best-seller and major book-club selection that was made into a popular motion picture. He retired from active service in the Navy in 1966 and is currently employed by the United States Senate.